27.86

COMETH UP AS A FLOWER

broadview editions
series editor: L.W. Conolly

COMETH UP AS A FLOWER

Rhoda Broughton

edited by Pamela K. Gilbert

broadview editions

Library and Archives Canada Cataloguing in Publication

Broughton, Rhoda, 1840-1920

    Cometh up as a flower / Rhoda Broughton ; edited by Pamela K. Gilbert.

(Broadview editions)
Includes bibliographical references.
ISBN 978-1-55111-805-5

    I. Gilbert, Pamela K II. Title. III. Series: Broadview editions

PR4174.B56C66 2010   823'.8   C2010-900103-6

Broadview Editions

The Broadview Editions series represents the ever-changing canon of literature by bringing together texts long regarded as classics with valuable lesser-known works.

Advisory editor for this volume: Juliet Sutcliffe

Broadview Press is an independent, international publishing house, incorporated in 1985. Broadview believes in shared ownership, both with its employees and with the general public; since the year 2000 Broadview shares have traded publicly on the Toronto Venture Exchange under the symbol BDP.

We welcome comments and suggestions regarding any aspect of our publications—please feel free to contact us at the addresses below or at broadview@broadviewpress.com.

North America
PO Box 1243, Peterborough, Ontario, Canada K9J 7H5
2215 Kenmore Ave., Buffalo, New York, USA 14207
Tel: (705) 743-8990; Fax: (705) 743-8353
email: customerservice@broadviewpress.com

UK, Europe, Central Asia, Middle East, Africa, India, and Southeast Asia
Eurospan Group, 3 Henrietta St., London WC2E 8LU, United Kingdom
Tel: 44 (0) 1767 604972; Fax: 44 (0) 1767 601640
email: eurospan@turpin-distribution.com

Australia and New Zealand
NewSouth Books
c/o TL Distribution, 15-23 Helles Ave., Moorebank, NSW, Australia 2170
Tel: (02) 8778 9999; Fax: (02) 8778 9944
email: orders@tldistribution.com.au

www.broadviewpress.com

This book is printed on paper containing 100% post-consumer fibre.

PRINTED IN CANADA

Contents

Acknowledgements

Tamar Heller has published an excellent library edition of *Cometh Up as a Flower* with exhaustive notes (2004), for which I am grateful. I generated my own notes, and then checked mine against hers. Where our opinions differed, I have noted it, and where her notes provided information I was not able to find, I have noted that also. I would also like to thank my graduate student and research assistant, Leeann D. Hunter, for her help in formatting and checking the text and her intellectual contributions to the ancillary material. Finally, I am grateful to the British Library Board for permission to reprint material from the Bentley papers in Appendix A3.

Introduction

Rhoda Broughton (29 November 1840-5 June 1920), one of the most popular novelists of the second half of the nineteenth century, largely dropped from view in the early to mid-twentieth century. She has only recently been rediscovered, but now a number of scholars have addressed her work, and Marilyn Wood's very welcome literary biography of Broughton, published in 1993, indicates that a formal revival can be said to have begun.[1] Driven by interest both in women writers and the genre of the sensation novel, the Broughton revival draws attention to a writer whose production significantly exceeds the bounds of a single genre or theme. Broughton was a prolific writer, producing 25 novels and many short stories during her lifetime, and her prose is lively and colloquial.

Broughton was born at Segrwyd Hall, near Denbigh in North Wales on 29 November 1840. Her parents were the Reverend Delves Broughton and Jane Bennett, and she had three siblings: two older sisters and one younger brother. She grew up at Broughton Hall, in Staffordshire, where her father took a position as a clergyman. She was educated at home by her father, who taught her Latin and Greek. When he died in 1863, she went to live in Surbiton, near London, with her sisters, and then moved again with her newly married sister Eleanor to Ruthin in Denbighshire. In the late 1870s, she went to live in Oxford with Eleanor (now widowed), where she lived for well over a decade and became a well-known (though not always well-loved) local personality. In 1890, she moved to London. Ten years later, she moved back to Oxford, but maintained a flat in London. She died of cancer at Headington Hill, near Oxford, on 5 June 1920.

Broughton began publishing novels during the heyday of the "sensation" genre and immediately made a splash as a sensation novelist, though her novels were not characterized by the kind of dark secrets and heavily plotted crime stories that were common in the writings of more typical sensation authors such as Wilkie Collins or Mary Elizabeth Braddon. Rather, her novels were considered sensational for their depictions of female erotic desire.

---

1 Marilyn Wood, *Rhoda Broughton (1840-1920): Profile of a Novelist* (Lincolnshire, UK: Paul Watkins, 1993).

Although often derided as a merely popular novelist of middle-class romance—Wilde famously, and ambiguously, praised her as having "that touch of vulgarity that makes the whole world kin," but warned her to stick to "Philistia," as the terrain she knew best[1]—she is also a novelist of manners and of character, in the tradition of Jane Austen. She did much to gain acceptance for explorations of women's desires—so much that she ceased to be shocking at all in later years and wryly observed that she "began life as Zola and finished it as Miss Yonge."[2]

Broughton debuted with two very influential novels in the 1860s, *Cometh Up as a Flower* and *Not Wisely but Too Well*. Both were published in 1867, and both were instant hits. *Cometh Up as a Flower* is shorter and livelier than *Not Wisely but Too Well*, which was lengthened in part to satisfy the publishing convention of long three-volume novels, despite Broughton's initial success with the briefer, breezier *Cometh Up*. One of the two best-known Broughton novels, *Cometh Up as a Flower* made Broughton's reputation and fortune. It came out as a two-volume novel with Richard Bentley and Son in 1867. Her first novel, *Not Wisely but Too Well*, was published in serial form in the *Dublin University Magazine* from August 1865 to July 1866. However, when she submitted the novel to the Bentleys for publication in bound volume form, the novelist Geraldine Jewsbury, a frequent reader for the house of Bentley, found it horrifyingly "sensual," and the publisher withdrew the tentative acceptance.[3] Broughton offered Bentley *Cometh Up as a Flower* instead, which he published.

---

1 Wilde, "New Novels" (*Pall Mall Gazette*, 1886). Although the term Philistine originates in Biblical references to a particular land and its people, by the late nineteenth century the term is often used out of its Biblical context. Philistia here refers to Matthew Arnold's christening of the middle classes as "Philistines" in *Culture and Anarchy* (1869). Wilde is identifying a stratum of British society that he feels is materialistic and deficient in taste. Reprinted in Robert Ross, *The First Collected Edition of the Works of Oscar Wilde 1908-1922*, 15 vols. (London: Dawsons of Pall Mall, 1969), 98-102.

2 Earl of Oxford and Asquith, *Memories and Reflections, 1852-1927*, vol. 1 (Boston: Little, Brown, 1928), 217. Emile Zola (1840-1902) was a French realist writer perceived as scandalously frank; Charlotte Mary Yonge (1823-1901) was a British religious writer of domestic novels who, for many, exemplified the unrealistic moralizing of the mid-Victorian period.

3 See Appendix A3.

The novel was an immediate success (as was *Not Wisely*, which Broughton published with Bentley's rival Tinsley). Subtitled "An Autobiography," *Cometh Up* has important resonances with *Jane Eyre* and other fictional women's autobiographies of the period. Author and critic Margaret Oliphant's famous *Blackwood's* review, which helped define the notion of the "sensation novel," attacks Broughton directly, calling the novel "disgusting."[1] What particularly inspired Mrs. Oliphant's ire was the heroine's frank discussion of her sexual attraction to the hero, and her dispassionate evaluation of her loveless marriage as a form of self-sale, in passages such as these:

> Half an hour after I am sitting on the green settee by the library fire, with the gentleman by whose library fire I am to sit through my life, with what patience I may.
>
> His arm is round my waist, and he is brushing my eyes and cheeks and brow with his somewhat bristly moustache as often as he feels inclined—for am I not his property? Has not he every right to kiss my face off if he chooses, to clasp me and hold me, and drag me about in whatever manner he wills, for has not he bought me? For a pair of first-class blue eyes warranted fast colour, for ditto superfine red lips, for so many pounds of prime white flesh, he has paid down a handsome price on the nail, without any haggling, and now if he may not test the worth of his purchases, poor man, he is hardly used! As for me, I sit tolerably still, and am not yet actually sick, and that is about all that can be said of me. (269–70)

Notwithstanding, or perhaps because of, this critical reaction, the novel was wildly successful and widely read.

Cometh Up as a Flower is simply plotted, but the typically melodramatic romance is undercut and made piquant by Broughton's racy colloquialism, unsentimental representation of sibling relations and marriage, candid treatment of women's desire and agency, and refusal to pose a conventional solution to the moral problems of the tale—the heroine dies, the villainess prospers

---

1 "Novels," *Blackwood's Edinburgh Magazine* 102 (September 1867), 257-80 (see Appendix C4). See also "Sensation Novels," *Blackwood's Edinburgh Magazine* 91 (May 1862), 564-84 (see Appendix C1).

unpunished. The representation of female sexuality is daring and important for this period—and caused the novel to be an immediate target for ongoing assaults on popular women's writing. The style was groundbreaking as well. An "autobiography" written by a heroine of good family with an informal, slangy voice, the narrative broke rules regarding the gentility of the woman narrator and writer. Nell behaves in a way her father brands as "unmaidenly" (72), both by accepting the attentions of a man not approved by her family (and without the presence of a chaperone), but also by declaring her feelings, both to the reader and, worse, to the object of her affections. The very fact of her having those feelings is shocking enough. She is represented as actively desiring her lover, and at one point, as proposing adultery. Nell also speaks openly of her loveless marriage as prostitution or sexual slavery. Her sister Dolly, a caricature of the ideal Victorian woman, is ruthlessly commercial regarding her own sexuality and marital chances. The novel decisively deromanticizes the marriage market in a way that looks back to the best novelists of manners, such as Frances Burney and Jane Austen, even while finally—if ambiguously—upholding the ideal of romantic love mid-Victorian novels such as those of Brontë or Dickens extol.

Recent Trends in Broughton Criticism

Broughton's fairly recent critical rediscovery has been gaining momentum. Unearthed along with other 1860s novelists designated "sensational," Broughton was, early on, mostly of interest to scholars doing feminist recovery of a lost tradition, who privileged the rebellious elements of her plots and characters. Interest in the sensation novel has grown rapidly, and a fine library edition of several such novels came out in 2004. They included *Cometh Up*, brilliantly edited and introduced by Tamar Heller. Work on the sensation novel was also driven by critical work on the body, and there has been a fair amount of focus on Broughton's treatment of physicality, including my own 1997 book that deals with two of her novels.[1] Heller's introduction returns to this issue and attends to Broughton's canny use of a rich web of intertextual references to self-con-

---

1 Pamela K. Gilbert, *Disease, Desire and the Body in Victorian Women's Popular Novels* (Cambridge: Cambridge UP, 1997).

sciously foreground the problem of having a woman narrate her own physicality; as she points out, Nell not only refers to Brontë, but George Eliot, and a number of other earlier texts and plots to dramatize the difficulty of a woman narrating a woman's sexuality. Like George Eliot, Heller notes, Broughton "strands her heroine at the intersection of tales of love rewarded and vice punished, competing stories of women's desire into neither of which Nell fits, and neither of which is appropriate to the more complex, unconventional narrative needed to 'tell her experiences as a body.'"[1] As her quotation of Virginia Woolf suggests, Heller sees Broughton as a significant early attempt to do what Woolf called for in "A Room of One's Own": to narrate the experiences of women as embodied beings, rather than, as Nell says she might be in the afterlife, a "bodiless ... sexless, passionless" essence (106).

Broughton is also known for her popular short stories, especially ghost stories, and several reprintings in various anthologies have received critical attention. Broughton wrote through the end of the century, when she was no longer seen as a rebel but as rather mainstream, though her wit and irreverence were undiminished. Emerging from work on the New Woman novel,[2] there has been some attention to Broughton's apparently rather jaundiced view of that figure, especially in her novel *Dear Faustina* (1897). We now have enough scholarship, both on Broughton and on the Victorian woman writer, to attend to the complexities of her work without our primary attention being engaged by the necessity simply of applauding (or apologizing for) Broughton's political stance on the woman question. Recent work has begun to attend to other themes in Broughton, such as the "sister narrative" (that is, a narrative with a significant focus on the theme of sisters). Lindsey Faber argues that, contrary to Helena Michie's observation that sister relationship plots "defer," but ultimately also "defer to," courtship plots, Broughton uses the sister plot to resist "a clearcut and conventional approach to her characters, her depiction of

---

1 Tamar Heller, introduction, *Cometh Up as a Flower*. In *Varieties of Women's Sensation Fiction, 1855-1890*, ed. Andrew Maunder, et al. (London: Pickering & Chatto, 2004), xxxv.

2 The New Woman novel refers to a genre of novel published mostly in the 1880s and 1890s that explored the changing roles and expectations of women, especially in regard to sexuality, education and work. See Carolyn Christensen Nelson, ed., *A New Woman Reader* (Peterborough, ON: Broadview P, 2001).

sister relations, and her ending."[1] In a recent article in *Women's Writing*, Lisa Hager notes that Broughton continues her fascination with the sister plot in her later works, and still uses the tension between sisters to critique both the solidarity of female relationships and heteronormative marriage as the alternative.[2] Certainly the most vivid and complex relationship in *Cometh Up* is between Nell and Dolly.

Genre

The 1860s, when Broughton began to publish, saw the recognition by critics and reviewers of a new craze in novel writing and reading: the sensation novel. Most sensation novels, such as William Wilkie Collins's *The Moonstone* (1868), Mrs. Henry Wood's *East Lynne* (1861), or Mary Elizabeth Braddon's *Lady Audley's Secret* (1862), focused on women with a dark, often criminal secret. They were often heavily plotted, and involved crime, bigamy, madness, and improbable coincidences. Further, they were set, not in far away castles on the continent, as gothic novels tended to be,[3] but in familiar domestic England, in homes like the reader's own. "Proximity" was thought to be part of what made the sensation novel so effective; as H.L. Mansel observed of the effectiveness of such mundane settings in the *Quarterly Review*, "it is necessary to be near a mine to be blown up by its explosion."[4] Indeed, *East Lynne* boasted a plot somewhat similar to the novel that intrigues Nell: a wife runs away from her husband and suffers extreme (indeed, astonishing) ills as a result.

---

1 Lindsey Faber, "One Sister's Surrender: Rivalry and Resistance in Rhoda Broughton's *Cometh Up as a Flower*," in *Victorian Sensations: Essays on a Scandalous Genre*, ed. Kimberly Harrison and Richard Fantina (Columbus, OH: Ohio State UP, 2006), 149.

2 Lisa Hager, "Slumming with the New Woman: *Fin-de-Siècle* Sexual Inversion, Reform Work and Sisterhood in Rhoda Broughton's *Dear Faustina*," *Women's Writing* 14 (2007), 460-75.

3 Gothic novels, such as Horace Walpole's *The Castle of Otranto* (1764), tended to be set in exotic locations, mostly on the European continent, and were filled with mysteries, conspiracies, and startling, often supernatural, events. Young women were often protagonists in these novels, and were sometimes stalked or imprisoned by the villains.

4 "Sensation Novels," *Quarterly Review* 113 (1863), 488 (see Appendix C3).

Sensation novels were wildly popular with readers and roundly condemned by critics, who tagged them as morally empty (or dangerous) narratives relying entirely on excitement of the readers' nerves and baser instincts. Indeed, the term sensation referred to the novels' supposed impact on their readers: they were to cause physical shock and excitement, bypassing intellectual and moral stimulation for cheap thrills. Further, these novels were thought to be crassly commercial, being produced quickly to satisfy a passing consumer desire, and written to formula. Again, for women to write novels that appealed to such appetites was more inappropriate than for men: "It is a shame to women so to write; and it is a shame to the women who read and accept as a true representation of themselves and their ways the equivocal talk and fleshly inclinations herein attributed to them,"[1] expostulated novelist and critic Margaret Oliphant, on the sensation craze. But women (and men) read them anyway.

Broughton's novel, though quite different in many ways from these sensation novels (it is not heavily plotted; though there is a forgery, it is not a complex web of crime, but sisterly interference in courtship; there is little of the crime and madness characteristic of the other novels in the genre) was immediately tagged as sensational, as were her other early novels. No doubt this is partially a result of their popularity and appearance at the same time as these other popular novels, also mostly written and read by women. But there is another reason: Broughton gives us desiring heroines, women actuated by sexual desire. The proper Victorian lady was generally (though not universally) thought to feel little sexual desire, and what she did feel was believed to be called into being as a response to male desire: marriage and love created a responsive feeling to the man's, but only after the emotional (and civil) commitment was in place. Broughton's Dick M'Gregor has often been faulted, and with reason, as a bit of a cardboard hero. We see little complexity in the character, and our sense of his appeal is largely based on Nell's response to him. Nell has a self-confessed weakness for big, handsome soldiers, and her attraction to Richard is primarily physical before it is anything else; likewise, her repulsion to poor Sir Hugh is based on his age and appearance, as much as, or more than, her sense

---

1 "Novels," *Blackwood's Edinburgh Magazine* 102 (September 1867), 257-80 (see Appendix C4).

that he is intellectually or culturally lacking (his perpetual conversations about manure and "fat cattle"). Sensation novels featured women whose strong desires caused them to violate social norms; some of these were desires for position and wealth, such as Lady Audley's, and some were sexual or emotional desires, such as Lady Isabel's in *East Lynne*. Broughton's tendency to quote from and make reference to other literary, religious, and musical works may be frustrating for today's reader, less familiar with those references, but they serve an important role in the narration. Nell constantly refers to her reading to make sense of her own situation. Often this serves the purpose of foreshadowing or revealing some complexity to the reader that Nell is not yet aware of. Sometimes, also, Broughton uses these references to call attention to the inadequacy of existing literature to address her experiences. Strongly desiring female characters seemed newly threatening to readers in the mid-century, as women were fighting for and being granted new rights to divorce and rights to their own property.

Broughton thus comments on the social and educational role of literature. Nell is, as she tells us, reared on storybooks wherein the guilty are punished and the innocent rewarded, wherein there are gentlemen and shop-boys and the differences are very clear. This has not been very good preparation for a world of moral complexity, economic change, and dubious fairness. Even the sensation novel Nell is reading when Dolly comes to her home, "all about a married woman, who ran away from her husband and suffered the extremity of human ills in consequence," prompts her to observe that she is still not sure she would have been "very miserable" if she had run away from her own husband with Dick (314). By the end of the novel, Nell recognizes the kindness of the Coxes and the goodness of her husband; she weighs the effects of her actions on the feelings of the people around her and finds compassion even for her hated sister. Broughton thus suggests that her novel is *not* simply a storybook, not a typical romance. It is something more realistic and with more to teach than such simple fare. Thus, Broughton attempts to distance herself from the judgment of critics on the popular novel as merely frivolous, or worse, immoral. This judgment was particularly hard on women writers, who were held to standards of modesty and indeed ignorance that made it difficult for an unmarried woman to write a novel dealing with human emotions without being tagged as unmaidenly—as, of course, Broughton promptly was. But there was a fine line between writing a serious moral story and the mission of the novel to entertain. *The Times*, generally supportive of Broughton, faults her precisely for her attempt to write a realistic story: "It is very true that poetical justice is seldom dealt out in real life, but for that very reason we like to have it dealt out in a story-book. We feel vexed that Nelly, after being cruelly deceived, should be left to die of decline, while her 'she-devil' of a sister—as King Olaf forcibly styles her—lives to marry a peer with 80,000£. a year. No childish audience, listening to a 'make-up' story, would allow us to conclude thus; and children are excellent judges in these matters."[1]

Besides its relation to the sensation novel, several other genre elements are influential in *Cometh Up*. One recognized (and mostly derided) by the novel's early critics and largely missed or ignored by contemporary ones is the tradition of the religious conversion narrative. The novel is written in the first person and often in the present tense, as an "autobiography," a convention that draws on readers' familiarity with *Jane Eyre*, another unconventional fictional heroine writing an "autobiography." Dissimilar though the novels might seem today, critics then identified both novels as expressing a similar rebellion against the conventional virtues. But the autobiographic form was often also used as spiritual autobiography, an account of coming to religious consciousness. Like *Jane Eyre*, our heroine does not seem at first particularly religious, yet there is a shared theme of religious awakening through the pangs of forbidden love (and of the discontents of poverty). Also, as in *Jane Eyre*, many critics found Nell's emerging religiosity unconvincing. There the similarity ends: as Jane triumphs, Nell is confounded by her sister's machinations. Jane's story ends on a bright note, whereas Nell's turns increasingly dark.

Nell's religious awakening is likely to be simply overlooked by today's reader, less attuned to such concerns. But in fact, the religious theme runs through the entire novel. Nell begins her story in spiritual immaturity: she has been instructed in religion, but that religion is less a matter of felt truth than a series of half-understood doctrines. Early in the story, as Nell is guiltily trying to distract herself from daydreaming of her handsome soldier in church, she

> tried hard to be as sorry for my sins as I said I was—tried to
> implore from that God, who was to me then but a dim awful

---

1 "Cometh Up as a Flower," *The Times* (6 June 1867), 9 (see Appendix B3).

abstraction, those good things for my soul ... to remember of how infinitesimally little account Richard M'Gregor and his beauty would be to me at the Judgment Day.

Often and often had I terrified myself with two vivid pictures of Death and Judgment as I lay wakeful on my bed. (84)

But this is a childish concept of religion as a series of rewards and punishments, much like her moralizing storybooks. After her father dies, she faces the practical effects of a life without a deep faith:

I *hated* to think of my father, not having that living faith accorded to some, which enables them to say from their hearts, that their dead ones are "not dead but gone before." My father *was* dead to me, dead as the old dog who died the other day....

Life seemed to me a great vast chaos, through which men stumbled and tottered to a big black pit at the end. (292–93)

Victorian readers, struggling with doubts raised by science and philosophy, as well as religious diversity, would have been alert to Nell's familiar narrative of unbelief and spiritual crisis. It is by giving up her anger and plans for vengeance—"Vengeance is mine; I will repay, saith the Lord," she muses—that she is able to regain her faith—"I yielded up my injuries unto Him, who claims the redressing of all the injustices that have been wrought since the world was. I had been clamouring for justice, bare justice. Alas, if bare justice is all I myself get, in that day when the world's long tangled accounts are made up, where shall I be?" (322). The conviction of sin, forgiveness of wrongs, and recognition of a higher power are all elements of conversion narratives.

Finally, the novel intersects with the dominant genre trend in the nineteenth-century novel, the realist *Bildungsroman*, or novel of development, in which a protagonist must mature and overcome both external social difficulties and internal character flaws to resolve the conflicts of the story.[1] Nell is clearly a sympathetic character and, as the narrator, encourages us to identify with her point of view. However, as Broughton allows us to know by Chapter Three that the story has not ended well, we are

---

1 Charles Dickens's *Great Expectations* (1861) and George Eliot's *Mill on the Floss* (1860) are both examples of this genre.

encouraged to look also in Nell's narrative for character flaws that might be the origins of her problems. Nell herself takes an increasingly remote stance, as she reveals the distance between her former girlishly frivolous self and her current experience as a young woman chastened by adversity and impending death. Part of our criticism of Nell emerges from the fact that Broughton does not allow anyone but Dolly to appear as villainous (and, as we will see, even Dolly's case is not simple). The much-adored father seems strangely unaware of his daughter's loathing for Sir Hugh, yet he is not held to any accountability for the pressure upon her. Sir Hugh's only crime is that Nell does not find him appealing; he is a loving husband who tries hard to please Nell, and Nell finally comes to appreciate his moral worth, if not his attractions. The reader often likes him much better than Nell does. The "vulgar" family down the street is quite kind to the impoverished Lestranges (and even among Victorian readers, poking fun at people whose hospitality one was enjoying was considered unmannerly). Nell is amusing, but not always thoughtful in the early part of the novel; we may forgive her innocence, but also judge her as callow and self-involved. (Broughton, though she highlights these faults in Nell, seems to have struggled with them herself; a scandal that alienated her from much of Oxford society erupted when she published *Belinda* in 1883, a novel that lampooned, many felt quite cruelly, Mark Pattison, a scholar who had been a great friend to Broughton until that time.) The novel is to some extent then an aborted *Bildungsroman*, in which Nell grows to maturity, compassion, and self-awareness, but is denied the contentment and full integration into society that is the destiny of the protagonist of a *Bildungsroman*; she achieves full consciousness only to lose her life. In its way, this can be read as a condemnation of the condition of womanhood as ringing as Jane Eyre's famous articulation of discontent with her lot.[1]

---

1 Jane articulates the frustrations of women's social constraints: "Women are supposed to be very calm generally: but women feel just as men feel; they need exercise for their faculties, and a field for their efforts, as much as their brothers do; they suffer from too rigid a restraint, too absolute a stagnation, precisely as men would suffer; and it is narrow-minded in their more privileged fellow-creatures to say that they ought to confine themselves to making puddings and knitting stockings, to playing on the piano and embroidering bags."

Love and Money

Love and money are key engines of conflict in the nineteenth-century novel, as protagonists balance commitments to self and society, and to ideals and the demands of material life. *Cometh Up* begins with the high themes of death and love— or sentimentality and desire, at least. Nell sits in a graveyard, musing on death, and there first sees the "good-looking" man who distracts her from perusing the gravestones. As the story unfolds, we realize that Nell is writing this autobiography in her last days, facing death in serious earnest. The handsome young man is dead as well. Nell's cavalier attitude towards religious pursuits—her boredom with her weighty Sunday reading of "A Narrative of a Mission to the Jews"—is slowly exposed as part of a general youthful lack of interest in serious things. But as the narrative continues, she transcends her disappointment in her situation and is able to move beyond her resentment of Dolly (though the reader might have more difficulties). She gives up her opportunity for revenge and destroys the evidence that puts Dolly in her power. Finally, she accepts death and repents of her earlier impulse to rebel against her good-hearted husband and commit adultery. But the novel that begins in Chapter One with death and love—the eternal verities—quickly turns to material issues in Chapter Two, which informs us that class and money are themes that will also dominate Nell's narrative: "We had a big house, but we were not big people—at least not now; we used to be, but we had gone down in the world" (40). The first conversation with Nell's beloved father shows us that "bills, bills, bills!" is the "song in this house from morning to night" (43). These material concerns are finally what define— and defeat— her courtship story.

Nell struggles to conquer her revulsion against Sir Hugh, but she displays continuing discomfort with her role as chattel. Still, the specter of prostitution haunts her behavior. Proper young ladies do not accept money from men who are not related to them by blood or marriage; to accept a gift of money, or even an expensive gift, from such a man, is considered to put them in the man's power and therefore to be an implicitly sexual transgression. Nell's acceptance of money from Dick for the watch is improper, but, as readers, we understand that she is innocent; in her inexperience, she believes him when he says he sold it for fifty pounds. This comic scene foreshadows a later and more painful one. She cannot accept money for her father from Hugh without engaging herself to him, yet he is deeply embarrassed when she refers to this fact. Despite his offer to simply give her the money, they both know it is impossible. The uncomfortable openness around the fact that marriage—a sacrament supposedly uniting two souls deeply in love—is primarily a financial affair brings into the open something that haunts the Victorian novel from its inception (in Jane Austen's *Pride and Prejudice*, Elizabeth quips that she began to love Darcy when she saw his estate, though she is horrified that Charlotte marries a fool for the financial and social advantage of being married and off the hands of her family). Yet few female characters of good family are as bald about the exchange as Dolly, who cries "is there any old lord between the three seas, so old, so mumbling, so wicked, that I would not joyfully throw myself into his horrid palsied old arms, if he had but money; money! money! money is power; money is a god!" (204). Certainly such a mercenary female would not marry well and flourish in most Victorian novels. Yet when poor Nell responds to Sir Hugh's proposal, she might as well be making what Victorian readers preferred to think of as quite a different kind of exchange, one of sex for cash: "I will—do as you wish, if—if—you will—lend me—give me—some money—*a great deal*; oh dear—oh dear!" (259).

The mercenary Dolly bears some resemblance to Mary Elizabeth Braddon's character Lady Audley (in *Lady Audley's Secret*, 1862), the ultimate sensation villainess—a beautiful, apparently ladylike, but cold and calculating opportunist, seeking to gain money in the only way a woman legitimately can: by marrying up. As the *London Review* explains it, "The description of Dolly, the wicked sister, has some artistic merit, but it would have fitted some Italian lady in the middle ages, of noble birth, and with a propensity for poisoning, better than the daughter of a kind old English rector."[1] Yet this was precisely the exciting charm of sensation novels: they situated crime at the heart of the English home and intimated that the charming, perfectly ordinary-seeming woman in its parlor might harbor dark designs, rather than relying on the expedient, common in the gothic novel, of situating crime on the continent, in a remote location, among

---

1 *The London Review* (16 March 1867), 324-25 (see Appendix B1).

mysterious and dramatic characters. After all, however, Dolly's criminality is fairly prosaic. She manipulates a courtship, which is what women are generally supposed to do. The interception of the letters and the forgery of Nell's signature carry her over the boundary of acceptable behavior, but unlike most sensation villainesses, she is hiding no discreditable marriage, has stolen no valuable heirloom, and unlike Lady Audley in particular, has murdered (or tried to murder) no inconvenient spouse. So is Dolly a materialistic monster or simply a pragmatist?

Dolly is easy to hate. She breaks the tradition of "good sisters" and narratives of family solidarity in the novel of the period. Certainly other novels portray quarreling siblings, and some prodigal—or downright bad—brothers, but the idea that the women of the family are its emotional backbone, supporting each other when the chips are down, is generally preserved. Here, however, we have sisters between whom there is simply no love lost. Dolly may consider that she is doing her duty by her sister and her family, but she certainly demonstrates little concern for her emotions. Dolly and Nell are refreshingly and believably unpleasant to each other in their daily lives. Some readers may find a spirited anti-heroine in Dolly's unsentimental ambition: Dolly is a Mean Girl, who also manages to be a Popular Girl with a minimum of resources or family support. While Dolly can be read as one of the great female villains of the period, her motives are surprisingly complex. They draw attention to the great paradox of attitudes toward love and money in the nineteenth century and especially its fiction. The nineteenth-century novel affirms romantic love and is overwhelmingly oriented toward courtship narratives. In fiction as in life, women, especially, were supposed to experience love devoid of any economic considerations. It was the role of the family of the young marriageable woman to carefully protect her from meeting economically or socially unsuitable men, so her heart is not given to an "imprudent" match. Yet, almost invariably, when such fictional romances take place against all the strictures of parents and friends in the nineteenth-century novel, the reader's (and the narrator's) sympathy is with the lovers. But if the family's job is to guard against such liaisons, Dolly is fulfilling her role as the older sister to a motherless girl. Dolly can be read as a dutiful family member fighting an uphill battle.

Broughton does not solve this puzzle. She leaves readers to

think through Nell's and Dolly's decisions and come to their own conclusions. The Victorian middle class, like the aristocracy, emerged from an older and honored tradition of arranged marriages; marriages served primarily to consolidate property, provide heirs, extend the social influence of the family, and cement economic relationships. It was a girl's duty to her family to marry well, just as it was the family's duty to provide a dowry and educate her to be a suitable match for the right new relation. The mother usually had primary responsibility for educating and marrying off daughters, but in the absence of a mother, the father or an aunt would look to such arrangements. Nell's father fails her in this, though her family name, an old one, and estate, even though decayed and encumbered by debt, are a kind of dowry. Hugh Lancaster, with his colonial wealth and adjacent estate, is clearly the perfect match from a practical point of view. Nell's whole family desires the match, and many readers might consider her blind pursuit of what Dolly, in exasperation, calls Nell's "big wax doll" (268) and considers a "childish besotment" (321) for a thoroughly unsuitable match, to be selfish. At the same time, emergent beliefs about the importance of companionate marriage and the idea that a young girl should be innocent of the taint of mercenary motives—business being the province of men—created discomfort around the treatment of her disposal in marriage as property, or as Nell baldly puts it, "so many pounds of prime white flesh" (269).

The status of Nell's body as both a commodity with a certain value and as a feeling, desiring embodiment of her subjectivity is highlighted by that body's vulnerability. Like many a Victorian heroine, Nell's looks improve over the course of the narrative—she describes herself as plain in the beginning of the novel but later acknowledges that she is beautiful—"worth my price" (275). Red hair had traditionally been considered unattractive in Britain, but an avant-garde group of mid-century painters who called themselves the Pre-Raphaelite Brotherhood—especially Dante Gabriel Rossetti and John Everett Millais—did much to popularize it by the 1860s through their use of striking red-headed models, such as Jane Burden, Fanny Cornforth, and Elizabeth Siddal.[1] So although Nell describes herself as plain in

---

1 Dante Gabriel Rossetti's (1828-82) painting "The Blessed Damozel" is a good example of this type of image. The model is Elizabeth Siddal.

the beginning of the novel, the reader of the time would already have been familiar with images of red-haired women as icons of beauty. Nell seems initially to be healthy and vigorous—she describes herself as large and tall, especially compared to Dolly and seems always to be running, jumping, and generally acting like an energetic teenager. But her brilliant coloring also invokes another familiar image of the period—the young girl of fair skin and bright blushes who succumbs to the great terror of Victorian adolescence: tuberculosis, also often called consumption. Tuberculosis was a scourge of the period—untreatable and fatal, it often struck down apparently healthy young people in their late teens and early twenties. Doctors did not know what caused it, but suspected that there was a hereditary component and a certain kind of physical and emotional type that was most vulnerable. As Nell's mother died young, and as Nell herself is precisely the type identified as likely to succumb, the novel signals a clear danger (see Appendix F).

The belief that love denied could cause a "decline" in health dates back considerably before the period (it is covered extensively in Burton's *Anatomy of Melancholy*, published in 1621, which Nell reads looking for "serious" learning). The consumptive heroine, declining as a result of thwarted affections, was a commonplace in the Victorian novel, with roots in contemporary medical theory (see Appendix F). Readers would have seen Nell's illness in part as proof of the depth of her feeling for Richard, and as a kind of justification for her insistence on romantic love over material considerations—the practicality championed by Dolly kills the truly loving, pure Nell. On a less exalted note, the nervous systems of women were thought to be particularly vulnerable to disease based on emotional or moral causes, and sensation and romantic novels were often tagged themselves as "contagious" causes of such nervous afflictions. In turn, these afflictions could also cause moral "ills." Victorian physician Thomas Trotter, M.D, in his popular *A View of the Nervous Temperament*, notes that the "passion of novel reading is ... one of the great causes of nervous disorders. The mind that can amuse itself with the love-sick trash of most modern compositions of this kind, seeks enjoyment that is beneath the level of a rational being.... To the female mind in particular, as being endowed with a finer feeling, this species of literary poison has often been fatal," resulting in, among other things, sexual depravity.[1] Victorian doctors generally believed in a strong mind-body connection in health and illness; sadness and melancholy led to ill-health, just as overstimulation through novels might do. Thwarted love could lead to consumption, and it was possible to die of a broken heart. So Broughton's burden as the writer of a love story is twofold—to show an idealistic, romantic girl crushed by material reality and to avoid, in that process, being accused of perpetuating a morbid sentimentality.

Class Attitudes in Historical Context

Although the novel is filled with accessible themes—the age-old plot of lovers parted, for example—there are also elements that are more historically and culturally specific. Class is a complex issue in the novel, and may be confusing particularly for North American readers today. Although Nell lives in "genteel poverty," paying the butcher with difficulty, she lives on a substantial ancestral estate. Her name is ancient, and she traces her heritage back to the Norman invaders of 1066. But all is not well with the family, and there is a certain archness with which Nell notes that "we had poured out our blood like water, under lion-hearted Richard, for the Holy Sepulchre; we had had fat abbey lands given us by King Henry of the many wives" (41). In short, the Lestranges were staunch Catholics when it suited them and made a transition to Protestantism when Henry VIII left the Catholic Church, for which the family was rewarded with lands seized from the Catholic Church. The latter days seem a descent into mercenary and frivolous pursuits: "we had married heiresses ... and it had been well with us. But, alack!" the Lestranges had gambled away their money and kept expensive mistresses, and so their lands had "passed into the hands of Manchester gents with fat, smug faces, who waged a war of extermination against the letter H" (41). The newly rich middle classes were buying up lands that impoverished upper-class families could no longer afford to set up country estates, thus beginning the process of gentrifying their own families. Manchester, as a center of cotton manufacturing, was a mill and factory town wherein the rapid

---

1 Thomas Trotter, M.D., *A View of the Nervous Temperament*, 3rd ed. (London: Longman, Hurst, Rees, Orme and Brown, n.d. [1812]), 94 (see Appendix F6).

expansion of the cotton industry made great fortunes in the early nineteenth century.

Readers of the period liked stories about aristocratic characters—though they also liked to think that such characters were somewhat morally lacking. Britons respected class hierarchy even as they questioned class privilege; as audiences are today, they were fascinated with the classes they thought of as above (and below) them even as they might censure the values identified with those classes. For British readers at the time, Nell certainly had more claim to the status of "ladyhood" than those "great bouncing dairymaids" down the road, whose *nouveau riche* father has made his money in trade, and moved to the country as part of a multigenerational process of gentrifying his family. Nell's casual snobbery dismisses these people, but presents them as good-hearted. However, though the mostly middle-class readership of the novel might well have shared her snobbish attitudes toward the newly arrived in their own class, such readers would also have disapproved of what was seen as the typically aristocratic irresponsibility and immorality that had dissipated the Lestrange fortune. Thus Broughton encourages us to think of Nell somewhat critically, if gently so. Her father's pro-Confederate stance marks him as a quite conservative Tory (the most conservative party in the UK at that time, associated with the aristocracy and traditional values), and by the time of the Civil War in the US, even many Tories were anti-slavery. (Slavery had been abolished in England in 1702 and Britain's colonial possessions in 1833; the British slave-trade industry was outlawed in 1807.) Nell treats the Civil War more as her father's hobby than a serious matter—she knows just enough to follow her father's conversation and has no political opinions of her own, as was considered appropriate for a young woman. However, she certainly retains a firm belief in class superiority that is perhaps more noticeable and probably more off-putting to readers today than it was then.

Nell's casual anti-Semitism is even more jolting to readers now, but it was widespread across all classes at the time. Readers today may wonder how a person might borrow money and then resent the lender for wanting it back; this, too, is part of Victorians' complex relation to money matters. A gentleman never borrowed from anyone of his own class, and on the rare occasion he did (or owed money on a bet), it had to be paid promptly on demand.

However, to loan money for profit was ungentlemanly for two reasons: it meant one had to earn money rather than inheriting it, and then it violated Victorians' sense of making money honorably, by offering labor or producing goods. Default on such loans, although illegal, usually did not prompt the censure that other financial irregularity did, and popular sympathy often went with the defaulter rather than the unfortunate lender. Lending was popularly associated with Jews, though there were certainly gentiles in the lending industry. In many cases, however, the word "Jew" was used interchangeably with "lender," regardless of the actual ethnicity or religion of the person described. (Anti-Semitism was widespread in Europe during this time, and although it never reached in Britain the extremes it achieved in Germany, or even in France, Jews were long subject to alternating suspicion and attempts at conversion during this period.) Nell's class position and her vexed relation to monetary issues thus serve as part of her characterization, immediately recognizable to Victorian readers. But her characterization also develops a central theme in the novel: its interrogation of the responsibility of the individual to her own fulfillment, to her family, and to the fortunes of that family. This issue is particularly problematic for women, whose position in the private, domestic world is supposed to insulate them from money concerns and to protect their purity. A woman exposed to the hard realities of the economic world is likely to end up a fallen woman. Yet a woman's only negotiable possessions are precisely her purity, which forbids her to make a market of her sexuality, and, paradoxically, her sexuality itself, which it is her responsibility to use to her family's advantage. Thus, the withholding and finally the giving of her body and her emotional loyalty are central to the heroine's narrative; indeed, traditionally, it was her only possible narrative, and marriage (or the failure to marry) its only end. Much of Victorian literature concerns itself with this difficulty.

Conclusion

Broughton continued to be highly productive. Her popularity was huge: she was widely known as one of the top women writers of the period, a "queen of the circulating library." Helen C. Black includes her in her revised collection of magazine articles about "notable women authors of the day," as late as 1906, and remarks:

"The fame of these [Broughton's] books went far afield. Some years ago a graceful tribute was paid to the author. Captain Markham, of H.M. [Her Majesty's] ship Alert, begged to be introduced, and told her that in a remote Arctic region they had by common consent christened an icebound mountain, 'Mount Rhoda,' in grateful acknowledgment of the pleasure which her books have given the officers of the ship on their perilous voyage."[1]

Broughton remains eminently readable today. Her informality, strong sense of voice, and ironic humor are as appealing today as they were when she first wrote—though less shocking. *Cometh Up* is an early novel and has an early novel's faults, as well as energy and strengths. Subsequent novels were often more complex, offering more fully developed characters and less obvious padding, but none exceed *Cometh Up*'s vigor and simple appeal. However, the novel is a product of its time, and so the scholarly apparatus of this edition is intended to enhance the accessibility of the novel. Broughton's novels are rich in allusions to and quotations from everything from Shakespeare to popular songs. Often, she creates a comic effect by switching abruptly from the register of "high" art such as Milton to the most ephemeral and banal of doggerel. This practice was part of the amusing and slightly shocking irreverence and sense of contemporaneity that attracted readers, especially younger ones. Broughton's readers of the period often shared a more homogenous culture and educational background than readers today and had the additional advantage of living in the popular culture of the moment that Broughton makes use of so deftly. This practice, along with her frequent use of slang, can make for occasional tough going for today's readers, especially students who are already grappling with an unfamiliar historical period. I have extensively footnoted the references for the reader for convenience, but they are often not required to understand the story, and readers who brave the onslaught of unfamiliar quotations and terms will find the narrative readable and fast-moving. Broughton has much to teach us about the Victorian period, but reading her should be, first and last, a pleasure. I have also included several appendices to allow the reader the opportunity to further explore some themes I have

---

1   Helen C. Black, *Notable Women Authors of the Day* (London: Maclaren and Company, 1906), 42. I have not been able to locate this mountain.

raised in this introduction: Victorian attitudes toward the sensation genre and this novel's reception, marriage and the question of the "marriage market," women's desire and sexuality, health, and the body. Broughton continues to gain the attention of readers and scholars, confirming the judgment of Victorian author, anthologist, and critic Gleeson White, who wrote Broughton that, "Historians of English fiction in the reign of Victoria will, one fancies, be compelled to consider your work more seriously than contemporary critics have done."[1]

---

1 Quoted in Michael Sadleir, *Things Past* (London: Constable, 1944), 89.

Rhoda Broughton: A Brief Chronology

1840 Born 29 November, third child of Rev. Delves
Broughton and Jane Bennett, at Segrwyd Hall near
Denbigh in North Wales; during Rhoda's early
childhood, the family moves to the manor house at
Broughton Hall

1843 Joseph Sheridan Le Fanu marries Susanna Bennett,
Rhoda's maternal aunt

1860 Mother dies

1863 Father dies, requiring Rhoda to leave Broughton Hall;
she joins her sisters in Surbiton

1864 Her sister Eleanor marries William Charles Newcome,
and Rhoda lives in their home at Upper Eyarth in
Ruthin, Denbighshire, for fourteen years

1865 Rhoda presents a manuscript to her uncle Le Fanu, an
editor at *Dublin University Magazine*

1865 *Not Wisely but Too Well* is serialized in *Dublin University
Magazine* from August 1865 to July 1866

1866 *Cometh Up as a Flower* begins serialization in the *Dublin
University Magazine*, continuing into January of 1867

1867 *Cometh Up as a Flower* appears anonymously, in two
volumes, as Rhoda's first novel in book form, published
by Bentley and Son; *Not Wisely but Too Well* is not
published by Bentley, due in large part to Geraldine
Jewsbury's critical objections and Bentley's resulting
demands for revision, and it is instead published, in
three volumes, by Tinsley

1870 *Red as a Rose Is She* is published

1872 *Good-bye, Sweetheart!* is the first publication for which
Rhoda claims authorship; publication of *Tales for
Christmas Eve* (reissued as *Twilight Stories* in 1879)

1873 *Nancy* is published

1876 Installments of *Gone Wrong*, a parody of Rhoda
Broughton's works, appear in *Punch* magazine from
March 25 to June 3; publication of *Joan*

1877 Rhoda meets novelist Henry James (1843-1916), and,
despite his unfavorable review of *Joan*, they develop a
lifelong friendship

1878 William Charles Newcome dies, leaving Eleanor a
widow; Rhoda and Eleanor move to Oxford, where
Rhoda's literary reputation makes her a controversial
figure; in Oxford, Rhoda meets Mark Pattison and his
wife Emilia Frances Strong
1880 *Second Thoughts* is published
1883 *Belinda* is published
1886 Publication of the two short stories "Betty's Visions"
and "Mrs. Smith of Longmains" and the novel *Doctor
Cupid*
1890 Rhoda and her sister Eleanor move to London;
publication of *Alas,* the last of her novels to be published
in three volumes
1891 Publication of *A Widower Indeed,* written in
collaboration with American author Elizabeth Bisland
(1861-1929)
1892 *Mrs. Bligh* is published
1894 *A Beginner* is published
1895 Rhoda's sister and lifelong companion Eleanor dies;
publication of *Scylla or Charybdis?*
1897 *Dear Faustina* is published
1899 *The Game and the Candle* is published
1900 Acquires a residence in Headington Hill near Oxford;
publication of *Foes-in-Law*
1902 *Lavinia* is published
1905 *A Waif's Progress* is published
1908 *Mamma* is published
1910 *The Devil and the Deep Sea* is published; Rhoda develops
friendship and companionship with novelist Mrs. Belloc
Lowndes (1868-1947)
1912 *Between Two Stools* is published
1914 *Concerning a Vow* is published
1916 Henry James dies
1917 *Thorn in the Flesh* is published
1920 Dies 5 June in Headington Hill; *A Fool in Her Folly* is
published posthumously

A Note on the Text

The original version of *Cometh Up as a Flower* was serially published in the *Dublin University Magazine* between July 1866 and January 1867. It was considerably shorter, at 28 chapters, than the 38-chapter version published by Bentley and Son in two volumes in 1867. This Broadview text is based on the full-length version published in 1867 by Bentley. Obvious typographical errors in that version have been silently corrected. Appendix A identifies all other changes from that version and also reproduces the original conclusion, which was not used as part of the two-volume version.

COMETH UP AS A FLOWER[1]
An Autobiography

"Is the old man yet alive?"[2]

In Two Volumes

---

1 Job 14:1-2. "Man that is born of a woman is of few days and full of misery. He cometh up as a flower, and is cut down." In this passage Job is lamenting the brief and often apparently unfair nature of life. He calls out to God to show him why he suffers as he does.
2 Genesis 43:27. Joseph, his father's favorite among twelve sons, was sold into slavery in Egypt by his jealous brothers. Years later, he had risen to power and was in a position to save his brothers, who did not immediately recognize him. He asked them first if the "old man" was still alive before he revealed his identity. The scene is emblematic of the affection between father and child.

VOLUME I

CHAPTER I

"When I die, I'll be buried under that big old ash tree over yonder—the one that Dolly and I cut our names on with my jagged old penknife nine, ten years ago now. I utterly reject and abdicate my reserved seat in the family mausoleum. I don't see the fun of undergoing one's dusty transformation between a mouldering grandpapa and a mouldered great-grandpapa. Every English gentleman or lady likes to have a room to themselves when they are alive. Why not when they are dead? Yes, when my time to make a decent ending has come, I'll have a snug hole grubbed for me right under my old friend the ash (the near one, isn't it?) and there I'll make myself as comfortable as circumstances will permit amongst the lobbies,[1] and the woodlice, etc. And Dolly (if she survives me, as I hope she won't, and as I am sure she will) shall plant a rose at my head, and a gillyflower at my feet, and daffydowndillies on each side of me, and there I'll sleep as sound as a top, and not dream a bit, whatever Hamlet says to the contrary."[2]

These remarks I made to no other audience than myself, consequently they were received without any marks of dissent. I did not say them aloud; for, within my experience, people do not soliloquise at the top of their voices, save at Drury Lane and Coventgarden,[3] but, as it were, to my *Philon Hetor*,[4] or dear heart. And as I soliloquised I leaned the rather frayed elbows of my venerable holland frock on the top of the low stone wall that parted our big hay meadow (the largest of the fields belonging to the Grange) from

---

1 Spiders.
2 See Shakespeare's *Hamlet* (first printed in quarto 1603) Act 3, Scene 1. Hamlet considers that while death may seem a desirable rest, it might also hold terrors of its own: "To sleep: perchance to dream: ay, there's the rub; / For in that sleep of death what dreams may come / When we have shuffled off this mortal coil, / Must give us pause."
3 Theater venues.
4 The Greek poet Pindar (522-443 BCE) frequently used this expression; he thus invokes the muse in Olympian Ode I.

the churchyard. It was the pleasantest hour, videlicet[1] 9 p.m., of one of the pleasantest days of the pleasantest month in the whole year, videlicet—May. There had not been a breath of wind all day, but at sundown a little whiff had arisen from no one knew where, except that from its fragrance and velvet softness, one felt sure that its original home must have been heaven. Rejoicing in it, the elms were waving their topmost crowns, and talking to one another, low and stately, in their own language, which none but themselves and the wind can comprehend. I think they were telling each other how strong the spring sap was running through their leafy veins, and how grateful was the touch of the dew-freshened flowers about their gnarled feet. And the grass, not green now, but clad by twilight in dim silver gray, was talking too, as any one might see, who watched its blades and spears bowing and swaying to catch each other's confidences.

Ours was a churchyard that it would have been a real luxury to be buried in. It inspired one with no horrible, hardly even melancholy ideas. One never thought of skulls or cross-bones, or greedy worms, when one looked at those turfy mounds sloping so softly; those mounds that the westering sun always gave his last good-night kiss to before he went to bed behind the craggy purple hill. Were one really dead, stowed away in one's appointed oak box, it would concern one, no doubt, not a whit whether one were huddled with other oak boxes into some ghastly pit, among the dark be-nettled grass of some city charnel, or laid down reverently in the fragrant earth, shadowed by some peaceable little gray church tower, such as ours was. But while one is yet alive, and one's oak box is as yet not a box at all, but the trunk of some branchy tree, one cannot realize this. Unconsciously we fancy that we shall smell the odorous mignonette and carnations that are revelling in the summer sunshine above our heads, that we shall hear the birds preaching our funeral sermons, and singing their own epithalamiums,[2] when spring comes back, that we shall shiver in the snow, and be chilled by the wintry rains.

During my meditations, my elbows had grown quite numb with resting so long on the cold stone, and of this I at length became aware. I raised them from their uneasy position, and rubbed them slowly and affectionately.

---

1 Namely or that is to say (corrupt Latin).
2 Type of pastoral poem associated with the celebration of marriage.

"I wish I were in the churchyard," said I (to myself, as before). "I could sit so comfortably on old Mrs. Barlow's big flat tombstone, and perhaps I might be inspired to compose an elegy that would make Gray's[1] hide its diminished head. If Dolly were here she would say it was indelicate and unladylike for a grown-up woman to be scrambling over walls. But as Dolly is not here, to the winds with gentility! There's nobody to see me except a few bats, and perhaps a ghost or two."

And so I clambered over, and got coated with lichens in the process, and made for Mrs. Barlow's tomb, sat down upon it, and fell into a reverie. I had read all the inscriptions scores of time; they were of the usual type.

"Affliction sore long time I bore,"[2] etc., decidedly bearing away the palm of popularity. Just opposite to me was an upright stone, with the somewhat halting, but highly impressive poetic effort, which is to be found in every graveyard over England, inscribed upon it—

"When the Archangel's trump shall sound,
And souls to bodies join,
Thousands shall wish their stay on earth
Had been as short as mine."[3]

For the twentieth time I was perusing this gloomy prophecy, supposed to be spoken by an infant of tender years, and was marvelling whether the gifted but unknown author intended the rhyme to be "*join* and *moine*," or "*jine* and *mine*," when I was startled by hearing the lych gate[4] behind me swing on its hinges. I turned my head round with a jerk, and the archangel and the prophetic baby went out of my head together. In the waning light I saw the figure of a man. If he were a ghost he was

---

1 "Elegy Written in a Country Churchyard" (1751), by Thomas Gray (1716-71).
2 The full text of this characteristic bit of verse, found on gravestones everywhere in England during this period, runs as follows, with some variation: "Affliction sore long time I bore / Physicians were in vain, / Till death gave ease, as God was pleased, / To ease me of my pain."
3 A typical gravestone verse for a child.
4 Roofed gateway to a churchyard, used traditionally as a resting place for coffins before burial.

a very substantial one, besides a ghost would not have banged the gate, and oh! I never heard of a ghost that whistled Meyerbeer's "Shadow Air!"[1] It could not be the sexton, for he was a hump-backed sexagenarian, who would as soon have thought of burying himself in one of his own graves as of courting rheumatism, amid the damp dews of a May evening. It could not be any one of the John Smiths or Robert Browns of the parish; for besides that the bumpkins in our parts are not given to indulging in the sentimental melancholy of pilgrimages to the tombs of their respective Betsys, and Anns, and Marthas, one glance, even though the light was waning, sufficed to show me that the new comer was a gentleman. He did not appear to have seen me at first, as he stood there in the church path, with his hands in his pockets, and a meerschaum in his mouth, "viewing the landscape o'er."[2]

I cannot bear being in the company of a person who is not aware of my proximity. I always experience something of the guilty feeling of a spy or eavesdropper, so I coughed gently, to hint to him that there was a young woman perched, ghoul-like, on a gravestone in his vicinity. Having so coughed, I was overcome with shyness, and durst not look round again, to watch the result of my manoeuvre. I suppose it succeeded, for he certainly manifested no signs of surprise, as he came close by me, in his deliberate saunter towards the church.

"What is he like?" asked the inquisitiveness of nineteen within my breast. "What's that to you?" said Decorum. "Everything," returned Inquisitiveness. I must have one peep. I had one peep. As he passed I looked up at him, and he looked down at me, and our eyes met. There was nothing impudent in his gaze, none of the fervent admiration with which, at a first introduction, the hero in a novel regards the young lady, who at a later period of the story is to make a great fool of, or be made a great fool by him. It simply expressed the moderate amount of curiosity with which a young Englishman regards a young Englishwoman whom he sees for the first time. "Are you pretty, I wonder? It's

---

1 "Shadow Air from Dinorah." Popular piano music in the 1860s, adapted from a piece by Giacomo Meyerbeer (1791-1864).

2 See "There is a land of pure delight" (1709), a hymn by Isaac Watts. Tamar Heller offers a different source for this: Hannah Wallis, "To Mrs. —, On the Death of her Husband" (1787).

almost impossible to tell by this light." So said those dark, gray eyes, and that was all they said. Why I did it I do not know, and cannot explain to this day, but with my usual stupidity I blushed crimson; forehead and throat and ears all shared the crimson glow. I became a lobster. Perhaps it was only my guilty imagination, but I fancied I detected a slight smile dawning under a great yellow moustache—a smile which good manners and gentlemanlike feeling strangled in the birth.

However that might be, he made no pause in his walk, but strolled on, and sat down on another tombstone somewhat similar to mine, a few yards further on, where he puffed away solemnly at his pipe, and kept his eyes to himself. I could have scratched my cheeks till they bled, in my righteous anger against them. "So missish!" said I, internally with much severity. "So school girlish, as if you had never seen a man before!" The ridiculousness of the situation tickled my fancy irresistibly; two people seated, each on their several tombstone, within bow-shot of one another, silent, solemn, and unsociable. I felt that I should disgrace myself by laughing outright if I stayed much longer, and besides, the hour was growing late, so I rose from my seat and dawdled towards the gate. As I reached it I heard a deep voice behind me say, "Allow me," and as he spoke, the stranger unlatched the gate, and politely opened it for my benefit. Then he took off his hat, displaying a head of curly yellow hair, and smiled. I was taken by surprise and covered with confusion. "Thank you." I mumbled, ungraciously enough, and made a somewhat gawky inclination, the effect of which was still further marred by the fact that in the very act of making it I trod on my own dress, nearly tripping myself up, and all but measuring my length on the ground in a profounder salaam than I had any intention of executing.

CHAPTER II

Though I ran nearly all the way, it was striking ten on the stable clock before I stood under the faint thick clusters of monthly roses that glimmered out of the dark ivy above the heavy, nail-studded, old oak door of my own. We had a big house, but we were not big people—at least not now; we used to be, but we had gone down in the world. People at whom fifty years ago we turned up our noses, now turned up their noses at us. We had come sailing over

the sea in beaked ships with Norman William; we had poured
out our blood like water, under lion-hearted Richard, for the
Holy Sepulchre; we had had fat abbey lands given us by King
Henry of the many wives, we had married heiresses, and had
gone mounting up to the top of fortune's wheel, and it had been
well with us.[1] But, alack! in these latter days we had been but too
well known at Epsom and Newmarket; we had been very much
at home at Crockford's when Crockford's was; we had wasted
our young affections and substance on operatic Phrynes; we had
run away with our neighbours' wives, and had generally misbe-
haved ourselves; and, in consequence, our many thousands had
dwindled to very few hundreds, and our fair acres passed into
the hands of Manchester gents with fat, smug faces, who waged
a war of extermination against the letter H, and used big words
where little ones would have done better.[2] So the poor old house
was very much out of repair, and there was no money wherewith
to patch up its stout old walls.

But all this time I am keeping myself waiting at my own hall-
door while detailing my family's genealogy. I stayed a moment
to bury my face in a bunch of pale roses, whose scent the night
air brought out pure and strong, and then passed into the dim
old hall. At this time of night it was as gloomy and ghostly an old
place as one would wish to see—very big, very dark, with heavy
beams across the low ceiling, oak panels sadly in want of varnish,
coats of arms that showed what brilliant marriages we had made
in the old times, mangy stags' heads with bulging glass eyes,
and rather damaged family portraits. It would have taken a vast

---

1   William the Conqueror came from Normandy to invade England in
    1066. Richard the Lionheart (Richard Plantagenet) reigned as king
    of England from 1189 to 1199. He is best known for his action in
    the Crusades and for his conflict with his usurping brother, John.
    King Henry VIII (1491-1547) is best known for breaking with the
    Roman Catholic Church and founding the Anglican Church, in
    part over a conflict resulting from his several marriages, two of
    which ended with the execution of his wives.
2   Epsom and Newmarket are famous for their horse races. Crock-
    ford's was a gentlemen's club, where there was often gambling.
    Phryne was a Greek courtesan of ancient times. "Manchester
    gents" refers to the newly rich who made their money in textile
    mills (also known as "cotton lords"), who were considered socially
    beneath the aristocracy. Not pronouncing the "h" at the beginning
    of a word was considered characteristic of the lower classes.

expenditure of gas to have lit it up properly, and in lieu of such expenditure one solitary composite candle blinked sleepily from the middle of the large ricketty hall-table, illuminating the Family Bible out of which I read prayers to the servants in an impressive and quasi-clerical manner every morning and evening, and leaving the rest of the apartment "to darkness and to me."[1] As I entered, I was met by a ricketty old man, who, somehow, seemed of a piece with the rest of the establishment, in whose superannuated old body centred the functions of butler, under-butler, groom of the chambers, valet, footman, and page, and whom my father kept on from a motive of compassion, and because he hated changes.

"Tea is ready, Miss," remarked this desirable body servant, emerging from the gloom into the little circle of pale light round the candle.

"Is it?" said I, nothing more original occurring to me to say, as I stroked down my untidy ruddy locks with my fingers.

Without further addition to my toilette, for I feared to keep my father waiting, I ran down two or three shallow, well-worn stone steps into the dining-room. It was likewise very big and very dark, with more panels that obtrusively proclaimed their destitution of varnish to each casual observer, and with more family pictures glooming down out of black frames, in their faded beauty, for beauty the Lestranges, man and woman, always had apparently in those old times, however degenerate they might be now. The table in the middle of the room, laid for two people, scantly furnished with light, and scantlier still with eatables, showed like an oasis in a desert of obscurity. My father was already in his old velvet arm-chair, and was sitting leaning forward with his head between his hands, in a pose sufficiently expressive. You did not need to see his face to tell you that here was a man careworn and weary, on whom the sun of his life's afternoon was beating scorching hot, a man with whom life was going awry—awry I should think it was; the old house was going down hill, and he did not like it; the brambles had sprung up rankly, and were choking the Lebanonian cedar; he and his were last where they used to be first, and he felt that it would be the death of him.

---

1 See Gray's "Elegy."

Brave as the Spartan boy,[1] he kept the vitals-gnawing fox hidden under his cloak, away from the eyes of the coldly prying world—a world often ill-naturedly curious in seeking out and putting its fingers through the tatters in its neighbour's coat—a world

"That would peep and botanize
Upon its mother's grave."[2]

I gambolled up to him in a kid-like manner. "Well," said I cheerfully, "I suppose the tea is quite cold, and you're quite cross, and I'm to have a real good scolding, aren't I?" Then I stooped and kissed the whitened hairs.

"Eh, what?" said he, thus suddenly called back from his joyless reverie to the contemplation of a young round face that was dear to him, and vainly endeavouring to extricate himself from the meshes of a redundant crop of curly hair, which was being flourished, in its redness, before his face. "Indeed, Nell, I'd forgotten your very existence that minute."

"What could have chased so pleasing an image from your mind's eye?" said I, laughing.

"What always chases every pleasing image," he answered, gloomily.

"Bills, I suppose," returned I, discontentedly, "bills, bills, bills! that's the song in this house from morning to night. Is there any word of one syllable in the English language that includes so many revolting ideas!"

"None except hell," said my father, bitterly, "and I sometimes think they're synonymous."

"Dad," said I, "take my advice, and try a new plan, don't worry about them any more, take no notice at all of them, we've got the air and the sunshine, and one another left, we ought to be happy, and if the worst comes to the worst, we can but go to gaol,[3] where we shall be nicely dressed, well fed, and have our hair cut, all for nothing."

---

1 Legend has it that the Spartan boy hid a fox under his cloak. The fox began to gnaw at his vitals, but he never complained, and so died without allowing anyone to know his misery.

2 See "A Poet's Epitaph" (1799), by William Wordsworth (1770-1850).

3 In the early nineteenth century, those who owed money could be jailed if it were not repaid; this practice continued until 1849, and so was not a real threat by the time of this narrative.

My ideas of a debtors' prison were evidently not derived from "Pickwick" or "Little Dorrit,"[1] inextricably mingled were they with my recollections of the felon's gaol at Nantford our county town.

Papa shook his head. "All very well to say 'don't worry,' Nell; as well say to a criminal on the scaffold 'don't be hanged,' or to a dead body, 'don't be buried'; to be worried or not worried does not depend upon an effort of the will, child."

I had by this time established myself among the cups and saucers. As he spoke, I held the teapot suspended in mid air, and paused. "Dad," said I, "doesn't it say in the Bible, 'sufficient unto the day is the evil thereof.'"[2]

"Yes, Nell; and it says too, 'man is born to trouble, as the sparks fly upward';[3] I do not doubt the wisdom or truth of the first, but the last comes home to my inmost soul, 'as the sparks fly upward!'" He looked up as he spoke, as though tracing the flight of the sparks.

"If you sigh like that," said I, pettishly, "you'll blow the candles out, and then there'll be no sparks to go up."

My father made no rejoinder, and we both ate in silence for some minutes. But at that period of my life I had no talent whatever *pour le silence*;[4] I would rather have harangued a cod's head than hold my peace. I began again.

"Dad."

"Well."

"Please to listen. I'm going to tell you something; come down from the clouds, or up from the pit, wherever you are."

"I'm all attention."

"Well," said I, narratively, "you must know that I found you so dull and unsociable this evening, that I betook myself to the churchyard!"

"Did you find anybody, I should rather say any of the bodies, particularly sociable there?"

"I rather like dead people's company, pa; they don't contradict

---

1   Novels by Charles Dickens (1812-70) in which the debtor's prison features significantly.
2   See Matthew 6:34. Jesus preaches that his listeners should focus on spiritual things rather than worrying about the worldly future.
3   See Job 5:7. Here, Job remarks that it is the nature of humanity to suffer.
4   For silence (French).

one, and one has not to make talk for them; but I saw something besides tombstones to-night. Guess what?"

"A pig?"

"No."

"A widow?"

"No."

"A ghost or two?"

"Fiddlestick!"

"My divining powers are exhausted, then," said my father, looking as if he should be rather thankful if I would leave him in peace.

"Guess again."

"Oh, plague take it, how do I know what you saw? one of our servants, perhaps, or some other sight equally strange and invigorating."

"It was not anything of ours, we have not got anything half so good-looking about the place, dad, it was a *man*!"

"What sort of a man, old Iken?"

"Well, if it was old Iken, old Iken is six foot high at least, and has got wavy yellow hair, and I have been labouring under a delusion as to his personal appearance for the last nineteen years."

"Young John Barlow, perhaps, come to see whether his mother's tombstone is put up right."

"No such thing, dad. It was no more John Barlow than it was John the Baptist, and that, you'll own, is not probable."

"Some counter-jumper[1] from Nantford, probably; they get themselves up much finer than gentlemen now-a-days," said my father, ruefully.

"Papa, don't you suppose I know gold from brass? don't I know a gentleman when I have the luck to see one? *My* friend had no ditchwater in his veins, he had a decidedly warlike air too, and you know, dad, you and I have a *penchant* for soldiers; haven't we?"

"I have a *penchant* for peace, my dear, if you would be kind enough to drink your tea, and let me indulge it. Probably this prodigy was one of the Burgoynes, if you are quite sure he was neither Iken Barlow[2] nor a pig."

"No, no, it was not one of the Burgoynes. I know them both.

---

1 Shop assistant (derogatory term).
2 This seems to be Broughton's mistake, conflating the two people.

John is crooked, and Charles squints; they are a pair of ugly little boys, and this was a *man*." My parent smiled benignly at my enthusiasm concerning the unknown's beauty.

"What's your definition of a man, Nell? John Burgoyne would be surprised to find he did not come under that head. I think in his own estimation he's something very little lower than the angels."

"He may be very little lower than the angels," said I, pouring myself out a second cup, "for I haven't the least idea how high the angels are; but he's a great deal lower than my man—two inches, I should think."

"It's a pity we cannot solve the enigma of his name, Nell. '*My man*' is rather a vague designation, isn't it?"

I laughed, not quite so musically as usual perhaps, because my voice was partially smothered in buttered toast.

"Yes, dad, and the worst of it is, it isn't true, either; he *is* not mine, and, what's more, he is not ever likely to be either. Oh, dad, I wish we could find out about him. You don't know how pleasant he looked; almost as nice as you when you've got your Sunday coat on."

"That gives an idea of majestic beauty I own," said my father, with a little gentle sneer at his own stooped shoulders and bowed head.

To my mind it did; in my eyes my father had the amaranthine bloom of ivy-crowned Dionysius.[1] Love looks beyond the withered husk to the fresh kernel, and I knew that to me his heart was always young.

"He was an elderly gentleman, was he?" continued my father. "I begin to think better of him. I fancied at first that he was some foolish young puppy, not come to years of discretion."

"Papa, I like puppies; there's much more life and fun about them than about mumbling old dogs. I don't mean by that that you are a mumbling old dog."

"I did not mean any insult to him, my dear, by calling him a puppy. I'd be a puppy again myself this minute if I could; I'd compound for puppy brains if I could get back puppy spirits with them."

"Are people always happier when they are young than when they are old, pa?"

---

1 The Greek god of wine and sexual ecstasy was traditionally crowned with ivy.

"Mostly, I think."

"Then I hope I shall die young."

Whereupon I fell a-thinking what an interesting young corpse I should make lying in the big four-poster in the red room, with my emaciated hands folded on my bosom, and a deluge of white flowers about me.

"You'll die, darling, when God pleases," said my father, with his dear old voice shaking a little. "Whether He takes you away from the evil to come, as He did your little mother, or leaves you to fight out the weary fight to the end, as it pleased Him that I should."

Then he rose, and I, running to him, stole my hand into his, and we left the room together in sober fashion.

CHAPTER III

The next day, the 18th of May, 18—, was a day of note in my life. I had been looking forward to it during the past week with a small portion of pleasant anticipation and a large portion of shy tremor. It was the day of my first dinner party. Yes, though I was nineteen years of age, I had never been at one of those solemn symposia which form the Englishman's idea of festivity. *But* twice or thrice during all my nineteen years had I exhibited my bare neck and arms to an admiring public,[1] and *once* I had been to a ball. That ball seemed to me the one thing of importance that had ever happened to me. I dated from it as the Greeks did from the first Olympiad, or the Romans, *ab urbe condita*.[2]

Dolly—let it be understood that Dolly is my sister, and my senior by four years—had rather got into the habit of repressing me—keeping me and what charms I had in the background, hiding my light,[3] if I had any light, under a bushel. As for herself, she

---

1 Evening dress for women was characterized by low-cut necks and bare arms. Nell is saying she has not yet been at many social events for adults.

2 From the founding of the city (Latin). In the original, the city is Rome, and hence carries the connotation, "since the beginning of civilization."

3 Compare Matthew 5:15. Jesus cheers his followers, telling them that just as people do not hide a light under a bushel, they must shine the light of their beliefs and good works on the world.

loved the world, technically so called, with all her heart, and soul, and strength, with the one-idea'd devotion of a Frenchwoman.

In the main, I was tolerably content to remain under the bushel where I had been deposited by sisterly care; having hardly tasted the fire-water of dissipation, I did not miss its stimulus. I stayed at home with my old daddy, and pottered about our pleasant, weedy old garden, cawed around by clamorous rooks, and where Jacob's ladder, and columbines, and white pinks, and lilies of all sorts and sizes flourished with a luxuriance I have never seen approached in trimmer parterres. O dear, old dad, when shall I walk hand in hand with you again? Will you call me your little Nell in Heaven? I do not want you to be a glorified saint, with an aureole round your head, and triumphant joy in your altered eyes; no longer full of that careworn, tender look. I thirst to see you just as you were, in the old hall garden, just as you were with your dear gray head, and your shabby old coat, and your poor sorrowful smile. I should not recognize you, exultant in your palmy crown, I who only knew you toiling along under your heavy cross.

Let me try and forget you, oh, my father; do without you, as one after another we have to do without our darlings here below. Let me go back to the old Castle Rackrent,[1] where I lived when I was not all alone. Lazy and dowdy I pottered about there, with my inconveniently abundant hair fastened up, in an unbecoming lump, at the back of my head, and my slim young body encased in such of Dolly's old clothes as I could induce to meet across me. Sometimes, indeed, it struck me that it would be pleasant to flaunt about in airy fashionable raiment, such as my sister rejoiced in, instead of in my sorry gowns, which made my figure look as if it went out wherever it ought to go in, and went in wherever it ought to go out. Once for a few days, I cherished the wild scheme of launching forth my small boat on the ocean of the world outside the old black and white house, with the casemented windows, and the queer gargoyle faces grinning down on us poor players[2] strutting out our little day beneath them. I even let

---

1 See *Castle Rackrent* (1800), a novel by Maria Edgeworth (1767-1849).
2 Compare Act 5, Scene 5, of *Macbeth* (first printed 1623), by Shakespeare. "Life's but a walking shadow, a poor player / That struts and frets his hour upon the stage / And then is heard no more: it is a tale / Told by an idiot, full of sound and fury, / Signifying nothing."

my fancy stray amongst troops of unknown, ardent youths, all of whom bore a resemblance more or less *prononcé*[1] to a certain penniless Captain Gordon, with whom, at the before-mentioned ball, I had danced eight several times,[2] thereby drawing down the vials of Dolly's wrath on my devoted head.

Once, and once only, I rebelled against my enforced hermitship, and we had a grand quarrel upon the subject. But Dolly being strong-minded, and I being weak-minded, I being the earthenware vessel, and she the iron one,[3] the dispute ended, as our disputes always did, by my *fondant en larmes*,[4] begging Dolly's pardon, and submitting.

"After all," said I to myself, leaning out of the window among the honeysuckle sprays, to cool my tear-swollen cheeks, "it is as it should be." Dolly was beautiful, and the Lestranges had always been beautiful, and it was right she should go forth and be a credit to the old house, and I was ugly, and the Lestranges had never been ugly, and it was meet that I should keep in the obscurity, for which alone I was calculated. But was I ugly? It was not very often that I asked myself whether the face that met me night and morning in my looking-glass was one calculated to make men's hearts ache, and their hot blood surge, or to lull them in a stagnant calm; but now and again the question would suggest itself, and clamour to be answered. Was I ugly? Hesitatingly, slowly, sadly, regretfully, I always answered in the affirmative. Sometimes I feared I was distressingly ugly. There was nothing neat, or smooth, or regular about my face, and oh those carrotty locks! How many sighs and inward groans they cost me.

One day I resolved to ask Dolly's opinion about my outward

---

1   Pronounced (French).
2   Dancing more than occasionally with the same partner was usually an indication of preference. Unless a young woman was being actively courted by the man, for her to show such a decided preference was considered inappropriate.
3   Compare Apocrypha, Sirach 13:2. "Burden not thyself above thy power while thou livest; and have no fellowship with one that is mightier and richer than thyself: for how agree the kettle and earthen pot together? for if the one be smitten against the other, it shall be broken." This is one of a series of proverbs exhorting the reader to stay among those whose beliefs, as well as whose station in life, are similar.
4   Bursting into tears (French).

woman. Dolly was not a very nice person I thought, not very easy to live with, and though she was my only sister, I did not care much about her; but for her judgment I had the profoundest reverence. We were sitting in the hall that winter morning, Dolly on a dark oak settle with a carved and writhen back, by the wide fireplace, in which a great log of wood was crackling and sputtering cheerily, and against the faded Utrecht velvet,[1] Dolly's bright blue draperies, and pure young profile, stood out clear and bright. I, who have a propensity for sitting on things that were not intended to be sat on, and for not sitting on things that were so intended, was squatting in an ungraceful but agreeable attitude, on the middle of a long table, that ran along under the windows over against her, hugging my own knees.

Dolly was a very fair woman to look upon; a small oval face, liquid brown eyes that had a way of looking up meekly and beseechingly, that no man less self-contained than St. Senanus[2] could resist, a little sharp cut nose absolutely perfect, a sweet grave mouth, and an expression nun-like, dove-like, Madonna-like; she looked as if her life must be one long prayer. I do not think it was though, or if it was it was a prayer said backwards. I gazed at her with a youthful enthusiasm, dashed with envy.

"Dolly," said I, "I wish I were as pretty as you."

"Do you?" said Dolly, not looking up from her work, for what was the good of looking meekly, beseechingly at me?

"Yes, I do," said I, "I'd pray for such a face every night among my other prayers, only I know it would be no good."

"Not the slightest, I should say."

"I wonder why God gives some people so many more gifts than others; will He make it up to the poor ugly ones in Heaven?"

"You'd better consult Mr. Bowles."

Now Mr. Bowles was our curate, and an individual for whom I entertained one of those unreasoning, unjustifiable abhorrences, often bred in the immature minds of the extremely young of the female sex, for some one of their acquaintance.

"Dolly," said I, reproachfully, "that's always the way you answer my questions. I'm sure I wonder that I ever ask you any."

---

1 A rich heavy velvet, made in Utrecht and favored for wall coverings and upholstery.
2 St. Senan (488-560) was an Irish saint who lived on Scattery Island, where no women were allowed.

"Don't, then."

"By-the-bye, Dolly," getting rather hot, and clutching my knees more firmly than ever, "do you think I am—ahem—ahem—so *very* ugly?"

"I never think about it," responded Dolly, coolly.

"But do think about it, this once, Dolly, please," I urged anxiously.

Dolly raised her sweet eyes, and surveyed my perturbed countenance calmly.

"I don't admire you," she said, dropping them again, "but that's no reason why somebody should not. Some people may like red hair and a wide mouth."

I yielded to destiny. I *was* ugly. I must try and be good, or clever, or eccentric, for it was very evident that pretty I could never be. I was ashamed of myself for having mooted the question. At the time I am writing of, Dolly was away from home on a visit to some admiring friends in a distant county, and to this fact was owing my introduction to the world.[1] Her absence was a matter of great, though secret rejoicing, both to my father and myself. We did not tell one another we were glad, but I think we were each tolerably well aware of the other's sentiments. Truth to tell, our Madonna kept us rather in order, and was somewhat of a thorn in the flesh to us. I sometimes caught myself wondering whether, in the event of Dolly's death, I should be enabled to cry a little and wear a decent semblance of grief. I hoped I should be, but I misdoubted myself somewhat. I need not have been disquieted. As I write, myself tottering on the verge of that last bed I so tiredly long for, Dolly is in the heyday of health and prosperity. Dolly will have that tear difficulty to contend with in my case; not I in hers. She will vanquish it, and will weep plentifully over this poor thin carcass, which indeed is ugly now.

---

1 It was customary to invite the eldest daughter old enough to be "out" to social functions, although often all of the daughters out would be invited. Dolly's absence moves Nell into this position by courtesy, but Dolly's habit of keeping Nell out of the limelight may also account for Nell's lack of invitations. Additionally, it was expensive to launch daughters into society, as they required an extensive wardrobe and other investments to prepare them for the social events they would attend—and their attendance often obligated their families to eventually host in turn.

CHAPTER IV

At about half-past six on the evening of that ever memorable day when I crossed the narrow brook between "womanhood and childhood fleet,"[1] my father's voice came sounding up the crooked oak staircase to my virgin chamber. "Nell, Nell, the carriage is waiting!" I was standing dressed, with all my worldly goods scattered higgledy-piggledy about me, making derisive faces at my own image in the glass, and wondering to myself whether any one in England was the owner of such obnoxious locks as mine; wondering likewise, whether it would be wrong to smash the mirror which told me such disagreeable truths.

"I'm coming, pa," responded I, still making passes at the pale, rose-filleted head I saw there. "Ugh, you fright! There's pa calling again. Where are my gloves? Oh, Heavens, where can they have gone to? Yes, pa, this very minute! What a potato face. It can't be helped. I *must* go." Thus ejaculating, I *élancéd*[2] myself downstairs. My father looked at me as I stood before him with an expression more doubtful than admiring.

"I don't know much about such things, Nell," he began, dubiously; "but is not your gown rather—what d'ye call it? I do not know how to express myself; is not it rather scant and shabby?"

"It *is* rather skimping, I'm afraid, pa, and I *did* let down two inches, and put in a new breadth too, but tarletane[3] is *so* dear now-a-days."

A look of mortified vexation clouded his kind old face as I spoke.

"I wish I'd known this before," he began; but I interrupted him.

"Please do not trouble about it," I said, hastily; "ten to one not a soul will know what I have on, or whether I have anything on at all!"

The cloud did not disperse; it deepened.

"I like you to look as well as other people, I don't want people to say that I'm too poor to dress my girls properly."

"They won't say anything of the kind, dad, unless they are nasty, purse-proud snobs; and if they do say it we shan't hear them!"

---

1 See "Maidenhood" (1841), a poem by American poet Henry Wadsworth Longfellow (1807-82).
2 Hurled (French, formed into an English past tense).
3 An open-weave, coarse cotton with a starched finish, like net.

"I don't want my little girl to be cut out by those fine Miss Coxes," persisted my father, thinking bitterly of the days when the said Miss Coxes' sire would have been glad to clean his boots for him.

I laughed. "Papa," said I, "if I were dressed in sackcloth and ashes, or in the brim of a hat and spurs, I should look more like a lady than those great bouncing, overdressed dairymaids, and after all, that's all that matters much."

A three miles' drive through the soft spring evening, along a turnpike road, with close cropped hedges on either side, whence the shears had lopped off all the pretty hawthorn flowers, leaving only dusty leaves; then we drew up before a Grecian portico,[1] on which the arms of the Coxes—arrived last month from the Herald's College[2]—were blazoned in full-blown glory; while a nondescript antique bird, half cock, half griffin, and supposed to be the Coxe crest, showed its ugly stone-beak and claws all over the house, in every nook and angle where antique bird could perch. Big footmen, all calves and crimson plush, on whose heads the dredging-box had done its work,[3] a blaze of light and Babel of voices, and then I, not knowing exactly whether I was on my head or my heels, found myself being presented by my father to a large woman, whose roseate arms were fettered with heavy gold bracelets, fresh from the jeweller's, and above whose pug face a tiara rose like a mural crown.[4]

---

1   A roofed entrance often supported by columns, here, Greek columns.
2   The Herald's College maintained, traced, and sometimes invented, family coats-of-arms. Newly wealthy families were often anxious to discover aristocratic relations among their ancestors. The pretentious entrance to the house underscores the family's social ambition and wealth.
3   Wealthy families retained footmen, male servants who opened doors, attended the family during travel, and served food. Long after other servants abandoned elaborate livery, or servants' costume, footmen retained theirs, often dressing in powdered wigs (the "dredging-box" is a device used to sift flour), colorful jackets, and silk stockings. Because footmen were originally responsible for protecting families on hazardous highways, footmen were traditionally very large, athletic men. Tall, gorgeously dressed footmen continued to be expensive and conspicuous accessories of the wealthy household long after their use as bodyguards was superfluous.
4   A crown given in ancient Rome to one who had vanquished a city (mural refers to the city walls).

Having got through the ceremony of introduction, I subsided into a chair, and gradually gained courage to look about me. A lofty, spacious saloon, oh, how unlike ours at home; wax-lit chandeliers, Cupids, and Psyches sprawling on the ceiling;[1] Carlo Dolcean Madonnas smiling insipidly, and Claudean landscapes flashing sunnily from the walls,[2] a general impression of gilding and ormolu and white paint. There was a very large party—substantial country gentlemen; lords and commoners, with bald pates and a prosperous stall-fed air, not unlike their own oxen; matrons with double chins, in the folds and creases of whose fat necks diamonds blazed fitfully; youths for whom Poole[3] had done his utmost; and girls like a flock of full-plumaged doves. Oh, those young ladies! I could bear the gorgeous dowagers; I could bear the irreproachable cornets, and baronets, and undergraduates, but the girls were too much for my equanimity. If my poor frock had looked scant and skimping in the hall at home, where it had the background of oak chairs and panels to set it off, what aspect must it have worn here, among the crisp *chef d'oeuvres* of Mmes. Descou and Elise?[4] It *was* ashamed of itself, I think, for it clung to me, limp and flabby, like a wet bathing dress; and to complete my discomfiture, I discovered that my hair was dressed in a fashion that had died the death at least a year and a half ago.

I was as much a stranger in this my own neighbourhood as a native of Kamtschatka[5] could have been, and knew not a soul. Several people (men especially) looked at me, and I attributed their notice solely to my outlandish attire.

"They are wondering who that bundle of rags, that scarecrow, is!" said I, bitterly, to myself. "Oh, Nelly Lestrange, you poor dowdy, how I wish you were back in your old holland gown, eating cold mutton for tea, in the dining-room at home!"

---

1 Cupid is the god of love; Psyche became his bride.
2 Carlo Dolce (1616-86) was an artist best known for religious paintings, and Claude Lorrain (1600-82) was a famous Romantic landscape artist.
3 Poole's was a fashionable Victorian Savile Row tailoring firm owned by Henry Poole and favored by wealthy young men.
4 Dress designers. Elise is probably Madame Elise and Co., Limited, Court Dressmakers, on Regent Street. Madame Descou seems likewise to have been favored by an elite clientele.
5 Kamtschatka is in Siberia and is often invoked as an example of the most out-of-the-way place imaginable.

I was very childish for my age, and I felt very lonely—so lonely that the tears came into my eyes as I sat contemplating my hands lying in their wrinkled eighteen-penny gloves upon my lap. Just as dinner was announced, a gentleman entered the room—a gentleman, the adornment of whose person had apparently detained him somewhat long. He was a tall, broad-shouldered man, with yellow hair—a man whom the armour of some strong King Olaf, some red-handed Jarl,[1] would not have misbecome. I recognized him in a moment; he was the hero of my churchyard adventure. My father, who was just in the act of conducting old Lady Blank to the festive board, looked over his shoulder, and smiled at me. I smiled too; and a minute afterwards I had quite forgot my limp one-skirted frock and ill-dressed hair. All my annoyances were merged in shy pleasure when I found that my Viking was under orders to take me in to dinner. But when he had so taken me, and had deposited me on a gorgeous velvet chair beside him, he did not seem in any violent hurry to cultivate my acquaintance. He ate his soup deliberately, and left me to the contemplation of his outward man. Perhaps he knew that he was pleasant to look upon, and trusted to that pleasantness to prepossess a stranger in his favour; perhaps he did not care whether I were prepossessed or no. I was soupless; so I amused myself glancing obliquely at my neighbour. Very curly Saxon hair—so curly as to excite in envious, lank-haired brother officers a suspicion (a base and unfounded suspicion) of the agency of tongs;[2] a beautiful bronzed face, with the scar of a sabre-cut running down the cheek, close to the ear; a beardless, whiskerless face; hairless, save for the heavy tawny moustache.

"I wish he'd speak," said I to myself at last. "Perhaps he has nothing to say; good-looking men seldom have the gift of tongues, Dolly says." I would as soon have thought of cutting off my head as of originating a conversation with a perfect stranger, so I held my peace, and wondered how he had acquired that scar. At last, as if he had read my thoughts, he turned towards me.

---

1 Viking warrior, martyr-king and patron saint of Norway. Nell
   seems to be dwelling on romanticized images of Olaf Trygveson,
   who was actually known to his peers as Olaf the Fat (995-1030).
   Jarl is Old Norse for Earl. The source for Nell's musings is likely to
   be *Heimskringla, The Chronicle of the Kings of Norway* (c. 1225), by
   Snorri Sturluson (1179-1241).
2 Curling tongs, or curling irons, heated by coals and used to curl
   hair.

"I'm afraid I startled you rather, last night?" said he, with a smile.

"Not much," responded I, briefly, turning my head half away, after the manner of shy girls.

"Did you think I was an evil spirit or a bogy, going about, seeking whom I might devour?" he asked, more familiarly. I suppose he saw I was young and a raw recruit in the ranks of the *beau monde*,[1] and consequently concluded that he might treat me as such.

"No, I didn't," said I, "because——"; and there I stopped, I was going to say "because you are too good-looking for a bogy," but I recollected in time that it is an inversion of the order of society for a young lady to pay broad compliments to an unknown gentleman.

"Because what?" asked he.

"Because——because——," said I, floundering about, and seizing desperately the first reason that occurred to me, silly as that reason happened to be, "because I never heard of a bogy with yellow hair!"

"My hair is not yellow," responded he, carelessly; "nothing half so nice; sandy decidedly."

"It is not my idea of sandy," I maintained, stoutly.

"What is your idea of sandy, then, may I ask?"

"Mrs. Coxe's is sandy," said I, with youthful rashness, looking towards the lady of the house, "and very hideous it is."

"I am sorry you think her so hideous," responded he, coolly; "she's my sister!"

I was covered with confusion. I would fain have slipped from my chair underneath the table, and spent the remainder of the dinner hour among the feet of the company. I reddened to the roots of my hair, which, as I have before mentioned, was red too. My shamefaced eyes sought my plate, and studied the parrot-poppy depicted thereon in glowing colours. I attempted no apology, but sat dumb-foundered. Then a deep voice, stifling much laughter, sounded close to my blazing ear.

"Never mind! I won't tell of you. By-the-bye, Mrs. Coxe is not my sister, and I only said so to frighten you."

I felt extremely angry, though profoundly relieved.

"How could you tell such a story?" I asked, reproachfully.

---

1 High society (French; literally "beautiful world").

"It was not a story, as you call it," he answered, with an almost imperceptible mimicking of my indignant intonation. "In one sense, she *is* my sister. We are all brethren, aren't we?—at least, we call each other dearly beloved brethren in the prayer-book every Sunday."

"That is very flippant," said I, gravely. I had a great respect for the prayer-book, and did not like to hear it mentioned so lightly. I fancied he looked slightly surprised that a country chit like me should venture to rebuke a man of the world like him, but he said nothing to that effect, and rather abruptly changed the subject.

"Is it one of the manners and customs of the young ladies in these parts to sit among the tombs towards nightfall?" he inquired.

"I don't know about other young ladies; *I* sit there sometimes."

"You are a strong-minded person, evidently; cart-ropes would not drag one of my sisters within half a mile of a churchyard after dark."

"Indeed! How many sisters have you got?——

"'Sisters and brothers, little maid,
How many may you be?' eh?"[1]

"'Sisters and brothers, little *man*,' it ought to be in this case, oughtn't it? Well, I've got two."

"Are they like you?"

"Not a bit; much better looking."

I felt incredulous, but I hope I kept my incredulity out of my countenance.

"Have you been here long?" I resumed, catechetically.

"Since last Tuesday."

"Are you going to stay here long?"

"That depends upon how I like my quarters. Is there anything more you wish to know?"

"Oh, I beg your pardon; I'm sorry I asked so many questions," I said, contritely, fearing I had committed a grievous sin against good manners.

"I did not intend to be rude, indeed!"

"Rude," said he, "nonsense! I should not think such a pretty mouth could say anything rude, if it tried."

---

1 See "We Are Seven" (1798), a poem by Wordsworth.

It was rather impudent of him, certainly, and I ought to have told him so, I suppose; but, as he spoke, the dark gray eyes looked full into mine, with an expression I had never seen in mortal eyes before; an expression that sealed my lips, and sent a sort of odd shiver—a shiver that had nothing to say to cold, through my frame. I felt that to the utter neglect of "beignets aux huitres"[1] (than which no dish can be delectabler), he was watching me, which did not add to my composure.

"Don't be angry with me," he said at last, in a tone that meant to be penitent, bending his handsome head down towards my downcast face. "I didn't mean to say it—it slipped out."

"I'm not angry," I said, with some difficulty, "that is, not very; but I'm afraid—you—think—I'm an ignorant country bumpkin, to whom you may say anything you like to?"

"Upon my soul, I don't," he replied, earnestly. "I think—well! it doesn't much matter what I think about you."

"You cannot think much about me," said I, "seeing that you have only known me for about a quarter of an hour."

"It doesn't take long to know some people!"

"They're so shallow, you mean?" suggested I, attempting to be arch.

"What a shame!" he said, "you know I didn't mean that; but have you never heard of a sort of inexplicable sympathy and attraction between two people at first sight?"

I had heard of something else at first sight, but I did not say so.

"I have nobody to sympathize with or to be attracted to, at home, except papa, and our old man servant, and the sexton."

"What do you mean? do you never go out anywhere?"

"Never. Dolly does often, but I don't."

"Who is Dolly?" he asked, rather amused at my *naïveté*; "or I suppose I ought to say who's *Miss* or *Mrs.* Dolly?"

"Dolly is my sister."

"Oh, older or younger?"

"Four years older; she was twenty-three last January, and I am nineteen this month."

"You are very candid."

"Am I? why should I not be?"

"No reason whatever; and do you and Dolly—I beg her pardon—*Miss* Dolly, live together, all alone?"

---

1 Oyster fritters (French).

"All alone! oh, dear no; we live with papa, of course; that is papa opposite."

How many more revelations concerning my family history I might have made in my young ingenuousness can never now be ascertained, for at this point I perceived Mrs. Coxe, inclining her head towards the old woman of exaltedest rank, at the other end of the table; whereupon we all sailed and floated and shuffled out of the room. How glad I should have been to have stayed with the gentlemen; protected by papa, and condescendingly chatted to by my blonde King Olaf. With my return to the drawing-room returned my sense of loneliness, my consciousness of shabby clothes, and my embarrassment as to the disposal of my hands. There was no wish, I am sure, among those dames and damsels to neglect or be unkind to the poor gawky young stranger; it was only the force of circumstances. One good natured, graceful Lady Alice tried her best to extract my ideas on the comparative charms of Brighton and Scarboro';[1] but finding I had no ideas on the subject to be extracted she desisted in despair.

All the other ladies knew each other very well, lived in the same circle, had the same pursuits, objects, interests. I, alone, shivered chilly outside the magic ring. I was like a ghost come back after the lapse of a century, to the house where he used to be lord and master and darling, who hears language that he understands not. What did I know about the Duchess of A.'s at home?[2] or dear Lady B.'s ball? I who had never to my knowledge set eyes upon a duchess, and whose sole experience of balls was derived from the inglorious Infirmary one of our little county town. However, I looked with unshaken faith to the coming of the gentlemen for bettering my condition, and better it that coming certainly did. If I had expected indeed that my large new friend would make any demonstrations in my favour, I was disappointed. He betook himself straightway to the piano, where a brilliant little brunette was trilling airy French songs in a voice like a bird's; there he stood with his back against the wall, now and then leaning forward to whisper two or three words into the pretty musician's ear, words that made the dark eyes sparkle more brightly than before.

---

1 Brighton and Scarborough are resort towns on the coast.

2 A lady's "at home" day was a weekly occasion, the day on which she received her visitors with refreshments. Such days were part of the usual round of social events in a community.

I felt an insane desire to sing too; I *could* sing; it was the one accomplishment I possessed, but nobody requested the pleasure of hearing me warble; so I sat chafing, with my talent hid in a napkin. Then a quartet of old fogies sat down to whist,[1] and dealt, and shuffled, and abused their cards, and quarrelled with their partners, as irascible old gentlemen will; and other bald heads got into groups, and bragged about their short-horns[2] to their hearts' content. And gradually the younger men sought out such women as seemed good in their eyes, and sat into their pockets, to the satisfaction of both parties; even dowdy I found favour in somebody's eyes.

Two or three men came and were introduced to me, and I attributed their notice to a praiseworthy feeling of compassion, having too unaffected a belief in my own ugliness to attribute it to any other motive. I tired my neck somewhat craning up at them as they stood black-legged around me, and they were very civil—one of them indeed, a jolly-looking, short, dark man, considerably past his *première jeunesse*,[3] whom I had heard addressed as Sir Hugh, civiller far, as I now see, than the occasion required. While we were making our *adieux* to the hostess on our departure, King Olaf left his brunette and her little songs in praise of love and wine rather abruptly, and gave me his arm to lead me to the carriage. We were in the hall alone together for a minute, and as he put my shawl round my shoulders, he stooped and gazed full into my eyes. Innocent and childish as I was, I could not mistake that expression, bewildering me with its bold, avowed admiration.

"Will there be any use in my going to the churchyard to-morrow evening?" he asked hurriedly.

"I'm sure I don't know," said I, turning away coldly; "it's nothing to me whether you go there or not."

"Is it not? I'm sorry for that," he said gravely; and I was sorry too, as soon as the words were out of my mouth.

And then my father called me, and I ran hastily away, and left him standing under the portico, with the carriage lamps gilding his severe Greek beauty.

---

1 A card game, related to bridge.
2 Their cattle—these are all country land owners, and breeding prize cattle was a popular pastime, as well as an economic activity.
3 First youth (French).

CHAPTER V

"The Federals have had another licking, Nell," said my father, in an exultant tone next morning, as I entered the dining-room in my usual elegant morning *négligé*[1] (and very *négligé* it was), and with my hands full of dear old-fashioned flowers, dark claret-coloured double gillyflowers, great heavy heads of lilac, and bottles of colour.

"Have they?" said I. "Brutes! I'm so glad."

We were great politicians, my father and I, and I could have stood a very stiff examination in the battles of the American war. If I had been left to myself I do not think I should have cared very much whether the Confederates conjugated the active or passive voice of the verb to "*whip*." I should have listened with equal indifference to the "tall doin's" of Abolitionists or Secessionists;[2] but I was truly thankful for any subject of public interest which could rouse my father from his melancholy, and moreover I loved him so entirely that what interested him, interested me too, of necessity. There is no relationship so delightful as that between father and daughter when at its best. Some thought of this kind ran through my head as I sat eating my porridge, and occasionally glancing at my father, whose dear old head was half buried between two sheets of the *Times*. It prompted me to say,

"Papa, I sometimes feel inclined to wish that Dolly would never come back, that she would live always with those Graftons, who seem to appreciate her so much more than you and I do."

"You should not say that, Nell," said my father from the banks of the Potomac, but his rebuke was of the very mildest description.

"Why should not I say so, if I feel it?—you and I are so happy together, aren't we, daddy?"

"Yes, very happy," answered my father; but even as he spoke he sighed.

Sighs are the gales that blow us to heaven, I sometimes think; they breathe unconscious weariness of the "here," and longing for the "there."

"I should like," pursued I, "things always to be just as they are

---

1 Informal, sometimes revealing apparel, nightwear. The word can also mean disorderly, neglected.
2 Nell's father follows the progress of the civil war in the United States, progressing contemporaneously with the events of the novel. His support of the South is characteristic of the kind of old Tory, aristocratic attitude that Broughton gives to the character.

now; you and I living here together, for ever and ever and ever, with our pigs and our chickens and our cabbages, only we'd have no money matters, and nobody to bully us."

"Your wants are nearly as few as Diogenes, Nell; indeed you haven't included a tub in your list of indispensables."

"You're my only indispensable, dad!"

"Poor little lass! you'll think differently some day when you've got a husband and children, and I'm dead and gone."

"When you're dead and gone," said I decisively, "I shall be dead and gone too, for I could not bear to live without you"; and I really believed it.

"Nonsense, child," said my father, smiling. "Did you ever see a stone thrown into the pond; there's a great splash, and a few circles on the water, and that's about all, isn't it? Well, when I die there'll be a great splash of tears and hullaballooing, and a few circles of tender recollections, and then the surface will smooth itself over, and it'll be all right again."

I was so overcome by this affecting metaphor, that a piece of porridge stuck in my weasand[1] and all but choked me.

"Like the remembrance of a guest that tarrieth but a day,"[2] said my father over to himself, reflectively, leaning his head on his hand, "that's about our tether, Nell; wet pocket-handkerchiefs, and long faces for a day, and then somebody new springs up, and fills up our vacant hole in this odd ant-hill, and we're jostled away into the limbo where so many better and wiser have been bundled before us."

I am soft-hearted—easily moved to tears. I was blubbering gently behind the tea-kettle now.

"Crying, Nell!" says my father, roused from his reverie by my sniffs. "Come, child, I'm not dead yet; wait till my coffin is ordered before you set to making lamentations over me."

"You're ve-ve-ry d-d-is-agreeable," said I, with moist indignation. "I've a great mind never to say anything to you again. You're always bothering about dying. I wish to heaven there was not such a word in the dictionary."

"If there was not it would be a very terrible world, Nell," replied my father, gravely; "every man with Cain's curse[3] upon his brow."

---

1 Gullet, throat.
2 Compare Apocrypha, Wisdom of Solomon 5:15.
3 See the story of Cain, son of Adam and Eve, who is cursed by God and banished after he kills his brother Abel in Genesis 4:11-16.

"Do let us talk of something else," cried I, peevishly. "I hate such moping sort of subjects."

"By all means; something gay and festive. The party last night, for instance," said the author of my being, ironically.

"It was not so bad as I expected," returned I, brightening up, and eradicating the moisture from my eyes with my knuckles.

"How did you get on with all those fine ladies?" inquired my father, kindly.

"Middling," said I, "I did not care much about them; I liked the men better. If I went into society, I should like to go to parties where there were no women, only men."

"That is a sentiment that I think I should keep for home use, my dear, if I were you."

"Should you? Well, perhaps so; but women are so prying and censorious. All the time you are talking to them you feel sure that they are criticising the sit of your tucker, and calculating how much a yard your dress cost. Now, if you're only pretty and pleasant, indeed, even if you're not either (I mentally classed myself under this latter head), men are good-natured, and take you as they find you, and make the best of you."

My father did not dispute my position.

"Talking of men," said he, "that Sir Hugh Lancaster seems to be a very nice young fellow; he and I had a great deal of talk together."

"Do you mean that little black man[1] you introduced to me?" inquired I, contemptuously. "Young fellow, indeed! Well, if he's a young fellow, Methuselah[2] was rather juvenile than otherwise."

My father sipped his coffee reflectively.

"Poor Methuselah," said he; "nine hundred and sixty-six years he had of it, hadn't he? How sick he must have been of the eternal millround—seed-time and harvest, summer and winter coming back near a thousand times, to find him hanging on still!"

I had nothing to suggest on the subject of the patriarch, so I held my peace.

"Did he do nothing worth recording all those ten centuries?" went on my father musingly, "that we're told of him only that he was born, and begat sons and daughters, and died."

---

1 Nell means that Sir Hugh is dark haired and complected, especially compared to Dick.

2 See the story of Methuselah, the man who lived for 969 years (although Nell's father cites it as 966), in Genesis 5:21-27.

"You've wandered some way from Sir What's-his-name, pa," said I, recalling my parent's spirit from the realm of barren speculations whither it had travelled.

"I'll come back to him, my dear, if you wish; only I don't think I know much more about him than I do about his prototype, Methuselah!"

"And to my thinking, he's hardly more interesting," added I, with which scant courtesy I dismissed the worthy baronet from my conversation and my thoughts.

I had often heard other motherless girls deploring their destitute condition; envying such of their friends as were in the enjoyment of a mother's care and supervision; but such sentiments, such regrets, met no echo in my heart—inspired me rather with strongest surprise and amazement. It was to me a matter of unfeigned and heartfelt gratulation that my mother had died in my infancy. As often as I came in contact with well-drilled daughters, nestling under the wing of a portly mamma, I hugged myself on my freedom; my father was more to me than ten mothers. If my mother had lived, thought I, I should have been only second in his affections, some one else would have been nearer his heart than I—an idea almost too bitter to be contemplated. If I had had a mother, I should have had to mend my gloves, and keep my hair tidy, and practise on the piano, and be initiated into the mysteries of stitching. My mother had been among the fortunate of the earth, having died while yet young and fair, and passionately loved, before the world had grown tired of her, or she of it. In the early morning of her life, ere the glow of prime had faded,

"The Almighty's breath spake out in death,
And God did draw Honora up
The golden stairs to heaven."[1]

Her name, I may mention incidentally, was not Honora, but it would spoil a very lovely line to introduce her real cognomen

---

1 Broughton conflates two poems here. "The Almighty's breath spake out in death" is from "The Nautilus and the Ammonite" (c. 1849), a poem by G.F. Richardson. "And God did draw Onora up the golden stairs to heaven" (note variant spelling) is from "The Lay of the Brown Rosary" (1840), a poem by Elizabeth Barrett Browning (1806-61).

of Dorothy into it, so I have ceded to the necessity which makes Anthony White appear for ever as Anthony Blue[1] on his tombstone.

Devoted as I was to my father, I could not always be with him; sometimes he preferred his own society and that of his books to mine, found more solace for his vexations in epigrammatic French essayists and German metaphysicians, whose rhapsodies about the beautiful and the sublime I could make neither head nor tail of, to my girlish cackle. Sometimes, but more rarely, he took long solitary rides about his heavily mortgaged farms on a sedate old cob,[2] with a docked tail and hogged mane, who, like his master, had seen better days. The soft May wind, and the invitations of the garrulous blackbirds and thrushes, had tempted him to set forth on such a ride one evening after tea, two days after my introduction to society. Consequently I was thrown on my own resources, and rather short of a job I was.

If I had followed my inclination, I should have betaken myself to the churchyard, to see whether my stranger might not be there again, as he had hinted (not dimly) that he might be, but two considerations checked me. If, on the one hand, he were to be there, I could not look him in the face for shame, and if, on the other hand, he were not—if I were to go to meet him, and he were not to be met—if I were to seek him, and he were not to be found, what words could express my degradation? Even if there had been no new charm about the fair old graveyard sloping westwards, the old one would have been quite strong enough to draw my heart and myself thither. I liked to go there in the soundless gloaming, and think of all sorts of grave dark things. When one is very young and very happy, one courts melancholy thoughts for the sake of the contrast they afford to one's own inner life; in later days such thoughts are less coy, need no courting, but run to meet us, embrace, and cling about us, even when we could well dispense with the pleasure of their society. But in youth, when the blood is rioting through the veins, life seems so strong within us as to be almost able to challenge the old scythesman to single combat, and worst him. At nineteen, death seems so immeasurably distant, we may have so many

---

1 I have been unable to locate a source for this reference, which appears to refer to a name being changed on a tombstone for the sake of the inscription's rhyme scheme.
2 A stout, short-legged horse.

miles of pleasant pasture-land and shady woodland to traverse before we dip our feet in the inky stream, into which whosoever steppeth straightway

"He forgets the days before."[1]

I was fond of sitting among those mossy headstones, speculating on the for-ever-ended histories of those dead people—those uneducated churls, who had been so below me in intelligence while alive, now so immeasurably above me in the knowledge that there is but one way of attaining to; fond, too, was I of marvelling after what various fashions they had battled through their lives; with what different degrees of apathy, despair, and heaven-born faith they had confronted him whom some call foe, some friend. But the churchyard and its attendant reveries being out of the question, I had to cast about for other occupation—occupation of a more practical kind. Our garden, as I have said, was a very wilderness. Chickweed and groundsel, and other abominations, intruded their plebeian heads among my crown imperials and sweet nancies, even tried to choke the nemophilas that were just opening their azure eyes, mirroring the sky. I stooped to dislodge a thistle which had impertinently insinuated itself into a bunch of sweetwilliams.

"I may as well garden a bit," I said to myself, "it will pass the time, and oh! how slow it is going now, even though I did put on all the clocks half an hour." So I fetched a pair of gardening gloves and a little mat, knelt down on the latter, and set to digging, and raking, and weeding with a will. It is pleasant to feel one's self useful, and doing some good in one's generation, and I, being ordinarily anything but a busy bee, found that to be laudably industrious was a new and delightful sensation. And as I grubbed, and watered, and scuffled, I ran over in my mind all the little incidents of my late dissipation, composed smart answers and brilliant repartees, which I might have made and had not at various points of my conversation with the gray-eyed stranger, and wondered, for the twentieth time, what he could have meant by staring at me as he had done under the gaslight in the hall. "Could he have thought me pretty?" I asked myself at last, being unable to find any other explanation for that long

---

1 See *In Memoriam* (1850), a poem by Alfred Lord Tennyson (1809-92).

eager gaze, the remembrance of which still stirred my silly little soul in the newest, queerest, joyfullest fashion.

At this preposterous suggestion I raised myself from my stooping attitude, dropped my trowel, and pushed back the flapping wide-leaved hat from my hot forehead. "Impossible!" said I. "Pretty, indeed! after what Dolly said, and Dolly's a good judge, ill-natured as she is! Nothing more unlikely. Certainly, living such a secluded life makes one magnify trifles, make mountains of molehills. I'm afraid, my good girl, that you are a sad fool!" These last words I spoke aloud, little thinking that I had any other auditors than the columbines and the damask roses which I had been tying up. Judge then of my surprise when my self-complimenting remark found itself answered. Somebody close at my elbow said, "Are you? I should not have thought it." I started as if a bullet had hit me, sprang to my feet, and confronted the object of my conjectures. There he stood, tall and straight, and strong as a young oak, on the gravel walk, between the prim box edgings, smiling broadly at my discomfiture.

"I'm sorry you have such a poor opinion of yourself," he continued, maliciously enjoying my confusion.

I made no answer to this remark, but struggled violently to compose myself, and to recollect how much I had said aloud; whether only the last clause of my sentence, which was comparatively harmless, or enough to have disgraced me for ever.

"Won't you ask me how I am? Won't you shake hands with me this evening, Miss Lestrange?" inquired my tormentor, resuming his gravity.

"I'm afraid I cannot," responded I, laughing constrainedly, holding up my hands in their earthy coverings to show him.

"I have no objection whatever to a little dirt; it's rather wholesome than otherwise, and I have tender reminiscences of the dirt pies of my youth."

I drew off my gauntlet with precipitation, and laid my hand (a long slim member) in his.

"It was rather cool of me, coming in here without anybody inviting me?" he asked, detaining my not unwilling, though rather embarrassed fingers, holding them as if he had forgotten all about them, and looking down (for though I was rather a tall girl, beside him I was small and short enough) at me.

"Oh no!" said I, "it did not matter at all, only you startled me rather."

"Did I? I'm so sorry; but you see I was just toddling about that field over there, in the most pitiable state, when I caught sight of some one (I felt sure it was you) burrowing in the ground, and I could not resist the temptation of coming to speak to you; a friendly human shape is a sight not to be despised in this desolate country. I could not throw away such a chance."

"Could not you?"

"*Could not you?*" said he, repeating my words rather reproachfully. "So that's all you've got to say to me? Why are you so hard, and cold, and stiff?"

"I don't mean to be," said I, naïvely, and I did not.

At this juncture my hat fell off the back of my head, and he had to release my hand to pick it up. Having restored my headpiece, he resumed—

"Why were you so cross the other night?"

"I was not cross."

"Yes, you were; very cross. I never saw any one much crosser. I could not conceive how I had vexed you; I asked myself a dozen times after you were gone, what can I have said to make that young lady so angry with me? only I'm afraid I did not say *that young lady.*"

"What did you say?" asked I, with female inquisitiveness.

"Never mind what I said. I did not call you by your name, for I did not know what it was, nor don't now; would you mind telling me what it is?"

"Nell."

"Nell! Nell! I like it; but were you christened *Nell*?"

"No-o-o," said I, dubiously. "I suppose not; I suppose I was christened Eleanor, but nobody but the servants ever call me so. What's your name?"

"Richard."

"Richard what?"

"Richard Harold."

"Richard Harold what?"

"Oh! you mean what's my surname? M'Gregor. I thought you knew that."

"No, I did not," said I.

Pretty names, I remarked to myself; but I like *Olaf* better; it's much more descriptive. I knelt down on my mat, and prepared to resume my gardening. But Richard Harold M'Gregor remonstrated.

"Please don't do any more of that horrid rooting and scraping," said he, seizing my trowel, and holding it high out of my reach; "you have made yourself quite hot already; do come and sit down on that stone bench, and talk a bit; have pity on a poor fellow who is dying for someone to exchange ideas with."

"I have nothing to say," responded I, but I complied with his request, without any demur, and sat down on the old bench with the little green mosses and lichens in the crevices of the cracked stone, while he stretched his lazy length at my feet.

"And so you spend your life in this rum old garden, do you?" inquired he, looking round, and taking a comprehensive survey of our roses, and cabbages and gooseberry bushes; all growing in friendly proximity.

"Yes," said I, "here, and in the house, and among the chickens."

"Rather dreary work, isn't it?" asked he, thinking, I fancy, what a contrast his own existence was to mine.

"I don't find it so," said I.

"In fact, you like it better than any other kind of life, I suppose."

"I never tried any other, so I cannot tell," responded I, sagely. "I should not like any life away from papa."

"You're very fond of him, then?" he asked, and I fancied I heard him mutter something like "lucky old beggar," under his breath.

"I should think so," replied I, emphatically.

"You cannot fancy ever being fonder of any one else, I suppose?" he inquired, pulling a blade of grass, and biting it.

"No-o-o, I think not," I answered, cautiously.

"I wish *I* had anybody to love me like that," he said, looking wistfully up in my face.

Of course he meant some sister, or mother, or friend, and of course I took it so; but innocent as my heart was, my detestable cheeks thought it necessary to hang out their ever ready flame signals again, giving me completely the air of having misunderstood his meaning, and being in the expectation of hearing him in his next sentence request the gift of my valuable affections. He was charitable; looked away, and ate more grass. Having given my cheeks time to cool, he looked round again.

"I think you and I should get on together," said he; "don't you?"

I nodded my head.

"I think so," I said, nibbling a daisy stalk.

"Shall we make a solemn league and covenant? shall we settle to be friends henceforth and for ever?" he asked.

I was rather taken aback by such suddenness of action.

"I don't know about that," I said, hesitatingly; "it would be rather awkward if, after having taken me for your friend, you found I was not so nice as you thought me."

I took it for granted, in my innocence, that he *did* think me nice. He laughed.

"Not so nice as I thought—eh?" said he. "Well, I don't think I mind running the risk if you'll do as much for me. Life is too short to waste in preliminaries."

"It *is* short," said I, sententiously.

"Horribly short!" replied he, with a sigh; "and if I like you and you like me, as I hope you do. *Do* you, by-the-bye?"

He raised himself on his elbow till his face was on a level with my knee, and awaited my answer.

"Yes, I do," I said, slowly, "what I know of you, at least—that is not much."

"Give me your hand, then, to seal our contract."

I felt rather flustered by the rapid strides our acquaintance had made within the last ten minutes; but I gave him my hand, and as I did so, my father, my adored papa, appeared round the corner. As he caught sight of the pretty *tableau vivant*[1] we had kindly got up in his garden to surprise him, he looked extremely astonished and considerably displeased. Nor was the poor man much to blame, I think, finding his favourite daughter sitting in the dusk of the evening with a man, whom, to his certain knowledge, she had seen but twice before in her life, lying at her feet and clasping her hand, apparently unforbidden. It is rather a truism to say that things that occur seldom impress us a great deal more than things that occur frequently. If there were a thunderstorm or an earthquake every day we should think nothing of those catastrophes. It was so very infrequently that my father was angry with me that I was in a state of proportionable awe and

---

1 Living picture (French). Actors often staged such scenes, sometimes referring to well-known art or stories. In the Victorian period, tableaux vivants were also performed as elaborate parlor games, as a variation on charades; the audience guessed what the players were representing.

wholesome fear when such a *contretemps*[1] did arise. I snatched away my hand and jumped up.

"Papa's coming," I gasped.

Mr., or as I afterwards heard he was, Major M'Gregor, did not appear much discomfited. He raised himself from his reclining posture, and went to meet my father. The latter on his part raised his hat very stiffly, and said, with a polite elaboration and distinctness which I thought very unnecessary, "How do you do, Sir? This is a *most* unexpected pleasure. May I take the liberty of asking your name?"

"My name is M'Gregor," said Richard, taking off his hat also, but not stiffly, and reddening a little, "and I must apologize for coming at such an untimely hour, but the fact was, Mrs. Coxe entrusted me with a message to your daughter, and after I had delivered it I took the liberty of asking to be allowed to see your garden, of which I had heard so much, and which Miss Lestrange was kind enough to show me."

A tissue of fibs! listened to by me, with open-mouthed, wide-eyed amazement. Could my hero tell lies? My father did not seem mollified. He said "Humph!" very gruffly, planted himself in the middle of the path between me and the stranger, and looked ostentatiously at his watch, as much as to say, "When is the fellow thinking of taking himself off?"

The fellow took the broad hint. "I'm detaining you," he said, politely; and after turning to me, and saying, with a fund of amusement in his face, "I hope you won't forget Mrs. Coxe's message," he again lifted his hat and walked away.

Papa and I followed slowly in his wake, I quaking, yet angry. My father was the first to speak.

"I don't like this sort of thing at all," said he, with irritation, "and what's more, it must not occur again. You're very young and inexperienced, Nell, and I dare say you meant no harm, but I wonder that even *you* did not think it was not very nice or maidenly to be out at nine o'clock at night with that big fellow sprawling at your feet, to say nothing of holding your hand!"

I felt disposed to weep, till he came to the word *sprawling*; that obnoxious dissyllable made me choke back my indignant tears.

"What was he doing with your hand?" pursued my father, still more severely.

---

1 Unexpected mishap or complication (French).

"I'm sure I don't know," stammered I. "I suppose he was going to bid me good-bye."

I really had not strength of mind to reveal the truth and expose the folly I had been guilty of, with regard to that most absurd proposition of friendship.

"Puppy!" exclaimed my father, fuming and working himself up into a passion. "He wants a good kicking, that's what he does. Uncommon free and easy, indeed! Walking into another man's garden, without saying '*by* your leave,' or '*with* your leave!' Those may be Manchester or Brummagem[1] manners, but they won't go down here, I can tell him."

"He is not Manchester or Brummagem," said I, gasping, and without the slightest feeling of the ridiculous.

"Well, Brummagem or no," retorted my father, "he won't come here again in a hurry, I can tell him!" and he stopped and struck his stick upon the ground to emphasize his remark.

"I should not think he'd wish to, after the way you treated him," I could not help saying.

"Perhaps not, perhaps not! So much the better!" replied my father, still at boiling point.

We had by this time reached the house. I stalked upstairs, with my head up, and on reaching my room, threw myself on my bed, in a passion of mortified angry tears.

I "*unmaidenly*," and he "*Brummagem*!" Which epithet was worst?

CHAPTER VI

I have lived now more than twenty years, and have seen much of the evil and much of the good (there is a good deal of the latter, after all) that there is in the world. I have often been led to ponder upon the comparative bearableness or unbearableness of the various burdens laid upon the shoulders of poor humanity. After much deliberation, after changing my opinion five or six times; after looking at the subject from every point of view; after considering all the *pros* and *cons*, counting one by one, as the Preacher says, I have come to the conclusion that the heaviest load under which

---

1 Vulgar pronunciation for the name of the town of Birmingham, which was, at the time, associated with shoddy goods, cheap or showy counterfeits or imitations.

man groans is poverty. By poverty I do not mean comfortable, decent poverty, which pays ready money, which keeps a parlour-maid instead of butler and footman, which walks instead of drives, buys cotton gowns instead of silk dresses for its wife, which sends its sons to Cheltenham and Cambridge, instead of Eton and Christ Church;[1] but the bugbear I have before me is poverty such as ours was—the poverty of living in a wide house—not with a brawl-ing woman[2]—but worse, with a very narrow income; the poverty which dares not look on from month to month and from day to day, before whose inner eyes bum-bailiffs[3] are ever present; the poverty which steals away our cheerful spirits; which renders us envious, and spiteful, and sordid; which makes our days a long torture, and our nights a long vigil; which saps the springs of our life, and sometimes ends by making us cut our throats to escape it. The death of friends is a far sharper grief, of course, while it lasts: then the light goes out in the heavens, and we sit among the ashes and curse the day in which we were born;[4] but the people whom we love *intensely*, whose existence or non-existence is of any very vital importance to our daily happiness, are so extremely few, that such devouring sorrows come ordinarily but three or four times in a life of sixty years. A sharp stab at rare intervals is better than a running sore festering perpetually.

On the morning after my unmaidenly behaviour, I was in the hall of our old house, and the morning sun was shining through the stained-glass windows (through Abel's head and Cain's legs,[5] queerly depicted thereon) on the faded Turkey carpet. As usual,

---

1 Eton was the top preparatory school for aristocratic boys, who would then go on to an Oxford College such as Christchurch. Cheltenham, though very exclusive, was one level down in prestige from Eton, and Cambridge colleges did not have quite the age or prestige that Oxford had.
2 Compare Proverbs 21:9. "It is better to dwell in a corner of a house-top, than with a brawling woman in a wide house."
3 Officials who served writs and made arrests. Nell fears that such officials may arrest her father or seize his property because of debts.
4 Compare Job 2:8. Job, afflicted with boils, sits in ashes and grieves. His wife advises that he curse God and die, but he refuses. Later, after other tribulations, he asks that God let him die (Job 6:8-9).
5 See the story of Cain and Abel in Genesis 4. Jealous of his father's blessing, Cain kills his older brother Abel. The scene is often depicted with Abel lying at his brother's feet.

I was sitting on the floor. I had a big darning-needle between my fingers, and was slowly and unskilfully mending stockings. It was an occupation I particularly disliked; it was a real penance to me; but having no lady's maid, I had to undergo it weekly. And as I darned and pricked myself, and grumbled at fate, I heard a door which led to the offices creak on its hinges, and saw a head peer inquiringly round it—the head of our old cook and housekeeper. She had been with us twenty years; she was as good a soul as ever trussed a chicken or concocted *entremets*,[1] and I loved her; but at the present moment she was to me a most unwelcome apparition. I had already ordered dinner, so I knew she could have come with but one fell object, namely, to get money for some of the numerous tradesmen who were kind enough to throng our doors.

"If you please, 'm, I want to speak to you," said the head, cautiously.

"Do you?" said I, with a sickening heart. "Come in then, there's nobody here."

Thus reassured, the head, and the body that belonged to it, came forward into the room, and both together stood before me—sleek, middle-aged, like a respectable tabby.

"Well?" said I, looking up from amid my hose, "what is it?"

"If you please, 'm, the butcher" (she pronounced the word as if the first syllable were the preposition *but*) "has come."

"Oh, indeed! How kind of him!" said I.

"Yes, 'm, he has; and he has not brought the right piece of beef. If you remember, you ordered the ribs, and he has brought the sir-*line*; he never brings us the prime pieces now either; he says he has to keep 'em for his larger customers."

"It cannot be helped," said I, resignedly. At nineteen, sirloin or ribs are indifferent to one.

"That's not all, 'm, I'm sorry to say," pursued Mrs. Smith, rather aggravated by my stoicism; "he's brought his bill again."

"I wish he and his bill were at Jericho,"[2] responded I, tartly.

"He says that this is the ninth time he has brought it in, and he wants to have it paid."

"Want must be his master," said I, briefly.

---

1 Side dishes or desserts.
2 See the story of Jericho, the famous site of a devastating massacre, in Joshua 6.

"But he says he *must* have it paid; that he's got a very 'eavy engagement to meet next week, and he cannot do without the money."

"They always say that," replied I, surveying ruefully a yawning chasm in the heel of my stocking.

"Indeed, 'm, I think they do; but, if you please, what am I to tell him? He's waiting."

"Tell him that I shall be most happy to pay his bill if he'll only show me how; that I cannot coin money; and I haven't got a farthing in the world, except the crooked sixpence on my chain, which he is most welcome to, if he likes to take it."

"I'm afraid I could not tell him that, 'm; but if you could manage to give him just a little something towards it—just to put him off a bit."

"I tell you it's out of the question," I said, eagerly. "I'm telling you the literal truth; I have not a halfpenny in the world. I gave you my last shilling last week, for that man that came with coals; and papa told me he could not give me any more till the end of next month."

"Eh, dear! it's a bad job—a bad job!" moaned our *chef de cuisine*, shaking her elderly head; "and I don't 'alf like going back empty-handed to the man—he's none too civil, I can tell you."

"None too civil, isn't he?" exclaimed I, indignantly, regardless of grammar. "The wretch! why don't you kick him out of the house?"

But Mrs. Smith's sense of justice revolted against this ladylike proposition.

"Nay, my dear," said she, mildly remonstrative, "we could not quite do that, I'm thinking. After all, the man's only come to look after his own, and if we was to turn him out o' doors, a pretty character he'd give of us, all over the place! Why, we should have the whole lot on 'em about our ears afore you could say Jack Robis'n!"

We remained silent a minute or two, Mrs. Smith rubbing her chin reflectively, as if to gain inspiration from that feature, or features—for she had two of them, while wild ideas of writing a book, for which emulous publishers should outbid each other, of marrying a certain snuffy old bachelor uncle of the Coxes, and making him settle three-fourths of his income on papa, coursed through my brain. At last Mrs. Smith spoke:

"My dear, would you mind speaking to your papa about it?"

I interrupted her.

"I should mind very much; I don't know anything I should mind much more."

"Well, 'm, you know something must be done, and perhaps he has got some money you don't know of—just a trifle would do, to stop the man's mouth for the present, and there's no harm in asking. *Do* now, there's a dear young lady! there he goes down the garden. Eh, dear! he stoops sadly of late."

"I *won't*," said I, vehemently, "and that's flat. He's in very bad spirits this morning as it is, and I won't do anything to add to his annoyances if I can help it. I'll see you and the butcher too, at the bottom of the Red Sea first."

Baffled in her little plan, Mrs. Smith stood the image of black despair in a lilac cotton gown, and bumbailiffs crowded thick and fast before my mind's eye. At last I said, gulping down my pride:

"Mrs. Smith, don't you think that if you were to go to him, and tell him that we are very sorry, but that we really don't happen to have any money by us at present, and if you were to speak very civilly to him, don't you think you might persuade him to wait till next week? by next week," I said, resolutely, "I'll get the money as sure as I sit here, by hook or by crook, by fair means or foul, if I have to steal it."

"I can but try," she answered, being the essence of good nature; "but I'm sadly afraid it won't be no good."

She disappeared despondent behind the swing-door, and I went back to my darning. Duns were such every-day visitors, that as long as I could keep them away from papa I bore their attentions with tolerable equanimity. After a considerable interval my messenger returned, with her visage somewhat shortened.

"Well?" said I, interrogatively.

"He's gone, 'm, drabbit 'im!" said she, with her one little pet imprecation—an imprecation which always rather puzzled me as to its precise signification, etymology, and derivation. What awful malediction was contained in the imperative mood of the verb "to drabbit?" "I've got him out of the house at last, though, indeed, I had hard work to manage it. He cuss'd and swore above a bit, that he did. I was ashamed out of my life that them girls should hear him; and he said, said he, 'Mrs. Smith,' said he, 'there's not another man in all ——shire as u'd been as patient and forbearin' as I've been,' said he; and here's his bill, 'm; he desired me pertickler to give it into your own 'ands."

I took it; £34 5s. 4½d.

"The halfpenny be demmed," said I, with dreary jocularity, quoting Mr. Mantalini.[1] "Well, will he wait till next week?"

"Not he, 'm; he would not hear tell of it nohow; he's coming again on Tuesday; he'd a come on Monday, only it's Nantford fair, and he says if he don't get his bill settled satisfactorily then, he'll go straight off to the master and 'ave it out with him."

"Pleasant!" said I, ironically. "I wish he and the baker and the candlestick-maker may all come to some horrible end soon, that I do! Spontaneous combustion, or something of the sort. They are the bane of my existence!"

However, I had got a reprieve, though a very short one; it's better to be going to be hanged to-morrow than to be hanged to-day. I was young and possessed of boundless spirits, which, when the immediate pressure of any anxiety was removed, rose elastic as an indiarubber ball, trusting implicitly in something turning up. I am bound to admit that nothing ever did turn up, but that did not lessen my faith in the *potentialities*, as Carlyle[2] would call them, of the future.

CHAPTER VII

Thirty-four pounds, five shillings, and fourpence halfpenny is a large sum for a person without present income or future prospects, to procure within three days. So I thought as I sat through that long forenoon, racking my brains to find out ways and means for obtaining that sum, or even a part of it. But I racked my brains in vain; no inspiration came to them; nothing turned up. I had nobody that I could borrow or hope to borrow from. I was, it is true, possessed of two well-to-do aunts, but they were vestals of the stingiest, who, as long as I could remember anything, had never given me or Dolly a farthing's worth, with the exception of two bone brooches, coloured crimson, and representing fruit and flowers; brooches vast in size, but infinitesimal in value, and

---

1 A character from *The Life and Adventures of Nicholas Nickleby* (1839), a novel by Dickens. Mr. Mantalini is always in need of money, which he wheedles out of his wife.
2 Thomas Carlyle (1795-1881) was an essayist and historian. He uses this term in the *Latter-Day Pamphlets* (1850).

which they had borne all the way, across sea and land, from Rome for us, as characteristic mementoes of the Eternal City. I felt that I had rather die than be beholden to their niggard charity.

I ran over in my mind all my few poor worldly possessions, to find something vendible among them; but to no purpose, I had no jewels, Dolly having appropriated all our mother's ornaments, before I was of an age to care much whether she appropriated them or not. The sole thing which I possessed, that could by any possibility be worth more than a few shillings, was a large unwieldy old watch, which had belonged to my maternal grandmother—a watch with a jewelled case with queer figures chased in gold upon it, and which I wore every day for want of a better, though it kept a time of its own, or, as often as not, no time at all. The idea of selling this ancient timepiece did occur to me, but I dismissed it as impossible. Who would buy such an old warming-pan? and, moreover, whom should I see to offer it to?

As the hours stole on I grew very down-hearted. Tuesday morning would be here directly, and with it the Furies, in the shape of that accursed butcher in his blue blouse. Despite all my anxious precautions, he would get access to my dear old father, and would dun and torment him, and make him even more miserable than he was now, though, God knows, there was no need for that.

My father and I had by this time quite made up our little differences; we never could be at war with one another for more than an hour; and we had taken our diurnal stroll about the premises, to inspect the stock, and say what we had said yesterday, and what we should say to-morrow about it. We had thought the red cow looking invalidish, and had ordered her a bran mash; we had, in imagination, sold five or six of our best porkers, and got fabulous prices for them; we had doomed the black pullets to an untimely death, and had administered his daily carrot to the old gray cob. And now my father had gone back to his books, and there would be no tearing him away from them for the rest of that day.

We dined at one, and did not have tea till eight; so that the afternoon spread in rather dreary perspective before my mind's eye; rather an inconveniently long period of time for a young lady who had no more pleasing occupation than that of meditating on her own and her papa's liabilities.

It was an oppressive, sultry sort of day, rather depressing to the spirits. The sun had gone out of sight somewhere, though there did not appear to be any particular cloud to hide him; and a dim, dull haze, which might be prophetic of either thunder, blight, or increased heat, enveloped all except the nearest objects. It was stifling in the house, and I betook myself to the garden, and strolled rather disconsolately between the luxuriant borders. But the garden did not please me to-day, I seemed to know every twig in it so intimately. I had not energy for gardening, and moreover, had memories connected with my last essay in that line which I did not care to dwell upon.

A low fence divided our grounds from a field of green corn, and over this fence I climbed, and sauntered through the young barley to a small fir wood at the other side of it. Ordinarily, I was not fond of taking solitary walks, having a wholesome fear of beggarmen, loose horses, etc.; but I did not dread an encounter with any such alarming objects among those tall quiet pines. It was very cool and shady there, and I enjoyed looking through the long vista of tree aisles and arches, without any brambles or brushwood to obstruct my view; while the fallen pine needles made a pleasant carpet for my feet.

Beyond the wood was a meadow all ablaze with buttercups, and beyond it a garrulous brook, which was the bound of my walk. Arrived here, I sat down in the grass on the hither side, and thought of the butcher. A little rude handbridge led over the hurrying, clattering stream, and on the other side of it, right opposite to me, rose a mill, and an old farmhouse, with a range of straw beehives and a plat of blue borage under the diamond-paned windows, beside it. The mill was at work, and the water came plunging and dashing and sparkling over the big wheel, as it turned round, dripping. I love a millwheel, and could watch it for ever; my eyes followed it with a sort of fascination, as it moved round and round interminably, with a noise, though loud, yet eminently soothing.

My attention was distracted by a little flock of yellow velvet chickens, coming pecketting down to the water's edge, with the old hen clucking fussily in the midst of them. Then the miller's wife came out with a bowl of something in her hand, and threw handfuls to them, and I wondered whether she fed her chickens on the same thing that we did ours; and then three large white ducks came swimming down the stream, paddling and quacking, and diving their sleek heads under water. But after a while the chickens wandered, scratching and picking, out of sight; the miller's wife went indoors, and I got tired of watching the ducks stand upon their heads. I yawned, and took one last glance down stream, before rising to go home.

Some way down, on the other side, I spied a man making his way through the thick alders—a man in brown velveteen, with a fishing-rod in his hand. During the last few days my heart had taken to thumping loudly whenever I saw a man in the distance, opining that it might be my new friend; and consequently I had to submit to severe disappointment as often as my hero turned out to be a gamekeeper, a day labourer, or even a cowman. The seat of my affections gave its usual thud against my ribs now, and this time it was justified in so doing; the man was Major M'Gregor. Presently he emerged from the alders, looking rather hot. Then he came over the ricketty bridge, smiling. He looked very goodly, and I thought so. To this day I think he was

"The goodliest man that ever among ladies ate in hall";

and most assuredly I thought so that day, when

"I lifted up mine eyes,
And loved him with that love that was my doom";[1]

for love him I did, though I have not said much about it, as it is no use dwelling on unpleasant truths.

Like a little fool as I was, I pretended not to see him, and turned my head, surmounted by its ragged brown hat, perseveringly down stream, and tried to appear immersed in the contemplation of the trout leaping half their own length out of the water, after the flies under the dipping alders, and then flopping back again. But all the same; I need hardly say that I heard his feet coming through the long sweet grass, as plainly as ever I heard cannonball or thunderclap.

"De do, Miss Lestrange?" said a jolly voice beside me, abbreviating the Briton's customary greeting to his fellow, after the manner of the young.

The brown hat and the reddened face it shaded veered round from the study of the trout, and two youthful and embarrassed lips responded, "How do you do?" in return, and a ladylike

---

1 See "Lancelot and Elaine" in *Idylls of the King* (1859), by Tennyson.

hand, in a most unladylike glove, perforated with many holes, went out to meet Major M'Gregor's large one—went out shyly, but gladly.

"I hope you did not intend to cut me,"[1] he said, laughing; "you looked away so perseveringly when I took off my hat to you on the other side, that I felt almost afraid of coming near you."

"I did not see you," I began, hastily; "at least—at least," and there I stopped, having expressed myself with my usual lucid coherency, and being fully aware of it.

"Well, never mind!" said he, good-naturedly, trying to put me at my ease. "I'll forgive you, if you did mean to cut me, on condition that you won't send me away now," and a pair of dark honest gray eyes looked at me in a beseeching and insinuating manner, to which at Lestrange Hall I had not been accustomed, and which I thought pleasant, though extremely odd. I plucked up my spirits, and determined to revolt against the dominion of gawkiness, and be sprightly.

"I could not send you away, if I had wished ever so much," I said. "This meadow is not mine, nor yet the grass nor the buttercups; you have as much right to be here, I suppose, as I have."

"But do you wish to send me away?" Silence. "*Do* you, Miss Lestrange?" Silence still. "*Do* you?" rather impatiently, bending down to look at my face.

I perceived his eagerness, and was elated by it. He wished me to say "No," so I would say "Yes." A spirit of graceful contradiction entered into me. Why should I not be *agaçante*, and *espiègle*,[2] and two or three other nice French adjectives whose exact meaning I should have been puzzled to define. So I looked up into his anxious countenance, and said, laughingly,

"Yes, I do wish to send you away."

"All right," said he, calmly; "then I'll go," and he picked up the fishing-rod he had tossed down on the grass, took off his hat, and went.

I have experienced a good many moments of mortification in my life—of course we all have—but I doubt whether I ever felt one more bitter, or more completely undiluted by any dash of sweetness. This was the result of my archness then. Why, oh why had

---

1 To snub him socially by treating him as if they are not acquainted— not greeting him, for example, or acknowledging his greeting.

2 Coquettish and roguish (French), respectively.

not I kept to my native stupidity? I had got on much better then. When I attempted to be funny, it was like a cow standing on her hind legs—nobody could understand what she would be after.

In the impulse of the moment, I sprang to my feet, intending to run after him, but I was held back by the remembrance of my mature age, and of what the best of fathers would say, were he to see me coursing round the big field after the "Brummagem young man," to whom he had so strong an objection. So I sank down on the grass again, and the silly tears stole into my eyes as I watched Richard walking huffily off, without looking once back at me. He did not walk particularly well, but much as dismounted dragoons[1] usually do; but to me his gait seemed that of an offended angel.

The trout might have leaped up into the trees above them, and sat there singing, for all the notice I should have taken of them now. A faint hope lingered in my breast that he might relent—might come back—that I might see him pushing through the alders and the wych-elms again; and in this hope I stayed there disconsolate till the dew fell, and the flowers went to sleep, and the June moon came up behind the fir wood. There I sat, thinking of dear, dear Richard, and of the butcher, and weeping over them both.

That was Saturday; need I say that next day was Sunday—day on which most people dine early, and many people have roast beef for dinner. Morning service at Lestrange Church began at eleven, and commenced with a hymn, which I led. My voice, as I said once before, was my strongest point—my strongest but one, perhaps. On mature deliberation, I think that my eyes were my strongest. Anyhow, it was a rich, full contralto, and some of the low notes were, I flattered myself, almost as deep as a man's.

Our choir was not a large one; it consisted of myself, two or three of our servants, who laboured under a fear of making too much noise, and consequently did not make enough; the clerk, and a young carpenter, who was too ambitious of introducing turns and trills and flourishes of his own composition into the simple old tunes. Often and often had I seen fit to skirmish with that too enterprising artificer. The church had two doors; a big and a little one; a big one, by which the bulk of the congregation came in; and a small one, by which we and two or three farmers'

---

1 A type of cavalry soldier.

families made our dignified entrance. In this hot weather both doors stood wide open, and the doorways made frames for pretty little pictures of waving tree-boughs, of weather-worn stone crosses, and of daisies opening their pink fringes upon the

"Grassy barrows of the happier dead."[1]

Exactly opposite the little door was our square pew, with its faded red moreen,[2] which the morning sun was trying to fade still more; with Sir Lovelace Lestrange's black and white marble monument glooming above it, and with many Sir Lovelaces, Sir Adrians, and Sir Brians sleeping beneath it. I had stood up, had cleared my throat, and had struck up the first line of "Jerusalem the golden." I loved that tune, it was so sweet, and so triumphant.

"I know not; oh, I know not,"

sang I loud and clear, while the birds outside tried to rival me; and as I sang, a tall fair-haired stranger stooped his head, and came in at the low door, close to me. For a moment I felt as if I must give up "Jerusalem the golden"[3] altogether—abandon it to the tender mercies of the trilling, roulading carpenter; but I mastered myself; I must go on, though twenty yellow-haired majors came trooping through the church portals. When one feels that a thing must be done, one generally does it.

"What radiancy of glory;
What bliss beyond compare,"

sang I, stronger and clearer than ever. I poured my whole soul into my voice. Love and excitement supplied the place of devotion. He should hear how I *could* sing, I thought, remembering that objectionable brunette at the Coxe's party, and her pretty little treble squeak.

1 See "Tithonus" (1860), a poem by Tennyson.
2 Heavy woolen fabric used for upholstery and curtains.
3 A Latin hymn, originally entitled "Urbs Sion Aurea" (c. 1146), by poet Bernard of Morlaix (also called Bernard of Cluny). Translated by John M. Neale (1858). Set to music by Alexander Ewing (1853).

As I laid down my hymn-book at the conclusion of the hymn, I felt that a casual observer would find some little difficulty in distinguishing which were my cheeks and which were the red roses in my bonnet. I did not yield to the temptation of taking one look, long or short, at the lion-hearted Richard (lion-hearted in thus a second time braving my revered papa), but I knew by instinct that he was in a pew over against me, in which Mr. Harris of the Home Farm had charitably given him a corner. I did not look at or towards him, and I tried honestly not to think of him—tried hard to be as sorry for my sins as I said I was—tried to implore from that God who was to me then but a dim awful abstraction, those good things for my soul, without which that soul would be so cold, so naked, so famishing—tried to remember of how infinitesimally little account Richard M'Gregor and his beauty would be to me at the Judgment Day.

Often and often had I terrified myself with two vivid pictures of Death and Judgment as I lay wakeful on my bed, in my dark room at night; but here in the full blaze of the summer sun, I could summon but faint shadows, indistinct reflections of such pictures before my mind's eye; here youth and joy and love seemed dominant, and to keep all darker powers, baffled and worsted, in the background. So I buried my head in my big old prayer-book, which had a dried pansy between two of its leaves, and a squashed fly between the other two, and caught myself praying earnestly, seriously, devoutly, for Queen Charlotte, the Prince Regent, and all the Royal family.[1] I had mentally resolved that morning to abstain during the day of rest from all harassing thoughts of Mr. Jenkins the butcher. Monday should be dedicated to the consideration of ways and means, to the begging, borrowing or stealing that obnoxious sum of £34 5s. 4½d. But to-day I would be free from sordid cares; I would try to keep my mind clear and clean from worldly thoughts. And I was moderately successful, as far as regards the butcher. But it was a very different matter when I endeavoured to close the doors of my mind against Richard; to observe the Sabbath strictly in my heart; his image pushed the door of that sanctuary *sans façon*,[2] and dwelt there, defying expulsion, during the long morning service.

---

1 The prayer book is quite old—George IV was Prince Regent from 1811 to 1820. Nell's many quotations from contemporary works place the time of the narrative in the 1860s.
2 Without ceremony (French).

All through the sermon I looked forward with childish impatience to the meeting in the churchyard, which seemed to me almost unavoidable. I pictured to myself how we three should stand in the church path under the ash tree. Papa rather grim at first, but thawing fast into his usual natural, dear old hearty manner; I, bashful and somewhat gawky, I feared, but in the seventh heaven; and Richard!!!

"Perhaps," thought I, exultantly, "papa'll ask him to luncheon, and if he does," subjoined cold reflection, "there's nothing but that old mutton bone." This last dismal idea lasted me through one whole head (the last one) of papa's brief and simple discourse.

"In conclusion," said my father—"in conclusion," echoed my heart, "there's nothing but the cold mutton." At the end of his usual twenty minutes, my father released us, and having pronounced the benediction, remained standing in the pulpit, putting his spectacles into their case, and eyeing somewhat hostilely the wolf in sheep's clothing that had stolen into his fold. Poor, naughty, handsome wolf! One lamb longed to go and put out a friendly paw to him; but lambs do not always know what is good for them. And then the little congregation trickled out by the two doors, and the farmers' wives shook hands among themselves, and the old women in black poke bonnets by themselves, and John Barlow slouched over to his mother's new tombstone, and read the inscription admiringly, having composed it himself; and then they all toddled decorously down the sunny road to the village. Behind them dawdled a disconsolate dragoon, casting, ever and anon, baffled and disconsolate looks behind him.

Meanwhile, I stood just within the church porch, tapping with my foot on the flags, above the buried head of another Eleanor Lestrange, chafing and fuming. It was my invariable custom to wait for my father, while he took off his gown, and usually, I had only about two seconds to wait. To-day the process of disrobing seemed a lengthier one. Perhaps it was only my angry imagination, but I could not help fancying that papa loitered purposely over his ungowning; purposely seduced old Iken into one of his long maunders.

"Toothless old nuisance," said I, stamping on Eleanor Lestrange's head harder than ever. But stamping and malediction, did not hasten the flow of old Iken's eloquence nor diminish my father's interest in it. At length it came to a sort of stop; and my father, cheerful and chatty, and I, disappointed and choking, sauntered down the path. The figure of Richard, diminished by distance to the height of a few inches, was slowly disappearing round the corner.

"What brought that fine fellow here to-day, I wonder?" said my father affably, looking after him. I made no response, but gnawed the ivory top of my parasol in a silent frenzy. There came no wolf to afternoon service at Lestrange church, and old Iken beginning another long rigmarole, was summarily repressed.

CHAPTER VIII

About five o'clock on that Sunday, I was passing through the hail, dragging my feet after me in a languid and dispirited manner, like the devil

"Trailing his nerveless tail
On the shore by the Red Sea sand,"[1]

when my father called to me from the library—
"Nell! Nell! is that you?"
"Yes," said I, and ran in.

He was sitting in his old arm-chair among his books, and looked up as I made my appearance at the door.

"Oh! it *is* you, is it?" he said. "I want you to do something for me."

"Yes," said I, expectantly.

"I promised to send old Widow Boyle some broth to-day, and I want to know whether you'll take it?"

"With the greatest pleasure," rejoined I, briskly, glad of some occupation, and of an excuse for deserting "A Narrative of a Mission to the Jews,"[2] which entertaining work had been my Sunday reading for the last seven years. Whereupon I vanished from my parent's eyes.

---

1 See "St. Medard: A Legend of Afric" in *The Ingoldsby Legends* (1840), by "Thomas Ingoldsby," pseud. for Richard Barham (1788-1845).

2 It was customary for the Sabbath to be passed in serious pursuits. The only reading considered appropriate was the scripture or religious tracts. Nell may be referring to "Narrative of a Mission to the Jews from the Church of Scotland in 1839" (1842), by Andrew Bonar and Robert Murray MacCheyne.

Having obtained from Mrs. Smith a small tin can, filled with a greasy-looking and untempting liquid, supposed to be mutton broth, and having received with meekness her exhortations not to spill it over my Sunday gown, I set off. Up a steep field of beans, and down a steeper one of clover, across a little common tenanted by a very thin donkey belonging to a tinker; then down a narrow lane, with high red sandstone banks and deep cartruts, and then I found myself at Widow Boyle's gate, with a mixed flavour of pigs and of that objectionable herb called southernwood, or old man, in my small nose. Having poured my broth into a bowl brought me for that purpose by Mr. Boyle's relict, and having received that gentlewoman's thanks, my tin can and I set off home again.

We went very slowly, I scrambling now and again up the steep red banks after big primroses, shining in clusters in their starry paleness. I gathered a great bunch of them, ruthlessly tearing them from the homes where God had put them. Then I sat down on the grass by the roadside, and set to making an orderly nosegay of them. Two children came by presently with more primroses; then two sweethearts—the man sheepish, the girl giggling; and then, oh then!—what in the world brought him there I never could make out—then a great big noble-looking young soldier, whose name was Richard M'Gregor. Apparently, he had not got over his huffiness, nor forgiven me; for he made as though he would have passed me, merely raising his hat; but I could not suffer that. Nature and impulse would have their way; this time I jumped up (and the primroses and the tin can jostled and hustled one another into a deep cartrut), ran across to him, and put out a most eager hand.

"Oh, please," I said, panting, "I hope you're not angry with me; I'm sorry I was so rude yesterday."

That man must have been colder than a statue who could resist two full soft lips begging with such pretty humility; and coldness of temperament was certainly not one of my sweetheart's vices or virtues.

The expression of huffy dignity melted out of his face—melted into the honestest, joyfullest smile.

"Who told you you were rude?" he asked. "I did not, I'm sure."

"No, but you thought so, or you would not have gone away so suddenly."

"What could I do but go, when you sent me?"

I hung down my head.

"One does not always *quite* mean what one says," I said, slowly.

"Does not one? I'm glad to hear you say so; you *did* make me rather unhappy. I'll tell you that now; though, perhaps, you'll only use your knowledge to torment me a little more."

"I don't wish to torment anybody," I said, gently. "I've told you already I did not mean what I said; I was only joking; I meant to have told you so after church this morning, only old Iken kept papa talking so long."

"I shall take the liberty of breaking old Mr. Iken's head for him next time I have the pleasure of meeting that old gentleman."

"He is rather tiresome," I said, "he's so deaf and stupid; but you believe what I said to you, don't you?" and I looked up earnestly at him.

"I don't know," he said, laughing; "I'll see about it. I'm of rather a sceptical nature; I never believe anything without proof."

"What proof can I give you?" I asked, eagerly.

He became grave.

"You can let me walk home with you?"

"Oh, certainly," replied I, with alacrity, "it's not five minutes walk from here to our gate."

His countenance fell a little.

"Not five minutes walk!" he repeated. "Well, anyhow, let us walk very slow, and make it ten minutes. Are those your flowers that are all tumbled about there? Let me pick them up for you."

I sat on the grass, and watched him as he did so, and gave him the biggest, sweetest primrose star I could find as a reward, at his request. Then his eyes looked into mine, and spake softly to them, and his lips said:

"Don't go yet, please. As you are strong, be merciful."

I was merciful; I began to feel a person of some importance, and accorded him this favour also, very graciously. Nothing short of a miracle could bring papa here, I thought.

"Don't you find Sunday afternoon awfully long?" he asked, yawning. "I never have the least idea what to do with myself down here. Coxe is a rare good fellow, but he is not an over-lively companion; and Mrs. Coxe (sandy-haired Mrs. Coxe, d'you recollect?) is a little too fond of the peerage to suit my taste."

I was a little nettled.

"If you find us so dull in this part of the world, I wonder you do not leave us. I cannot imagine what keeps you?"

"Cannot you?" he said, a little coldly. Then he went on in the same tone as before—

"Come, confess that you go to bed an hour earlier on Sundays than other days (everybody does), and that you are a little tired of reading sermons all day."

"I don't read sermons all day," I responded, gravely. "I read one to the servants, and sometimes, not very often, one to myself; but most of the afternoon I'm feeding the chickens, and seeing the cows milked, and that sort of thing."

"That does not sound very lively."

"One does not need to be very lively on Sundays," I answered, rather dogmatically.

"Does not one? I do not much know what one ought, and what one ought not to do; I wish you'd teach me."

"Teach you what?"

"Oh, I don't know; it does not matter what—anything. I should like to be taught by you."

I looked down, and plucked nervously at my flowers. Is this the way young men always talked to girls, I wondered?

"You would not be a very hard schoolmistress, would you?" pursued he, leaning his head on his hand, with his hat tilted over his eyes.

I laughed a little.

"It's a good idea my teaching anybody anything. I'm the greatest dunce in Europe."

"You are a very pretty dunce," he said, slowly and emphatically. The colour rushed into my cheeks. It could not be right to allow him to say such things to me—such pleasant, untrue things, especially. I flashed an indignant look at him, and gathered up my flowers, preparatory to going.

"You ought not to say such things to me," said I, vehemently, "it's not right. I'm not pretty, and you know I'm not; and you're either laughing at me, or you think I'm a poor countrified simpleton, who will believe anything you like to tell her."

He flushed a little too, and half rose from his reclining posture.

"I wish to Heaven there were more such countrified simpletons," he said, speaking with as much vehemence as I had done. "You always *will* misunderstand me,—always *will* think that I mean to insult you. It may be impertinent of me—I know it is, but I cannot help it. I forget my manners when I am with you. You *are* pretty—awfully pretty, and I cannot for the life of me help telling you so. There! be as angry with me now as you please."

He was excited, and reddened through all his sunburntness, as he uttered this last clause resignedly, awaiting a fresh burst of wrath from me. But no such burst came. I stood dumbfoundered. Here, then, was one of those eccentric individuals mentioned ironically by Dolly. Here was some one in whose eyes red hair and a wide mouth were recommendations. There was an awkward pause.

"Well," he said, softly, at last, rather embarrassed, "are you very angry? Have I sinned quite past forgiveness?"

"Oh, I don't know, I'm sure," I said, in confusion, turning away my burning face, "I—I—don't suppose you have *sinned*, as you call it, at all—only you startled me a little. I'm not used to having those—those sort of things said to me, and—and I think I'll go home now."

I rose as I spoke, and armed myself with my can.

"No, *please* don't," said he, very eagerly. "I'll promise not to be rude again. I'll bite my tongue out first. Only *do* stop five minutes longer. I've got so many things to say to you."

"You must say them some other time," I said hurriedly.

"Ay, that's the rub!" he answered, standing before me, with an anxious look in his gray eyes. "What other time? Am I always to have to trust to chance? May I never come to see you in your own home?"

I looked down and kicked a little pebble about.

"Why do you ask me?" I said. "How can I tell?"

"Who can I ask then?—your father? You know how pleased he was to see me the other night. He was longing to kick me out of the garden; I saw it in his face. Can you deny it?"

I hesitated, and swung my tin can backwards and forwards.

"I don't deny it," I said at last, slowly, "that is to say—I don't mean about the kicking; but I think he thought that you—that I—ought not to have stayed there in the garden without him. I don't know why he *was* displeased, I'm sure. I don't think we did much harm."

I looked up innocently at him, to gather his opinion on the subject of our common iniquity, and I really believe that I was not aware that my big blue eyes looked rather well with that air of childish inquiry in them. Richard *was* aware of that fact; looking back now, with the advantage of increased experience of that queer biped, man, I think he was.

"Harm!" said he, warmly. "I should think not indeed. He would be a pretty brute that could do you any harm. There? if I'm not offending again—breaking my promise, and making pretty speeches. By Jove, I cannot help it."

I dissected a primrose carefully.

"Papa is so very, *very* seldom angry with me—hardly ever, but he really was displeased that night. He said it must never occur again."

Richard stroked his tawny moustache meditatively.

"I'm not sure that he was not right. I have no doubt he thought I was taking a great liberty—which I was—and trying to get up an underhand—ahem!—ahem!—acquaintance with you, which I was not. I never like doing things underhand. I should like to come and call on him to-morrow, only I don't well see how I could. Tell me, did he call me any very hard names behind my back that unlucky evening?"

The ragged brown hat was unable to conceal the scarlet hue that my youthful and ingenuous countenance assumed at this awkward query. My blushes during this interview succeeded each other so rapidly that they almost made one continuous blush.

Face and figure, the cut of his clothes, and the tone of his voice, all were so very *un-Brummagem*, that I could not induce my lips to frame the obnoxious epithet that my sire had applied to him.

"Never mind," he said, laughing carelessly. "I see he did. Well, perhaps he'll think a little better of me some day. We must live in hopes."

"I think," said I, shyly, "I'm sure he'd like you if he were to know you better."

"I'm glad you think I improve upon acquaintance; perhaps *you* did not think much of me then, when we meditated together, yet severally, among the tombs in that pretty churchyard of yours?"

I responded not, but took out my watch to see how the time went. I was always ashamed of having no watch but that ancient warming-pan I have before described, and now endeavoured to shade it as much as possible from Richard's critical eyes with my long, slight fingers. My companion caught sight of a broad, yellow face between my shielding digits.

"What a handsome old watch!" said he, quite respectfully, to it. "An antique isn't it?"

"I know it's antique," quoth I, pouting, and scenting ridicule where ridicule was not. "A great deal too antique to please me; so antique, that all its inside is worn out, and I have to set it every two hours, but I cannot help it. I have not got any better, so I must wear it, and I wish you would not laugh at it."

So I, rapid and injured, disregarding punctuation: to me, Richard:

"If I was laughing, it was a convulsive grin—a contortion of the facial muscles. May I look at it? Thanks. Yes, it is an antique, and rather valuable one, I fancy. This sort of chasing is very rare now-a-days. A connoisseur would give you a lot of money for it."

"Would he? you don't mean *really*?" I said greedily.

"I do indeed; the way I know anything about it is that *the mum*—my mother, I mean—is as mad as two hatters, poor old lady, on the subject of articles of *virtu*,[1] as she calls them; and I hear so much jargon about them at home, from her and the girls, that I have picked up one or two scraps of information, whether I would or no; my mother would go wild over this turnip, though it *is* an uncommon ugly one."

Hope with her anchor,[2] and a fat man with a cleaver, danced a jig before my mind's eye.

"Do you think—have you any idea—would your mother *buy* it, do you think?" I stopped, quivering at my own audacity.

"You don't mean to say you want to sell an old heirloom like that? why I'm sure it must have belonged to your people for centuries."

"I don't know about that," said I, with great *sang froid*,[3] "and I don't care much either. It belonged to a grandmother of mine, whom I never saw, and whom I daresay I should not have liked if I had seen her; I hate old women generally."

"I'm fast getting new lights on your character," said Dick, "what a mercenary person you must be! Are you sure that you have not got some Hebrew blood in your veins?"[4]

---

1 Collectibles, fine arts.
2 Hope was often represented as a woman with an anchor, just as Justice is represented as a woman with sword and scales, and often a blindfold.
3 Composure, cold blood (French).
4 Broughton here participates in a form of anti-Semitism that was common, though not universal, in the period. Jews were associated with money-lending, and particularly lending of an unsavory sort.

"Oh no, *indeed* I'm not mercenary," I cried, sorely distressed. "Please don't say that, and I do assure you we never had anything to say to the Jews, but I do want some money *very, very* badly just now."

A mist of tears came before my eyes as I thought of my old daddy, worried into his grave before his time, by sordid cares. If ever astonishment depicted itself on a human countenance, it did then on the pleasing exterior of that much amazed dragoon. Then an inkling of the truth dawned upon him; perhaps he called to mind some of the many rumours he must have heard of our poverty, which was indeed not unknown to fame. For a minute compassion, sincere, surprised compassion, clouded his glad young eyes.

"If you do really want to get rid of it," he said, kindly affecting to ignore my tearful eagerness; "I can easily take it up to town with me next time I go. There are lots of shops where I could dispose of it for you with the greatest ease, if you'd only give me time; there's no great hurry about it, I suppose?"

"Oh, but indeed there is," say I, clinging to this new hope like a drowning man to a straw; "if I don't get the money to-morrow, it will do me no good. I—I—want it for a particular purpose—to—to buy something for myself." This I said in my astuteness, to put him off the scent of the butcher.

"*To-morrow!*" said he, opening his gray eyes very wide, "that is a short allowance of time; why, in the first place, I should have to go up to town about it."

"Would you? Oh, but indeed I could not think of putting you to so much expense and trouble for me," I said compunctiously.

"Trouble, a fiddlestick; I shall be glad of an excuse to air my brains a bit; I think some of the fluff and flue of Coxe's cotton mills is getting into them; but *by to-morrow!*"

"Tuesday morning would do: Tuesday morning early; but indeed I'm asha——"

"Will you be so kind as to be silent? Silence is woman's best ornament; do you know that? and I see that you are going to say something foolish. Well, I'll make no rash promises, but I'll do my best, and glad of the job!"

"You're—you're very good to me, and I'm sure I cannot imagine why," said I, and up went my blue eyes in a reverent rapture to his face.

"I *am* good, a very good boy indeed. I wonder you never found that out before, but if I do succeed, as I hope I shall, how am I to let you know I have?"

"Ah, to be sure!"

"Would you mind meeting me here, or somewhere else to-morrow evening? I'm sorry to trouble you, but I don't see how else it's to be done."

"I'd rather not," said I, in a mumbling manner.

"Why?"

Many pebbles kicked about, the lid of the can removed and replaced three several times. "If I were to ask papa's leave, he'd say no, and if I did not, it would be sly underhand!"

"Probity personified! Must I then come to Lestrange, and run the risk of being turned out again by an enraged parent? I'm 'exceedingly brave, particular';[1] but I really don't think I'm brave enough for that."

I smiled a little and shook my head.

"Must I go to the backdoor then, and bribe one of the 'young men or maidens' to take a message to you?"

"No, *certainly not*," with emphasis.

"What must I do then? I'm amenable to orders." No suggestions for a while, then I, with diffidence—

"Could not you—would you mind sending the money, if you have any, in an envelope; by post, I mean?"

"I *could*, certainly, but as you said just now, I'd rather not."

"I thought you said you were amenable to orders," said I, with an attempt to be smart, which sat, I felt, rather ill on me.

"So I am to most orders, but not to this one; the exception, you know, proves the rule; come, let us split the difference. I won't ask you to leave your own grounds, just come and meet me at the bottom of your garden, where that hedge of lilac bushes is, you know. I won't detain you a minute, I promise, and upon my soul, *I don't bite*; say yes, *do*; y-e-s, yes; you cannot conceive how easy it is to pronounce."

"Yes."

"Well, you *are* laconic, but it's very good of you, all the same,

---

1 See "Commodore Rogers," a comic poem: "Commodore Rogers was a man—exceedingly brave—particular; / He climbed up very high rocks—exceedingly high—perpendicular" (author unknown). Commodore Rogers was an American naval hero of the nineteenth century.

and I'll never tease you again, hanged if I will. On Wednesday I'm coming openly in the eye of day, to pay my respects under Mrs. Coxe's wing. I daren't come without Mrs. Coxe, and as it is, I shall feel something like a naughty little boy come to beg pardon."

As he spoke I had been detaching my watch from the chain, and now gave it into his hands.

"I *will* go now," I said. "Don't keep me a minute longer, or perhaps pa may be after me."

"Not a minute—but stay, don't forget to be in the garden somewhere about nine to-morrow. No great hardship surely, these spring evenings. Star-gazing is——"

"Good-bye," said I, cutting short the thread of his eloquence, and holding out my hand.

"Good-bye," said he, squeezing it till all my fingers seemed crushed into one painful mass. But I bore it like a man; not a groan revealed my agony.

"Then like a blast away I passed,
And no man saw me more."[1]

CHAPTER IX

Is it possible that one is through the whole course of one's life the same individual being? Is one possessed of but one individual soul? Does it not rather seem that each man or woman is in himself or herself a succession of individual beings, possessing, one after another, several successive souls? Our body is the same body at fifty as it was at five, and as it will be at seventy—the same, subject only to the changes and modifications made by time, weather, sickness, or mode of life. Wonderful as it seems, the fat, pink, dimpling baby body is the same as the withered old yellow carcass tottering into the long expecting tomb; but our soul—is it the same? I trow[2] not. Our estimate of things and people, our habits, tastes, dispositions, at certain periods of our life are so radically different from, and totally antagonistic to,

1 See "The Lays of Ancient Rome" (1842), by Thomas Babington Macaulay (1800-59).
2 Trust (archaic English).

what they are at other such periods, that I think it is hardly possible that their variations should be accounted for by any of the alterations that it is within the province of time, sorrow, or any change of inner or outer life to effect.

Perhaps, at certain epochs in our history, separated by varying periods of time, a new soul (in our sleep, may be) passes into our body, each successive soul sadder than the last. A more nonsensical, puerile idea never entered a human head, I'm aware; but here it is, and I cannot cast it out. *Can* I, *can* I be the same individual soul, the same *ego* as that girl who stood one May morning on a ladder, nailing monthly roses up against the hall windows at dear old Lestrange? There I stood, in a faded green muslin,[1] with a hammer in one hand and a nail in the other, humming softly to myself as I hammered. A party of young starlings stared at me from their residence under the eaves, and opened their great yellow mouths wide, expecting me to pop worms into them, as their mamma was in the habit of doing.

"The summer hath its heavy cloud;
The rose leaf must fall,"[2]

I sang under my breath to myself. "Rose leaf must fall," indeed. I wish it did not, for they make a sad litter on the border; I must make some *pot pourri* of them. I suppose the roses in Eden never fell or withered. What an odd idea. I wonder how that was managed. Were there always fresh roses coming out, and the old ones flowering on eternally? How the bushes must have overblown themselves.

"But in our land joy wears no shroud,
Never doth it pall.
Ne—ever do—oth it pa—all."

---

1   Soft, lightweight open-weave cloth.
2   From a song popular in the mid-nineteenth century. Harriet Beecher Stowe quotes it at length in her novel, *Dred: A Tale of the Dismal Swamp* (1856). Tamar Heller identifies the probable source as "I Have Come from a Happy Land: The Hindoo Girl's Song," music by Robert Archibald Smith and words by W. Kennedy (1858).

A strong wind had been blowing all night, that had loosened half the rose boughs; but now all was still—still and calm as the sleep of the just. Far off I heard the dull, drowsy burr of a threshing machine at work, and the bow-wow-ow of a little dog that felt himself insulted, coming from a distant farm; nearer, our gardening man, mowing the dewy lawn, and beheading a thousand daisies; nearer still, two wood-pigeons in our wood, telling their sweet prosy love tale to one another interminably—cooroo, cooroo, cooroo, cooroo; nearest of all, the important busy humming of a big bumble bee, going in and out of the campanula bells, stealing her honey drops from each.

I look back on that May morning, and on myself at my pretty play-work, as Eve must have looked back upon the pastimes of Paradise. I am not separated from that time by any great crime, as she was from the period of her happiness; but I think the yearning regret that filled the universal mother's bosom for the lotos-scented airs that breathed about the banks of those mystic eastern rivers, was akin to the eager longing (never to be gratified now) with which I inhale in fancy the rough western breezes blowing round old Lestrange.

I suppose it rained there in those days; I suppose it snowed, and was foggy, and cold, and dreary there in those days as much as other places—perhaps more; but I cannot realize that now; to me it seems as if those gnarled old trees were always crowned with a glory of green leaves; as if those walls were always sunlit; as if the pinks and the sweet peas and the lark-spurs flowered there all the year round. I did not think myself particularly happy in those days. That is the worst of this life, one never tastes its sweets while they are in one's mouth; it is only when they are gone, and we are chewing the bitters, and making wry faces over them, that we recognise them for what they were.

I took it as a matter of course that I was young and healthy and cheerful; to be so was the normal state of humanity, I thought. Sickness and sadness were abnormal, exceptional; why should I trouble my head about them? I had my annoyances, too; wore threadbare clothes and was gawky; and sometimes went to sleep with tears on my eyelashes—tears caused by my old daddy's stooping head and thin gray hair.

It was market day, and along the broad highway that skirted our grounds rolled gigs and tax-carts by dozens. I was continually turning my head to admire the smart bonnets of the farmers' wives, which distracted my attention sadly from my work.

Occasionally a horseman varied the programme—a farmer's boy taking a rough cart colt to water, the parson jogging along on his old roan pony, which in superannuated fatness yielded the palm to none save papa's; then a county neighbour, lazy and plethoric, ambling by to a justice meeting. Presently came a sharper, brisker sound—a long swinging trot. Round veered my head again, and simultaneously the sound ceased, and I perceived that the horseman had stopped at our gate, and was struggling to open it with his whip-handle, a measure which his steed did his best to prevent.

The steed had the best of it, too, at first, and would have had to this hour, if he had not good-naturedly given in. "Who can it be?" said I to myself. "Benbow's clerk, I suppose." Now, Benbow was my father's attorney, and his clerk was the chiefest among my bugbears, coming not infrequently on mysterious errands that cast a gloom over the establishment. I stood poised in air on the topmost rung of the ladder, and watched with interest. Under the elms came man and horse, the leaf shadows waving a shifting, dancing pattern over them till they reached the lower gate, not a hundred yards from where I was. Recognition here was certain, that is to say, if the man happened to be known to me. He was so known; but if he had been the "Mickle De'il"[1] himself I could not have fled with more precipitancy at his aspect. I sprang from the ladder, ran into the house, through the cool drowsy hall, where the double-chinned, powdered Miss Lestranges, and the fat-faced, wigged Master Lestranges were smirking at nothing but the walls, as usual, headlong into the sanctum where Mrs. Smith sat, muddling her old head over rows of illegible figures, doing those eternal accounts that never would come right.

"Mrs. Smith, Mrs. Smith!" cried I, panting and aghast, "Sir Hugh Lancaster is coming down the drive, *now*, this minute, and I *know* he's coming to luncheon."

Despair on a thin young face is pathetic; on a fat, elderly one, ludicrous. I laughed, but my mirth soon sank into a wail.

"Pa's so hospitable, he's certain to ask him. I never can get him to remember that there *never* is anything for luncheon."

My companion resented this insult to our commissariat.

---

1 Mickle means big, powerful, supernatural; De'il is "Devil" (Scots).

"*Now, Miss Lestrange! Nothing?* Why, there's always the mutton, and it was only yesterday—no, the day before—that I sent you in a lovely dish of fry."

"Is there any fry to-day?" My heart leaped at the thought of intestines.

"My dear, how could there be, when you ate it all o' Saturday? and that plaguy ould butcher has not been near the place since; and for my part, the less he comes the better I'm pleased."

"I shall give the butcher," said I, superbly waving my arm, "a lesson he'll not forget in a hurry."

"I'm sure I wish you could, 'm," said my companion, a little incredulously; "but had not we better be *schaming* something for luncheon?"

"Scheming the tops of our heads off will not put any meat in the larder; are there any fowls?"

"Ye—es; there's four or five of them ould Cochy hens: but they're walking about upon the yard, and it's after twelve now."

"Heavens!"

"There's the mutton," quoth she, recurring to that accursed joint.

"The mutton, Mrs. Smith!" said I, reproachfully. "I wonder at you; that mutton has come in every day for the last fortnight to my certain knowledge, and it's literally and actually nothing but bone."

"There's eggs and bacon."

"Eggs and bacon! Merciful powers, is it come to this? My good woman, do reflect a minute, and you'll see the absurdity of your proposition. Think of inviting Sir Hugh Lancaster to eggs and bacon! I'd as soon ask him to take a slice of dirt pie with me."

"Well, my dear, as good as 'im 'as made their dinners off 'em afore now, and been thankful. Who is them Lancasters, after all, I wonder? Cock 'em up! Not 'alf as good gentry as your pa, as eats whatever's set before him, and makes no fuss about it neither."

I stared glassily at her, and then at the ceiling, and then at the flies on the window, but nowhere did I see roast joints or succulent *entrées*. What was the use of letting one's fancy run riot among impossible dainties? Out of nothing, nothing can come. I rose in despair from the cane-bottomed chair on which I had precipitated myself, and emphasizing each clause of my sentence with my hammer, I said solemnly,

"Eggs and bacon it must be then; but I wash my hands of them and of you. I won't witness our disgrace; I'll go to bed sooner than appear at luncheon. If I'm asked for, tell Collins to say that I'm ill; I *shall* be ill; it's enough to make any one ill."

Hereupon I went and stole on *patte de velours*[1] past the library, where I heard Sir Hugh's jolly voice holding forth, and my father's (hardly less jolly for the time) responding. I betook myself to my little upper chamber, looking westwards, whence I had so often watched the great sun go down, sat down on the edge of my bed, forgot my troubles, and built air-castles. Of these edifices Richard was châtelain and I châtelaine;[2] in them papa had the best suite of rooms, and from them Dolly was utterly cast out.

The hall clock struck one very gravely, as it always did. I slid from my bed to the floor, embraced my knees with my arms, and re-commenced building. The clock struck half-past. Five minutes more, and then the door opened, and Mrs. Smith entered with a plate of thick bread and butter.

"I thought you'd be famished up here all by yourself, my dear," said she; "but indeed I don't see why you should not go down: I don't, indeed."

"Quite out of the question, madam," replied I, rather indistinctly, with my mouth full of bread and butter; "by-the-bye is luncheon in?"

"I just sent it in before I came up, and a very nice luncheon too; a piece of cold roast mutton, and a beautiful dish of mashed potatoes, and plenty of eggs and bacon."

"Plenty!" ejaculated I faintly, thinking of the small and elegant dishes I had seen at the Coxian feast, "about how many?"

"Well, 'm, I thought as there was not to say much on the mutton, and as the hens is layin' pretty tidy just at present. I thought I'd better make it 'alf a dozen!"

At this juncture another knock came at the door, and Mary, the housemaid, introduced herself.

"Please, miss, master begs as you'll go down *direcly*."

---

1   Velvet paw (French); also, the cat's paw with claws retracted.
2   A castle owner (French). Châtelaine is the feminine form of the same noun, and tends to have the meaning of housekeeper, or mistress of the keys. (Housekeepers or the wife of the master, depending on the size of a household, would have possession of all the keys to the house and its valuables locked up within it—the silver, the wine-cellar, etc.).

"What!" cried I in a fury; "did not I tell Collins to say I was ill, if I was asked for?"

"Yes, miss, and so he did, but your pa said he did not believe as 'ow you was very bad, and he desired his love, and he begged you'd come down just to obleege him, if only for five minutes; I think I understood as the gentleman was asking for you."

I laid down my bread and butter, and groaned. Mrs. Smith, with great presence of mind, seized a brush, and tried to plaster down my hair at each side of my face, and Mary gave two or three severe tugs to my dress, in the well meant endeavour to lengthen it, and then I went. The gentlemen were already in the dining-room, and I felt overpowered with shyness as I opened the door and entered. As I took my seat at the head of the table, I gave one comprehensive glance at the arrangements. Our table was a very big, wide one, and the leg of mutton, which had never been a large one, was now "beautifully less."[1] It showed like a dim speck on the vast ocean of table-cloth. I could not make the same complaint of the eggs and bacon; they filled the eye, and overpowered it; they seemed to me to be like the sand that is by the sea-shore in number.

"I hope your head is better, Miss Lestrange," said Sir Hugh, politely; he had wisely eschewed the mutton, and was eating a fat rasher with apparent relish.

"My head?" said I, raising a pair of bewildered blue eyes from my plate.

"Yes, to be sure, *your head*," put in my father, a little impatiently. "Collins told us you had a headache, and Sir Hugh is kindly asking after it; can't you understand?"

"Oh yes, I remember—oh, thanks—oh yes, it is quite well; pretty well, I mean, much better, thanks!" So I, incoherent and scarlet. Sir Hugh left me in peace after that, for which I called him blessed; left me at leisure to admire the simple hearty hospitality with which papa offered our meagre viands to our guest. He made no flimsy apologies for the poverty of the entertainment; he did not try to affect that the fare was worse than it usually was; he was vexed indeed, as I, who knew every line of his countenance, discovered at once, but I would have defied any stranger to detect it.

---

1   Compare "Henry and Emma" (1708), a poem by Matthew Prior (1664-1721). The line "Small [or Fine] by degrees, and beautifully less" is frequently quoted and misquoted.

Sir Hugh was a short man, but otherwise not ill-looking. He had a jolly countenance, not encumbered with any particular expression, a jolly laugh at anybody's service; enough brains to carry him decently through his very easy part in life, and not enough to make him feel uncomfortably wise in any company. Nobody had ever heard him say a clever thing, or a spiteful one. Mothers chased him, and he eluded their pursuit with so much good humour that they liked him all the better; daughters smiled at him, and he smiled back at them, but he smiled universally, which was discouraging; nobody ever accused him of having ever had his affections blighted, and yet now his dark hair was grizzling fast, and his big red house was mistressless still.

He did not love anybody in the world much, not even himself, and he liked everybody. Misfortune left him alone, because I really believe she could not find a vulnerable spot in him. Presently he spoke to me again. I think he had been casting about in his mind for a remark to make for some minutes before the remark arrived, but was not quite sure on what subject I could talk. Was a little doubtful whether I could talk on any subject.

"So your sister's coming home, I hear?"

"Yes."

"Jolly for you having her back?"

"Ye—es."

"So dull being by one's self, isn't it?"

My courage was rising, the string of my tongue was loosed.

"No, I don't think so; I like being alone; one's thoughts are always pleasant company; pleasanter far than most of one's friends."

"Ha, ha! you mean that for a hit at me, I'm afraid; but really now I never can make out what women can have to think about, except their crochet work; what are your pleasant thoughts about, I wonder?"

I resented this catechism suited to the intellect of a five years' child.

"Nothing worth mentioning," I said, tartly; "neither fat cattle nor guano!"[1]

He looked puzzled for a minute.

"Well, I suppose not. What made you pitch upon two such

---

1 Excrement, usually of bats, used as fertilizer.

unlikely subjects? Oh I see! You think they are about the only subjects I am fit to talk about; ah, very good, very good!"

My father rose, looking rather vexed.

"Don't get into the habit of making rude speeches, Nell, I advise you; a sharp woman is the most odious animal in creation; come, Sir Hugh, shall we take a turn about the place?"

Sir Hugh looked as if he would have liked to have said something good-natured to me, but could not make up his mind what, and contented himself with smiling encouragingly, and then followed my father, leaving me to feel as small as ever snubbed young woman need do.

CHAPTER X

At eight that evening, the blue summer sky hid itself behind low hanging gray clouds; at a quarter past eight, a small fine rain was pouring steadily down, settling itself to a good night's work; at half-past eight, I twisted a great coil of my red hair round my head, and slipped two wooden bead bracelets, given me by Dolly in a paroxysm of generosity, one birthday, over my wrists; these were all the preparations for meeting my love which my resources allowed of. At five minutes past nine I ran down into the hall, took an old shawl from the cloak-stand, and was searching for an umbrella, when I heard my father's slow step crossing the library floor. Instantly I disappeared. I put the shawl over my head, and ran down the gravel walk, over the shining pebbles, to the trysting place.

There was an ornamental wooden gate in the lilac hedge; a gate separating our Eden from the profane outer world of the hay meadow. I peeped over this gate, and all about the lilac bushes; not a soul was there; my heart sank; "He cometh not," said I, quoting Mariana.[1] I gazed disconsolately through the rain for exactly three minutes, at the end of which time I spied an object looming dimly through the misty air; it might have been a horse or a cow, a house or a haystack. It was none of these; it resolved itself into a large laughing young man, in damp velveteen.[2]

---

1 See "Mariana in the Moated Grange" (1830), a poem by Tennyson.
2 Cotton fabric made to resemble velvet, worn for hunting and other outdoor activities.

"Before your time," said he, gaily, as he came up, "see what it is to have sold your watch; it's five minutes to nine still." I gave him no greeting; I only looked up at him with dumb anxiety. "What, not a word for me! I don't think I shall tell you at all, if you look so eager; it would not be good for you! Well, is the lion to come in to the lamb, or the lamb to come out to the lion?"

"Oh, the lamb—oh; I—I mean—I'll come out to you." I unlatched the gate, and passed out into the long wet meadow grass, which felt much like stepping into a tepid foot-bath. "Well," said I, breathlessly, clasping my hands as if he was my God, and I was praying to him.

"Well, Miss Lestrange, what?"

"Oh, you know what I mean, have you any news for me?"

"News! oh yes, lots; the funds have fallen to 84; and the Bishop of —— is dead; and the eldest Miss Coxe is going to be married—to me—at least, so I heard this morning."

"If you asked me out here, only to make game of me, I may as well go home," I said; my not angelic temper succumbing under this process of aggravation.

"*I* ask you to come out this damp evening, and run the risk of catching a bad cold? *I* make game of you? God forbid."

I turned away in mute indignation.

"What, you really are going? Well, I'm sorry for that. It's so jolly standing chatting here in this puddle; but it *is* rather a wet evening, isn't it? seasonable though, for the time of year."

I fumbled at the fastening of the gate, blind with rage. "Your wit, sir," said I, my voice trembling with passion, and drawing myself up with as much dignity as my limp old gown would admit of, "may be appreciated by Mr., Mrs., and *Miss* Coxe, but it won't go down at Lestrange. I wish you good evening."

"Good evening, Miss Lestrange," said he, opening the gate for me to pass through, and baring his handsome head to the rain. "By-the-bye, would you be so kind as to take charge of a small parcel which I believe belongs to you?"

He pulled a small roll of bank-notes from his pocket as he spoke, and gave them to me. I hesitated. Should I throw them back with scorn into his teasing face, or should I gratify my intense curiosity to know how many there were of them? Curiosity prevailed, as I fancy it always has done, where women have been concerned, since the day when Eve was roused to inquisitiveness concerning that fruit which must have been a great deal more inviting to eye, and smell, and touch, than any apple that ever ripened, or she would not have run such tremendous risks for the sake of it. It was no Ribstone pippin, I feel assured, that served humanity that dirty turn, rather some juicy perfumed eastern pulp.

I unrolled the notes, with fingers rendered awkward by greedy haste, separated and smoothed out each one; pleasant were their crisp watered faces unto me. Will there be £10, £20; either sum would be a nice little sop for Cerberus.[1] So I thought, and then I counted one, two, three, four, five. Five times ten are fifty. FIFTY POUNDS for that most despicable of old turnips, whose interior was, so to speak, a dead letter; one of whose hands was a mutilated stump, whose movements were so erratic that no man could calculate from hour to hour what its next freak would be, and which was unwieldy, unbeautiful, and everything that was undesirable. Now and then, in these latter days, a strong qualm of doubt shoots through me, that never did that old warming-pan see the inside of Wardour Street, that that £50 came out of the not too well lined pockets of poor open-hearted Dick M'Gregor. No such doubts had I at that time, to trouble my blissful young serenity; in those days I believed everything I heard, everything I was told, and almost everything I read. For a minute I stood, with drooped head, remorse driving small penknives through and through my heart; then I put out both hands, and said "O—h!" under my breath.

"Well, Miss Lestrange, what have I done wrong now? Anything fresh? I'm not witty now, surely, am I?"

"Oh, don't, don't," I cry, whimperingly, and I cover my face with my left hand, and grope for my pocket-handkerchief with my right, while the shawl takes the opportunity of slipping off my head, down into an improvised pool among the buttercups; and there I stand, thin-clad, bare-headed, in the steadily pouring rain.

He picks up the shawl and shakes it.

"Are you too hot, Miss Lestrange? as you appear to be casting away your garments wholesale; if I might give an opinion, I should say that this was neither the time nor the place for taking a vapour bath."

---

1 The three-headed hound that guards the underworld in Greek mythology. To "give a sop to Cerberus" was to give him something to stop his mouths long enough to pass him.

I take away my shielding hand from my face, which I lift shy and burning towards his.

"Oh, please, don't mock at me any more. I *cannot* bear it; I thought you were only turning me into ridicule, and I—I—haven't a very good temper, I'm afraid, and I—I—oh! if you only knew how I felt, I'm sure you'd leave me alone."

Whereupon I fell to weeping sore, for no particular cause. Oh, my Dick, my bonny, bonny sweetheart! how goodly you were then! are you goodlier now, I wonder, in that distant *Somewhere* where you are; or when we meet next, shall we be two bodiless spirits, sexless, passionless essences, passing each other without recognition in the fields of ether? God forbid that it should be so; oh, my King Olaf, as I called you first, in my girlish romance, and I cleave to the old name still. Oh, strong fair Norseman! did you rise from your warrior grave under the icy Northern waves, and come back among men only to shame the punyness of your descendants; and have you gone back thither again to your sleep beneath the green billows?[1] There comes no voice out of the void to answer me.

★ ★ ★ ★ ★

Tears played the good speed with Richard. In justice to myself, I must distinctly state that I was not aware of this fact, but was, on the contrary, grievously displeased with myself for having been beguiled into weeping. Had his grandmother, his maiden aunt, his laundress, or any old beggarwoman in the street cried at him, he would have been seriously disturbed at it. How much more then when a really good-looking young woman was making her nose and eyes of a flame colour in her anguish at his cruelty. The smile died out of his jocund young face as if it had been an exorcised demon; nothing could be more surprisedly, pitifully penitent, than the expression of his blue-gray eyes; he looked like a big dog that is very much ashamed of himself for having been betrayed into bullying a little one. For a minute he was quite at a loss what to do; then he bethought himself of my shawl, which he wrapped round my shoulders, saying hurriedly, meanwhile:

"There! there! don't cry, don't cry! poor little girl! it was a

---

1 Some dead Viking warriors were placed on funeral ships, which were set ablaze and then adrift.

shame to make her pretty blue eyes red, wasn't it? but I didn't mean to vex her, indeed I didn't. I'd cut off my right hand before I'd hurt a hair of her sweet head."

He had bandaged me up so tight in his eagerness that I could hardly stir; I laughed through my tears.

"You've tied me up so tight that I cannot move my arms; I'm like a mummy."

He laughed too. "So I have, poor dear Nell! what an ill-used little girl she is!"

He bent over me to re-arrange my shawl, but when he had disposed its shabby old folds to his mind, he kept his arms about me. The rain dripped from his hat, and from his curly yellow hair, and Heaven's tears washed his bronzed cheeks; I looked up at him with shy rapture; at that brow "that looked like marble, and smelt like myrrh,"[1] at the honest, kindly, beautiful face; looked into his passionate eyes, and forgot the rain, and the long tangled grass, and my own mortifying silly behaviour, forgot everything in my new-found wonderful bliss.

"Am I teasing you now? shall I leave you alone, as you asked me just now? Must I? I will if you wish me; I should dislike extremely having to do it, but I will in a minute, if you tell me."

So he whispers, while his gold locks and my russet ones blend agreeably together. I had not the slightest desire that he should leave me alone, but I said neither yea nor nay.

"Poor little pussy-cat, is she very anxious to get away? does not she like being kept a prisoner? won't she stay with me one little minute? she'd have to go far before she could find any one that would love her better!"

For all answer, I lay my head on his breast, which the inclement weather has rendered rather a moist resting-place, and my cheeks put on their rouge, which the May showers vainly endeavour to wash off. He kisses me softly, and I forget to be scandalized.

"Do you know, Nell, I do really like you rather, joking apart."

"Indeed!"

"Yes, I do; it's rather nice, don't you know? having a foolish sort of little girl to kiss and make love to, and bully now and then; I haven't near done bullying you yet, miss, if you think that."

I raise my head, and make a feint of going. "If that's the way you're going to treat me, I'd better leave you this minute."

---

1 See "The Worst of It" (1855), a poem by Robert Browning (1812-89).

"Do by all means *if you can*; by Jove! how blue your eyes are, quite China blue, like tea cups!"

"What a pretty comparison!"

"I didn't say they were pretty; they're very big and babyish, and they pretend to be very innocent looking; but *pretty*! not exactly."

"I won't stay another minute."

"You're not going for two hours yet, good; and nor then without paying toll; twenty kisses, and as many more as I'm good enough to accept."

I make no relevant answer to this shocking announcement. I only burrow my countenance into his drenched velveteen shoulder, and murmur to it "O—h."

"Are you pretty comfortable, Miss Lestrange?"

"Yes."

"Nice growing weather, as I said just now, when you were in such an awful rage with me."

"Oh don't, *don't* remind me of it!"

"Yes, indeed, Miss Nell, you may well hide your face; that temper, unless checked in time, *may* (mind I don't say that it *will*, because our laws are so lenient now-a-days), *may* bring you to the gallows."

"What! for murdering you?"

"Yes, for tearing my fine eyes out, or biting my nose off, or some such atrocity; oh, you darling; how have I managed to get on all these eight and twenty years without you?"

The warm rain pattered and plashed on our faces; the big white lilac bush bent above us its dripping leaves, and fair large flower-clusters brushed our cheeks, and gave out its strong pure scent freely to us.

"Heaven is crying pretty freely over our courtship, Nell," Dick says presently. "I hope it's not ominous."

"Hush! speak lower! I hear the gravel crunching!"

"Nonsense!"

"But I do, indeed. Sh! sh! sh!"

We listen; there is undeniably a faint noise, as of gravel ground beneath a yet distant heel.

"It's papa; he very often comes out after tea; but I thought the wet would keep him in to-night. If I run very fast I shall be out of sight before he gets round here; he has not got to the garden-house yet!"

"Da——I mean hang him; why could not he stay indoors till we came to fetch him?"

I laughed. "Good night; let me go, quick!"

"Not unless you say 'good night, darling.' I'll keep you else, till the governor comes round here, and then begin to talk very loud; by Jove, would not the old gentleman look alive? well, is it coming? 'good night, darling,' or such a blowing up from Sir Adrian."

I made the required concession with less bashfulness than might have been expected of me, and then took to my heels, and reached my room, panting, dishevelled, crimson, but in safety.

CHAPTER XI

Anathema Maranatha[1] be upon him, whether he be black or white, young or old, gentle or simple, philosopher or dunce, bond or free, who says we are not intended to be happy in this world. Can our God be of so refined a cruelty as to have created so many millions of human beings, just to worry their lives out? Can he have framed them into such an ingenious compound of matter and spirit? Can he have given them such vast capabilities of being glad and being sorry, merely that he may the better torment them? Can he have made us out of spite, as Caliban opines of his god Setebos, in Browning's fine poem?[2] If he had done so, why did he make the period of our sufferings so short? why did he not make us eternal? then indeed (were he such a monster of *barbarity*, as is presupposed by this hypothesis), might he have worthily wreaked his hatred upon us. Our religion, as Pascal[3] remarks, is the only one that inculcates on its votaries not only awe and reverence, but love towards the Deity.

Could it reasonably ask us to give our hearts to a capricious, malignant demon, who had put us together, only that he might mangle us? Moreover, would not such a demon in all probability have got tired of his cruel game, having had so many hundred

---

1　See I Corinthians 16:22. Paul announces these words as God's curse on unbelievers.

2　See "Caliban Upon Setebos; or, Natural Philosophy in the Island" (1864), a poem by Robert Browning.

3　Blaise Pascal (1623-62) was best known as a mathematician and essayist.

generations on which to practice it? Would not he probably be turning his devilish power of inflicting anguish into some new channel; testing it upon some other family of defenceless sufferers? To no demon's malice do we owe our creation; our God meant us to be boundlessly, flawlessly happy; *that* we never can be now, thanks to ourselves, but moderately, temperately, soberly happy we may still be, if we go the right way to work; happy, partly in present fruition, far more in expectancy; happiest in the very fact that at the first blush has a sorry aspect—that all our happinesses here are but transitory; mere types and shadows of worthier substances, never to be grasped till this mortal has put on immortality.

Perfectly contented we never can be here. Kick as we may against the fiat which forbids it; struggle and strain as we may to attain that unattainable good; it is an impossibility, from the very constitution of our souls, which are ever unconsciously, involuntarily, looking onwards, onwards, from year to year, from hour to hour, from minute to minute.

"I shall be satisfied, but, oh, not here!"[1]

Fully satisfied on this earth can our spirits never be; they being of so high a nature; cast in so noble a mould that nothing less than God can fill them. Somebody, I forget who, remarks, on the rarity of hearing any one exclaim, "How happy I *am*!" "How happy I *was*!" and "How happy I shall be!" are frequent ejaculations, but to hear man, born of woman, felicitate himself on his present condition, is uncommon indeed. So it must ever be till the restless hungry soul be laid asleep in light.

My happiness that night was not temperate, moderate, sober, it was limitless, frenzied, drunken. The pace was too good to last, as I might have known, had I not been nineteen, and somewhat of a greenhorn, even for that immature age. I wonder I did not catch my death of cold, I'm sure. It never occurred to me, either to go to bed or take off my wet clothes. Hour after hour, I sat with drenched garments clinging close round me, with my dank thick hair streaming loose about my throat. I might have been Ophelia, barring flowers and the insanity.[2]

---

1   Tamar Heller identifies this as a poem ascribed to O.L. Turner.
2   See Shakespeare's *Hamlet* (first printed in quarto 1603). Ophelia goes mad and drowns herself, holding a bouquet of flowers.

There I sat by the open casement window, with a box of mignonette under my nose; with my candle first flickering in its socket, and then departing this life with a grievous stink, and with the summer dawn broadening across the pearl-gray sky. I had fallen neck and crop into love; it had not taken a minute doing, but for all that, it was as thoroughly done as if I had been walking in deliberately and gingerly for the last dozen years. Quite unexpectedly, when I was neither looking for nor thinking of any such thing, I had found a most precious stone, a pearl of great price,[1] and I must needs look at it on all sides, weigh it, and consider gravely to what best profit I could put it. One thing was certain, to no one's lot could it ever have fallen to have discovered so big a pearl; others might have hit upon smaller ones of the same genus, but in size and colour mine must be, have been, and ever will be unique.

The rain had ceased, and one star stole from behind the soft dense cloud-curtain, and trembled and shook in the distant ether. I fixed my excited sleepless eyes upon it. Had that far world any inhabitants? any beings like ourselves? men and women? were there any red-haired girls and handsome fair men there? If so, could there be any one living there now experiencing felicity equal to mine? most unlikely. Had any one in *this* world ever been possessed of such perfect bliss? Was papa as happy when he brought mamma back first to the dear old house, in the days when they planted that Westeria that covered half the south wall now? Mamma in a sad coloured gown, with a waist under her arms, leg of mutton sleeves, and bob curls,[2] which was the aspect under which my deceased parent always presented herself to my mind's eye, being the form under which she was represented in a miniature that had hung, ever since I could recollect anything, over against papa's chair in the library? I decided not.

Was Dolly anything like as happy, when she was engaged to that pink-eyed young man of immense property, who died of consumption a week before his intended wedding day? I taxed my memory to recollect any ejaculations expressive of ecstasy given utterance to by my sister, when in the rapturous position

---

1 Compare Matthew 13: 45-6. Jesus uses several parables to describe faith. In this one, salvation is likened to a valuable jewel: a merchant finds a pearl of great price, and so sells everything to obtain it.
2 Fashions of the late 1820s and early 1830s.

of betrothed to that poor, three-quarter-witted young Crœsus.[1] The nearest approach to anything tender that I could recall as having proceeded from her, was "that he was not quite such a fool as he looked."

When he died, I remembered that she cried a little, and went into mourning, and said that she wished she had been his widow, poor dear fellow, for that widows' caps were so becoming, and she should have liked to have paid that tribute of respect to his dear memory.

"What should I do if Dick were to die?" said I aloud, leaning my elbow on the sill, and addressing my question indifferently to the star and the mignonette box. Fall down dead on the spot probably, fall on his dead body, and die kissing him.

"As Hero gave her trembling sighs to find
Delicious death on wet Leander's lip."[2]

To me it seemed, then, that to stand by and see Dick die, I living meanwhile, and surviving him, would be a physical impossibility. But if, by some miracle, I were to be unable thus to rid myself of life; if it were still to keep its undesired hated hold upon me, why—I'd take poison. Nothing could be simpler; arsenic, for instance, such as we set for the rats, and which made them swell to such a size, run so greedily to the spring to drink, and die there. "Should I swell so, and be so thirsty before I died?" I wondered. I hoped not. It was not a romantic thought, but it thrust itself in among its more sentimental brethren.

The pearl-gray sky turned red, then lilac, then rose, then azure. The sun came forth in his might, and the birds began talking volubly all at once, singing hymns and pæans, and blythe good-morrows one after another. I rose from my seat, and began pacing up and down the room, with my hands locked together.

Why was I so happy? What had I done to deserve it? Why was God so good to me? Did He like me better than other people? Could it be that He chose favourites capriciously among his creatures? Had He so chosen me? or had He only given me this great boon to punish me more heavily by taking it away again? I fell on

---

1   Greek king of Lydia, from 560 to 546 BCE, whose wealth was legendary.
2   See "A Life-Drama" in *Poems* (1853), by Alexander Smith (1830-67).

my knees, and begged and entreated God to visit me in any other way He should see fit; to send any loathsome agonizing sickness upon me; any form of suddenest, awfullest, cruellest death, but not to rob me of my yellow-haired lover. In what way this hallowed, chastened, pious prayer was granted, you oh my unknown friends shall see hereafter.

As I rose from my impromptu devotions, I inadvertently put my hand into my pocket and drew out the bank-notes, which I had till that minute forgotten. I kissed each one separately, since Richard *might* have touched it, locked them all up in a drawer with my Sunday bonnet and my best Bible, and then at length, when other decent folks were getting up, I took off my clothes, laid down and slept profoundly, till roused by the entrance of Mary, the apple-cheeked, with my hot water.

That day was marked by two incidents, both black in hue; that day papa went away for a week's visit to an old chum, and that day Dolly returned. I think the two occurrences stood somewhat in relation of cause and effect to each other. I think that my father, with a cowardice unworthy of his age and station, fled at the approach of his lovely Dorothea. Dear old gentleman, I forgave him his desertion, because I sympathized so with the occasion of it. I poured out his tea for him, packed up his clothes, and put sprigs of lavender among them to remind him sweetly of his old home and his little daughter, gave him my blessing, and sent him off.

"Good-bye, dad," said I, hanging about his neck. "Don't catch cold, and don't leave any of your pocket-handkerchiefs behind you, and don't leave me very long to Dolly's tender mercies, and come back soon."

Dolly arrived shortly afterwards. From the upper regions I heard her advent—heard the wheels of her chariot, "low on the sand and loud on the stone,"[1] rolling to the door. I went down with laggard steps to receive her. The noon sun was beating on the hall door, making the iron knobs red hot; beating, too, on the aged and dilapidated Collins, who stood on the flagstone, with his ugly old head wagging like a mandarin's, partly from ague, partly in greeting to the returned Dorothea. The cab stood piled with luggage in the blinding glare, and the poor cab horse, with its lean head drooping, feebly tried to swish away the flies from

---

1 See "Maud" (1855), a poem by Tennyson.

its thin flanks with its tail. I stood in speechless, loveless admiration, as Dolly daintily descended, fresh and trim, as if she had been travelling in cotton wool and silver paper, in a bandbox, instead of in dusty railway and mouldy chaise.

"Well, Nell," said she, presenting her cool peach cheek to me, "how are you? Much the same as usual, I see—hair arranged with a pitchfork and dress with a view to ventilation."

I said nothing smart in reply to this fond greeting, because, as Johnson candidly avowed to the obsequious Bozzy, "I had nothing ready, sir."[1] I followed Dolly meekly into the house, taking great care not to tread on her train. She had addressed to me but half a dozen words. I had not been above five seconds in her company, and yet she had compelled me to descend to the old standing ground miles below her. In her absence, I felt myself to be a lovable, admirable, rational woman; once again in her presence, I returned to my old station of *gauche*,[2] charmless, witless school-girl.

CHAPTER XII

Luncheon over, we betook ourselves (the weather being too hot to go out) to the hall, and there prepared for an afternoon of coma. The blinds were pulled down

"On purpose to keep out the light,"[3]

but stealthy arrows crept through, and lay along the faded blue and red patches of the Turkey carpet, and the dim worsted work of the straight-backed chairs. It was profoundly still; one could *hear* the silence, which was only broken by the buzzing of the flies on the window-pane. Dolly had thrown herself—nay, not *thrown*, for that suggests an idea of violence never conveyed by Dolly's roughest movement—had sunk into a rocking-chair, and sat swaying gently to and fro.

---

1 Samuel Johnson (1709-84), writer and wit, was often accompanied by his biographer, James Boswell (1740-95), who took down memorable sayings in Johnson's conversation.
2 Awkward (French).
3 Unknown source.

Miss Lestrange never read, and seldom spoke in the family circle; I think she thought it a waste of time. She knitted now, mute as Anderson's poor pretty mermaid,[1] and meditated on heavenly themes, to judge by her countenance. I sat on a bench by the long table in the window; a tall bench, whence my legs dangled like gallows' birds, while my elbows rested on a big book, of which I read a page and a half. The book was Burton's "Anatomy of Melancholy,"[2] and it did not interest me in the least. I had selected it as being one of the biggest and most ponderous volumes in the library, as having likewise a ponderous title, promising to be good for edification. I, arguing, with faulty logic, that from so weighty a tome I must needs extract much weighty matter.

Truth to tell, I was deeply dissatisfied with myself, and with the weedy unstocked condition of my mind's fair garden. Dolly did well to despise me; I was but a poor creature, and despicable; foolishest, childishest, among women. I knew absolutely nothing; I had not the least idea what the Bill of Rights was about, nor who fought the battle of Fontenoy,[3] or any other battle either. Dick would despise me too when he came to know me better; would get tired of me, and find me insipid. Whether a more accurate knowledge of dates would make me a more original companion, I did not stop to inquire. To remedy my deficiencies I turned to Burton, and asked him to tell me something about something; tell me a few facts, was my cry, like the little turnip in Kingsley's "Water Babies."[4]

"Knowledge is Power," is a true aphorism, I suppose; but, after all, what is all human knowledge? The sum of our knowing is to leave a deeper, hopelesser conviction of our utter unknowingness.

---

1 In Hans Christian Andersen's "The Little Mermaid" (1837), the mermaid trades her voice for a human form, out of love for a human man. He marries another.
2 This book by Robert Burton was published in 1632. It is a detailed multi-volume treatment of the disorder of melancholy, which at that time encompassed many physical as well as psychological disorders.
3 This battle was fought in the Austrian Netherlands in 1745, over the Austrian succession. Scottish forces were involved.
4 *The Water Babies* (1863) is a children's book by Charles Kingsley (1819-75) in which he satirizes contemporary theories of education. The turnip is trying to learn "general knowledge," which consists of memorizing disconnected facts, but forgets them as soon as it hears them.

What a *chétif*[1] scrap of a science is mastered by the greatest proficient in, the foremost pioneer of that science? How the ripened spirits of the departed wise, bathing in wisdom's clear fount above, must smile, looking down on the smatterings of learning, on the strength of which we dub ourselves philosophers and pundits. Solomon, saith the Book of Kings, knew three thousand proverbs, and his songs were a thousand and five.[2] Doubtless; and yet assuredly there must have been ten times three thousand proverbs that he knew not—a hundred thousand songs never sung by him.

In the morning of this our little life, we set forth on some one of the many paths that lead to knowledge's citadel. The way is steep, but we are resolute; it is hedged with briars, and encumbered with great stones; the briars scratch us, and we break our shins over the stones, but we struggle on with a good courage. Our road is becoming smooth; we shall reach the prize in time. Then Death lays his numb hands on our hearts, and we are still, and the path is closed to us for ever. Is it for ever, though? Are not the pitiful incompleteness of our labours here, the fragmentary character of our best efforts, strongest, convincingest proofs of our soul's undyingness? Shall we not trace out in a nobler sphere that same path we loved on earth? the *same*, only with the briars cut down and the stones cleared away? Will not our poor crooked lives be rounded into Wisdom's perfect circle? Our Elysium is no occupationless, pleasureless *Ner wana* of swinish, plethoric repose;[3] in our asphodel meadows we shall each of us have some mighty problem to work out, some godlike scheme to effect; and our brains will not tire, our eyes will not ache, and our hands not fail in the doing.

To what a distance have I strayed from myself and my self-disgust? I have been up to heaven and down again. Burton's very detailed and minute analysis of the corporeal humours, which

---

1 Sickly or weak (French).
2 See I Kings 4:32. The passage catalogs Solomon's wealth, both material and of learning: "And he spake three thousand proverbs: and his songs were a thousand and five."
3 In Greek mythology, Elysium is the abode of the blessed after death; *Ner wana*, or Nirvana, is the afterlife of those liberated from the cycle of rebirth in Hinduism or Buddhism, often interpreted as including the non-existence of an individual self in a peaceful union with the divine.

are melancholy's parents and grandparents, failed to enchain my attention. An idea struck me.

"Dolly," said I, and my sudden word cut the silence sharply.

"Well?"

"Do you know much, Dolly?"

"What do you mean?" measuredly came the words from her lips.

"I mean, do you know much about any sensible sort of things? Are you very well up in history and biography, and those sort of things?"

"Had not you better add 'Shakespeare and the musical glasses?'[1] I suppose I am about as well informed as most other people."

Click, click, go her needles.

"Do you know enough to be able to teach me I wonder?"

"Probably; my acquirements would be small else."

I pass by the sneer on the other side; it was but my ignorance's due.

"I wish you would give me lessons in something, Dolly; we used to learn German together once. Do you remember? Why cannot we begin again?"

"Thank you very much, but I'd infinitely rather be excused."

The long gray stocking grows under the swift white fingers; she ruffles her smooth brow in the agony of counting stitches.

"I'd do my best to get on; I'd do whatever you told me; I do feel my ignorance so oppressive, Dolly—quite a heavy burden."

"I'm extremely sorry to hear it, and I'm sure you'd make a delightful pupil, but I think, on the whole, I should prefer not. I don't want to qualify myself for a governess just yet, though I daresay that's what I shall have to come to."

I was baffled, and returned discouraged to my atrabilarious studies. Audible silence again for an hour or more; then the lower iron gate is heard creaking on its hinges, the gravel grating under approaching feet, and voices talking. Dolly is not above

---

1 Playing with glasses partially filled with water in order to make music was a popular pastime and way of teaching about music to children. By the mid-nineteenth century, musicians also played them professionally. "Shakespeare and the musical glasses" is a phrase used to mean trivial but elegant conversation among well-read, fashionable people.

mundane curiosity; she rises and peeps softly round the curtain. "Mrs. Coxe," says she,

"But no livelier than the dame
That whispered 'Asses' Ears' among the sedge,"[1]

"and a *man*" (with slight animation), "good-looking too" (with interest), "*very*" (with symptoms of excitement), "who is he? do you happen to know, Nell?"

"N-o-o-o," I stutter, "I don't think so."

"You *do* know," says she, paling a little with anger, "and why you should think it worth while to lie about such a trifle I cannot conceive; if his name is ever such a mystery I don't doubt I shall fathom it without your help."

No more in that strain; the key changes to a "pathetic minor," for Collins entering announces "Mrs. Coxe and Major M'Gregor." Dolly's tongue was an instrument of great compass; it could play any tune, from the Hundredth Psalm to "Wapping Old Stairs,"[2] and discourse excellent music. I did not, assuredly, expect my lover to kiss me, or take me in his arms then and there, but I felt a thrill of cold disappointment when I found him shaking hands with me in the same commonplace manner that Sir Hugh Lancaster or Mr. Bowles the curate might have done. He was presented by Mrs. Coxe to Dolly, who smiled pensively, and cast down her eyes.

I made no attempt to entertain our guests, but clave[3] to my tall bench and my folio. I remember I read one inverted sentence over six times running, without a glimmering of its meaning penetrating to my brain. Dick came over presently, and looked over my shoulder.

"What light literature have you got there?"

I turn to the title-page and point gravely, Burton's "Anatomy of Melancholy."

"H'm! cheerful kind of title! and is that Mr. Burton himself? Rum old party, isn't he?"

The curled Greek head stoops lower; the amber moustache touches my ear.

---

1 See "The Princess" (1847), a poem by Tennyson.
2 Popular Victorian song circa 1860, author anonymous.
3 Past tense of cleave.

"Did you get home all right last night, Nell?"

"Yes."

"Did not catch a cold?"

"No."

"Nor get a blowing up?"

"No."

"That's all right; where's your father to-day?"

"Gone into Berkshire for a week."

"H'm! when the cat's away you know; and so that's Miss Dolly, is it?"

"Yes, isn't she lovely?"

Thus I ask, unknowing that never will man, come to years of discretion, be betrayed into the smallest commendation of one woman's beauty to another.

"Oh, I don't know; I haven't thought about it; I suppose I have been thinking too much of how lovely somebody else is."

"Who?" ask I, looking up with innocent inquiry; but somehow I read in the deep loving eyes who it is, and I begin to fiddle nervously with good Master Burton's yellowing leaves. Dolly's voice breaks upon my trance; it comes cooing softly across the hall.

"Nelly, dear, will you kindly run and get my portfolio of Bournemouth[1] sketches; Mrs. Coxe is good enough to say she should like to see them; do go, there's a dear child! they are in the left top corner of my chiffonier; you cannot miss finding them."

I rise and go reluctant; I misdoubt me concerning Dolly and her sketches. They are not in the left top corner of the chiffonier, nor indeed in the chiffonier at all, and it takes me ten minutes' diligent search to find them. When I return the position of affairs is changed, which does not tend to the ameliorating of my temper. Dick is balancing himself on a three-legged stool within six inches of Dolly's knee, and she (her knitting dropped, her soul in her eyes) is gazing at him with mournful absorption, while he narrates some trivial incident of everyday life.

I move a small table in front of Mrs. Coxe, place the portfolio upon it, and retire to my distant corner, fully expecting my handsome Gilderoy[2] to come and share my solitude. Whether

---

1   Coastal resort town.

2   The handsome hero of a popular and very old ballad. Gilderoy is executed for a crime he did not commit. One popular version uses verses by Thomas Campbell that were adapted to music in 1856.

he would have done so or not is a question now to be classed with such as "What would have been the course of English history had Queen Elizabeth married Philip of Spain? or had Richard Cromwell been the man his father was? or what would have been the fate of Norwich, if the man in the moon[1] had not come down too soon?" Whatever Dick's intentions were, Dolly was too prompt for him.

"Oh, Mrs. Coxe," cried she, sinking on her knees, in the prettiest attitude of despair, beside that lady, who, being short-sighted, was holding one of my sister's artistic efforts within a quarter of an inch of her snub nose, *feeling* its beauties with that sensitive feature, "Oh, Mrs. Coxe, I could not possibly think of letting you examine my poor little daubs so critically; you'd find as many faults in them as there are stars in heaven. They ought to be looked at at the distance of half a mile at least. Major M'Gregor" (diffidently, with a slight tremor in her voice), "would it trouble you very much, or *could* you, *would* you be so very kind as to hold up this *one*, only *just* this *one*, at the proper distance, for Mrs. Coxe to see? There, oh thanks so much. Nothing could be better! Oh, *how* good you are!"

Poor Mrs. Coxe screws up her eyes, and peers, and succeeds in discerning a confused blotch of blue and green and yellow.

"H'm! h'm! yes! yes!" says she, knowing that say something she must. "What a fine bit of colouring! and how well you have managed that patch of light on the hill-side!"

"It isn't a patch of light, Mrs. Coxe—it's a white cow," says Dolly, sweetly, correcting her.

Mrs. Coxe has her back to me, but by the wobbling motion of her big blue feather, I see that she is discomfited. I grin a ghastly grin.

"It's a shame to detain you so long, Major M'Gregor, isn't it?" asks Dolly, speaking with some little effort, in her coyness, at having to address a stranger again. "Nelly is show-woman generally, and a very good one she is too, but somehow she seems a little knocked up with the heat or something to-day."

"I'm not the least knocked up,"[2] growl I, "brief and stern," as the skipper in the song.

"Aren't you, dear? I'm glad of that; I thought you were. You

1 A Mother Goose rhyme.
2 Exhausted (slang).

see, Major M'Gregor, you're the only gentleman to-day, and we think we have a right to make a sort of slave of you—don't we, Mrs. Coxe?" The soft fawn eyes seek his with timid deprecation, and then droop suddenly, and the velvet cheeks deepen in colour to the hue of a dogrose's heart. Dick, of course, protests that if there is one employment he loves above another it is holding up water-colour sketches at arm's length for his hostess's inspection. If it is an irksome task to him he disguises his tedium under it uncommonly well. I meanwhile bite my nails, my lips, the top of a pencil, and anything else I can lay my teeth on. There are about a hundred sketches, and on each one Mrs. Coxe has to make comments; some few as fortunate as the one I have recorded; some more, some less so. At length they come to an end, and our guests rise to depart. I take a sudden resolution; nobody shall hinder me; the bit is between my teeth. I would open the hall-door myself for our visitors.

"Nelly, dear," coos my sister-cushat,[1] "will you ring the bell for Collins to open the door?"

"No," said I, doughtily, "*I will not*; I'll open it myself."

Dick was looking at her, and she could not scowl prohibition at me; but I think she made a little memorandum of it. However, I gained my point; ran and opened the heavy door while Dolly remained in the inner room. Mrs. Coxe passed out first, and having so passed was good-natured, and "never looked behind."

Dick loitered, and (Mrs. Coxe's extensive back being turned) took my face between his two broad hands.

"Bad luck, Nell! bad luck!" he said, a little disappointedly; "not five words with you to-day!"

"No," said I, and my countenance was troubled, "nor you won't either, now Dolly has come home!"

"Dolly be blowed!" said he, irreverently. "We must pack her off pretty quick if she spoils our sport, mus'n't we? but she won't, I'm sure; she looks good-natured; she'll help us."

I shook my head.

"Give me one kiss, pretty one, to take away with me; nobody's looking!"

Our lips met—met joyfully, clingingly; parted grudgingly, loathly.

"*One* more, Nell!"

"No, no, no! Mrs. Coxe will turn round."

---

1 A cushat is a ring-dove.

"Mrs. Coxe will do nothing of the kind; Mrs. Coxe is a sensible woman, and minds her own business."

"Indeed, *indeed*, you ought to go and open the gate for her," I said, wrenching my countenance out of his hands.

"In a minute! in a minute! no hurry. Nell, you're looking rather pretty to-day, only your cheeks want pinching or doing something to, to put a little colour into them."

"They never have any colour; it would not look natural."

"Well, then, I suppose I must put up with them, ugly as they are! Nell, where will you come and meet me to-night?"

My eyes clave to his face, and feasted on its beauty. I would have gone to meet him in a dungeon, in a charnel,[1] in death's stronghold itself. The door to the hall opened softly, and he dropped my hand like a hot potato. Enter Dolly, not a whit discomposed by her position of Mar Plot.[2]

"I thought," she said, suavely, "that this might be your stick, and that you had forgotten it!"

So speaking, she held up a walking-stick for his inspection. It had been in papa's possession a full twenty years, and she knew it.

"Oh, thanks, thanks; no, it isn't mine; I've got mine here. Well, I won't keep you out in the sun any longer—good morning!"

Thus he departed. My wrath surged and boiled like broth in a pot.

"You knew that stick wasn't his, Dolly?" quoth I, irefully.

She shrugged her shoulders.

"Hein![3] if I did, what then? One little ruse is as good as another, isn't it? Your little ruse was the hall-door, mine was the walking-stick, that's all; quits, don't you see?"

I did not see, nor did I vouchsafe another word to Dorothea that evening.

CHAPTER XIII

"For lo! the winter is past; the rain is over and gone; the flowers appear on the earth; the time of the singing birds is come; and the voice of the turtle is heard in our land."[4]

---

1 Slaughterhouse.
2 A busybody, someone who spoils plans ("mars plots").
3 Equivalent to "Hmmm?" (French).
4 Compare Song of Solomon 2:11-12.

It is not the fashion to quote canticles I am aware, but I cannot help that; it seems to me the exquisitest, joyfullest love song ever penned. It translates the spirit and essence of the spring into words. Spring out of doors, and spring in my heart, the turtle's voice was heard there too.

> "This world is very lovely, oh, my God,
> I thank Thee that I live,"[1]

say I, spontatively, descending suddenly from the "Song of Solomon" to that of Mr. Alexander Smith. I could spout tomes of verse to-day; I cannot amble peaceably along the high road of prose; it is too level, too dusty, I must go cantering up the green slopes of poetry. I am craning my long young neck out of the morning-room window, which is barred, and there is only just room for my head to get egress between the bars; but the May air imperatively demands to be sniffed—so with my nose aloft, I am sniffing "bouquet de printemps,"[2] an odour which if it could but be corked up in bottles and sold, would make the fortune of any rival of Piesse and Lubin[3] instantaneously. "I thank thee that I live," repeat I piously, in recitative, while my round white chin rests on the knuckles of my two hands.

"Thank Him that you live!" says Dolly, from the table where she is turning over the pages of *Le Follet*,[4] "do you? well then I must say that you are thankful for small favours. Life in an old barrack, with no present income, and no future prospects hardly seems to me a theme for Hallelujahs; for weeping and gnashing of teeth rather."

"I would not gnash my teeth if I were you, Dolly!" say I, with sarcasm, which is a weapon I but seldom use, as it mostly cuts my own fingers when I lay hold of it, "or you may break them, and that would seriously diminish your value in the market."

"Market, indeed!" echoes Dolly, interrupting herself in the

---

1 See "A Life-Drama" in *Poems* (1853), by Alexander Smith (1830-67). The "turtle" is the turtledove.
2 The fragrance of spring (French).
3 A firm which manufactured scent, located in London.
4 A publication which contained fashion plates, showing the latest modes of dress.

perusal of a *toilette de promenade*.[1] "This little pig does not go to market, and very sorry she is for it too; she might have all her teeth drawn and knocked out, or gnashed out, and nobody would be the wiser. Alas! alas! there are no pig dealers in this Sahara."[2]

"Why on earth do you come back to this Sahara, that you are always sneering at? who asks you? who wants you?" inquire I in a rage, withdrawing my head from between the bars, and grazing my ears.

"One must come home now and then," replies Dolly, quietly;— *she* never gets into a rage; she thinks it *rôturier*,[3] "or else people would say that one had been turned out of doors for misconduct, or that one's papa was in gaol, or that one emanated from the Foundling,[4] or something equally distressing."

"Thro' plea—sures and pal—a—ces tho—o—o I roam,
Be it ev—er so hum—ble, there's no—o place like home,"[5]

warble I, lifting up my voice, being utterly unable to abstain from metre to-day.

"As for palaces," says Dolly, closing *Le Follet*, "they have not been much in my line; except the Bishop's, indeed, when we go to propagate the gospel, or the negroes, or something there; and as for pleasures, one has to forage for one's own little bit of amusement certainly; but I quite agree with you as to there being no place *like* home, not the least like; for utter destitution of paint, and decent cookery, and hot water pipes, and all the appliances of modern civilization, this baronial residence is undoubtedly unique."

Blasphemy, flat blasphemy, wasn't it?

"*You*," say I, drawing myself up to my five foot six inches, and sputtering in my desire to get out my words fast enough, "*you* put paint, and *good eating*, (very scornfully), and hot water pipes

---

1 Walking dress (French).
2 The African desert was used as an archetype of barrenness.
3 Common, vulgar (French).
4 Thomas Coram established the Foundling Hospital in London in 1739 for orphaned and illegitimate children.
5 See "Home Sweet Home" in *Clari* (1823), a play by John Howard Payne. The quotation is actually "Mid pleasures and palaces ..."

above honour and glory, and Cressy and Agincourt[1] and ——,
(my historical knowledge exhausts itself here), and all that sort
of thing; *I* don't!"

Dolly says, "Agincourt a fiddle!"[2] a sentence, the construing
of which will tax the acumen of the New Zealand commentator a
couple of thousand years hence;[3] to which remote period this immortal work will undoubtedly descend. "Agincourt a fiddle! Does
the knowledge that one lot of mouldy old men poked at another
mouldy old lot in the ribs with pikes four hundred years ago make
me feel the draughts less, or you look less like a scare-crow?"

"By the tombs of my ancestors!" always seemed to me the
weakest oath ever invented; "by the tail of my dog," or "by the
whiskers of my cat," would be to me every bit as impressive and
binding. "*You* are not everybody," reply I, shortly, which though
not much to the point, was undeniably true.

"I wonder now," pursues Dolly, speculatively, stretching out
her arms lazily, and yawning—"dear! how sleepy this weather
makes one—I wonder now whether that mighty man of valour,
what's-his-name, that was here yesterday, I wonder whether he
has any forbears."

"Oh yes, lots," say I, hastily, whisking my face round for my
sister's scrutiny, and then I reflect that I have spoken without
authority, and that M'Gregor may be as innocent of a grandpapa
as his friend Coxe, for all I know to the contrary.

"How do you know that?" asks Dolly, sceptically, "does he
carry them about stuffed with him?"

I laugh explosively, "Not that I know of; no more do we, and
yet we have them all the same, but—but M'Gregor is a good
name you know, quite—quite historical."

"If you come to that, so is *Coxe*; there were Cocks that strutted out
of the Ark, and pecked and crowed on the top of Mount Ararat."[4]

---

1 Famous battles in 1346 and 1415, respectively.
2 "A fiddlestick!" was a derisive term for something trivial—here,
   Dolly is contemptuously dismissing Nell's attempt to invoke the
   glories of her family's past.
3 Nell imagines a traveler from New Zealand coming upon the
   manuscript in the distant future. Tamar Heller identifies the source
   here as Thomas Babington Macaulay's "Ranke's History of the
   Popes" (1840), in which he imagines a future traveler from New
   Zealand touring the ruins of London.
4 Compare Genesis 6–8. After the Flood, the waters recede and
   Noah's Ark comes to rest on Mt. Ararat.

I lean my cheek, which is growing as red as the wattles of any cock that ever was hatched against the cold iron window bars to cool it, and say with diffidence, "But—but—Sir Walter Scott?"[1]

"Oh, ho," says Dolly, drawing a deep inspiration, and shaping her pretty red mouth into the form for a whistle, from which unfeminine phonetic exercise she however refrained. "Oh, ho! he's a Rob Roy[2] is he? a mighty freebooter? We must be looking after the cows and pigs, or he'll be making a raid upon them to prove his descent!"

"I don't *know* of course," say I modestly, "any more than you; I only thought"—grasping the friendly bar spasmodically, "such an uncommon name, so pretty——" mumbling off into unintelligibility.

"He cannot be anybody *much*," pursues Dolly disparagingly, taking up a pencil and beginning to scribble faces on a bit of paper, "or he would not be staying with the Coxes; the Coxes are working up, undeniably; as undeniably as we are working down, but they have not got up many rungs yet. I suppose they think that they will begin with decayed gentlemen, and hoist themselves up on their shoulders into the society of prosperous ones; rather sharp of them."

"Lord Frampton dines with the Coxes, and so does Sir Hugh Lancaster," cry I eagerly; earnestly desiring that I had Richard's letters patent of nobility in my pocket to pull out, and fling in triumph on the table, under Dolly's unbelieving nose.

"Pooh!" says Dolly, demolishing my poor little plea, with one inflection of her voice, "Sir Hugh is a hail fellow well met with every pettifogging little attorney in Nantford, and Lord Frampton remembers that Parliaments are septennial, and would dine with old Nick, if he would give his second son a plumper;[3] and besides *dining* is a different thing; that god-like animal, man, is always governed by his stomach, don't you know that? And worthy *Calico's*[4] Burgundy and made dishes are worth undergoing a

---

1   Prolific and respected historical novelist and poet, Sir Walter Scott (1771-1832) specialized in novels of Scottish history.
2   Rob Roy is the hero of the novel of the same name, a highland clan leader forced to become an outlaw.
3   That is, support his son in the Parliamentary elections, which take place every seven years.
4   Inexpensive cotton fabric. The reference here is to the Coxes's Manchester roots, as fortunes were made in Manchester from cotton mills.

little *infra dig-ness*[1] for; but this man is evidently on quite an *ami de la maison*[2] footing."

There is a minute or two of silence, during which Dolly goes on making spirited little fancy sketches, with a black nibbed pencil; she is so handy with her fingers—and I sit biting my nails like giant Pope,[3] and cudgelling my small brains for some remark of Dick's tending to prove that he was not on terms of intimacy with the Coxes; that it was either business, or good nature, or convenience that had brought, and now kept him there; with all my cudgelling this was all I could cudgel out,

"He thinks them vulgar himself, Dolly, I'm sure; he said one day that Mrs. Coxe was too fond of the peerage."

"Did he?" replies Dolly, "how ill-bred of him. A man must be rather low before he will go and stay weeks in a tradesman's family, and be a tame cat about his house; but he must be lower still to abuse his hosts behind their backs to a perfect stranger; that does not sound like *sang pur*."[4]

"The King can do no wrong," the old Divine Right Tories[5] used to say. "Major M'Gregor can do no right," appears to be my sister's version.

"It was not abusing her," cry I hotly, "to say that she was fond of the peerage, any more than it would be abusing you to say you were fond of dress or society, or your own way, as you are; it was only stating a fact."

"I thought," says Miss Lestrange, very calmly, "that you adduced that speech to prove that he was no great friend of the Coxes; if it was not intended for abuse it proves nothing."

The honeysuckles are thrusting themselves in so forwardly

---

1 Beneath one's dignity (Latin).
2 Friend of the house (French). This means that he is sufficiently intimate with the family to come and go without an invitation.
3 Compare *Pilgrim's Progress* (1678), an allegory by John Bunyan (1628-88). This giant, representing the Catholic church, had killed and eaten people in earlier days, but at the time of the narrative, he is senile and feeble and can only sit in the mouth of his cave and grin and bite his nails at the pilgrims who pass by.
4 Pure blood (French).
5 The Tories were a political party, ancestors to today's Conservative party. The Divine Right Tories supported the Divine Right of Kings against the transfer of power to parliamentary authority. The phrase was current in the eighteenth century.

at the casement, sending their delicatest, divinest odour up my nostrils, which are inflated like Vivien's when Merlin called her ugly names, with "sharp breaths of anger."[1] They are sad radicals those honeysuckles; they would do just as much for an old fish-wife, they are saying all they can in their refined smell language to soothe me, and reconcile me to the humble *locus standi*[2] of my lover. They are humble themselves; they twist their pale coronets to crown every hedge; they are flecked with the common summer dust, and plucked by little ragged children to stick in earthenware mugs in the dim cottage windows.

"Rob Roy is a new acquisition. He did not grace these wilds when last I was at home; he was still sporting among his native thistles, I suppose. Have you known him long?"

"Ye—es; at least—I suppose—not very long."

"How long?"

(How long, indeed! according to the almanac of the soul, a life-time, longer than old Parr's,[3] an Æon; according to the prosaic humdrum almanack of the pocket-books, about a week or ten days.)

"I think—about a fortnight," I answer, slowly. My head is turned away, but I feel with some sixth sense that Dolly has sus-pended her art labours and is looking at me, but I flatter myself that with all her knowledge of physiognomy, she will be puzzled to extract much emotion from a washed-out brown holland back, and a huge loose knot of bronze hair.

"And where," continues Dolly, with a malicious little laugh, "may I ask, was the favoured spot where so much valour and so much beauty first met?

"'We first met at a ball, where our hands did entwine,
And I did squeeze his hand and he did mine.'[4]

"Was that it?" Dignified silence on my part. "I wish, my good child, that you would be so kind as to turn your countenance round this way, and not act as if you had a face each side of your head, like Janus."[5]

---

1 See "Merlin and Vivien" (1857) in *Idylls of the King*, by Tennyson.
2 Status, standing (Latin; literally "place to stand").
3 Thomas Parr, an Englishman born in 1483, claimed to have lived for over 150 years.
4 Unknown source.
5 Roman god of gates and doors, depicted with two faces. Often figured as presiding over the past and future.

I have been so much accustomed from my youth up, to put in practice the injunctions of that ingenious quatrain,

"Go where you're told,
Do what you're bid,
Shut the door after you,
Never be chid";[1]

(only that the last line is not true in my case, as I frequently am chid), that I comply.

"Where was it?"

"In the churchyard," in a very low, reluctant voice; it seems profaning the sanctity of that first blest interview to let in the garish day of Dolly's sneers upon it.

"What a cheerful rendezvous. Has old Iken's mantle, or rather spade, fallen upon Mr. M'Gregor; was the canny Scot turning an honest penny digging graves?"

"I wish he had been digging yours, and you were in it now," say I, but to myself. Moses was the meekest man upon earth, but it is my firm belief that he would have turned and rent either Aaron or Miriam,[2] if they had attempted to badger him in the way my sister was badgering me.

"Was it on a Sunday?"

"No."

"What took you to the churchyard, then?"

"My legs."

"Ah! how humorous; and if it is not an impertinent question, who introduced Sandy—is his name Sandy—to his Nell?"

"Nobody."

"Ah, to be sure! No doubt a friend of the Coxes would dispense with such preliminaries. I suppose in calico circles such checks upon the graceful freedom of social intercourse are voted superfluous."

My angry passions are rising like well-leavened bread; like a river after autumn rains; like quicksilver in fine weather.

"I suppose," says Dolly, leaning back her little snooded head[3]

---

1 Mother Goose nursery rhyme.
2 See the story of Aaron and Miriam, siblings to Moses, in Exodus.
3 A snood is a net, usually knitted, that holds hair in place in a bun at the back of the head or low on the neck.

among the sofa cushions, and surveying me from under the blue-veined marvel of her white lids—"I suppose that like Artemus Ward and his Free Lover, you mutually ejaculated, 'You air my affinity,' and rushed into each other's arms."[1]

The cup is full and brims over; the kettle has overboiled; the river has risen level with its banks, and is pouring madly over them.

"No!" say I, jumping off the window seat and stamping, "we did not; and if we had, we should not have asked your leave. You may rush into the arms of any man or devil in England, and the sooner the better! God knows I would not stop you. I'd push you on, though I should pity Satan himself if he got you, so stop your sneers at people whose shoe-strings you are not worthy to tie!"

I had vague Scriptural ideas running in my head, you know, or I should have remembered that Dick was not in the habit of wearing shoes, and "whose shooting-boots you are not worthy to unlace,"[2] would not have sounded half so withering. Dolly unbuttons her languid eyes, that look out of place anywhere but in a Seraglio,[3] about the hundredth part of an inch. Being "threeped at,"[4] as the servants call it, is for her a new sensation.

"That'll do," she says, coldly, "it's too hot for towrows.[5] Stamp a little harder on these worm-eaten old boards, and you'll find yourself in the cellar, reclining in one of the empty wine-bins."

The tornado of my wrath is moderating to a stiffish breeze, as, after having wrecked half-a-dozen vessels, and dismasted half-a-hundred, an equinoxial gale is content to fret and bluster itself into comparative peace; but in both cases the sea still seethes and works like must.

"I really thought," continues Dolly, gravely, having laid aside her mocking tone, "I really thought, Nell, that you could take a joke better; for you could hardly suppose that I meant *really* that a Lestrange would submit to any familiarity from a Coxian

---

1 See "Among the Free Lovers" in *Essays, Sketches and Letters*, by Artemus Ward, pseud. for Charles Farrar Browne (1834-67), American humorist.
2 Compare Mark 1:7. John the Baptist preaches that he is only the forerunner of one mightier than he (that is, Jesus), whose sandals he is not worthy to untie.
3 Harem (Italian).
4 Scolded (Scottish and northern dialect).
5 Uproars, noisy disturbances.

protégé.[1] No, no; we do not hold our heads so high in the world as we did, but it will take two generations more to bring us down to *that* depth; that would be fulfilling the prophecy, 'they that were clad in scarlet embrace dunghills' with a vengeance."[2]

I hardly relish this bold trope, being moreover guiltily conscious of having fulfilled the prophecy and embraced the dunghill.

"No! no!" fanning herself gently with the advertisement sheet of the *Times*; "everything after its kind; like and like; *Cocks* and Hens, and Lestranges, and gentlemen; probably from the docile way in which that man trots about at Mrs. Coxe's apron strings, and fetches and carries for her, he must be engaged to Amaryllis; they are going to try and mix a little poor blue blood, if it *is* blue, which is open to question, with their own full bodied red."

"He would not touch Amaryllis with a pair of tongs," cry I, digging my nails deep into my pink palms and making them pinker still.

"H-m," with a cynical motion of the shoulders, "hungry dogs eat dirty pudding, and Amaryllis' *dot*[3] would go far towards re-stocking the kail yard[4] that I suppose he has somewhere in Auld Reekie."[5]

"You see further into a milestone than most people,[6] that's evident," I say, derisively.

"No, I don't; I only see what's under my nose, and heaven forbid my setting up as a matchmaker; the vulgarest amusement a vacant mind can have; but, somehow, the world's pulse does not seem to beat in this remote corner; one has so little to think about that one is reduced to silly gossipy speculations about one's neighbour's concerns."

"I'd speculate something a little more probable while I was

---

1 One who is protected or mentored (French).
2 Compare Lamentations 4:5. The prophet laments the fall of the people of Zion, who are brought so low that although they were brought up in scarlet, that is in wealthy circumstances and fine robes, now are poor and "embrace dunghills."
3 Dowry (French), the money a woman brought to her marriage.
4 Cabbage garden or kitchen garden.
5 Edinburgh, capital of Scotland. "Reekie" means smoky.
6 This saying suggests that the person pretends to know things that cannot be known or to have a superior understanding to others. I have found the saying used elsewhere in this period, but have not discovered its origin.

about it," is my indignant comment, and being unable to trust myself either to say or refrain from saying more, I move towards the tall sombre door, and pass through it into the dim wide hall.

CHAPTER XIV

I don't think I like the word *Nature*, it sounds hard and dry and unfriendly; a chilly abstraction instead of the homely familiar assemblage of green fields and hedges and muddy lanes, and cows and donkeys, and rivers that it is intended to represent. However, I suppose until our language grows richer by a more satisfactory term, I must be content to make use of it. Dear mother Nature, after all is said and done, is far pleasanter than most specimens of Human Nature. She has been bespattered with a great deal of ill-fitting praise and undeserved abuse, for not sympathizing sufficiently with the howlings and throes and yearnings of aspiring and dyspeptic bards, for not howling and yearning with them, but after all she is quite sympathetic enough. She does not indeed disfigure her pretty face with crying for us when we die, why should she? She will die herself some day, she knows; but when our own kind cast us out, she takes us to her motherly breast, and wraps her fresh, sweet-smelling earth-cloak about us. And then, while we are yet alive, what a friendly companion she is; not too demonstrative, and such a good listener; lets us say what we please, never contradicts us, nor gives us bits of advice, or pieces of her mind.

I pick up my hat (it cost seven pence half-penny originally, and has been in wear three summers) from off the settle and pass through the swing door and the offices to the kitchen, with the raftered ceiling and huge broad fire-place. A very thin curl of blue smoke is going up its wide throat now; we need but little fire to do our minute portion of cooking. Times are changed since oxen were roasted whole, and old October[1] brewed at Lestrange. When the last Lestrange came of age, I don't think even a chicken was roasted whole in honour of the event; well! we shall be extinct next generation, and time for us!

---

1 Nell is referring to the days of wealth and feudalism when the Hall would have had great harvests and brewed its own beer.

"The old order changeth; giving place to new,
And God fulfils himself in many ways."[1]

Mrs. Smith is sitting in one sunny window, a little orange tree
in a pot that she has raised from a pip stands on the sill; it has shot
up very tall and drawn from the heat of the kitchen. Mrs. Smith
is shredding beans into a willow pattern dish. Coming events cast
their shadows before, and we are evidently going to have beans
and bacon for luncheon. Beans cost nothing and bacon not much,
so they are a very favourite and frequently recurring *mets*[2] in our
bills of fare. I stand by her for a minute or two in silence; so, finding that like a ghost, I require to be spoken to first, she lifts up her
kind homely face, and says,

"I'm afraid you're a bit lonesome to-day, my dear, your pa
gone and all; I 'ope 'e's got all right to his journey's hend; I don't
put much faith in them ould trains, and Miss Dolly is not much
company for you, is she?"

"No," say I, taking up one of the empty pods, and looking at
the short white down upon it; "but I don't want company," and
then I leave her with the warm sun streaming in on her little sickly orange tree, with its dusty dark leaves, on her black net cap
and faded purple ribbons, and on her pale smooth beans. I pass
through the house-yard, where a scullion, "fat and foolish" as the
one that was scouring a fish kettle at Shandy Hall when the news
of Master Bobby's death arrived,[3] is pumping into a bucket, with
her great red arms, and where the old tom-cat is crouching on the
top of the wall, with his tail curled round his toes, one eye shut,
and the other keeping wily watch upon the movements of a very
young, naked, and clumsy bird on the beech bough above him.

There was a little book came out some years ago, which I
believe had a great run among the spinsters of Britain, entitled
"Work: Plenty to do, and how to do it,"[4] and with an emblematic
beehive blazing on its small blue back. I had no work to do, and
should not have done it if I had. How would the ingenious author

---

1 See "The Death of Arthur" in *Idylls of the King*, by Tennyson.
2 Food, dishes (French).
3 See Volume VIII, chapter 7 in *Tristram Shandy*, a novel by Law-
   rence Sterne (1713-68).
4 *Work! Or Plenty to Do and How to Do It* (1853), by Margaret Maria
   Brewster.

have dealt with me? The gate into the ten acres stands open, and I enter. Our hay is not cut yet, it will be a month yet before the grass and the flowers' sweet death make all the land one nosegay; a month before, from my bed-room window in the early morning, I see the long row of haymakers bending to their scythes; before I see their ladies wearying their strong horn-hands with tossing the hay in the warm dry air, and raking it together with their big blunt-toothed rakes through the long summer days.

I made hay houses up to a very very few years ago, went on making them until my commanding height and Dolly's ridicule compelled me to relinquish my unseemly sport; even now, though I have been to a dinner party, and set up a lover, my soul hankers after the forbidden fruit.

Regardless of the injury I am doing to the crop, I throw myself down full length, shaded by a sycamore, which ought not to be in the hedgerow and is. The grasses are so very tall, they stand up inches above my prostrate form; I can see the little summer flies walking up the stalks of the ladies' smocks, and into the faint sweet flowers.

I clasp my hands at the back of my head and lie very still, so still that a little blue butterfly settles on my breast, and opens and closes its white-lined wings slowly in the sun; and green dragon flies go whirring confidently past, almost brushing my nose as they sail gauzily by. There is a path through this field, a right of way; in litigation about which, my worthy grandpapa, whose money always burnt a hole in his pocket, spent hundreds fifty years ago, but very few people ever pass along it. Nobody is passing along it now, this midday is as utterly mute as any midnight.

From my low bed I look straight into the sycamore; I see the coy little shadows playing hide and seek; see wonderful quivering lights; see the leaves in all the bravery of their new attire—some have put it on but this morning, and here and there Heaven's blue eyes looking through the green windows. The yellow light and the staring up make my eyes ache at last, so I turn them away and look through the grass forest round me, through "the oat grass and the sword grass" off far away to the horizon. I always fancy that the bridge at the World's End, at which the youngest of the three prince brothers in the fairy tale invariably arrives,[1] must be somewhere over there.

---

1 Stories featuring three princes, the youngest of whom successfully crosses a bridge at the end of the world, abound in variations of a common European folktale.

A very busy bee mistakes my right eye for a flower, and attempts to go into it; complimentary but not pleasant; to prevent the recurrence of such mistakes I close both eyes. When any one in a moderately comfortable position of body, and with any sin less than murder on his soul, takes to closing his or her eyes on a drowsy windless May day like this, there can be but one result; the result accomplishes itself in my case, and I fall asleep. Heaven knows what I dream about, some ridiculous *pot pourri* of impossibilities; but all of a sudden I jump half out of my skin, and start up. A man stands beside me; not Dick nor Sir Hugh, for what should they be doing trespassing in our ten acres? but

"A little glassy-headed, hairless man,"[1]

Collins, in fact, in that striped linen jacket and generally *dégagé*[2] costume in which he usually blooms through the forenoon.

"*How* you startled me!"

"If you please, ma'am" (for Collins, though of indisputable antiquity and not in the best repair, has sufficient remnant of good feeling and resemblance to a decent servant not to say "if you please, *Miss*"), "if you please, ma'am, there's a genelman in the library, and Miss Lestrange sent me to look for you to come to him."

"A gentleman!" I cry, with as much animation as if I were a second Miranda, whose acquaintance with gentlemen was confined to her papa and Caliban,[3] "and Miss Lestrange sent for me?"

"Yes, 'm; told me to 'unt heverywhere for you."

(Dick, of course, I say to myself. Well done, Dolly, your bark is worse than your bite.)

"And what is the name of the gentleman?" to make assurance doubly sure.

"Well, 'm, I were hout when he come, so *Hann*[4] went to the

---

1 See "Merlin and Vivien" in *Idylls of the King*, by Tennyson.
2 Casual (French).
3 Miranda has been marooned on a nearly deserted island since she was a baby, and has never seen a human man other than her father, in Shakespeare's play, *The Tempest*. Caliban was a monstrous creature native to the island.
4 Ann. In addition to dropping the initial "h" from words, the lower classes were often perceived to overcorrect by adding an h to a word beginning with a vowel. Nell emphasizes her servant's overcorrection.

door, and she says she could not take her hoath, but if she was to die next minute she should say it was Sir Hugh Lankyster."

"Sir Hugh Lancaster!" with infinite disgust, "then why on earth did you not say so before?"

I throw myself down again in a pet.

"You may go; I shan't come."

"But if you please, 'm, Miss Lestrange——"

"What do I care for Miss Lestrange! Say that you could not find me."

Collins retires, discomfited, and as the last glimpse of his bald head and round shoulders disappears round the corner, I change my mind; chiefly, I think, because I see that there is no one to try and do it for me. "Half a loaf is better than no bread," and a man, even though he be not *the* man, is better than nothing. Cleopatra was but true to the instincts of her sex when she said,

"I have no men to govern in this wood,
That makes my only woe."[1]

I effect a compromise with my dignity, by walking as slowly as I possibly can to the house, and entering the library with an air of ostentatious indifference.

"Here you are! That's all right," says Sir Hugh, jumping up, and in that jolly tone which is peculiar to him.

"Jolly" is Sir Hugh's own epithet, as "venerable" is Bede's, and "pious" Eneas's.[2] Other people may be, and no doubt are jolly, venerable and pious, though perhaps not all three at once; but these three men are the representatives *par excellence* of these qualities. Hugh reminds one somehow of the tone of Dickens's books;[3] there is a broad, healthy geniality about him; he is like a wood fire on a frosty day.

"Did Collins find you?" asks Dolly.

I say, surlily, "Evidently, or I should not be here."

---

1 Cleopatra, Queen of Egypt, during and after the reign of Julius Caesar. Here, she is the speaker in "A Dream of Fair Women," by Tennyson.

2 The Venerable Bede (673-735) was a medieval monk and scholar. Aeneas, a character in *The Iliad*, survives the siege of Troy. He is distinguished by his sense of duty and reverence for his family. He is generally introduced with the adjective "pious."

3 Charles Dickens (1812-70), novelist and journalist.

Dolly never wrangles in public: she remembers to *laver* her *linge sale*[1] at home, and not give her acquaintance the benefit of it.

"Where were you?"

"In the Ten Acres. I was asleep, and he woke me, and gave me *such* a start" (pouting).

"Taking a siesta, were you?" says Hugh; "best thing to be done to-day; melting, isn't it? My bailiff, who is very weather wise, says we are to have thunder before many days are over."

"I'm sure I hope so," Dolly says, languidly, "for it would cool the air, and prevent our all being reduced to little spots of grease."

"I'm sure I hope not," growl I, contradictiously.

"Why?" asks Hugh, who, I suppose, thinks that I must resemble the rooks,[2] who say nothing without cause (caws).

"Because it frightens me out of my wits. It is not a pleasant idea that you may be alive and well one minute, and as black as a coal and as dead as a door-nail the next."

Sir Hugh shows all his front teeth—and they really are his own, I do believe, his own by right of birth and not of purchase—in a laugh; he is as easily moved to mirth as a child at a pantomime.

"It doesn't sound very cheerful, certainly, when you put it so forcibly; but it is such an infinitesimal chance—a million to one. You don't mean to say that you do really funk—that you are really frightened at thunder. I should have thought that you were afraid of nothing."

"I am, though. I always tie something over my eyes, and go down into the cellar. Don't I, Dolly?"

"I can't say that you are remarkable for *physical* courage," replies Dolly, with a slight emphasis on the word; "but it's an unnecessary quality in a woman; only makes Jaels, and Judiths, and Madame Rolands of them,[3] doesn't it, Sir Hugh?"

---

1 Wash her dirty laundry (French), i.e. take care of her private problems.
2 Birds in the same family as crows, who make a cawing sound.
3 In Judges 4 and 5, Jael kills Sisera, the leader of an enemy army, by driving a spike through his head as he sleeps. The beautiful Judith, in the Book of Judith, one of the books of the Apocrypha, gains entrance to the tent of the leader of the Assyrians, Holofernes, by stratagem. As he lies in a drunken stupor, she cuts his throat, leading to the victory of Israel. Madame Roland (1754-93) was a famous figure in the French revolution, and was finally guillotined herself for protesting its worst excesses. Dolly lumps in two heroic figures from Biblical sources, much admired and often painted in this period, with a French revolutionary, who was a considerably more ambivalent figure.

Sir Hugh says "he supposes so," and the electric topic seems exhausted.

Dolly and I are sitting on the sofa, side by side.

"My dear child," says the former—in that maternal, elder sister, guardian angel strain which makes casual old lady callers remark that "Miss Lestrange is like a mother to her younger sister"—"what have you been doing with yourself? You are covered with bits of grass, and sticks and stones enough to make a rook's nest. She is a regular Madge Wildfire,[1] isn't she?"

Sir Hugh thinks it would be rude to me to agree with Dolly, and rude to her to disagree with her; so he holds his tongue and looks wise, as if he could say a great deal, but would not. The window is exactly opposite, and Dolly is looking out of it. Suddenly she rises and walks quickly, but without ungraceful hurry, over to it.

"Don't you think it would be pleasanter to have this blind down a bit? The sun does beat so very powerfully on this side of the house in the forenoon"; and without waiting to collect our suffrages on the subject, she pulls it down. "Do you know, Nelly, poor Sir Hugh has had such a disappointment this morning. He came over to have a talk with papa about those dwarf espaliers.[2] You won't mind trying to be a bad substitute, will you, and taking him to see them?"

"Why can't you go yourself?" ask I, not too civilly.

"*I*," (with a laugh and a shrug). "What do I know about dwarf espaliers? I'm a regular cockney in all gardening matters."

"Never mind, it will do just as well any other day. I don't want to bore Miss Eleanor," says Sir Hugh, good-naturedly, but looking rather vexed, for he is a great and zealous gardener, and no one likes to feel themselves shirked.

I recollect myself, and call to mind how sharply my father took me up for snubbing Sir Hugh the other day.

"Oh, no; I don't mind much," I say, ungraciously enough. "Come along."

"Go through the garden door, it is open," says Dolly, following us out to see that we take her advice.

---

1 A character from the novel *The Heart of Midlothian* (1818), by Sir Walter Scott, who becomes crazed after having been seduced and abandoned, and having suffered the death of her child.
2 Espaliers are structures on which a plant may be bound and trained to grow.

"You had better come too, Dolly," I say.

Hugh does not back my invitation.

"No, no," (with a sweet benedictory smile, which seems to say, like the "heavy father" in the fifth act of a melodrama, "Bless you, my children"). "Two are company and three are none; and, besides, the sun makes my head ache."

"How much better your rhododendrons do than ours," says Sir Hugh, stopping as we pass a great sloping bank of lilac blossoms, "can't make it out."

"We got plenty of bog earth for them from Brindley Heath," I say, looking down at my boots, and wondering whether my companion has yet discovered the yawning rift in the side of the left one.

"I see your father has let the land up to the very windows."

"Yes, he had to," I say, with a sigh; somehow, I don't much mind Hugh knowing our poverty.

We walk on silently for a minute or two. I think that Hugh is wishing it was not an insult for a rich gentleman to offer a poor gentleman money.

"What a jolly old place it is. I wish I could pick it up, and pop it down half a score miles nearer Wentworth."

"Do you?" in rather a dissentient tone.

"Yes, I do. Why, you see my mother is getting into years. It's a long way for her to come pounding over here. She is not so active as she was once, and I want you and her to know each other better."

"Me *and Lady Lancaster*! Why, on earth?" I should not have been more astonished had he expressed a wish to see me and the Duchess of Cambridge on terms of intimacy (*bien obligé*,[1] but I think that that cast-iron old lady would hardly be a meet playfellow for me). Hugh looks straight before him; I think he thinks me inconveniently innocent.

"I wish you'd let us put you and your sister up at Wentworth, while Sir Adrian is away; you think my mother rather alarming, don't you; and she does cut up rough now and then, certainly, but what old woman doesn't."

"I suppose they mostly are rather cross," I say, sedately, "and old men too!" I add, from a feeling of equity to my own sex.

"If you do come, you must come soon," continues Hugh, as

---

1 Much obliged (French).

we tramp together over the daisies that flourish unspudded upon our sward, "for in a fortnight or three weeks the old lady is off to town!"

"Are you going with her?"

"Oh yes, of course; though there's nothing in life I hate so much. Swelling about St. James's Street, in one's go-to-meeting clothes, and being squashed as flat as a pancake on some old dowager's stairs, aren't much in my line; I'd a deal sooner be sowing marigolds or planting potatoes; beastly hole, London!"

Sir Hugh is bucolic, you see; he has not Pope's admiration of "the town."[1]

"Dear me, how odd!" exclaim I, with genuine surprise; my views of the Metropolis are formed on the Whittingtonian and streets-paved-with-gold plan.[2] "I should like to go to London of all things; I want to see the Tower, and the British Museum, and the Wax Works."

Sir Hugh bursts out laughing.

"God bless my soul! what an extraordinary notion; you'd hardly find it pay, I think, travelling a hundred and twenty miles to see Rush and Palmer and Townley,[3] staring at you like stuck pigs."

I never have any great opinion of my own sapience, but I perceive that in my last observation I have considerably exceeded my usual standard of silliness, and so I am relieved in finding that we have reached our goal, the *potager*.[4] Having called our old gardener, who is involuntarily practising the virtue of temperance over a hunk of cheese and an onion, to my assistance, I stand by for about ten minutes, and listen not without amusement to Sir Hugh and him mangling the French words with their clumsy British tongues, while I entertain myself consuming in-

---

1 Alexander Pope (1688-1744) was a poet, essayist, and wit.

2 Dick Whittington is a character in a children's story dating to at least the beginning of the seventeenth century. He is based (loosely) on the real Richard Whittington who served three terms as Lord Mayor of London: 1397-99, 1406-07, and 1419-20. He first went to London believing the streets are paved with gold. Nell's idea of London is also a childish one; she wishes to see the most popular tourist attractions.

3 All criminals in high-profile cases, whose images were very likely to have been on display at Madame Tussauds, a famous waxwork museum.

4 From the French word for soup, meaning vegetable garden.

fantine peas. I have embarked on my seventeenth pod, and the others are deep in *Bons Chrétiens* and *Beurrés d'Alemberg*,[1] when the sound of footsteps and voices in a duet, approaching, make me turn my head. Hugh does ditto.

"Hallo! here's your sister come out, after all! And who on earth has she got hold of? a good many yards of him anyhow! Why it's M'Gregor, as I'm alive! I did not know that you knew him." Dolly is holding up a little gray parasol, and has tied a small *fichu*[2] over her head; she has a white gown on, and her modest eyes are cast down; altogether one would say that she was about to be confirmed. M'Gregor comes *mowing* along beside her; rarely, rarely can a plunger[3] walk.

"Why, M'Gregor, my dear fellow, how are you? I thought you had mizzled from these parts a week ago; why have not you been to look us up?"

Major M'Gregor takes his hat off to me; I am in disgrace apparently; not good enough to be shaken hands with.

"I did say something to Coxe about it, but he did not seem to care about lending me a nag, and I'm not particularly partial to pedestrian exercise in the dog days."

"You are amongst the poultry[4] still?"

"Yes."

"Anything up there? calicoes lively?" asks Hugh with delicate *persiflage*.[5]

"Bless your heart, my good fellow, the army's no where, they won't look at a soldier! Bulls are the only admirers of scarlet cloth now-a-days!"

Hugh turns to take a last fond look at the pear trees.

"What a sun trap this garden is," says Dolly; her *fichu* is not a very efficient turban and she has a righteous horror of freckles, "let us go home again now that we have found you, you were so long over your gardening that we thought we must come to see what you were about, though we were not quite sure of our reception, were we?"

---

1 Types of pears.
2 Triangular neckerchief, sometimes worn over the hair, or at the chest.
3 Cavalry man (slang).
4 In the countryside.
5 Banter, teasing (French).

"This sort of thing," says Dick, laconically pointing to a gooseberry bush beside him.[1]

"Exactly, very graphically put." I am too indignant to deny.

"What's very graphically put?" asks Hugh, rejoining me at this moment, but nobody answers him, and we all walk back to the house; *ego et rex meus*,[2] or Hugh and I ahead, and the others following at a little distance.

Sir Hugh's mare, bright bay with white stockings, is being walked up and down the gravelled sweep by Collins, for stablemen have we never a one.

"Poor old girl!" says Hugh, going up and patting her sleek flank, "you're not so young as you were, but no more is your master if it comes to that, but you are as handsome as paint, isn't she?"

"*He* has a very thin tail," say I, and from this remark the amount of my knowledge of horseflesh may be inferred.

The others come up by and bye, and Dolly exclaims, "Oh, Sir Hugh, you'll stay for luncheon, won't you? It's very shabby of you running away from us in such a hurry."

I stand aghast, with my mouth open, fly-catching.

"No, thanks, no," replies Hugh, rather hastily. He remembers the shin of mutton, and does not agree with the proverb that "the nearer the bone the sweeter the flesh." "I never touch luncheon, at least not once in a month; spoils one's dinner. Good-bye, Miss Lestrange; good-bye, Miss Eleanor; see you again soon," (how cheering!) "good bye, M'Gregor, give us a call, old boy, some day, when you are short of a job."

Off he rides, and we three stand looking after him, admiring the set of his coat behind and his mare's rat-tail.

CHAPTER XV

Providence makes use of humble instruments sometimes to fulfil its behests, to prove which many good little books and *leaflets* (as Spurgeon and Co.[3] have christened very young tracts) are

---

1 Playing gooseberry meant being a chaperone to a courting couple, or being an unwelcome third person.
2 I and my king (Latin).
3 Possibly Charles Haddon Spurgeon and his colleagues, who published short religious pamphlets.

written and printed. Providence makes use of Collins now in my favour, for as Sir Hugh and his war-horse—she is an old charger—vanish through the upper gate, he mysteriously summons Dolly to receive his confidence on some momentous theme. It was to tell her (as I heard later) that we were out of beer—we mostly were out of most things somehow—so that she may not be led away into offering Major M'Gregor any. *Manent*[1] my follower and I.

"It seems one down t'other come on, with you, Nell," the former says, rather bitterly.

"Don't talk about what you don't understand," I say, saucily, my spirits rising like an indiarubber ball; "when people come to call upon a person, the person must be civil to them, musn't she? *You* come into the garden without being asked, but *other people* aren't so forward."

Dick laughs, but not very satisfiedly.

"Don't remind me of my delinquencies; if I live to be a hundred, I shall never forget your father's face that day. It said 'trespassers shall be prosecuted' as plain as it could speak, didn't it? Well, have you anything particular to do this evening?"

"Have I ever anything to do?"

"Come and meet me then by the brook, by those alders, below the mill, will you?"

We are standing close together, and he lays his hand on my shoulder in his eagerness, to the amusement of Mary the housemaid, who like Jezebel, is "tiring her head"[2] at an upper window. I have not sufficient guile to try and enhance the value of my consent by hesitation, so I say, "Oh yes, how nice; what time?"

"Well we dine at seven to-day instead of eight; Coxe is going up to town by the night mail, so I can get away a bit earlier; but I'm afraid it won't be much before half-past eight, that's very late, isn't it? But you know it is daylight till ten now, and then there's the moon."

If there were neither sun, nor moon, nor planet, and only one tallow candle to illuminate our interview, it would not make much difference to me.

---

1 They remain (Latin).
2 See Kings 9:30. Jezebel was a famously beautiful and wicked queen of Tyre who was killed by Jehu; it is she who displayed herself in the window while adorning herself.

"Half-past eight then?"

Dick has only time to execute a nod, pregnant with meaning as Lord Burleigh's,[1] when Dolly reappears.

"I won't ask you to luncheon, Major M'Gregor, as I know it's no use," says Dolly.

How did she know it? There must have been a little confusion of ideas in her mind, I think. She knew it was useless to offer him any beer, because there was none, and I suppose that was what she meant. Dick feels himself dismissed. He has not the *tabouret*,[2] or right of sitting on a stool in Queen Dorothea's presence.

"Why, I rather agree with Lancaster, that it spoils one's dinner; and at Coxe's, dinner's no joke, I can tell you; it requires the powers of an alderman, and would tax even them. Poor Coxe! He means well, and I suppose it is old-fashioned hospitality, but it is rather trying. Good morning."

He fires off a look of intelligence at me, which seems to say "Remember," as plainly as King Charles the First of blessed memory did to Bishop Juxon.[3] I return it by a minute but knowing nod. I feel rather important, and a little dissipated, with the consciousness of a secret assignation on my mind.

"What was it you and Sandy were laying your heads together about, just now? You appear to 'love greetings in the Market Place.' Collins must have been edified," says Dolly, would-be playfully, but I detect the "clawses at the end of her pawses."[4]

"He was telling me about his passion for Amaryllis, to be sure," reply I, with charming archness; "asking my advice as to Gretna Green[5] and a post-chaise."

---

1 A gesture that implies a great deal of meaning. The phrase comes from the description of a gesture (a nod) of a character in *The Critic* (1779), a play by Richard Sheridan (1751-1816).

2 A low stool (French). The privilege of the tabouret was the permission to sit on such a low stool in the presence of the queen.

3 Charles I was put to death in 1649. Bishop Juxon administered the last rites and accompanied him to the place of execution. "Remember!" was his last word, spoken to Juxon.

4 An old joke: "A sentence [or, sometimes, a document] has *pauses* at the end of its *clauses*, but a cat has *clawses* at the ends of its *pawses*." The origin is unknown, but the earliest example I have found of this is from 1858.

5 Town just over the Scottish border to which English couples often eloped, as looser marriage laws enabled couples to marry more quickly there.

"Nonsense! What was it?"

"Brekkekekkex! Koax! Koax!"[1] I answer, quoting Aristophanes, though without knowing it; and Dolly, finding that a servile war has broken out, and that I am in a state of open insurrection, desists.

I was sadly in want of some one to confide in that day. What is the good of possessing the consciousness of being about to do something as exciting, and daring, and *hors de règle*[2] as walking down the Burlington by oneself of an afternoon, unless you have some one to share that proud consciousness with you. What is Tilburina,[3] stark mad in white satin, without her confidant, also stark mad in white linen? I should certainly have unbosomed myself to Mrs. Smith, the recipient of all my confidences, from my aversion for Dolly and Mr. Bowles, to my grief for the death of the little black duck that the rats ate, had it not been that the bread not having "*rose*" (arbitrary past participle of the verb to rise), she was not in the best of humours, and paid small heed to me, when I threw out two or three remarks of an introductory nature as feelers. So I had to content myself with warbling

"Come into the garden, Maud,"[4]

all over the house, and wondering whether the household did not guess at the personal application of the song. Once and again a qualm of conscience broke off my singing, as I thought of my father. If he were displeased with me for sitting with a young man in our own garden at *seven* o'clock in the evening[5] (for I really don't believe it was later), would not he, *a fortiori*,[6] be far more displeased with me for sitting with the same young man, at a spot, a quarter of a mile beyond our grounds, at nine o'clock?

---

1   See "The Frogs" (fourth century BCE), a play by Aristophanes. The frogs, who are the chorus, introduce their discourse with this sound, meant to resemble croaking.

2   Outside the rules (French).

3   See *The Critic* (1779), a play by Richard Sheridan (1751-1816). In it, the characters discuss another play, the Spanish Armada, in which Tilburina is a character.

4   See *Maud* (1855), by Tennyson.

5   Nell originally specifies that her father first finds her with Richard at nine o'clock.

6   All the more (Latin).

My father's notions of propriety were rigidity's self. A woman's virtue, in his code of *les convenances*,[1] should be a stiff vestment of buckram and whale-bone; he would have liked his daughters' modesty to be inferior only to that of the young lady in "Mr. Midshipman Easy,"[2] who affirmed, that to shake hands with a man made a cold shudder run down her back. Shall I not go, then? Stay at home, and mend stockings, and listen to Dolly, "damning" her friends "with faint praise," and regaling me with Rochefoucauld[3] and water. What? and leave poor Dick to kick his heels in the damp grass in dress-boots? No, no; if it is a sin to disobey a parent, it is also a sin to break one's word, and when one must commit one of two sins, one may as well choose the pleasantest.

All the same, you will understand, please, that I liked my father a hundred times better than Dick, and always should. I was not, I think, one of those fiery females, whose passions beat their affections out of the field. And really I don't think that Englishwomen are given to flaming, and burning, and melting, and being generally combustible on ordinary occasions, as we are led by one or two novelists to suppose. Foggy England is not peopled with Sapphos.

My thoughts having once travelled to my dad, stayed with him for ever so long. Had he lost any of his pocket handkerchiefs yet? six of them were not marked. Had he remembered his gout, and abstained from port wine? exchanging the *cuisine* of Lestrange for that of any other house, was, to a human creature, what being turned into a field of deep clover, after having been regaling on half-a-dozen bents is to a cow. Is he having a little rest from his burdens, a little time to gather up strength, and fortitude, and endurance? He had told us not to forward his letters to him, and indeed, when I looked at their big blue envelopes and the character of their superscriptions, I did not wonder at his not being in any hurry for a better acquaintance with them. I determine to write to him; I don't write a letter once a quarter, so it is a work of some labour.

---

1 The [social] proprieties (French).
2 Novel published in 1836 by Frederick Marryat.
3 Cynical commentator François, Duc de La Rochefoucauld (1613-80) is best known for his observations in a book originally published in French in 1665, and later translated into English as *Maxims*.

"Darling Dad,

"It seems such a long time since you went, I can hardly believe that it was only yesterday; I hope you'll come back soon,
at least I mean I hope you won't if you find it pleasant where
you are. I hope they make a great fuss with you; not so much
as I do, I'm sure! Dolly is come back. She looks very well, and
has got a whole heap of new clothes; she is about as pleasant
as usual. Sir Hugh Lancaster was here this morning; he came
over to talk to you about the dwarf espaliers. (I had to look
in the dictionary to see how *espaliers* spelt itself.) He seemed
quite disappointed to find you out, and pronounced the
French names almost as badly as you do. Major M'Gregor,
the man you did not like, was here too. The cob is very well,
and so are all the fowls, except the hen with the top-knot,
which has broken her leg tumbling down the ash hole. I don't
think I have anything more to tell you, except that I send you
twenty kisses and a great deal of love, and that
"I am always,
"Your most loving NELL."

Tea in the kitchen at Lestrange seems a jovial meal; at least
to judge from the peals of laughter that even through the double
doors reached our ears now and then. I believe that Collins is
humour itself, in unofficial hours, and *Hann* of great worth in
repartee. Tea in the dining-room is a silent feast; Dolly is buried
in thought, and makes only one remark.

"I think you said that Sir Hugh was at luncheon here the day
before yesterday, didn't you?"

"Yes."

The house seems to fall asleep after tea; as fast as the palace
of the sleeping beauty.

"Not a sound,
Not even of a gnat that sung";

nor could the slumbers of the sleeping beauty herself be sounder
than Dolly's as I peep at her through the library door, as,

"She lieth on her couch alone."[1]

---

1 A misquote of Tennyson's poem, "The Daydream" (1842).

As the time for my dereliction of duty draws near, I "wash and anoint myself, and change my raiment,"[1] or rather, as the fashion of oiling oneself like a machine is not prevalent in these Western regions, I confine myself to the other two. Then I steal through the garden door, and fly through the pleasure grounds, with as much velocity as if I had been projected from a cannon's mouth; *ventre à terre*[2] I go, till I reach the fir wood. Not a breath of air! Every wind from Boreas to Zephyr[3] is asleep in its cave, like bears in winter; and yet—how they manage it I don't know—there is the same little gentle sighing in the fir tops that there always is; they must do it themselves without the wind, it must be their "song of love and longing," like Shawondasee's to the dandelion in "Hiawatha."[4]

As I cross the threshold of Nature's solemn little pine temple, I drop into a respectful walk, as men take off their hats when they enter a church. On emerging from the wood, coming out of church, I see cavalry in the distance. Courage! I'm not first at the trysting place to-day. I perceive the cavalry before it perceives me, as it is manœuvring among the alders. Is not it humorous of me calling my lover *it*; as humorous as Mr. Peter Magnus signing himself "*Afternoon*."[5]

I come tripping bashfully over the buttercups and the meadow sweet, which are washing their faces before going to bed, and are so obliging as to wash my ankles too.

"I was afraid Sir Hugh had come to see some more pear trees," says Dick, with a smile, and drawing a breath of relief as we meet.

I feel a boundless capacity for impertinence unfolding itself within me.

---

1 Compare Book of Ruth, 3:3. Ruth's mother Naomi plans for her to marry Boaz, and so tells her to wash, "anoint herself" and put on her "raiment" or clothing before she meets him.
2 Belly to the ground (French).
3 According to Greek mythology, the North and West winds, respectively.
4 Henry Wadsworth Longfellow's epic poem based on Native American legend and history, *Hiawatha*, was published in 1855. Shawondasee was the South wind.
5 In Dickens's novel *The Pickwick Papers* (1837), Peter Magnus says that as his initials are p.m., he sometimes amuses his friends by signing as "Afternoon." This is presented as rather a bad pun, and not as amusing as Peter Magnus imagines.

"Yes, indeed, there would not have been much chance for you then; he's a '*baronite*,' and you are '*a shade or two wus*,'[1] as you must allow; but fortunately for you, I don't think his dear mamma would let him come out so late at night for fear of getting his feet wet."

"As you are yours," says Dick, looking down at my boots, which are all shiny with the dew. "Is he coming to-morrow then?"

"Perhaps so; who knows what luck is in store for one?"

"He seems to bestow a good deal of his company on you; how long is it since he was at Lestrange last?"

"The day before yesterday," reply I readily.

"Humph! cannot understand a fellow making himself so much at home in another man's house, a man might as well keep an inn."

"Who was it?" inquire I, with the air of a person desirous of information, "who was it that came to call at Lestrange with Mrs. Coxe yesterday, and by himself to-day, have you ever happened to hear of such a person?"

We are walking along slowly side by side, past the alder bushes, further down the brook, where we need not stand in awe of the miller and the milleress's *espionage*. Dick has got a light overcoat over his dress clothes, which are very plain; no embroidered shirt-front or jewelled studs. Dick is twenty-seven and has passed the jewelled age, which is as regular a period in the history of man as the wood, the bronze, and the iron, are in geology.

"*I'm* different," says Dick, gravely.

"Are you?" ask I, looking up naïvely. Next minute I am sorry I said it, for I see that he is vexed.

"If *you* don't see it, of course it is not so," he answers coldly, and sticks his nose up in the air, and looks as tall as a steeple.

"I do see it, of course; in the first place you are twice the size of him; he is such a dear little duodecimo edition of a man, I could rest my chin on the top of his head with the greatest ease imaginable."

---

1   See "Pretty Polly Perkins of Paddington Green" (1864), a song composed by Harry Clifton (1832-72). Polly Perkins refuses to marry a milkman. Instead, "In six months she married, this hard-hearted girl, / But it was not a wicount, and it was not a nearl, / It was not a baronite, but a shade or two wuss, / It was a bow-legged conductor of a Twopenny Bus."

Dick's nose descends from the clouds, and he passes his arm around me. "I'll go down on my marrow-bones before you, and then you can do the same to me; it *is* a nuisance, being such a lumbering great brute, nobody ever gives you a mount."[1]

We have reached a spot where, two months ago, a great girthed oak spread its arms to the air and its roots to the stream. Where it stood, there it lies now; all along by its friend, the brook, that sings a little pretty dirge for it. We have had to cut down every stick of timber on the property; every stick, except trees as valueless as the hollow elms in the avenue, that are too old even to make paupers' coffins.

"Let us sit down, Nell," says Dick. "I think we may defy the eyes of the mill now, and I don't suppose they've got opera glasses."

"It's to be hoped not," I say laughing; "I shall have to run the country if they have," which being interpreted means that *both* Major M'Gregor's arms have disposed themselves around me now.

"I never thought I was given to jealousy before—I always thought Othello[2] the biggest fool out," he says, while the honest gray eyes look rather wistfully into mine, and I see myself reflected in the dark pupils; "but I don't know, I don't feel easy about that fellow, somehow; why *do* you plague me about him?"

"How should I know it would plague you?" I ask very gaily. "You seemed such very dear friends to-day, 'my dear fellow'ing and 'old boy'ing each other, that I thought you would be pleased to hear that he was a dear friend of ours too."

"I knew him in India; all through the Mutiny with him; he is the deadest shot I ever clapped eyes on. They used to get him to pick off those black devils; he bagged a good deal of black game!"[3]

---

1 People do not like to loan Dick their horses because he is considered too heavy.

2 Jealous protagonist of Shakespeare's play of the same name (first printed 1622).

3 The Indian Rebellion of 1857. The rebellion started among native troops of the British army in British India, and was thus called a mutiny, though it quickly spread beyond the military. A number of Britons died, including several women and children. The British response was brutal and targeted military personnel and civilians alike. Contemporary British attitudes were inflected with what we would today identify as racist assumptions, although race was only beginning to be thought of as a fixed biological category in this period, rather than as primarily related to different geographic locations and cultural histories. The "black devils" Dick refers to here were natives of India.

"Were you great friends, then, *really?*"

"Oh average! we always hit it off very well; he is a very good straightforward fellow, though he won't set the Thames on fire; he can ride a bit too; and he has got a modest competence of something under £30,000 a year; *that* covers a multitude of sins."

"I suppose it does; I wonder what it feels like?" I say with curiosity.

"Do you know, Nell"—says Dick, and I see his wide white forehead oddly white, when contrasted with the brownness of the rest of his face, contracting a little as with some pain—"do you know, Nell, I have not sixpence to bless myself with; that I am as poor as Job?"

I nod. "Yes, I know!"

"Who told you? Lazarus'[1] reputation precedes him apparently!" (Very sharply.)

"Nobody."

"How on earth did you find out then? Do I look poor? Is pauper written on my face?"

I rub my cheek gently against his shoulder.

"I felt sure you were poor; nice people always are! rich men are always short, and old and ugly." (I am thinking of the one Dives of my acquaintance.) The sun is dead, but has left half his beauty behind him; at the mere memory of him, the whole western sky is a-flame, there are no watery lilac tints streaking the rich crimson that faints away into pale clear gold and dusky blue. "And at evening ye say it will be fair weather to-day, for the sky is red." The rosy flush is catching at the tops of the churchyard yews, and striking up along the old gray tower like a thought of heaven in a weary life. At our feet, the little burn goes wimpling down to the distant river; a small swift current in the middle, and under the bank little amber pools, where the tiny baby fish can shelter their semi-transparent bodies from the sun. The big ones are swaying their slender bodies 'gainst the stream, which has force to make the "lush green grasses" on its banks bend downwards with it, long and drenched like the hair of a drowned maiden.

"I suppose," says my impecunious Plunger, rather dolefully, looking down and tugging at the ends of his moustache which are

---

1   See the story of Lazarus and Dives in Luke 16:19-31. Lazarus is a beggar ignored by Dives, a rich man. When they die, Dives suffers torments, while Lazarus is compensated for his suffering on earth.

not waxed, "I suppose, if I had done what was right and honour-able, I should have sheered off as soon as I found I was getting hit;[1] but it's an awful grind doing one's duty. If it would but lie in a pleasant direction for a change, it would have more chance of having some attention paid to it; and I really did like you so much, Nell, that duty or no duty, I had to tell you so. By-the-bye, what does your sister think about it?"

"Think about what?"

"About you and me."

"I don't know what she thinks about me, I'm sure; nothing particularly flattering, I fancy. But she thinks that you must be engaged to Amaryllis Coxe; at least, she said so this morning."

"To Amaryllis! God forbid!" says Dick, fervently. "I'd rather a millstone were hanged about my neck, and that I were drowned in the depths of the sea. By-the-bye, Amaryllis, or *Ammy*, as her sisters tersely call her, is not unlike a millstone either in weight or shape. Your sister put the saddle on the wrong horse that time, didn't she?"

"She was so positive about it, too, that I thought I must have made some mistake. I was beginning to make up my mind that I must look out for a fresh situation."

"I see. That partly accounts for the pear trees; a Roland for my Oliver;[2] a Lancaster for my Amaryllis. But seriously, Nell, doesn't she *see* how the land lies? I should have thought that it did not require spectacles."

"There's none so blind as them as won't see,"[3] I reply, oracularly.

"And you did not tell her?"

"Not I; I never tell her anything."

Dick looks puzzled.

"That was it, I suppose, then. I thought, of course, that you knew all each other's secrets—my sisters always do." (Dick has not realized the fact that there are sisters and sisters.) "So I be-gan to say something about you to her this morning, and she shut

---

1 Dick suggests that as he is not financially well prepared to marry, he should have left town as soon as he felt he was falling in love with Nell.
2 Roland and Oliver are characters in the *Song of Roland* (c. 1100), a medieval French poem. Although they are initially rivals, they become friends. The saying, "a Roland for an Oliver" means one gives as good as one gets.
3 Proverb.

me up rather; did not seem to know what I was driving at, you know; began to speak of something else."

The flush is dying out of the sky's cheek; the remembrance of the dead sun is growing faint as the memory of the human dead weakens beneath the weight of the crowding years; the buttercups have gone to sleep, each with his little cup full of dew; and the cows are making up for the time they wasted at noon, when they stood knee-deep in the brook, and combated the flies, by feeding now as if for a wager; we hear their short quick bites in the evening stillness; and the stream goes whispering on, carrying little sticks, and green leaves, and fallen cherry blossoms from the mill orchard higher up, as a present to the gray distant sea.

Dick's and my hat are making each other's acquaintance at our feet, and the rising moon is turning our respective red and yellow *chevelures*[1] silver, as the old bugbear with the scythe will do for us by and bye, if we wait patiently. I don't believe that Dick will ever be an old man. I cannot fancy him with his handsome mouth fallen in, and his handsome eyes melted out; cannot picture him hobbling about in a list shoe, mumbling his dinner with the wrecks of those strong white teeth, and having to be roared at before he can hear what is said to him.

"The sound as of a hidden brook
In the leafy month of June,
That to the sleeping woods all night
Singeth a quiet tune,"[2]

says Dick, in his deep voice. Dick can take a capital bass.

"Do you ever read poetry, Nell?"

"Oh, yes; very often. I have read 'Lara,' and 'We are Seven,' and the 'Lord of Burleigh,' and the 'Needy Knife Grinder,' and 'Samson Ago—Ago—something,'"[3] reply I, glibly.

Dick smiles.

---

1 Heads of hair (French).
2 See "The Rime of the Ancient Mariner" (1798), a poem by Samuel Taylor Coleridge.
3 "Lara" (1814) is by Lord Byron, "We are Seven" (1798) is by William Wordsworth, and the "Lord of Burleigh" (1842) is by Tennyson. "The Needy Knife-Grinder" (1791), a burlesque of Robert Southey's pro-revolutionary verse, is by politician George Canning. "Samson Agonistes" (1671) is by Milton.

"Homer, Plutarch, and Nicodemus,
All standing naked in the open air."[1]

"What has that to say to it?" inquire I, wondering what put that indelicate and irrelevant couplet into his head.

He pinches my cheek.

"Nothing; only I thought that your pieces of poetry seemed to have about as much relationship to one another as those three elderly gentlemen."

"You asked me what I had read, and so I told you," I say, rather injured. "It is not my fault that they are not related to one another, any more than it is that you are not related to the great Mogul."[2]

"It was very rude of me," apologizing, though the offending smile still lurks. "Tell me something else about your studies, and I'll swear to be as grave as a judge."

"There's nothing to be told about nothing," say I, with chagrin. "Papa knows everything; Dolly knows most things, and I know nothing. That's the state of the case. You thought it fair to tell me that you had no money, and I think it fair to tell you that I have no learning and no brains to get any."

I turned away my head, and the tears, always within hail in my case, come stealing into my eyes.

"I don't believe the last, and I don't care a straw about the first," says Dick, putting his hand under my chin, and bringing my rueful countenance round within reach of his eyes.

"Perhaps—perhaps—" say I, still rather lachrymosely, and making the remark to his shirt-front, on which I have been good enough to deposit my rough, chestnut head, "perhaps you'll try and teach me something. I asked Dolly once, but she would not."

Dick laughs and strokes my hair.

"*I!* I can teach you the platoon exercise, and how to make cartridges, and shall be very glad to do either if you think they would help you; but I don't think that my capabilities go much further."

---

1   Several versions of this bit of doggerel float through nineteenth-century literature. It probably originates in "The Groves of Blarney," by Richard Milliken (1767-1815).

2   Probably Jahangir, ruler of Northern India legendary for his wealth, brought to British attention in the seventeenth century, though this term could refer to any of a series of these rulers. It also refers to the largest diamond ever found in India.

The church clock strikes ten; tells the dead people that they are an hour nearer their release—so clearly and sweetly each beat comes sounding over the quiet land. I resume the possession of my own head, and jump up.

"I must go home, else I shall be locked out."

"There *would* be the devil to pay, then," says Dick, standing up, too, and stretching like a big Newfoundland.

"I shall be late for prayers as it is, and I always read them."

"Oh, you *can* read, can you, ma'am?"

"Yes, I can manage anything under five syllables."

"Why does not Miss Lestrange act parson? You seem to have no idea of the rights of primogeniture."

"Dolly does not like prayers. She says that they are a great farce, and that she cannot see why if a person wants to say his prayers, he cannot say them to himself, without dragging in all the household to help him."

"They'll have a holiday from family worship at Lestrange to-night, then, I take it."

"Yes, sure to. Well," (with a long sigh), "it has been very pleasant. Good night."

"I'm willing to bid you good night any number of times, but if you think you are going to get rid of me here, you are mistaken. It's Lancaster's turn now. How do I know that he may not be dodging round the corner somewhere?"

So we stroll away together from the silvered sedges, and the poor barked tree, and the spot where we have been doing our best to lay in a stock of rheumatism, and swelled joints, and shooting pains for our riper years, the pennilessest, improvident-est, happiest pair of sweethearts in Great Britain. Walk as slow as we may, and no tortoise can beat us, ten minutes bring us to the parting gate. There we pose ourselves in the attitude of the famous "Huguenot" picture.[1]

"I don't think you can come to much grief, Nell, between this and the Hall door. Good night, my darling. You are *my* darling, and not Lancaster's, aren't you? God in Heaven bless you!"

"*Yours*, if you'll have me; if not, *nobody's*," I say, very earnestly;

---

1   Sir John Everett Millais's wildly popular painting, *A Huguenot, on St. Bartholomew's Day Refusing to Shield Himself from Danger by Wearing the Roman Catholic Badge* (1852), is probably what Nell has in mind.

and then we kiss each other twenty times, where we first kissed, beneath the big white lilac bush.

CHAPTER XVI

A household where woman reigns alone, freed from the dominion of her natural enemy; an entirely female establishment, leavened by no admixture of the masculine element, is a very dreary thing. So I found to my cost during that long, long week.

The man of a family may be, and often is, a very inferior animal to his woman-kind; made of infinitely poorer, commoner clay; he may be a coarse, surly brute, all body and no soul worth speaking of, or a soul wrapped up and enfolded in swine and turnips, or in gray shirting, or brown sugars, or pill-boxes and blisters. Even so, the sound of his heavy boots on the stairs, of his gruff, untuneful voice, mixes harmoniously and healthily with the women's noiseless, catlike footfalls and shrill treble pipes. Good is his unbeautiful face at dinner; good are his dull anecdotes, that yet bring a whiff of the outer world with them; yea, good are his very hat and dreadnought in the hall.

Women's minds are apt to get narrowed, soured (the best women's have an undeveloped tendency that way), if they have not some male intellect to rub against, and be wholesomely jostled and buffered and sweetened by.

How dumb the old house seemed that week! I don't think Sir Adrian, Sir Guy, and Sir Fulke can be much dumber as they "lie in glory" under the chancel of Lestrange Church. Outside, the thrushes and blackbirds sang, the cocks crowed, the dogs barked, the ploughboys whistled, and I caught myself wishing earnestly that they would all come indoors, and make their pleasant noises in the hall, in the ghostly galleries, in any room or rooms they pleased, just to break the weary silence, the silence as of a house where a shrouded body lies coffined, a tenantless rigid clay image. Dolly sat through the long hours, motionless as a statue, tinted with life colours, like Vishnoo[1] contemplating his own attributes and god gifts in the shining heart of the Swerga.[2]

---

1 One of the three aspects of God, in Hinduism.
2 The Hindu underworld.

My fingers itched sometimes with a profane longing to box her ears, to upset her out of her chair, to do anything unseemly, just to shake her out of her frozen content with herself and that endless gray stocking, which was of dimensions suited to a manly leg, and yet not destined, as I knew, for our papa's wear.

"Satan finds some mischief still, for idle hands to do,"

is about the most veracious couplet ever indited by Mr. Watts of busy beeical memory.[1] Even if he leaves our hands unprovided with work of his; leaves them to hang down harmless by our sides, or folded in our laps, he makes up for his forbearance by giving our minds double tasks.

How rigidly must those early Eremites,[2] those holy men who loved their souls so much, and soap and water so little—how rigidly, I say, must they have adhered to their Lenten fare;[3] upon how few bitter herbs, upon what undiluted water must they have dieted themselves, if they did really succeed in keeping all earthly imaginings away from those lichen-curtained rock crevices where they were wont to stow their lean tormented bodies out of harm's way. To lock the door against those ideas, "earthly, sensual, devilish," that throng the portals of an empty soul, must have been even a harder job than the exclusion of the lizards, newts, and other "miscreated forms of life" that frequented those dank, agueish abodes.

My mind misgives me concerning those bearded, ragged, vermined saints, that their bald-shaven pates enclosed thoughts as naughtily mundane, and as mundanely naughty as any of their helmeted and wigged coevals; that that hair cloth (stranger to the washing tub) covered hearts that beat to as worldly a tune as any devil's jig. Man's spirit is so essentially irreligious, so honestly God-hating, that, leave it to itself for one minute, it turns its

---

1 Isaac Watts (1674-1749) was a nonconformist minister and didactic poet, perhaps best known for "Against Idleness and Mischief" (1715), which begins "How does the busy little bee / Improve each shining hour."

2 "Eremites" means "hermits"; Nell probably has in mind a particular sect of Christians who lived as hermits and practiced self-denial.

3 Lent is the period of fasting which precedes Easter; Lenten fare is thus a scant, self-denying diet.

back upon its Maker; runs away from Him swifter than a jagged lightning flash, "anywhere, anywhere."[1]

Montaigne[2] counsels an infrequent use of prayer, because, saith that chatty old heathen, man's soul is so rarely in a suitable attitude for addressing its Creator. The premises are right, though the conclusion is wrong. What do we see in the depths of our tall hats when we gaze so devoutly into them in church? When we lean back with folded arms in our corner of the family pew, while the parson is

"Bummin' awaay loike a buzzard clock ower our heads,"[3]

are we thinking of Heaven's high King, and our position relatively to him; or is not rather our fancy running riot among our pleasant sins? We call them to us, one by one; we look into their dear faces, and give them a parting hug, whilst God's messenger is giving his parting warning or promise to us. These remarks are somewhat out of place here; but they would do nicely for the backbone of a sermon when I have leisure to compose one. It may be objected by some one that the pleasant sins of an innocent-minded girl of nineteen must be few and far between; that I (such as I have described myself) could barely have had enough iniquities to meditate upon, to fill up many of those vacant hours.

Iniquities, perhaps not! sins, perhaps not, according to the lax worldly interpretations of the term; but of silly, witless, profitless conceptions and whims I had a great store. There seemed to be nothing but feeding times to look forward to that week; from breakfast to dinner, from dinner to tea, we travelled sluggishly, with no emotion livelier than what the sight of minced collops or hasty pudding was calculated to call forth.

If one of the chimneys would but catch fire; if that unsafe

---

1 "Anywhere, anywhere" may be from Thomas Hood's popular poem "Bridge of Sighs" (1843) about a woman who, having been seduced and abandoned, commits suicide by drowning herself in the Thames: She is "Mad from life's history / ... Swift to be hurled— / Anywhere, anywhere / Out of this world!"

2 French thinker and essayist, Michel Eyquem de Montaigne (1533-92).

3 See "Northern Farmer. Old Style" (1865), a poem written by Tennyson in Northern English country dialect. It is coupled with "Northern Farmer. New Style," in which a farmer admonishes his son to marry for money.

garret, where the man hanged himself in Queen Anne's days,[1] would but fall in; if even one of the dogs would but have a fit, or puppies, or anything; if *anything* would but happen! thought I. Something *must* happen before long; even if I myself had to pull the strings that set the machinery in motion. I began to have a morbid longing to do something startling, something that would break the gelid monotony of my existence. In my pretty vacant head—I can talk of its prettiness now without airs of mock modesty; now, I say, when it is as much a thing of the past as Helen's or Aspasia's[2]—I began to cast about what action at once extremely eccentric and extremely naughty I could perform.

Should I slay Dolly in some new and ingenious manner? should I practise some picturesque form of suicide? should I drown myself in the garden pool, and be found with my long red hair inextricably entangled among the duckweed? or should I choose some sequestered spot in which to "snip my carotid," and be discovered beautiful but gory, with an explanatory billet[3] in my lily hand?

I was saved from the difficulties attendant upon the selection of either of these enticing endings by the occurrence of two small incidents which diverted my plannings and imaginings into other channels. The first incident regarded the butcher; the second, Sir Hugh Lancaster and "that other." The butcher may be dismissed *paucis verbis*.[4] He came, he saw, whether he conquered or was conquered I am not very clear.

One morning I stood by the garden pool, looking down rather ruefully at the duckweed, and hoping that it would not get up my eyes and nose and ears when I should commit myself to its shining breast in despairing yet becoming self-slaughter, Dick having proved faithless, or having been killed in the wars. What wars, whether French, Kaffre, or Sikh,[5] I had not decided; there being, at the time I write of, an equally remote probability of our picking a quarrel with either of those nations. Among onion beds and cabbages, and through the well-sticked peas came Mrs. Smith in panting haste, and with woe in her eye.

---

1 She reigned from 1702 to 1714.
2 Women in Greek mythology legendary for their beauty.
3 Note (French).
4 With few words (Latin).
5 Kafirs are particular African tribes, but the term was often used indiscriminately by Britons to designate all Africans. Sikhs are a religious group originally from Northern India.

"Oh, my dear, Miss Nelly, the *butcher*!" As the war-horse is popularly supposed to snort at the trumpet blare, so snorted I at that fear-breeding name. "I've spent all the breath in my body trying to make him let it stand over till next week; them pigs oughter bring your pa in some money then; but he won't hear till it, he's in the room now (ellipse for housekeeper's room) stormin' shameful, that he is!" I picked up a stone and flopped it into the pond, making a hole in the duckweed. "I've been to Miss Dolly, and tried to get her to go down to him; she's such a rare good'un to palaver[1] folks, she is! I thought she might make somethin' of 'im, but she did not seem to care nothin' about it. She said if he threaped the roof of the 'ouse off, it wasn't none of her business." I fished for a floating piece of becka bunga[2] with a stick, coveting its small blue star flowers. "Put not your trust in princes," said I, gravely, that is, in Miss Dolly, who, if she isn't a princess, ought to be one.

"If I'd 'a known," said Mrs. Smith, expanding her fat hands to catch the pond breezes, "all I should ha' 'ad to put up with, along o' that man, I'd 'a seen him eating snails at Jericho,[3] with a two pronged fork, afore I'd 'a let 'im inside our doors; they're the independentest lot about 'ere as ever I see, *that* they are; there ain't no doin' no good with them, nohow."

I let pass, without criticism, the redundancy of negatives in my housekeeper's last clause. I was still immersed in hooking up wet lengths of water-weed.

"And what the *jouse*," (*sic*) perorated Mrs. Smith, rising into sublimity, as she stretched a drab stuff arm to Heaven. "I am to say to that ould *blaygaird*,[4] I know no more than the babe unborn."

My piscatory efforts were by this time crowned with success. I had tugged up great sprays of greenery, and now grasped them lovingly in my bare white hands, while they dripped abundantly over my dress.

"Pretty things," said I, invoking them inwardly, "are my eyes

1 Talk.
2 Veronica beckabunga, a water-plant.
3 See the story of Jericho, the famous site of a devastating massacre, in Joshua 6.
4 Nell is emphasizing her servant's manner of speaking again: "jouse" is "deuce," a common euphemism for the devil, and "blaygaird" is "blackguard," a villain.

as blue as you, I wonder? I must ask Dick." Then aloud. "*I* know what to say to him, Mrs. Smith, though you and the unborn babe don't; and what's more, I *will* say it before I'm ten minutes older." Whereupon I left the pond, and the becka bunga, and the potherbs, and ascended lightly to the upper chamber, where I kept unrevealed to Dolly, to Mrs. Smith, or other living soul, poor Dick's bank-notes. Armed with them, and with his bill, I repaired to the encounter with the "fat greasy kill-cow," as Southey[1] christens one of that fraternity. I entered the "room," as Mrs. Smith called it—the room, *par excellence*—with my head up and my nose in the air. Oh for those fine old days when the fowls of the air built their nests in Justice's disused scales, when the Sieur[2] Lestrange might take twenty lances and transfer as many fat kine as seemed good in his mind's eye from his lowborn neighbours' premises to his own.

Happy, happy days, when gentlefolks lived at ease and duns were not. So, in I stalked, with my chin superciliously elevated, and my money in my sack's mouth. There he sat, the vile *rôturier*,[3] red-faced, vituperative, with a glass of beer beside him, which Mrs. Smith had given him as a peace offering. There he sat swilling our beer (that smallest, sourest of all malt liquors), and reviling us.

"I believe you want your bill paid," I said, haughtily, while Mrs. Smith gave my gown a great jerk of dismay at my lofty deportment, from behind.

"I *rayther* believe I do, miss," responded my creditor. "I've been a wantin', and a wantin', and a wantin' it any time this last twelve munse, but it don't seem much good a wantin' hanything in this 'ouse."

I tossed down his bill, and four of my bank notes with it.

"Give me change, please," said I, superbly, "and be quick about it."

As I spoke, I think a feather might have floored the great man-mountain before me. Two round eyes, stolid, unspeculative as his own oxen's, stared ever rounder and rounder at me; he did not move hand or foot.

---

1 Poet Robert Southey (1774-1843) was a Romantic poet who became poet laureate of England.
2 Lord (French).
3 Plebian, vulgar person (French).

"Be quick, please," I said again, very imperiously, and gave a little stamp. He escaped apoplexy by a near shave that time; after all, there was the money, and that was all that was his business, "though *sewerly*[1] it was odd how them Lestranges managed to get hould on it." So he thrust a hand as big as a fillet of veal into his pocket, and counted out the change, and then, calling for a pen, scratched his receipt.

"Now," said I, with my eyes flashing in my triumph, and the Lestrange blood burning in my fair cheeks, "leave the house this instant," and I waved my hand towards the door, "and never set foot within these doors again, do you hear? Go, this minute."

He was cramming his bill and his notes into his breeches pocket; then he prepared to obey me.

"I'm a-goin', miss," said he, grinning; "don't you be a-puttin' of yourself about; and I do hope as you'll find some one as 'ull serve you satisfactory, and bring you all the best *jints*, and not expect to get a farden[2] for them neither, that I do. Good-day to you, miss."

He was a low fellow, wasn't he? but I'm not sure that he had not the best of the argument.

CHAPTER XVII

Few, indeed, were those of the families dwelling round Lestrange that had not contributed a combatant to the siege of Sir Hugh Lancaster. Lestrange itself was no exception to the general rule; we had sent forth our eldest hope, or rather she had sent herself forth to the fray, and, after a protracted campaign, had returned to us, worsted, indeed, but in good order. She had never fought in the foremost ranks, nor had she ever been amongst the leaders of the Crusades, being too wary for that; but for all that she had laid lines of circumvallation, had set up battering rams, and pointed cannon as sedulously as the noisiest, vapouringest of her rivals.

But the lines had been laid so stealthily, the battering rams brought up so quietly, and the cannon pointed so noiselessly, that when she returned discomfited, having been compelled to

---

1 Surely.
2 Joints, i.e., meat, and farthing, a coin of very small value.

raise the siege, none knew the fact, none knew that there had been a siege at all, except the besieged town itself, and one that viewed the carnage from afar, to wit, myself.

Dolly, unlike the bulk of her nation, knew when she was beaten; once thoroughly foiled, she never renewed the attack; whether by escalading, mining, or any other mode, she kept her scaling-ladders for walls more accessible; she laid up her javelins and cannon balls to hurl against iller-defended ramparts.

In Sir Hugh, I think, must have been lacking some one of the ingredients that go to compose a man; he was the sole individual of his species that ever I met with who appeared totally impervious to the beseechments of those maddening eyes that ordinarily upset the manly reason from its throne, and made the manly head giddy and staggering, as with strongest new wine. He did not appear even to see them.

Dolly was very civil to him after those days, and cooed pretty little speeches to him when they met, but she never missed an opportunity of giving a sly little stab behind his honest back, and she "hated" him with the hate of "hell."

Had Sir Hugh and Dolly been cast upon some desert island, it is my belief that each would have kept to their separate half, each have had their own banyan trees, and fountains, and caves; they might perhaps have exchanged nuts and roots, and other savage delicacies, but their intercourse would have been confined to that till some night, when the tropic moon was bathing in the plunging tropic waves, Dolly would have stolen to Sir Hugh as he slept under the feathery palm trees, and have cut his throat with a sharpened stone, or strangled him with her strong white fingers; she would then have taken off his handsome signet-ring and his hunting-watch, thinking it a pity that they should be wasted; would have buried him neatly in the shelly sand, that he might not infect the torrid air, and would then have sat down and watched "the sunrise broken into scarlet shafts,"[1] with calmly waiting eyes.

That dreary week came to an end, and still papa made no sign of any intention of returning to his leathern arm-chair, and his handsome daughters, and his duns. One morning, Dolly and I sat as usual at our *tête-à-tête*[2] breakfast; most refreshing was she

---

1 From Tennyson's poem "Enoch Arden" (1864).
2 Private, intimate (French; literally "head to head").

to look upon, as she sat there calmly eating her bread and butter, the sleep not yet quite gone out of her heavenly eyes. Her hair was all swept back, tidily and comfortably out of her way, behind those ravishing little ears, and gathered up into a delicious ingenious sort of twist behind, the mysteries of which no manly mind could pretend to fathom. Her dress, simple enough, was of some thin, cool summer stuff, of a rich, bright Forget-me-not blue, and round her dear little white throat hung a gold locket, in which lurked the photograph of the latest victim. She turned over her unopened despatches with slight leisurely fingers, and made comments on their exteriors before opening them.

"A bill," she said to the first, tossing it away. "Another from that stupid boy! what a bore! I shall have the trouble of writing to him again"; and No. 2 was passed carelessly by. "Lady Lancaster's hand, I declare!" The bread and butter is dropped, the envelope is torn open, and Dolly becomes immersed in the contents. I likewise have a letter—a letter written in a big bold hand, with a very broad-nibbed quill-pen, and about two words, or one long one, in a line. Thus it ran—

"My Darling,—My leave will be up on Friday; I have tried to get extension, and failed. They're up to the 'urgent private affair' dodge now, so go I must, I suppose. Will your father be home before then? I want very much to have a talk with him, on what subject I think you'll guess. Write to me one little line, my pretty one, and say something kind, for I'm awfully low at the thought of going.
"Your very fond
"R.H. M'Gregor."

Before opening this document, I had had a very good appetite, and had surveyed the viands with a hungry eye; now I felt that one mouthful would choke me. My hands were trembling, and my cheek flushing when Dolly's calm voice wafted these few words to my ear, "Do you wish to read this?" she held out Lady Lancaster's note, inscribed with niggling little characters, and headed with a monster monogram, in which half the letters of the alphabet twisted their legs and bent their backs against each other.

"Dear Miss Lestrange,—My son tells me that you and your sister are quite alone at Lestrange. Will you come to us to-morrow for

three days, as we have a few friends coming to us? Please excuse such a short notice, as I did not know you had returned before.
"Yours sincerely,
"A.J.K.N. LANCASTER."
"P.S.—Major M'Gregor, whom I think you know, is to be among our party."

Lady Lancaster's characters were of the crabbedest, "scribbled, crost, and crammed," "hard to mind and eye," as Merlin's charm;[1] any word might have been any other word: "friends" looked like "fiends," "house" like "louse," "quite" like "guts," and "days" like "dogs." However, I mastered the gist with great rapidity, and left the minor difficulties for after-consideration.

"Shall we go, Dolly?" asked I, and I covered my mouth with my hand, to hide the broad smiles that would come rippling, dimpling over it. *Hei mihi!*[2] What a capacity for pleasure feeling one has in one's green youth! To feel either pleasure or pain is a sign of weakness; if we could ward off things noxious, hateful to us; if we could procure at will things profitable, jocund, we should never experience either sensation, but rest in a calm, immovable nothingness.

"I joy because the quails come; would not joy
Could I bring quails at will,"[3]

or something to that effect, says Browning's Caliban. Our sources of enjoyment grow fewer, and dwindle at every fresh section of our lives.

In childhood we enjoy everything, from the devouring of uncleanly compounded lollipops upwards, everything except being washed and saying our prayers. In youth we enjoy most things; the screws and springs of our earthly machine are in such prime order; the wheels of that chariot that will drive so heavily by-and-bye, run so smoothly and glibly, that we think they must needs be running to some pleasant goal, as they are in such a hurry to get over the ground to it. In manhood we enjoy many

---

1   See "Merlin and Vivien" in *Idylls of the King* (1857), by Tennyson.
2   Ah, me! (Latin).
3   See "Caliban Upon Setebos; or, Natural Philosophy in the Island" (1864), a poem by Robert Browning.

things, though each year knocks off one or two from the shortening list; in old age we enjoy few; the wheelless, springless waggon lumbers toilfully along a rutty road, and in death—nay, in death, I know not what we do, nor what we leave undone—yea I know nothing concerning it.

My hand is on the thick black curtain, whose warp is darkness, and whose woof is grief; when next the hedges, burgeoning now, are putting forth their sprouting green, I shall have raised the curtain, and have found out what there is behind it; but, oh, my friends, I cannot come back to tell you; if I shriek with agony, if I laugh with rapture at what I find there, you will not hear me.

"Shall we go, Dolly?" said I.

"I don't know what *you'll* do, I'm sure; *I* shall go."

"There's no reason why I should not go too, is there, Dolly?" I went over and knelt down by my sister, and put up my small white face to be kissed. I was so happy that I loved everybody, even Dolly (with a spurious sort of affection it is true). Dolly stooped a reluctant pink velvet cheek towards mine; she looked upon two women's kissing one another as a misapplication of one of God's best gifts.

"No reason whatever," said she, with cold cheerfulness, "except that you have nothing but rags to go in."

I rose hastily from my knees, with my desire for osculation quite quenched.

"All the better for you," said I, a little bitterly, "I shall make a better foil than ever."

"I'm quite satisfied with you as you are," Dolly said; and with this parting shaft she withdrew.

Twelve hours more, and I am transferred from the ancient domicile where the rats and we hold a divided sway to the substantially hideous brickdust coloured pile, where Hugh Lancaster and his household gods dwelt with his mamma, well content.

Two aged coach-horses (whereof one was spavined and the other had string-halt,[1] and both were overfull of grass), yoked to our triumphal car, *i.e.*, a dilapidated yellow-bodied barouche,[2] hung high in air, in which papa and mamma had taken their wedding tour,

---

1 Both diseases of horses. Spavin causes lameness, and spring- or string-halt causes leg spasms.
2 A four-wheeled carriage with a collapsible top. The style described here was popular in the early years of the century.

bore my sister and myself to Wentworth Park. It is ten o'clock, and the brave and the fair are all assembled in the yellow drawing-room. There are a good many people, but not a great many.

The gentlemen have just torn themselves from Sir Hugh's '47 port, and are huddling, most of them, about the door, black-backed, white-throated, with the Briton's inborn grace in each of their attitudes. The ladies, in blue and pink and purple, and fine twined linen, and with many natural productions in the shape of flowers and butterflies and feathers, and beetles about their heads, are dotted about the yellow satin. The yellow satin is Lady Lancaster's very own taste; she matched it by her cheeks, and then lavished it on sofas and ottomans and chairs. It makes most people look hideous by night and jaundiced by day.

Let me give a short descriptive list of the company among whom I find my lot for the present cast: Sir Hugh, in broad-cloth and high good-humour; his mother in wrinkles and Point d'Alençon;[1] a thin viscount with a handsome wife, who bore a year of her lord's income on her fat back; a man in barnacles,[2] supposed to be a genius, because he never spoke, and had one or two nasty tricks; a puisne judge,[3] who to his acquaintance's exceeding dolour, was very much up in political economy; a tall young man, who had a bad cold; and a short one, who wore death's-head studs and made jokes; an agreeable old gentleman, who did not believe in anything particular, and had a certain proclivity towards *double entendres*;[4] a young lady, with sharp shoulder blades, and another with a sharp tongue; a widow with a great many bugles[5] about her, who rather relished the agreeable old gentleman's innuendoes; a big fair man of the name of M'Gregor, and two artless virgins of the name of Lestrange. The judge has got the cheerful old sceptic into a corner, and is inflicting a new form of the question[6] on him.

"We must ameliorate the condition of the rural poor, my dear

---

1 A kind of lace.
2 Glasses.
3 Judge of the common law courts.
4 Statements that can be understood to have a double meaning; often one of the meanings is indelicate or socially inappropriate in a sexual way.
5 A kind of bead.
6 Interrogation by torture, an ancient practice discontinued long before the time of the novel as barbaric.

sir, that's what we must do," he is saying, very confidentially, as if he was telling some pleasant secret. "We must set sanitary reforms[1] on foot throughout the country; that's what I've always been saying. I can tell you" (lowering his voice) "that the utter neglect of sewage in many of the agricultural districts would surprise you, it would indeed."

"Yes, yes, I dare say, no doubt," replies the unhappy heathen uneasily, edging away from his captor, and looking as if he did not much care whether there was one sewer throughout the length and breadth of Britain or no. He has got a succulent anecdote which he is panting to pour into the widow's rosy ears.

"I bet a dabesake of yours the other day," quoth the man with the catarrh to the man with the skulls, "he was a cordet in the dideth; they had some dickdabe for hib; the *Dose*, I think it was."

"The *what*?"

"The *dose*, because he had such a big dose, you dow," touching his own afflicted feature, explanatorily.

"What a cold that poor man has got!" says the viscountess, with fat compassion.

"Does not he wish he was in bed, poor wretch?" says the sharp young lady, pertly. The shoulder-blades agitates her fan softly, and sighs behind it.

"Aren't you tired of standing?" breathes Dolly, low as the south wind when it blows the down from the clematis, to a large and stately person who is leaning over her.

"Is that a hint for me to go?" responds the large person, making no movement, however, towards so doing.

My sister says, "Oh, no!" semi-audibly, and the thick white lids sweep down over the modest eyes. Dolly is sitting on a prie-dieu,[2] right under the big, hundred lighted chandelier, and the waxlights are blazing down full on her shimmery sheeny garments, on her round, pearl-white shoulders, and on the coral lengths that go twisting in and out of her blue black hair. Dolly is doing no harm at all, none whatever; only she is looking up under her eyes in a way I know, a way I cannot do myself, and that I hate.

Dick rests his arms on the back of the prie-dieu, which is diverted from its original use this evening; he looks very handsome

---

1 Sanitary reform—the disposal of sewage and supply of clean
   water—was one of the great political questions of the day.
2 A low padded stool, originally used to kneel on for prayer.

and a good deal out of sorts; his yellow moustache droops close to her ear, as he talks low and rapidly to her, occasionally looking up to scowl at me.

For myself, I am in a position which I would willingly cede to any one else in the room, should they propose an exchange. I am seated on a sofa (yellow of course), by Sir Hugh, and we have a picture book on our laps (half on mine and half on his), and he *will* keep his head very close to mine, pull away as I will; and the consequence is, we have, to a casual observer, a very lover-like and *flirtatious* air.

Over against me is a big mirror, in it I catch occasional glimpses of myself. I see a little head "brow-bound" with the "burning gold"[1] of its own ruddy locks. I see great blue eyes that look childish and troubled, and about to cry, and I see a good sized but withal pretty mouth quivering distressedly. We are looking at prints from Landseer.[2]

"Jolly kind of dog that," says Sir Hugh, "ain't it? had one just like it myself once, only mine had more tan about the muzzle; best sporting dog I ever had. Came to awful grief, poor brute, though, got caught in a trap and had to be shot. I never was so cut up about anything, I don't think."

"Perhaps so," I murmur, with utter irrelevancy.

"Perhaps what?" cries Sir Hugh at sea.

"Did I say perhaps anything—oh, so I did. I—I don't think I quite understood what you were saying." Truth to tell, I am straining my ears to catch Dolly's remarks. My ears do not look very long ones, but they are long of hearing.

"Does not Nelly look nice to-night?" She was sighing in her honeyed way. "What would not one give for that freshness of sensation? We old people have *effleuré*[3] all our pleasures, haven't we?"

Dick's answer is addressed to the back of her head, so I lose it.

"Half child and half woman? Ye—es, I think so, combining the amusements of both ages too, isn't she, lover and picture-book."

---

1 See "A Dream of Fair Women" (1833), a poem by Tennyson.
2 Sir Edward Henry Landseer (1802-73) was an artist particularly known for his pictures of animals.
3 Grazed, abraded (French), here meaning, already experienced, having become jaded.

Dick bit his golden moustache, and his gray eyes flashed angrily.

"She must be mighty easy pleased, if Lancaster's conversation can afford her *amusement*."

"Oh, I don't know; she is young, and—well, perhaps—but indeed, Major M'Gregor, I think that facility of being pleased and attracted, is a very enviable possession. If one had it, one would never feel lonely in society, as one sometimes does now, doesn't one?"

One swift satanic shot from the dark, passionate sympathy-craving eyes; a shot that reached his senses, I think, though it missed his heart.

"Do you sig, Biss Seybour?" asks the cold in the head of the shoulder-blades.

"Sometimes—to intimate friends—now and then; do you?"

"Do; but I'be very fod of it. Do you dow a sog called 'Baggie's Secret?'" Miss Seymour bites her fan in perplexity.

"'Baggie's Secret?' No-o, I think not; who's it by? Oh, '*Maggie's* Secret,'[1] to be sure; how stupid of me!"

Miss Seymour does know it, loves it, and will sing it if he wishes. My Hugh and I have reached the last of our dog portraits.

"H'm! come to an end, have they?" says Hugh, trying to split the last leaf in two with his broad thumb. "Never mind, there's lots more, somewhere."

He rises to seek more pabulum[2] for my mind and eyes, and I stretched out an eagerly detaining hand.

"Oh, *please*, won't it do another time? I think I've seen almost enough pictures. I'm—I'm a little tired."

The worthy baronet regarded me with surprise plainly written on his broad brown face.

"Tired! nonsense! are you? Have some sherry and soda? Mother, here's Miss Lestrange so knocked up she can hardly move; what are we to do with her?"

Lady Lancaster and the Point d'Alençon happily do not hear; are rather hard of hearing indeed.

"Oh, don't, don't please! it's nothing, only the room is a little hot; isn't it?" cry I panting.

---

1 Tamar Heller identifies this as a popular song by Charlotte Alington Pye Barnard (1830-69).
2 Bland cereal used to feed babies, by extension, bland or undemanding intellectual nourishment.

"Ah, yes; so it is, now you mention it; quite like an oven; I never can get mother to have the windows open; come into the next room, it's much cooler there, and we shall have it all to ourselves."

What an inducement! thought I. The waxlights blaze steadily oppressive; the singing girl's voice comes harshly to my ear; the yellow satin glare tires my aching eyes, and across blaze and glare I see a Greek face, a very cross Greek face, scowling prohibition at me. Oh, why is he scowling at me? what have I done? what can I do? "We shall have it all to ourselves," repeats honest Sir Hugh, with his jolly voice not a note lowered. The heathen escaped from his corner, is getting to the point of his spiced tale; its cayenne is tickling the widow's palate; she is chuckling behind her black-edged pocket-handkerchief. The air is faint with patchouli and ess bouquet,[1] and heavy scented gardenias.

I feel a hysterical lump rising in my throat, and the angry Greek face is clouding before my eyes. I am going to cry! I am going to make a scene! I am going to make a beast of myself! I rise hastily, and upsetting a light cane chair, and two Chinese gods in my passage, pass hurriedly down the room, through the folding doors into the cool empty saloon beyond, while Hugh, sore amazed at my indecent haste, follows hard upon my heels. Dolly's voice, pseudo compassionate, pseudo motherly, pursuing, stings me. "Poor Nell! that *empressé*[2] manner is very pretty, isn't it?"

CHAPTER XVIII

"Live as long as you may," says Southey,[3] "the first twenty years are the longest half of your life." It is a reflection so trite as to be made by every living soul capable of that mental process ycleped[4] thought, that one of childhood's days is equal in duration to five or six of man or womanhood's; that one of childhood's years is a sæculum, a mighty æon, whereof the beginning is distanter from

---

1 A perfume, made with essences, often used to scent handkerchiefs.
2 Zealous, eager (French).
3 Poet Robert Southey (1774-1843) was a Romantic poet who became poet laureate of England.
4 Called or named (archaic English).

the ending than are the Tudor days from ours. Was the case the same, I marvel, with those giants in age that flourished and withered before the Flood?

Those unfortunates, on whom was inflicted the penance of a thousand years of labour and sorrow, did their earlier days spread and stretch themselves in the same disproportionate fashion? Did they grow to maturity, I wonder, as soon as we do? Were they full grown at twenty, middle-aged at fifty, and were their remaining eight or nine hundred winters devoted to old age? Oh, monstrous notion! A land peopled with dotards! a world full of gray heads and gouty feet,[1] and age-palsied intellects. The alternative, though more probable, is *assez drôle*,[2] in its necessary and legitimate consequences.

At a hundred years old, those ill-starred ones were still spinning tops and dressing dolls, if antediluvian dolls there were; at two or three hundred, they were making love, and getting into those scrapes to which hotheaded youth is liable; at five hundred they were thinking of settling down to the serious business of their lives. Were the memories of those ancients strengthened in proportion to the length of time they had to be exercised upon?

Did they remember in their eighth or ninth century, what they said and did in their first and second, or were they in their later days oblivious of the actions and passions of their youth? Could a man in King George's reign have any very distinct recollection of what he was thinking about in King Alfred's?[3]

"I know not; what avails to know."[4]

I have heard it affirmed by sane people and have read in divers books that breakfast forms the cheerfullest, sociallest réunion of English home life. Whosoever stated that fact, whosoever wrote it, I take upon myself to deny it. *Tout au contraire*,[5] that interest-

---

1 Gout is an acute inflammation of the joints, often of the toes or ankle. It is often associated with the intake of rich food and alcohol and is more frequent in the elderly.
2 Rather funny (French).
3 King George V (the latest George at the time of the novel) ruled from 1820 to 1830. King Alfred reigned from 871 to 899.
4 See "The Questioning Spirit" (1847), a poem by Arthur Hugh Clough (1819-61).
5 Quite the contrary (French).

ing animal, man, so curious in many of his habits, is at that hour at his worst. A remnant of sleepiness, unknown to themselves, clings to most people; they have not warmed to their day's work. If the new organizing of society were intrusted to me, I should make it as indecorous to breakfast in public, as it is now considered to perform one's ablutions in the presence of that vague personage the world.

Whether social or not, breakfast is over at Wentworth; much kippered salmon and cold tongue have been consumed, and a little slack conversation has been kept up. Dolly, knowing that there is a time for all things, has molested no man with her eyes, has contented herself, at least, with two or three quite trifling glances at Dick, whom Fate has deposited at her side. Breakfast then is over, has been over an hour or more, and most of the tenants of that red brick Elysium, Wentworth Park, are standing and sitting about the hall, pulling on gloves, reading the *Times*, and settling disputed claims to pot hats.[1]

Before the door, out in the spring sunshine, stand many horses, *malely* and femalely saddled;[2] likewise a double dogcart[3] with a pair of light-hearted chestnuts. Most of the ladies are in riding habits; the widow among the number, and very like an overripe gooseberry she looks. I am unclad in riding gear; I have never bestridden (or the feminine equivalent for bestridden) anything nobler than a jackass; never shall possibly. It is evident we are all on the verge of some expedition. Most of us, it is true, would rather stay at home; to many of us indeed a pic-nic is verily and indeed the accursed thing.

Two or three of the men are yearning to throw a fly in the trout stream, that goes purling, twisting, flashing through Sir Hugh's fat meadows—

"Thro' the meads where melick groweth."[4]

---

1 Bowler style hat with a low round crown.
2 Women used sidesaddles.
3 A dogcart was a two-wheeled vehicle with a ventilated box under the seat for hunting dogs. A regular dogcart normally held two people; a double dogcart would be a larger, more luxurious version. The main point here seems to be that it is an open, rather than a closed carriage.
4 See "The High Tide on the Coast of Lincolnshire" (1863), a poem by Jean Ingelow (1820-97).

Two or three more would far fainer be a peppering of rooks, and a ratting with pink-eyed terriers than squiring of dames along a dusty road. No matter! The trout, speckled, pink-fleshed, silvery, may, jumping, gulp down live flies in peace to-day. No fictitious fly framed of delicatest feather and finest silk, will this day beguile them.

We are to be amused, all of us, *nolentes, volentes*,[1] not in our own way but in Lady Lancaster's. I am among the very few *volentes*. I am not looking my best this morning, having been crying most of the night, and there is a red rim round each eye; but of red rims, red noses, and haggard cheeks, I am careless, for I am sitting on the topmost one of the flight of stone steps that lead up to the hall door.

Dick is stretching his long length, like a big Newfoundland, one step below me; he is looking at the chestnuts, and smiling and saying:—"Won't we put them along at a tidy pace, Nell? We'll take the shine out of them?"

By one brilliant *coup*,[2] I have retrieved last night's disasters; at least I think so.

Five minutes back, Dick was leaning against the door post, looking glummer than glum. Nobody was nigh save me. Dolly was up stairs, Sir Hugh was rating[3] one of his grooms. What an opportunity for prompt action! I go up and put my hand on his arm. "Dick," said I (I had never called him Dick before), "Well?" (very glum), "What have I done? why are you angry with me?"

"I am not angry," (with averted head, but slightly thawed intonation).

"If you're not angry, do drive me in the dogcart to-day, instead of riding; you know I cannot ride; *do, dear* Dick!"

As I make this indecently forward proposal, my voice shakes, and my heart thumps like a steam ram. Dick's head veers round like a weathercock in a high wind.

"Won't I just? if I have the chance; what a little darling you are! but you see the cart is Lancaster's—not mine, and perhaps—"

Sir Hugh coming up, interrupts him.

"You're for riding, I suppose, ain't you, M'Gregor? Carriage exercise isn't much in your line; at least it used not to be, and there's the roan all ready for you."

---

1 Whether not willing or willing, respectively (Latin).
2 Stroke, blow (French).
3 Scolding (slang).

"Oh, thanks, old fellow," responds M'Gregor, "but if you don't mind, I've rather a fancy for tooling these chestnuts along. I don't seem to care much about peacocking along the king's highroad."

Sir Hugh's countenance falls.

"All right," says he (his face says "all wrong"), "just as you like, only you'd better keep an eye on that off mare; she is the very devil to pull when there's anything behind her; don't blame me, Miss Lestrange, if you find her flourishing her heels in your face."

Dolly standing near, overheard. She was holding her habit up delicately with one hand, and slashing a small Balmoral boot[1] with her whip.

"Had not you better get your cloak, Nell?" she suggested, "we may be late coming home."

"Perhaps I had," said I, and upstairs I ran, two steps at a time. Dolly followed me, made a remark or two upon my dress, and upon no other subject, and then went down again. I was a long time finding my cloak; having discovered it at last in the depths of a trunk, I redescended to the hall. Dolly is gone; the riders all are gone, but the dog-cart is still there; Sir Hugh is still there, and Richard is not there! I stare blankly.

"Why I thought Major M'Gregor was to drive me?"

Sir Hugh's mirth runs over in laughing eyes and a broad grin.

"Yes, so he was, but your sister made it all right; awfully jolly of her, wasn't it?"

"How—how do you mean?" I gasped.

"Why she told him you were rather nervous about horses, and that you funked[2] rather at what I said about the mare; that was all my eye, you know. She's as quiet as an old cow."

"Well, go on," said I, digging my teeth into my under lip.

"Well, he stuck to it like a man for a long time, till at last she had to tell him—jolly girl she is—that you had hinted to her— she said you did not like to speak out—that you'd rather have me for a Jehu;[3] he gave in, then, in a minute, like a sensible fellow. Come, hadn't we better be starting! Mind the wheel?"

---

1 Laced-up ankle boot popularized in the 1860s for outdoor activities.
2 To be frightened.
3 See the story of Jehu, the tenth king of Israel famous for his fast and reckless chariot-driving during the battle in which he took the throne, in II Kings 9.

My heart, like Nabal's,[1] turns to stone within me. I get in mechanically.

"Give her her head," shouts Sir Hugh to the groom, and off we go. The chestnuts are a showy, high-actioned pair, and step well together; full of oats, are they? swiftly do they bear us along.

> "We by parks and lodges going,
> See the lordly castles stand;
> Summer woods about us blowing
> Made a murmur in the land."[2]

Only we did not see any "lordly castles," because there were not any such on the Lancaster estate. Instead we passed by many a substantial farm and homestead, with barns and stacks, and trim out-buildings, that told of a good and well-to-do landlord. Hugh points out his possessions with complacency as we bowl past them.

"D'ye see that copse over there, with the lot of scrubby brushwood there, down in the hollow?"

"Yes."

"Well, that's the very best cover in the county;[3] always find there; never missed once last season."

"Oh."

I am determinedly sulky, and register an inward vow that no sentence longer than a monosyllable shall be extracted from me. The hedges are white with hawthorn; on the orchards the rosy snow of the apple blooms lies thick, the blackbirds are singing, and Sir Hugh's heart is merry within him.

"Nice little box that, isn't it?" says he presently, indicating with his whip a snug cottage, buried in cherry trees and laburnums. "My governor built it for an old bailiff of his. I've got a lot of greyhounds there now for coursing."[4]

No comment whatever.

---

1 See I Samuel 25. The unpleasant rich man Nabal unwisely refuses David, who will later become king, goods that he asks for, insulting him. David plans to kill all Nabal's men. Nabal's wife Abigail heads off the disaster by giving David goods, prophesying that he will be a great ruler and promising to become David's wife. When Nabal hears this, his heart becomes like a stone. Ten days later the Lord smites him and he dies.
2 See "The Lord of Burleigh" (1842), a poem by Tennyson.
3 The best place to hunt foxes; Sir Hugh never fails to find a fox there.
4 Racing.

"Do you like coursing?"

"No."

Our destination is a certain show place, fourteen or fifteen miles from Wentworth, a place that appertains to a certain earl, who has so many houses, show and not show, that he is quite puzzled to know which to live in. The equestrians reach the bourne to which all we travellers are hastening[1] sooner than my Hugh and I do; they are able to take advantage of bridle paths and wood paths and narrow lanes, in which, if we attempted to traverse them, we and our four-wheeled vehicle should stick. So our delicious *tête-à-tête* has lasted an hour and three-quarters ere we reach the great wrought iron gates that give ingress to Wilton Towers, and roll through the park among the oak-clumps and the fallow deer and the thick deep bracken. The place of rendezvous is by the side of a mere,[2] much affected by coots and wild ducks and Canada geese—a piece of water more remarkable for extent than beauty.

Here we find our associates mooning and loafing about, like unburied spirits on the hither side of Styx;[3] heavy and displeased are most of them. Of such a *fête*[4] as the present one, the eating part, the fleshpots and flagons form the marrow, the pith, the kernel; hitherto these ladies and gentleman have been put off with husks and rind; and very cross it makes them. We pull up under a spreading horse-chestnut which is tossing its white spikes in the sunny breeze.

"Stop a bit," says Sir Hugh, throwing the reins to the groom, "don't be in a hurry; I'll lift you down."

My sole response is to hurl myself to earth. The velocity of my spring precipitates me to the ground, and of me, it may truly be said, in the words of the poet—

"Humpty Dumpty had a great fall."[5]

Half a dozen men rush to pick me up; but I am beforehand with them, and rise to my feet with two great green patches on my

---

1 Compare Shakespeare's play, *Hamlet*, printed in quarto in 1603.
2 A swamp.
3 In Greek mythology, the river that separates the underworld and the land of the living.
4 Feast, party (French).
5 From a nursery rhyme.

dress, where my knees have saluted mother earth. When things come to their worst they always mend, which is not to be wondered at much, considering that there cannot be a *worser* than worst.

The only thing is, it is so difficult to know in this world when our fortunes have reached their nadir; there are so few depths that have not a yet deeper deep beneath them—heat and horse-flies, and midges, and the headachy snappishness which is the result of heat, formed the lowest abyss to which poor humanity in our persons was called upon to descend to-day. Half an hour after my *culbute*,[1] life, I think, wore a cheerfuller aspect in the eyes of most of that roasted assemblage; Wilton Towers seemed a desirabler demesne, and even the twelve miles ride home a more bearable prospect.

At the expiration of that wonder-working thirty minutes (the two grooms being the *Dei ex machina*),[2] a white tablecloth lies like an exaggerated snow-flake, beneath an oak-tree, big enough to have sheltered a dozen blackguard King Charleses in his great leafy heart.[3] Spoons and forks flash in the sunshine that filters through his thick green cloak, tall sloping-shouldered bottles cool themselves in the mere; there is a scent of mint sauce on the breeze, and the young acorns, looking down out of their cups, see beneath them baked meats, frequent as those which adorned the obsequies of Hamlet,[4] King of Denmark, and yet were enough (they must have been a little stale, mustn't they?) to "coldly furnish forth" his widow's marriage banquet. Pasties were there,

"Costly made,
Where quail and pigeon, lark and leveret lay
Like fossils of the rock, with golden yolks,
Imbedded and injellied."[5]

---

1 Fall (French).
2 Plural of "deus ex machina," or "god from the machine" (Greek). In Greek and Latin drama, often an actor representing a god would be lowered onto the stage by means of a machine. This would typically occur at a moment of crisis or insoluble difficulty which would then be resolved by the god by supernatural means.
3 King Charles II eluded the troops of Cromwell in 1651 by hiding in an oak tree.
4 Play of the same name by Shakespeare, first printed in quarto in 1603. The character referred to here is not the protagonist, but his murdered father.
5 See "Audley Court (1842), a poem by Tennyson.

Juicy chickens, and juicier lamb, lobsters lurking redly in crisp lettuces, and pastry enough to furnish a cook shop.

Oude ti Qumos edeueto daitos eases[1]

Round these cates[2] we sit *accroupis*,[3] on the short fine grass, and feast to the sound of "the long ripple washing in the reeds."

"Capital Sauterne,[4] this!" cries the disbelieving old bachelor, holding up his glass to the light, to see the foam bead sparkle diamond-like. "I wonder where Lancaster gets it; I've tried half a dozen places, and never could get hold of anything decent."

"It *is* nice," owns the widow, sipping.

"By-the-bye, *apropos* of Sauterne, did I ever tell you of a *bon mot*[5] of Lord ——, the late man, you know, not the present?"

He travels a little nearer to the bereaved one, along the turf, and his wicked old eye twinkles (he has not had the heart to unpack any of his little anecdotic wares, for her benefit, hitherto).

"No, I think not; tell me now, *do*."

"I'm almost afraid, but it really is too good to be lost."

His voice sinks to a *susurrus*, a *chuchottement*, either of which words is more onomatopoeic than whisper. The widow lends him her ears, and I see them reddening under the combined influence of the Sauterne and the *bon mot*, which was, I think, a very *mauvais mot*.[6]

"Nice little cob of yours, Lancaster—that black one," says the lean lord; "easy as an arm-chair. Do you ever hunt him?"

"No," says Hugh; "he's hardly up to my weight, particularly over a stiff country like this; he'd be just the thing for you, and he's A1 at timber."

---

1 Greek in Latin characters, from Homer's epic, *The Iliad*, Canto I, line 468: "they feasted, nor was any man's hunger denied a fair portion." The full quotation in the serial version was *Oude ti thumos edensto daitos eases* (Ουδε τι θυμος εδευετο δαιτος εισες). The book version corrected edensto to edeueto, but introduced other errors; "qumos" should indeed be "thumos," for example.
2 Food, especially luxurious delicacies.
3 Squatting (French).
4 A white wine.
5 Witty remark (French).
6 Bad or improper saying (French).

(All the Lancastrian geese are swans.[1])

"Is there any *bustard*?" asks the youth with the influenza.

"Biss Seybour wadts sobe bustard; Atcha! Atcha!"

"Bless you," murmurs Miss Seymour, under her breath. The benediction being called forth by the sneeze, not the demand for mustard. I, of course, am next to my host; I always am; people begin to leave that coveted post vacant for me; I made a feeble effort to shirk it at the beginning of the entertainment, but was foiled. Hugh is drinking bottled beer, and making brilliant remarks, and sharing his *petits soins*[2] pretty equally between the silent dove beside him, and the not more silent doves in a pie before him. Dick M'Gregor and Dolly Lestrange seemed to have hardly more appetite for their luncheon than I had; they could not well have had less.

Flirting is, in one respect, like wit; it has never been satisfactorily defined; it is less fortunate than wit; in that it has not yet found a Bishop Barrow[3] to expend pages of gorgeous eloquence in describing it; no object, they say, looks exactly the same in two pair of eyes, nor are any two people's notions on the subject of flirting precisely alike.

Dick and Dolly, however, fulfilled all the conditions required by all the different ideas of all the different people then present, on this vexed theme. Firstly, they seemed to have a very great deal to say to each other; secondly, they did not seem to have anything whatever to say to any one else; and thirdly, what they had to say to one another, they appeared compelled to say in a stealthy and secretive manner. Dick's face was troubled "as if with anger or pain,"[4] as he lay reclined, like a young river god, among the yellow irises by the rushy margin of the lake. His hat was off, and the sun was busy weaving an aureole like a saint's round his curly head. Poor fellow! there was not much of saintly repose, and there was a great deal of earth's unquiet passion in that honest angry face.

I never knew any woman who could compare with Dolly Lestrange in the art of drawing out and waking into rampant

---

1 To say that all someone's geese are swans is to suggest that he or she esteems her friends or belongings more than they deserve (the person thinks all his or her geese are swans).

2 Little attentions (French).

3 Isaac Barrow (1630-77) was a mathematician, theologian, and classicist noted for his eloquent prose.

4 See "The Grandmother" (1859), a poem by Tennyson.

life any spice of the devil which might be lurking latent in a man's soul. She was waking Dick's devil now; I saw her—saw the evil spirit gradually shaking off its sleep, and coming with a lurid light into those eyes that had looked before only vexed, and pained, and thwarted.

Dolly was not a fine woman,[1] as they say, at all; not *beef to the heels*, by any means; in a grazier's eye, she would have had no charm whatsoever. She looked very girlish and simple now as she sat on the grass, leaning on one slight arm, her slender figure looking slenderer than its wont even, in her dark tight-fitting habit, out of which her throat rose, like a lily stem from its sheath.

"Les yeux noirs
Vont au purgatoire,"[2]

you know she is saying, in her low tender voice; "poor black eyes! that's treating them very badly, isn't it?"

"Your eyes are not black,—brown surely?" says he, with interest.

"No, black, I think—aren't they?"

She raises them full of innocent wondering inquiry, and fixes them on his; rests them there unabashed; neither speak for a minute; then Dolly, in a half whisper—

"The moon will be up as we go home to-night, won't it? we shall see it in that pretty brook we came down by, shan't we? but, perhaps—oh, I forgot——"

She stops, as though in confusion.

"Forgot what?" he asks eagerly.

"I forgot that I mightn't—mightn't be riding with—*you*, might—be riding with somebody else; and then I thought——"

"Thought what?"

He bends closer to catch a glimpse of the down-drooped head.

"Oh, nothing—nothing; it was only that—that I thought I should not care much about the brook, or the moonlight, or anything else—*then*."

---

1 "A fine woman" was a phrase used to refer to women who were attractively large.
2 Black eyes go to purgatory (French). From an old saying: "blue eyes go to heaven, gray to paradise, green to hell and black to purgatory."

The great velvet orbs passionate, passion rousing seek his again; seem unable to tear themselves away. What man can stand it? Dick cannot. I see the broad low brow flushing. I see his eyes *answering* hers; speaking that mysterious thrilling fire-language that surely the devil invented.

"Why should not we ride home together?" he says, softly.

She plays with the wide-open iris flowers, with the stiff, wet iris stems that lie in her lap.

"You might have got tired of me, mightn't you? is that *quite* an impossible hypothesis? Do men never tire of women? I think I've read somewhere that they *have* done such a thing before now."

"Never of *some* women; wasn't it of a woman that it was said—

"'Age cannot wither her, nor custom stale
Her infinite variety?'"[1]

She shakes her head with pretty incredulity. "Cleopatra was Cleopatra; if her case had not been a unique one, her story would not have come down to us; we cannot all, or indeed any of us, expect to have her luck." She sighs, and I see under the dark blue cloth of her bodice, her heart fluttering.

"You live on air, Miss Lestrange," sounds Sir Hugh's deep voice, as he regards me remonstratingly,

"With his heart full of love
And his mouth full of pie."[2]

"No, I don't," I respond snappishly, like a little yelping cur, with his tail between his legs, snapping at a big dog's nose, "pickled salmon is not air that I'm aware of." The fact is, I have got some pickled salmon on my plate, and am sorely bested to know how to dispose of it, for swallow it, most surely can I not; I could as soon swallow Hugh. I should like to hurl it, and the platter that contains it, and any other crockery within reach, at Dolly's sleek shapely head; but that may not be. Unguessing of the storm in a tea-cup beside him, in a state of blissful unconsciousness,

---

1 See Shakespeare's *Antony and Cleopatra* (first printed 1623).
2 See "The Witches Frolic" (1840), a comic poem by "Thomas Ingoldsby," pseud. for Richard Barham (1788-1845).

Hugh takes up the thread of his discourse, begins a new thread rather, for—dear fellow—he is a little discursive.

"We shall have to *do* the house just now, I suppose; walk through a mile and a half of execrable pictures; I will say that for Lord Stencliffe, he has got more vile daubs and bad copies together than any other man in England."

(Oh for that cut glass decanter to aim at the bridge of Dolly's nose! oh to make those black eyes black eyes indeed!)

"H'm! has he?"

"I wonder why one ever comes to see these sort of places. I never heard any one say they liked it—did you? it's an awful bore, isn't it?"

"Yes, it is; most things *are* awful bores in this world, I think—and people too!"

Sir Hugh laughs lazily; champagne and sunshine, and a heavy luncheon will induce a certain blandness of manner and indisposition to take offence; he laughs as one laughs at a parrot swearing, or at the rage of anything equally impotent.

"Ha, ha! most people means *me*, I suppose; why are you always so down upon me, I wonder?" I gaze straight before me into space, and feign deafness.

"Never mind!" he says, good humouredly. "I've a pretty tough hide, and I'd rather be pitched into by *you* than kissed by anybody else!"

Hugh never thought it necessary to lower his voice when he said anything tender. The expression "love whisper" never could be applied to his amatory commonplaces; love-shout or love-bellow would be more applicable; any one that chose to listen might hear; he was not saying anything he was ashamed of. Dick does hear, and draws his smooth brows together into a frown. Dolly does hear, and says, with a pretty, playful, dimpling smile—

"Lovers' quarrels! Poor little girl! I hope he is not trifling with her!"

The poor little girl, listening, winds her pocket-handkerchief tight round her fingers, till it is converted into a ropy, stringy rag, and then bites a piece out of it. *Fête champêtre*[1] has a pleasant sound, but I think the sound is pleasanter than the reality. I think, in sober earnest and in literal truth, it is sweeter far to have one's legs beneath the friendly mahogany, where lively

---

1 Country feast.

grasshoppers cannot get up them; in a cool dining-room, where one enjoys immunity from phlebotomizing gnats and midges.[1]

The Wilton flies and gnats drew much human blood that day, but we bore our being "let blood" meekly; it was part of our appointed torture. Meekly also we bore the house, and the Dutch Madonnas, and the Lelyan and Knellerian portraits,[2] and the lying anecdotic biographies tacked on to each by that obesest of housekeepers; meekly also the chapel, with the place where the family sat, the place where the ladies' maids sat, the place where the footmen sat; meekly also the gaudy new window to Lady Grace's memory, where a very big blue St. Peter, and a rather big red St. John, and a green impotent man, stood huddled together in close proximity, with a gate anything but "beautiful," picked out in yellow in the background. Everywhere Hugh followed me like St. Nicholas's pig.[3]

CHAPTER XIX

"Time is but a parenthesis in eternity,"[4] as somebody (I always forget the sayers of grand things) grandly says; if so, what must each of our lives be? A parenthesis in a parenthesis, and a very short parenthesis too. Our life is but as a very little boat tossed on the sea of infinity; it is a small breathing space between the tussle with life at the beginning and the tussle with death at the ending. Poor little lives! What immeasurable self pity fills one, when one thinks of our poor little farthing rush-lights, that often before they are half burnt, great Death blows out. And yet all our reflections and lamentations and moralizations on the brevity of our abiding here, does not do anything towards making one dull minute seem shorter, or greasing the wheels of one tedious hour.

---

1 A phlebotomist draws blood, usually for medical testing.
2 Dutch painting was widely collected in the sixteenth and seventeenth centuries. Sir Peter Lely (1618-80) was a famous Dutch portraitist. Sir Godfrey Kneller (1646-1723) was German born but Dutch trained, and was court painter to English royalty during the reigns of four sovereigns.
3 Nell may be thinking of St. Anthony (of Egypt), often pictured with a pig.
4 Misquoted from *Christian Morals* (1716), by Sir Thomas Browne.

Did the assured knowledge that my existence was but an imperceptible speck in the fields of space make that long long road between Wilton Towers and Wentworth Park seem a quarter of a mile shorter that night? Not it. Endless appeared to me the lengths of moony turnpike, the wood-shaded windings and twistings among Lord Stencliffe's great quiet oaks and beeches.

Whether it was all love and no champagne, or all champagne and no love, or half love and half champagne, or three quarters love and one quarter champagne, or one quarter love and three quarters champagne, I cannot say; but certain it is that Hugh became inconveniently tender—tender in the moonlight, tenderer far in the shade. I, in my own mind, ascribed an undue preponderance to the champagne element, and suffered agonies of apprehension lest the grooms behind should overhear his amorous platitudes.

"Jolly and big the moon looks, doesn't it? like a Cheshire cheese!" The moon, the sacred moon, the be-songed, be-sonneted moon, the moon that Romeo sware by, and that Milton saw

"Stooping thro' a fleecy cloud"[1]

like a Cheshire cheese!

"How poetical," I said, sardonically.

"No, it isn't poetical, I know. I'm not up to the dodge of poetry. I don't go in for those kind of things. I would though, if it would make you like me any better."

Cupid and the vintage of Epernai[2] have infused a certain sentimentality into the dark middle-aged eyes that contemplate me.

"How soon shall we be home?" I ask, abruptly, looking at him discomfortably, and thinking how plain the crow's feet come out in the moonlight.

"Home! Why we've hardly set out yet. We haven't got to the fourth milestone by Thorny Hill, you know!"

"*Haven't* we?"

---

1 See "Il Penseroso," meaning "The Thinker," (1645) a poem by John Milton.
2 Cupid is another name for Eros, god of love. The vintage of Epernai is champagne (Epernai is in the province of Champagne, France).

"What are you in such a hurry to get home for! I feel as if I should not mind going spinning along here for ever behind such tidy cattle and with *you* beside me!"

As he speaks we reach a toll-gate, and the sleepy toll-keeper descends in a slight and sketchy attire, suitable for the wooing of Morpheus,[1] opens the gate for us, and shuts it again behind us. We are coming to a part of the road which runs parallel to the railway for a quarter of a mile. Rather a dangerous bit of road, for this reason, there is but a narrow strip of field intervening between it and the line; and people with fidgety horses have found before now the disadvantage of such close proximity to a possible locomotive, at full speed.

We are going along at a spanking trot through the dumb May night; there is not a sound but what we make ourselves. Suddenly the sharp shriek of an engine, as it issues from the tunnel through the Marston Hill at our backs, cuts the stillness.

"Hang it!" says Hugh, "there's a train coming. I hope to God they won't bolt!"

I turn my head, and see the great dim bulk, with the red lamps at the buffers like glaring eyes, devouring space a hundred yards behind us. Then it comes roaring, puffing, thundering by. For a second the chestnuts stop and stand motionless, shivering with terror; then quick as thought, as lightning, they wheel right round. Snap goes the pole, and off we go, tearing down the road we have just come along. The broken pole swings to and fro, kicking and banging against their legs, goading them to madness; thud, thud, come the off mare's heels against the splash-board.

"*Damn*," says Hugh, under his breath. "Sit still, Nell!"

No need to give me that injunction. I could not budge an inch if I was to be shot for it. Stock still I sit there, clutching the side of the dogcart with one hand. The elm tree boles flash by, white in the moonlight; past race the dim harebell carpets beneath them; past rush the hawthorn-crowned hedges. We are nearing the toll-gate.

"By G——," says Hugh, hoarsely, "the gate's shut!"

I see him setting his teeth; he plants his feet against the splash-board, and pulls with all the force of his strong wrists. I see the veins rise in knotted cords on his hands, in the intensity of his

---

1 Greek god of sleep.

exertions. To no purpose; there is no perceptible diminution of their mad speed! With heads down and mouths like iron, on they rush; in two minutes we shall be crashing into the gate, knocked to smithereens probably. Suddenly Hugh gives one vigorous tug to the right rein; I see what is coming, and stretch out my hand involuntarily to clutch him—to clutch anything—then—smash we go into the hedge bank.

When I discover myself again, for my body has outrun my spirit, I find myself standing on my head in a clump of violets. I reverse myself as soon as possible, that is to say, I return to the position nature intended for me, and erect myself upon my legs again. I look about me, but at first am too giddy to make out anything; everything goes whirling round, and there is a buzzing, surging sound in my ears.

Then I see Hugh likewise picking himself up from among the thorny hedge, where he has been making his downy bed. Down the road the horses go, galloping wildly, dragging the dogcart on its side along with them. In the ditch sprawls one groom, rather stunned, and from the field on the other side comes the voice of the other, shouting a doleful inquiry as to whether we are killed. Hugh comes staggering, rather dizzily, over to me.

"Are you hurt, Nell?" (very anxiously), no trace of champagne.

"No—o—o, I think not. I—I—believe I'm going—to—to—die!"

I have a recollection of the aghastness of Hugh's countenance at this announcement; then a vision of his arms stretched out, and my tumbling into them, and then my spirit went away for a space, as spirits will sometimes, though whither they go has never, by ancients or moderns, been satisfactorily explained.

As soon as my soul comes back from that trip—how long it is absent I know not—I begin to sneeze violently, and my eyes water profusely, which is the less to be wondered at, as I find a very large bottle of strongest salts[1] held right under my nose, and sending its pungent vapours up my nostrils. I push it away, and look about me. I am in a room I never was in before, an inn parlour evidently; a small room where stalest tobacco and stalest beer contend for kingship over the dominion of smell; a very big-patterned brown and yellow paper on the walls; Lord Stencliffe

---

1 Carbonate of ammonia, used as a restorative in case of faintness. This was often carried by ladies in small decorative bottles.

in a cocked hat and red coat, and with a battle furiouser than Armageddon, of which he is apparently unaware, raging behind him, over the chimney-piece; Adam and Eve *au naturel*,[1] over the sideboard; the woman of Samaria,[2] very embonpoint,[3] in a corner; a broken lustre and two crockery lambs on the mantelshelf, and three or four horse-hair chairs.

I myself am lying on a very hard horse-hair sofa; a tidyish elderly woman is standing over me, brandishing a brandy bottle, and oh horror! oh shame! oh infamy! Hugh's arm is under my head, and his face with the middle-aged eyes and the crow's feet—his face—its mahogany streaked with blood, is within two inches of my nose; he is hanging over me like a mother over her baby.

"Feel better?" he asks, concernedly.

Instantly I struggle into a sitting posture.

"Yes, thanks, I'm all right again now, I think; hadn't we better be going home? is the carriage mended?"

Hugh laughs.

"Mended! not exactly! I have not heard tale or tidings of it yet; if the traces have not broken, it's some way beyond Wilton by now, I should think. I have sent Jackson after those brutes, but I'm hanged if I know when he'll be back again."

I gaze blankly at him.

"How are we to get home then?"

"Ay, that's the rub," he says; "they have not got any sort of a trap that can take us, here. I've sent Smith (he was the other groom) walking to Wentworth, and I told him to go as quick as he could, and get them to send the brougham[4] for us."

"How soon can it come?"

He takes out his watch and calculates.

"He's been gone about a quarter of an hour, and it's five minutes past ten now, and it's eight miles *good* to Wentworth—an hour and a half, two hours and a half—three hours; it *may* be

---

1   Nude (French).

2   See John 4:4-42. The woman of Samaria encounters Jesus at a well. She is puzzled that he asks her for water, as Jews did not customarily do so. He responds by offering her his faith, which is not merely for Jews but for all. It was a favorite scene for illustrators; Nell sees that the artist took the opportunity to paint the woman as attractively fleshy.

3   Plump (French).

4   A one-horse closed carriage.

here in three hours, that is, if he ever gets there; but he was rather muzzy when we left Wilton, and that *spill* has obfuscated his intellects still further, I'm afraid."

The calmly, cheerful way in which Sir Hugh makes this promising statement *roiles*[1] me—to use a word sanctioned by Clarendon, though fallen from its first estate now—considerably.

"If you thought there was a doubt about his getting there, why on earth didn't you go yourself?" snapped I.

"And leave *you*?" says Hugh, reproachfully, still kneeling beside me.

Neither words, tone, nor attitude are lost upon the goodwife, as I see. She coughs a little, and looks or makes as though she is looking towards the plump Samaritan dame in the corner. I vault from the sofa, as if the spirit of a flea had passed into me, and walk across the room; my legs feel stiff and sore, and I experience an inward longing that Hugh would have the sense to leave the room, and enable me to examine into the number and extent of my casualties.

"Won't the lady take anything?" asks the female Boniface,[2] demurely.

The lady declines, but the gentleman says—

"Take anything! of course she will! Why, it'll be hours before we get home again; bring in some tea directly, and something to eat; chops, or ham and eggs, or anything, it does not matter what, and—have you got any decent beer?"

When did an Englishman forget to pay his orisons to his great and beneficent god, malt liquor? Of course they *have* decent beer, more than decent, admirable beer, at least so our elderly friend asseverates, and Hugh signifies his intention of migrating to the bar to partake thereof. The landlady and he pass into the little flagged passage, and close the door behind them. I, left to myself, sit down by the window, curse my fate, and those unmannerly blood mares, and count the bruises, great and frequent, on my shins. Presently the hostess returns with a clean tablecloth and tea things.

"The gentleman'll soon be back, 'm," she says, consolatorily, to me.

"I daresay."

---

1 Agitates or annoys (archaic spelling of "roil").
2 Here, not the saint, but an innkeeper.

"He's just gone 'alf a dozen yards down the road to see if he can see hanythink of the man and them brutes of 'osses."

"Oh, has he?" with ostentatious indifference to the communication.

"Do you feel quite yourself again, mum?"

"Quite, thanks."

She arranges a black-glazed tea-pot and two cups and saucers, and then recommences her attack.

"I was so thankful when you come to yourself when you did, mum!"

"Were you?"

"Yes, 'm, because of the gentleman, I mean; I never see a gentleman so put about, about hanythink; no, never. I thought he'd agone off his 'ed a'most."

I see her glancing stealthily at my left hand.

("I should not have cared much if he had," said I, internally.) "Perhaps he'd never seen anyone faint before?" I suggested, aloud; "perhaps he thought I was dead!"

"Well, indeed, mum, when you fust come in it gev me quite a turn, *that* it did; 'e was a carryin' of you in his harms, and your 'ead was a 'angin' down over 'is shoulder, and your mouth was hopen, and your face was as wite—as wite as that table-cloth; I did raly think you was a corpse at fust."

I relapse into silence, and vultures gnaw my heart, *I*, in Hugh's arms, with my head hanging over his shoulder, and my mouth open! Disgusting tableau! Not only disgusting, but public; witnessed by the two grooms and the landlady, certainly; by a barmaid and a host of boozing boors, probably.

Hugh returned in about a quarter of an hour from his unsuccessful quest after his refractory cattle, and we sat down to tea. It was horribly honeymoonish, as I felt! I poured out Hugh's tea, and he helped me to mutton chops. I did not feel the least inclined for eating, but it was something to do, better than staring at my *vis-à-vis*. When the landlady came in to clear away the tea-things, she found us both sitting on the little window seat, quite *loverly*, looking out on the gooseberry and currant bushes, and the sweet basil and mint and marigolds. My Othello,

"Somewhat declined into the vale of years,"

was pouring tales of

"Moving accidents by flood and field"

into the ears of a most unwilling Desdemona.[1]

"What a funk I *was* in when you said you were going to die! I thought I had killed you. What *should* I have done if I had?" he ends, sentimentally, reverting from his Sebastopolian and Lucknowian[2] experiences to our late perils by dogcart.

"What *would* you have done?" I replied, sarcastically, "why I suppose you'd have had the *body* (me I mean) conveyed in here, and then you'd have had some beer, and then you'd have posted off to Wentworth to break the news to Dolly!"

"*That* I shouldn't."

I don't know whether he intended me to ask what he would have done; if he did I did not gratify him, but stared out at the gooseberry bushes, and tried to count the nascent gooseberries on the nearest one. Having no further pretence for staying, the goodwife left the room, to my regret. I miss her chaperonage, the whisking of her sage green stuff dress, and the cheerful clink of the teaspoons, which sufficed instead of conversation. When she was gone the stillness irked me; it is not a cooling or a soothing process sitting at dead of night alone on a narrow seat with a man who *will* keep edging an inch every five minutes nearer you, and who never moves his eyes from your face.

"I wonder that woman did not know who you were," I said, for the sake of saying something. "She talked of you as *the gentleman*."

"Not to know me, you think, argues herself unknown;[3] well, she's a stranger in these parts, that's it—poor old girl! She was sorely puzzled to make out our relationship to one another, wasn't she?"

"I should have had the greatest possible pleasure in explaining to her that there was not any relationship whatsoever," I answer drily.

Hobnailed boots stump along the flagged passage into the little bar; men are talking and drinking there; the barmaid's tee-

---

1 Othello, the protagonist of Shakespeare's play of the same title, won Desdemona's love by telling her of his adventures (first printed 1622).

2 Sebastopol was the scene of the famous final battle of the Crimean war (1855), and Lucknow was the scene of a famous battle in 1857, during the Indian Rebellion.

3 Compare Book IV of *Paradise Lost* (1667), an epic poem by John Milton.

hee, inharmonious, as the laugh of the uneducated always is, rewards their sallies, and mingles with their haw-haws; they are smoking evidently, for tobacco smoke—bearable now, because fresh—creeps under the door, and assails our noses.

"How does the time go?" I ask restlessly.

"Five and twenty past eleven."

"Is that all?" (with great disconsolateness of tone).

"Does the time seem to you to go so slow, *Nell*?"

His arm is, I find, establishing itself on the sill behind me.

"Yes, dreadfully slow," I say, impatiently; "and don't call me *Nell*, please—I don't like it."

The house grows silent, the guests return to their homes, and to the rods their expectant wives have got in pickle for them; the aborigines retire to bed. Hugh and I are virtually alone together—alone with the stars and their mother, the night. Oh, grave, sweet night! how solemn you are! type and figure of death! I know not which is solemnest, a calm or a stormy night; it is but the difference between an angry God and a God at rest. How often have I watched the stars overspread

"The cool delicious meadows of the night,"[1]

and longed with hot impatience to be floating, upborne on spirit wings, through those soft dusk fields, finding out how far they spread, and what treasures of delight they hold in their airy depths. Night brings back, vivid and clear to us, the faces of our dead ones; gaudy day scares and chases their pale eidola, but in the night remind us of the look they wore, of the words they spake, ere they

"Folded their pale hands so meekly,"[2]

and laid their heads on the Reaper's breast. In the night we think steadfastly of our departure; we realize that it will be; that some day we shall surely get that letter signed with the sign manual of the Great King, that letter that bids us set our houses in order, bids us kiss our tearful wife and little ones, bids us rise up and come

---

1 See "A Love-Poem" in *Poems* (1853), by Alexander Smith (1830-67).
2 See "Footsteps of Angels" (1838), a poem by Henry Wadsworth Longfellow.

away, for *He* needs us. At night we probe the soul-wounds that the turbulent brawling day has inflicted; we lay to them the salve of humblest prayer and deepest penitence, we make up our accounts with God. But if we would conjure up our dead, solitude must be the Witch of Endor,[1] whose incantations arouse them for us; if we would ponder in sober seriousness upon our sins there must be no distracting thought, no distasteful company, no impertinent irritations to mar the influences of night and silence.

In that ever-to-be-abhorred night I speak of, I was not alone—not alone, though I would have given one or both my ears to have been so. I was harried by the company of a man, my indifference for whom was fast merging into loathing. Poor Hugh! there was nothing loathable about him, as I see now, on calm retrospection—nothing, except his efforts to act basilisk[2] or charming serpent, a part for which his eyes and the whole cast of his countenance singularly unfitted him. I begged him to take off his watch and lay it on the table, that I might not have to be perpetually appealing to him to know how the time went. Restlessly I rambled up and down the room, every moment seeking information from the impassive China face of my familiar. Stock-still stood, or seemed to stand, the hands; the progress of the minute was as imperceptible as that of the hour-hand. I could not sit quiet; it seemed as if I were on wires, or had a fit of the crebles.[3] I turned my uneasy eyes helplessly round; what could I do to curtail my sufferings? A few books lay on the little sideboard—a few books and a tumbler full of daffodils. I perused the titles eagerly. A Bible and a prayer-book, a tattered primer, Alleine's "Alarm to the Unconverted," and Cumming's "Great Tribulation," the two latter presented to Martha Harris by her kind friend, the Rev. Mr. Smith.[4]

Anybody's "Tribulation" was an attractive title to me now; it woke my sympathy. Was not I in great tribulation myself? Perhaps

---

1 See I Samuel 28: 4-25. At the request of King Saul, the Witch of Endor conjures up the dead prophet Samuel.

2 A legendary creature who turned its victims to stone with a look.

3 This seems to be a slang term for fidgety nervousness.

4 Joseph Alleine's book *An Alarm to Unconverted Sinners* was published in 1671 and went through many reprints well into the mid-nineteenth century. John Cumming's book *The Great Tribulation; or, the Things coming on the Earth* was published in 1859. Such books were often given as Sunday school prizes or as gifts.

it might frighten me, or amuse me, or shock me, or do something towards making me forget that dreadful watch and dreadfuller man. I get through half a page, and then recur to my old wonder, "how's the time going?" I rise and look. Half-past one!

"It ought to be here by now, oughtn't it?" I say, looking dolorously across the flare of the tallow candles at Lothario.[1]

"It will soon, I dare say," he replies, cheerily. "Probably they were all in bed when he got there, and it would take some time knocking them up, and putting the horses in."

I bring the "Great Tribulation" over to the table, and bend my eyes resolutely on its gloom-breathing pages. The print is very small, and the prophecies are of a nature to make the stoutest heart quail, the limpest hair stand on end; they seem to me only consumedly dull. I look up one page and down another; look to see where the chapter ends, and whether it looks pleasanter further on; then I yawn; then I take a peep at Hugh. He is leaning his elbow on the table, and his brown hand is shading his brown eyes, which are taking an inventory of my charms apparently. Some impulse prompts me to say sharply,

"I wish you would look at something besides me!"

"Why should not I look at you, if I like?"

I turn over the pages with quick irritation.

"Because—because it is tiresome and stupid, and you might find something better to do!"

"There's not much to do here, good or bad, and I don't want anything better."

I turn my back upon him, and peruse a paragraph of an uncomplimentary nature about the *Beast*.

"Nell!"

"I asked you not to call me Nell."

"What am I to call you then? may I call you Eleanor? Miss Lestrange sounds so stiff."

"You need not call me anything."

Tick, tick, tick, goes the kitchen clock; somebody is snoring overhead.

"Why *will* you turn your back upon me?"

"Because I hate being stared at," I reply, pouting.

"By *me*, I suppose that means; it would be a different tale if it were that long-legged M'Gregor."

---

1 Seducer in *The Fair Penitent* (1703), a play by Nicholas Rowe.

This is the first trace of jealousy and spleen I have yet discerned in easy-going Hugh Lancaster. I wheel round with great velocity.

"You've no right to say that," I flash out vehemently; "no business to say it; it's mean of you."

"Mean!" he cries angrily; "that's the very first time any one ever applied that word to me!"

Then he subsides; I think he perceives the absurdity of our sitting there, storming at one another, at dead of night, in that dreary little pothouse.

"Never mind!" he says; "you're a privileged person; you may say what you like."

The candles burn low in the brass candlesticks; the morning wind—wind that carries away so many ebbing lives on its chill pinions, arises; the stars die, and—

"O'er night's brim day boils at last."[1]

"That idiot has lost his way, as I thought he would," says Hugh, whose weather-beaten face looks haggard and grim in the dun misty light.

"Yes," said I, reproachfully; "and if you'd gone yourself, as I wanted you, we should have been back hours ago."

"It was your fault," he replies, rather downcast by my persistent snubbing. "Cannot you forgive me for liking too much to be with you?"

He says it so bluntly and so humbly that I feel compunctious. I stand by the window, and watch the dawn's birth. I can almost see the wind

"Waking each little leaf to sing."[2]

Even a hot day often comes in coldly, and sitting up all night is not warming to the blood. I shiver.

"Are you cold?" Hugh asks.

"Yes, rather, and my arm smarts a little; I wonder did I bruise it when I fell."

I pull down my sleeve, and consider my maimed limb. What is there in nature or art so pretty, so appealing to the senses

---

1 See *Pippa Passes* (1841), a verse drama by Robert Browning.
2 Probably misquoted from John Keble's poem, "Morning" (1866).

as a beautiful arm? Mine was beautiful, round and firm, and polished like marble, that some god had kissed into warm life; with dear little nicks and dimples about elbow and wrist. I find a big black bruise, and two or three long red scratches on the soft cream-white flesh. "It hurts," I say, looking up rather ruefully at my companion, somewhat after the manner that a dog does that has got a thorn in his foot, when he comes limping up, with upheld paw, to any one he thinks in his doggish mind, looks friendly. Mahogany faces can look loving and pitiful just as well as alabaster ones, though they don't do it so becomingly. Hugh's did now. Oh the perversity of this human nature of ours. Why, in the name of common sense, could not I look loving too? Why could not I feel loving? Why could not I tumble straightway into his honest ready arms, as he stood there with

"The lights of sunset and of sunrise mixed"[1]

upon his face: stood there, unkempt, unshorn, grizzly as a mechanic on a week day? To fall into his arms was to fall into the arms of £12,000 per annum, and a house in May Fair.[2] It included the ideas of clover for life; fine clothes, high feeding, and other delights. "Poor little arm," he says, "we must get some plaster for it; let me kiss the place to make it well!"

His moustache just brushes the surface, has not time to do more, before I snatch it away as from a hyena about to mumble it; snatch it away from £12,000 a year, as if it had been twelve brass farthings paid quarterly. "Leave me alone, *do!*" I cry, fierce as a young tigress, looking volumes of outraged virtue at him; "will you never understand that I *hate* you?"

Hugh pales, as men do in any strong emotion; it is their equivalent for women's "*torrent de pleurs!*"[3]

"I have been rather dull of comprehension," he says, "but don't be alarmed; I understand now *fully!*"

We retire to two different corners, and glower at one another. The house awakes and shakes itself; girds up its loins for its day's work; the barmaid and the ostler are heard exchanging matutinal gallantries in the bar, and the landlady enters

---

1 See "Love and Duty" (1842), a poem by Tennyson.
2 A wealthy and fashionable neighborhood in London.
3 Flood of tears (French).

slip-shod, curl-papered, to "know what will be for breakfast?" Breakfast! Oh, ye gods! shall we then have to undergo another grievous *tête-à-tête* repast? Shall I again pour out Hugh's tea? Will he again help me to ham and eggs? As I thus ruminate (despair creeping coldly over me) even while Mrs. Harris urges lamb chops on Hugh's notice—even while the savour of bacon, incipiently frizzling, insinuates itself through the walls, I hear the sound of wheels.

Eagerly I run out to the inn door, and stand with hand shading my eyes from the morning sun, while the Blue Boar swings above me. Surely, surely, I know those big bays, and that sociable—behind which and in which old Lady Lancaster and her yellow wig make their weekly pilgrimage to church. I rush back to Hugh, crying joyfully, "The carriage is come! hurrah!" and fall to youthful caperings and actions, expressive of intensest relief. I know now with what accent a shipwrecked mariner shouts, "A sail! a sail!"

Hugh looks askance at me and my gymnastics; then comes out, and damns his servants; wishes to know why the devil they have not come sooner, and what the deuce they mean by their d——d impertinence? In fact he is in a towering rage, such a rage as they have not seen him in since he came into the property, twenty years ago. It surprises them a little, and amuses them a good deal.

The explanation of their non-appearance before, is easy. Smith, as his master had divined, had lost his way; never had been very clear about it, and had dropped into the Red Lion, three quarters of a mile further on, to refresh his memory; consequently had not reached Wentworth till an hour and a half ago.

Mrs. Harris has to eat her fried bacon and drink her coffee herself; the bays, under Hugh's Jehuship, deposit us at the bottom of the flight of steps at Wentworth hall door, exactly as the clock strikes nine. Nobody is down yet, and I flee along the corridors and lobbies unobserved to my own room, where I lie down on my bed, and straightway fall asleep, and forget my troubles, and that nightmare pothouse!

End of Volume 1

CHAPTER XX

"Our birth is but a sleep and a forgetting;
The soul that rises with us, our life's star,
Hath elsewhere had its setting,
And cometh from afar."[1]

Is that true? Have we existed in other states of being as many poets and many non-poets dimly conjecture? Is this life our beginning though we know it not to be our ending? or is it only one of a series of existences through which we pass? Now and then flashing reminiscences—reminiscences of things we know positively not to have happened in this life—dart across our minds, recognition in a smell or a sound of something we have met with, something we have had to do with, somehow, somewhere, somewhen. Whence can such reminiscences, such recognitions come, but from some pre-existence? Our draught of Lethe[2] has not been quite deep enough.

But even without those dim hintings at recollections of a former state, our utter forgetfulness of ever having been in life, under any form before our present one, is no argument against the existence of such a previous life, for what faintest remembrance have we of our first year? Does any glimmering of memory illumine those days when we lay on our nurse's lap, sprawling, making faces, sucking?

Are there only a certain number of old souls which continually go in and out of an ever new succession of bodies? And if we did exist in some former state, was it a higher or a lower one? Were we beasts or angels? Have we fallen or risen?

There is no light *whatever* on the past. Thank God there is in the Future enough to enable us to walk soberly, heedfully, warily, on towards the fuller light, which will dawn on us on that—

---

1 "Intimations of Immortality" (1807), a poem by William Wordsworth.
2 In Greek mythology, Lethe was one of the rivers in the underworld. Drinking its waters gave forgetfulness.

"Marge beyond the tomb."[1]

Southey, in his "Doctor,"[2] makes his hero maintain, half in jest and half in earnest, that he was able to recognize, in the personal appearance, habits and dispositions of many of those around him, the different animals which, in a former state, their spirits had inhabited.

Truly there is none of us who cannot point out a pig or two, a sheep or a mule, among his acquaintance. If Dolly had ever pre-existed, it must have been in the shape of one of the feline tribe; not a comfortable old tabby sitting staid beside the hearth, and putting up her head to be tickled, but a tigress or a panther, sleek, lithe, beautiful, stealthy. There lacked to her but the eyed skin, the outward beast form; her spirit had remained the pard-spirit[3] of her former life, when she lived in jungles; tangled, torrid swamps, and lay in wait to pounce on deer, and kid, and man.

Turning day into night, I slept on, till the afternoon, till the sun came round to my side of the house, and woke me, blazing down hot and full on the bed whereon I lay through the uncurtained, unshuttered windows. When I did wake, it was to the consciousness of a sufficiently bad headache. For some little time I lay motionless, on the border land between sleeping and waking; feeling nothing much, wishing nothing much, thinking of nothing much except myself as a mere animal; my headache, my vertigo, and my heat. I was fully roused at length by the door handle turning softly, the door opening, and some one coming in. Some one came over to the bed, and bent over me; some one was Dolly.

"Awake, are you? have you quite recovered your adventure?" she says, in a key so sweet and low, that it does not jar on my aching cranium, as almost any other sound would. She would make the divinest sick nurse, would Dolly. My senses come back to me, full and strong. Dolly has treated me despitefully; there shall be no peace with her; war to the knife with Dolly. I fixed my eyes steadily upon her, from among my tumbled pillows.

"I don't want to speak to you," I said, "you tell lies!"

---

1   Compare lyric 46 from *In Memoriam* (1850), a poem by Tennyson.
2   The poet Robert Southey also wrote a multivolume work of fiction called *The Doctor* (1834-37).
3   A pard is a leopard.

"Do I?" said Dolly, unruffled. "I daresay; I never yet met a person who did not, and I hope I never shall, for they would necessarily be very disagreeable; a certain amount of fibs is essential to the existence of society; did you never hear that?"

I refuse to be led from the concrete to the abstract.

"You made mischief between me and Dick. You prevented him from driving me to Wilton," I cry, with raised voice, knives running through my head under my exertions.

"If Dick, as you call him, has forgiven me, don't you think you might?" she says, gently.

If Dick had forgiven her! How that quiet implication stung me! I roll my head restlessly from side to side.

"What object could you have had in doing it? Had you any object at all, or was it only pure malice?"

Dolly smiles and sits down on the side of the bed; she perceives we are going to have a squabble, and she does not see why we should not have it out comfortably.

"What a foolish child you were not to get into bed," she says with affability; "lying down in one's clothes does not rest one in the least; now, you know, to-night you'll look quite green."

"Was it pure malice?" I reiterate, disregarding this digression.

"Nobody but a fiend would think of doing anything out of pure malice, I should say," returns my sister, sedately, "and I'm not a fiend yet, that I know of; malice had neither part nor lot in the matter."

"Did you want to ride with him yourself?" I ask, vehemently; "are *you* fond of him too?"

Dolly smiles again; a little amused, compassionate smile, and shrugs her shoulders.

"Am I given to being fond of men, merely for being long-legged and poor, which I confess seem to me the most salient points in your dear Dick's character?"

"Any one would have said you thought he had a good many good points in his character, who saw the way you looked at him yesterday," I cry, choking with indignation.

"My dear, did I make my own eyes? Can I help it, if they have any peculiar way of exercising themselves; Providence made them, and Providence must answer for their vagaries."

"If you have such a contempt for poverty, why did you waste so much time and trouble; why did you tell lies, and make me perfectly miserable, merely to get that which, when you had got it, you thought worthless?" I asked bitterly.

"My good child, for once I was unselfish; cannot you believe that?" asks Dolly, playfully, and laying her cool slim hand on my burning forehead.

"I had no plans for myself whatever; certainly no designs on our mutual friend, with the crack-jaw Scotch name; it rather bored me than otherwise ambling along beside him, for heaven knows how many hours, in the broiling sun!"

I am dumbfoundered, and lie staring at her with boundless wonder in my wide open eyes.

"What upon earth did you do it for, then?" I gasp, slowly; "once for all, tell me what object you had, or whether you had any?"

"Will you have some Eau de Cologne on your head?" she asks; and as she is sprinkling scented drops over me, "An object?" says she, "yes, to be sure; who but an idiot ever does anything without an object? I have no objection whatever to tell you mine either, if you'll listen to it like a sensible woman, and not scream at the top of your voice, as you have been doing for the last quarter of an hour; if you *must* know the truth, I intended you to drive with Sir Hugh. Was not it charitable of me? He looked so disconsolate, poor little wretch!"

"Why did you want me to drive with him?" I ask in blank astonishment.

"Because, my dear, I wish and intend that you should drive through life with him; because I hope, before I die, to see you Lady Lancaster."

"*That* you never will," I cry, with flaming cheeks, starting up in bed, and fumbling with the counterpane.

"Ah! perhaps not; at present you prefer the idea of riding in the baggage-waggon after Daddy Longlegs, with several little M'Gregors, male and female, clinging about your skirts!"

So Dolly, softly inhaling Eau de Cologne as she speaks. I fling myself back among the pillows, and am thankful for the shade afforded by my loosened hair—a shade which partially veils the blush that I feel creeping all over my body.

"How coarse you are!" I murmur.

"Very likely," says Dolly, "common sense always is coarse; but my being ever so coarse won't make the baggage-waggon an easier mode of conveyance, nor will it pay Romeo and Juliet's butcher's bills."[1]

---

1 Romeo and Juliet are the doomed lovers of Shakespeare's play of the same name (first printed in 1597).

"What is it to you whether they are ever paid?" I am embold-ened by the protection of my tangled locks to ask; "why cannot you let us be happy in our own way?"

"*Us* be happy, indeed!" says Dolly, a little contemptuously. "Are you so sure about Romeo? because I'm not; Romeo likes coats from Poole;[1] he likes billiards and Château Lafitte, and actresses;[2] of course he does; he keeps them in the background now, but you are even a greater ninny than I take you for, if you cannot believe that they are there, out of sight somewhere. Will he be content, do you suppose, with poky lodgings and a dirty parlour maid, and shoulder of mutton and rice pudding, even with you to sweeten them?"

I writhe in silent anguish; but her logic is unanswerable. What equivalent am I for billiards and Château Lafitte, and actresses?

"It's something quite new your taking such an interest in my concerns," I say presently. "I cannot see what it would matter to you if I were to run away with a tinker."

"I don't think a tinker's arms would quarter well with the Lestranges'," says she, laughing, "and I should not like to have to allude to my sister Madame la Chaudronnière."[3] Then falling into gravity again, "I don't pretend to any great disinterestedness in the matter; my motive for endeavouring to prevent your mar-rying Major M'Gregor, is no particularly tender regard for your interests; it is simply this, that by marrying a pauper, as, from all I can make out, I believe our worthy dragoon to be, you will drag down our family, and me of course with it, even lower than it has already fallen, though it seems pretty nearly at the bottom of the ladder as it is."

I toss about restlessly. I feel that there is a flaw somewhere in her worldly wisdom, but I cannot detect it.

"Whereas," pursues Dolly, rising and pacing up the room, "if you marry Sir Hugh——"

"Never," I cry, interrupting her; "I'd rather be flayed alive! Ugh! married to Hugh! I should be dead of disgust in a week! Faugh!"

---

1 Poole's was a fashionable Victorian Savile Row tailoring firm owned by Henry Poole and favored by wealthy young men.
2 Dolly means that he likes the expensive and decadent habits of upper-class bachelor life: gambling on billiards, drinking expensive wine, and keeping pricey mistresses (actresses and other female performers were often assumed to be sexually available as "kept" women).
3 Mrs. Ironmonger (French).

Dolly pauses before a cheval-glass, and considers herself—not with vanity—for vanity in her was not, but reflectively, appraisingly; looked at her small snaky head; at her coiled cables of ink-black hair; at her tall, svelte figure.

"Don't you see, you stupid child, that I'm only giving you the advice that I always give and take myself?" she says. "Am I more in love with Hugh's attractions than you are? not I; as I see him, he's a good-natured, wooden-headed old booby; but for all that, if he were to come in here this minute (don't be alarmed, he'd hardly be so ill-mannered) and say to me, 'Miss Lestrange, will you marry me?' or, 'Dolly, will you be mine?' wouldn't I respond, 'Yes, dear Hugh, *that* I will, and thank you kindly'; I'd swear to love, honour, and obey, not *him*, not *him* (with a gesture of contempt), but his £12,000 a year, his French cook, and his opera-box, and I'd keep my vow, too!"

"I wish to goodness he *would* ask you!" I groan.

"Is there," pursues Dolly, warming with her theme (it's not often she thinks it worth while wasting so much breath on anything female) "is there any old lord between the three seas, so old, so mumbling, so wicked, that I would not joyfully throw myself into his horrid palsied old arms, if he had but money; money! money! money is power; money is a god!"

I sit with my legs dangling over the side of the bed listening.

"It may be yours," I say; "it is not mine. What do women want with power? What would they do with it when they had got it? Love is worth all the power in the world!"

"Pooh! I did not know that any one after sixteen or before sixty, believed in that venerable old imposture now-a-days; love is another name for selfishness!" says Dolly, recommencing her walk, and sweeping up and down.

"It cannot be selfishness to live altogether in and for another person," object I, thinking that I have nailed her there.

"Worldly wisdom and sordid common sense," continues she, "would make you marry Hugh, sacrifice your own passions, give a lift to the poor old family, the depression of which is breaking papa's heart—it's a pity you've always made such a fuss about your devotion to him, isn't it—and relieve him of more than half his cares; on the other hand, *Love*, noble, beautiful, be-poetized *Love*, will make you hurl yourself at the not particularly delighted head of that big Scotchman—you will have no money, no position, no power for good or evil, but your passion will be gratified;

you will be put in possession of that very luxuriant moustache, and those very broad shoulders, and having them, you can afford to let papa's 'gray hairs go down with sorrow to the grave,'[1] as somebody's in the Bible did; cannot you, dear?"

She opens the door and passes out; I call after her, "Dolly, Dolly, come back!" but she either does not or will not hear.

CHAPTER XXI

"Macbeth has murdered sleep!"[2] and Dolly had murdered mine. Much good to shake up the pillows, to smooth the coverlet, and turning round compose oneself resolutely to the continuation of one's unfinished snooze; much good to think of a key, or the wards of a lock, or the legs of a chair, or anything else as intensely unexciting.

I am Orestes, and Dolly has hounded on the Erinnyes on my track.[3] My Furies are—like the original ones that pursued Orestes,—three in number, viz.: Dick's poverty, as impeding our union, and docking his luxuries, (of which I grudged him but one item), not as affecting myself, for from my youth up I had been hard up, and should not have known what it felt like to be otherwise; Dick's jealousy of Hugh; and Dick's flirtation with Dolly.

I had not sense enough to see that I need not worry myself about all three at once; since any two of them were exclusive of

---

1 Compare Genesis 42:38. Like the epigraph to the book, this refers to the story of the jealous brothers who sold Joseph into Egyptian slavery. Here, before Joseph, unrecognized by his brothers, saves them from being prosecuted as spies, he asks them for a hostage to show their good faith. They ask their father permission to give the youngest son Benjamin, his favorite after the lost Joseph, as a hostage. The father weeps and tells them that if Benjamin does not return alive, his gray hairs will go down with sorrow to the grave. Joseph eventually saves the whole family.
2 See *Macbeth* (first printed 1623), a play by Shakespeare.
3 From Greek mythology and history, best known through plays by Aeschylus. Orestes avenges his dead father by killing his mother's lover, who plotted the crime with Orestes' mother. But he also kills his mother, and this offense against nature causes him to be persecuted by the Erinnyes, or Furies, three avenging goddesses. Their names were Tisiphone (avenger of murder), Megaera (jealousy), and Alecto (rage).

the third, as for example, that if Dick was going to jilt me, his want of money would in nowise prejudice me: be rather a matter of rejoicing,—or, that if Dick was jealous of Hugh, he was the less likely to be in love with Dolly.

All three of them, Megæra, Tisiphone, and Alecto, crowd their ugly faces round, and grin at me, and I have not strength to combat them.

After about a quarter of an hour, which seems to me about two full hours, I jump up. I have no watch, as you know, but I hear a clock ticking on the landing outside. I open the door, and peep out. Only five o'clock! An hour and a half till dressing time! I will go down. Fortune favours the brave, and I suppose also the fair, as they are mostly put in the same category, and I *might* meet Dick in the passages, or the stairs, in the billiard-room; as Christabel says, "All may yet be well!"[1] (though that is rather an ill-omened quotation, for all was not well in *her* case), and at the worst, the society of my fellow-creatures, even though they are not *Dicks*, is pleasanter than my own.

At the morning-room door I stop and listen; not with any eaves-dropping intention, but simply to try and detect those tones that I foolishly imagine would wake me "Had I lain for a century dead!"[2] Lain for a century dead indeed! It is all very well, and a pretty conceit to say so in a love song, but it will require a louder than human voice to re-form those scattered dust particles into the marvellous image, of which the great God Himself condescended to be the model.

The tones I seek are not detectable; I hear instead ever so many women's voices; young and old, croaky and mellow. Nearly all the women, half of the Wentworth party, are scattered about the many cornered room, in groups of twos and threes. Each is provided with a cup of tea, and all have apparently just come in from walking; judging by the large show of Mrs. Heaths' and Mrs. Browns' hats that are lying about, and by the display of a great many pairs of trimmest Balmorals. Lady Capel (the fat

---

1 Misquote of the original "May Heaven be praised if all be well!," a line from "Christabel," (first published 1816), a poem by Samuel Taylor Coleridge. All is not well in her case because Christabel is cursed; the poem is unclear whether she is a kind of vampire, or under the sway of an evil spirit, but she does harm to the family that shelters her.

2 See "Maud" (1855), a poem by Tennyson.

Viscountess) stands by the table, in a charming little point-lace bonnet, chatting with Miss Seymour. I think it makes her feel comfortable to look at anything so thin.

She has had the post of honour this afternoon; and has been out driving with Lady Lancaster in the sociable. Honour and pleasure are not Siamese twins in this world. Our hostess, also bonneted (in the literal and not metaphorical sense), is *button-holing* another philanthropic old woman, on the subject of the Shoe Black Brigade.[1] As I come in, she turns round and utters an exclamation of surprise, "Come down after all! So glad! Your sister gave us such a sad account of you, that we were afraid we were going to lose you for all the evening; there does not seem much the matter now, does there?" patting my cheek as she would have patted the cheek of the Hottentot Venus,[2] if Sir Hugh had seen fit to throw his Sultanic Majesty's pocket-handkerchief to her.[3]

"You are quite a heroine, my dear!" says Lady Capel kindly, "we are all dying to hear your version of this unlucky *contretemps*!"[4]

"Men are so stupid!" cries the sharp young lady, whose name is Miss Gifford, coming over from the other side of the room, "they never know how to tell a story; they always leave out all the details, which are the most important parts."

"It must have been a great shock, and—*very* embarrassing,"

---

1 A charitable organization formed in 1864 to provide employment to street children as shoe shiners.

2 Saartje Baartman, a young Khosa woman from Southern Africa who was exhibited as a public spectacle in both England and France. Baartman, who became known as the Hottentot Venus, was brought to Europe in 1810. Spectators were particularly interested in her large buttocks. After her death at a young age, her genitals were preserved in France. The connection of African and other native peoples with what was considered to be both exotic and barbaric culture and sexuality was a common fascination of Europeans in this period. The exhibition of human beings as spectacles was not unusual, and continued in Europe and the US well into the twentieth century. Her remains were finally returned to Africa in 2002.

3 Europeans were also fascinated with eastern cultures, and especially the concept of the harem, which was the topic of a good deal of fantasy. It was a popular belief in Europe that the Sultan of the Ottoman empire would indicate which of his many concubines he would sleep with by tossing her his handkerchief.

4 Accident, embarrassment (French).

says Miss Seymour, in that whiny-piny voice, with which an inscrutable Providence has seen fit to visit her.

"I should have put on my seven-league boots,[1] and set off walking home!" says Miss Gifford smartly. She would have done nothing of the kind, as indeed she would have given all her back hair, and two or three of her fingers for a six or seven hours' nocturnal *tête-à-tête* with Sir Hugh.

"It was very fortunate that it was not one of the other young men," says Lady Lancaster, stiffly; "it certainly was a trying position for a young woman to be placed in; and you could not have found yourself in better hands than my son's."

I receive this assurance in silence, and bite my lips. Perceiving that I am *pro. tem.*[2] a small lion,[3] and am expected to roar in my humble way, I execute a slight *mugissement*.[4] "I don't know much about it, except that the horses were frightened at the train—they had been rather frisky all along, I thought—and then they ran away, and upset me into the hedge bank. I don't know where they upset anybody else, and then I suppose I fainted, for I don't recollect anything else, until I woke up in that inn-parlour. Ugh!" (with a shiver of aversion at the remembrance).

"Poor child, it must have been very disagreeable!" Lady Capel says good-naturedly, fat women mostly are good-natured, whether it is a cause or an effect I cannot say.

"Dreadful!" I answer emphatically, "I never was so miserable in my life!" Lady Lancaster takes my emphasized remark as a personal affront.

"You should have been very thankful, my dear, that your life was spared," she says rather rebukingly, "and that you were with a person who would be sure to take such excellent care of you!"

"What on earth did you do all those hours?" puts in Miss Gifford, rather quickly, to save us a sermon, "talk, or go to sleep, or play picquet![5] oh, I suppose they had not such a thing as a pack of cards in the house, had they?"

"I looked at Sir Hugh's watch half the time, and read an awful

---

1 In European folklore, these magical boots allow the wearer to travel very quickly—seven leagues with each step.
2 Temporarily (Latin; short for pro tempore).
3 Celebrity (slang).
4 Roaring (French).
5 A complex card game distantly related to bridge.

book about the End of the World and the Third Vial[1] the other half," I answer rather grimly.

They all laugh except Lady Lancaster.

"What a picture!" "How wretched!" "I cannot imagine anything more dreary!" "And what did Sir Hugh read? Drelincourt on Death?"[2] (this is from Miss Gifford).

"He read nothing!"

"Poor man! he was worse off than you even; how did he amuse himself then? smoked? took a nap?"

"He did nothing, he sat quiet."

"You don't seem to have been very sociable," remarks Miss Gifford, with sprightliness, "nor to have taken much pains to entertain one another."

My thoughts fly back to poor Hugh's well-meant efforts to entertain me, and I feel myself blushing.

"Did nobody miss us?" I ask hastily, fiddling with my tea cup, "was no one ever coming to look for us?"

"Oh, I believe there were people hunting for you all over the country half the night, only they did not manage to find you somehow; weren't there Lady Lancaster?"

"They went the wrong road," replies our hostess, sitting very upright, and looking over her spectacles, "that was how the mistake arose. Hugh never was known to come by that lower road in his life before; it is three miles longer too; I cannot imagine what possessed him."

I *can* imagine, and I dive under the table after an imaginary pocket-handkerchief.

"Aren't you very much shaken and bruised?" asks Miss Seymour, making up her face into a sympathetic shape.

"Oh, yes! I'm black and blue from top to toe."

"My dear child! why did not you say so before?" says Lady Lancaster, very kindly, though fussily, as 'tis her nature to, "and I would have sent my maid with some arnica for you; it's the best thing in the world for contusions and sprains, and anything of that sort. I'm afraid, dear, that if you are so stiff and sore, you will not be equal to much dancing to-night."

---

1 See Revelations. At the end of the world, the angels pour out seven vials of God's wrath. The third turns all the water to blood.

2 Charles Drelincourt's cheery tract, *The Christian's defence against the fears of death* (first published in English 1675).

"Dancing!" repeat I, pricking up my ears, as a horse does, when in the distance he hears the horn and the hounds giving tongue.

"Haven't you heard of it?" says Lady Capel, "why, we have all been on the *qui vive*[1] all day about it; we have been making decorations, and hanging up flags and standing on step-ladders ever since breakfast, haven't we?"

My thoughts revert to my one ball, and Captain Dashwood, who has become a very hazy misty figure of late. He was a "heavy"[2] too. I seem fated to be the prey of the Cavalry.

"We are not very much dancing people generally," Lady Lancaster says in her stately slow way, "it is many years since there was a ball in this house; it was quite a sudden idea, but my son thought perhaps it would amuse the young people."

"How very kind of him," I say very gratefully, while my eyes begin to shine like carriage lamps.

"It is quite a small affair! only nine or ten couples, but every-body is in town."

Lady Capel sighs. Fain, fain would she be there too, but the Newmarket Stud, and a long course of point-lace bonnets have necessitated the letting of the Capellian mansion in Park Lane this season.

"Small impromptu dances are always the pleasantest," she says politely, "the only thing is that in the country gentlemen are not to be had for love or money."

"It is indeed very true!" says Lady Lancaster, shaking her head, and her marabou feathers with it, as solemnly as if it had been *question* of the famine in India. "The young men of the present day cannot be content to stay at home and look after their properties; they must be running about to Egypt and Palestine, and half a dozen other places that they never thought of in my younger days," (very likely not, for it took eighteen months to get to India in her younger days).[3] "I consider that it's quite

---

1 Alert (French).

2 A heavy dragoon, i.e., of the armored cavalry.

3 Nell is probably referring to the advent of steamships, which first began to cross the oceans in 1819. Shortly after this novel was published, in 1869, the Suez canal made it possible to go directly from the Mediterranean to the Red Sea, dramatically reducing travel time to India. Prior to this time, travelers from Europe had to sail around the continent of Africa.

one of the greatest evils of this generation; one of the signs of the latter days!"[1]

"A very unpleasant sign!" think I, if it is to entail a Spurgeonic[2] dance on me this evening. Lady Capel sees my countenance falling.

"You need not be afraid of lacking partners," she says, nodding to me; "for I heard Sir Hugh saying that he had invited a number of the Scots Greys[3] over from Nantford."

"My son is a host in himself," says Lady Lancaster; "he is a very energetic dancer!"

There is nothing, from the writing of a book on the Differential Calculus to making cabbage nets, that "my son" cannot do in his mother's opinion.

"How many are we in the house?" says Miss Gifford counting. "Sir Hugh, one, Lord Capel, two. Does *he* dance, Lady Capel?"

"When he is wanted; he does not think it fair to stand in the young men's light!"

The dressing bell rings.

"Dear me! I had no idea that it was so late!"

"We dine at seven to-day," says Lady Lancaster, explanatorily, and then we all separate to make ourselves beautiful for the Scots Greys.

CHAPTER XXII

We are to dance in the dining room; the hall has a stone floor, and Lady Lancaster objects to the dismantling of any of the other rooms; consequently we are to dine in the hall. Lady Lancaster makes many apologies to us; hopes we don't mind, but we must be prepared to rough it a little, which means that we are to eat a first rate Russian dinner, and drink unexceptionable wines half an hour earlier than usual, and in a different but equally comfortable room to that in which we usually feast.

---

1 That is, the coming end of the world predicted in Revelations.

2 Charles Haddon Spurgeon (1834-92) was England's best-known preacher for most of the second half of the nineteenth century. His most famous work is a commentary on the Psalms of the Bible, in the multivolume *The Treasury of David*. Nell seems to be suggesting that she fears spending her entire evening listening to Lady Capel sermonize.

3 The particular regiment to which both Dick and Sir Hugh belong.

Blessed! for ever blessed! be the manner and custom which compels the host to take the woman of highest rank into dinner. In no company more exalted than that to be found in an alms-house, or a charity school, am I likely to be the woman of highest rank, so, for once, I escape Hugh. Though he manœuvres to have me on his other side, I counter-manœuvre and more success-fully to avoid him. Fate assigns me the young gentleman with the death's-head studs, Mr. De Laney, an artless child who helps to make the British Grenadier

"The terror of the Umbrian,
The terror of the Gaul,"[1]

and who prattles away to me about Windsor and Canada, and muffins, and skating on the Rink, and shooting Cariboo. Dick is on the same side of the table, further down. By leaning back in my chair, and peeping behind my guardsman, the widow, the sceptic, and Miss Gifford, I catch a glimpse of a broadcloth back, and a yellow love lock or two; he has been dipping his head in cold water, apparently, for it is curling more furiously than ever. But neither a man's back-hair nor his back afford much insight into the state of his temper and feelings. I certainly neither lived to eat, nor ate to live that day; great excitement is utterly exclu-sive of hunger.

"No, thanks! no, thanks! no, thanks!" say I again and again, as gorgeous gentlemen in plush and calves,[2] poke fish and flesh, and fowl, in every appetizing disguise under my nose.

"Are you a Catholic, Miss Lestrange?" asks my little boy at last. He is not a bad little boy; cheery and equally ready for a Fenian[3] invasion, and a valse[4] with a pretty girl.

"No; why?" ask I, opening my big eyes.

"Because it seems to be a Fast Day with you, and it *is* Wednesday, so I thought you must be a Holy Roman."

I laugh a little.

---

1 From a poem by Horace, translated by Thomas Babington Macaulay in *Lays of Ancient Rome* (1842).
2 Footmen wore uniforms made of plush (velvet) and displayed their muscular calves in silk stockings.
3 Irish revolutionary movement of the mid-nineteenth century, named after the legendary Gaelic hero, Finn MacCool.
4 Waltz, a dance, or the music associated with it.

"No; only I'm not hungry."

"I'm afraid you are seedy."[1]

"No, I am not."

"Dancing is very hard work; one requires a great deal of support to stand it at all!" with a grin on his jolly wide mouth, and he acts as if he believed what he said. Not even our brave defenders can eat for ever, however; about ten o'clock we are most of us gathered in the drawing-room. The men are struggling into their gloves; one, who pretends that he takes ladies' size, has burst one pair, and is on the eve of bursting a second; two or three of the youngest and conceitedest have retired to endue fresh ties.[2]

Carriages are beginning to be heard; the Coxes are the first to arrive. Horses next door to thorough-bred, that must not be kept standing one second; a coat of arms as big as a dinner plate on each panel; cockaded servants,[3] (for Mr. Coxe is a volunteer, and inexpressibly laughable the podgy little millionaire looks going through the goose-step, and shouldering arms, in his invisible green uniform); this is the way in which the British tradesman visits his friends in these happy days.

Mr. and Mrs. Coxe make their entry *arm-in-arm*, and as they are both fat kine,[4] they have some difficulty in getting through the door. Mr. Coxe has on that crimson velvet waistcoat, from which not all the prayers, tears, and entreaties of his wife and daughters can avail to divorce him.

Behind the parent birds come the pullets and cockerel; Mortimer Spencer De Laney Coxe, Gentleman Commoner at Oxford, with his name down for Boodle's,[5] the "Junior Conservative," and half a dozen other crack Clubs, but of the shop, shoppy,[6] with his

---

1 Tired, or a bit ill.

2 In other words, to retie their neckcloths. Fashionably dressed young men were very careful of their neckcloths, which were elaborately arranged.

3 A cockade was a rosette worn as a badge of office or on the livery of servants of an office holder. Traditionally, a black leather cockade is worn to denote service to the Crown.

4 Cattle.

5 An upscale gentleman's club.

6 Compare I Corinthians 15:47, "The first man is of the earth, earthy; the second man is the Lord from heaven." Nell again points to the Coxe family's background in trade and therefore below those of inherited landed wealth in status.

sister Amaryllis and the rear brought up by Lily, who has the highest colour, and Violet, who has the loudest voice in A——shire. Lady Lancaster in her pearl-gray satin—Mrs. Coxe's pink moire-antique[1] cost just as much a yard, but it has not the same imposing effect,—rises and says very majestically, "How do you do, Mrs. Coxe?" It is the first time that the Coxes have been within the doors of Wentworth, and I think for a minute or two they wish themselves well out of them again.

Despite my distaste for old women, I cannot help admiring the old lady. She is like an old queen receiving a deputation from some of her faithful burgesses. She is a tiresome old woman, and teases one's life out about the Zulu Indians and the Millennium[2] and "my son," but she is a lady to the backbone. Coxes may buy up the old houses and the poor old lands, and almost the old pedigrees, but they cannot buy the "grand air." Hugh has not got the grand air, but he has a very good-natured air, which has more the knack of making people feel comfortable than his mother's grand one.

"Dye do, Miss Coxe? very glad to see you! Dye do Miss Lily? I hope you feel equal to a great deal of exercise to-night, for we don't intend to let you go home till this time to-morrow." Then the Scots Greys arrive in their drag;[3] half-a-dozen of them come herding into the room, knowing no one, and hanging together like a swarm of bees.

Hugh takes them up, and presents them to his parent, who shakes hands with the Colonel, and executes a magnificent reverence to the others, which reverence frightens one cornet of a timid disposition and tender years nearly into fits.

---

1 Silk treated with heat and pressure-rollers to give it a rippled pattern.

2 The Zulu were a tribe in Africa against whom Britain was to fight a war in 1879. Tamar Heller points out that the British brought indentured Indian servants to work in sugar plantations in Zululand in the early 1860s. The phrase "Zulu Indians" may be a reflection of this practice, or Lady Capel (or Nell) may simply be a bit confused. Africans and Indians (both from India and from North America) were the targets of missionary efforts; given Lady Capel's concern with the latter days and the Millennium (the era to be initiated by the second coming of Christ after the latter days), she is probably concerned with such religious issues.

3 Large carriage with seats both inside and out.

Then the arrivals come thick and fast; people who do not go to town at all; and people whose purses are only equal to a month or six weeks at the height of the season, and who, consequently, have not taken flight yet. Papa and mamma, boys and girls, here they all are.

About half-past ten, Sir Hugh gives Lady Capel his arm, and leads her to the dancing room; each man chooses the woman he loves, or the woman to whom he has just been introduced, or the woman whose father has asked him to dinner, and we all troop after them.

I don't wish to see a more cheery scene than the Wentworth dining-room—transmogrified with pink calico and union jacks, and wreaths of evergreens and flowers, till it hardly knows itself—presented that evening, just before the dancing commenced, when the waxlights—becomingest of lights—were all lit and blazing softly, mellowly, from their sconces along the walls where dresses were rustling gently, and there was a buzz of talking; when the hook-nosed chaperones, (why, I wonder, do the noses of most British matrons at a certain period become hooks?) in their many coloured silks and satins were settling down on their benches, like a flock of brilliant but venerable tropical birds, contented with the prospect of an evening of vicarious enjoyment, and looking forward with trusting faith to the supper hour; when all the girls, with one or two hopeless exceptions, were looking pretty, and when the fiddlers were tuning up and causing their instruments to emit queer little squeaks, discordant prelude to a harmonious after-piece. My faithful Grenadier boy has bidden me for the first dance, which turns out to be a quadrille,[1] rather to his disgust.

"I did not mean to ask you for one of those stupid square things!" he says, "it's the worst compliment you can pay a woman to ask her for a quadrille!"

"For the *last* quadrille," I say laughing. "You have not done that at all events!"

Sir Hugh has been rushing about wildly, saying a civil thing to each of the old women, and making good-humoured jokes to a percentage of the girls; now he comes up to me, where I sit on a scarlet bench alone.

---

1 A dance performed by two couples together, involving a frequent exchange of partners.

"You are engaged for this next valse, *of course?*"

"Yes."

"Is not it anybody that you can cut?"

"Oh, no! no!"

"Give me the next then, won't you? We have made it up, haven't we?"

"I did not know that we had ever quarrelled!"

"All right then; *mind* you keep it for me."

He writes his name on my card, as men always do write on these occasions, so that no human being could decipher it, and then rushes back to his duties. I told Sir Hugh a fib; I am not engaged for the next dance. Several people have asked me for it, but I have told the same fib to them all; I am keeping it for one who does not seem inclined to come and claim it. There is a little pause between the two dances; a little lull between two pleasant storms; people seem to be shaking up together very comfortably. The strange warriors have made acquaintance with some of the native women, and are exchanging beads and looking-glasses.

The Miss Coxes are in great request; Miss Violet—such a jolly girl! it does not in the least matter what you say to her—is holding a little court near the door, well away from Lady Lancaster; her *bon mots* do not reach me, but the applause that follows them does. Close to me, the young man with the catarrh[1] is coughing noisily; his cold has taken a new turn; he can pronounce his M's and N's, but he has purchased that power at the expense of as roaring a cough, as the poor lady's in the epitaph.

"If you would but try jujubes,"[2] I hear Miss Seymour saying, with feeling.

"No good at all!" replies the sufferer, huskily. "I've eaten a box and a half already."

He seems very sorry indeed for himself as men always do, if they have a finger-ache.

"Go to bye-bye, my dear fellow, I advise!" says little De Laney heartlessly; "put your feet in gruel and drink hot water, and you'll be all serene to-morrow morning."

---

1   A cold.

2   The name is taken from the fruit of the same name. It was used as food and could be pulped and made into lozenges for the treatment for sore throats.

The invalid looks cross, and mutters something about its being all very fine.

"Not fine at all! if you intend going on barking that way all the evening, for you'll drown the band," and then he goes off laughing.

"I'm afraid you'll think me a very fidgety old woman," says Lady Lancaster to a young matron, who has inadvertently placed herself near an open window, "but aren't you a little imprudent to be sitting in such a thorough draught? nothing so likely to give cold; we old people have learnt by bitter experience you know, particularly when *décolleté*[1] too——"

I hear no more, for the band clashes out; big fiddle and little fiddle, harp and bones, off they go. There is a movement among the company; non-dancers clearing out of the way, men looking for their partners.

My heart begins to beat so fast, that I feel choking. "Perhaps he cannot see me where I am sitting." I stand up, and push gently forwards into the front of the circle forming round the dancers, while my legs tremble under me.

The ice is broken; one adventurous couple has set off on their course of insane gyrations, quickly followed by another and another, till the whole room is filled with whirling clouds of tulle and tarlatan, enveloped in which, manly legs vanish to re-appear meteor-like for an instant and then be swallowed up more completely than before. I dig my fingers into my poor bruised arm, and don't feel the pain I am inflicting on myself one bit. "Won't he come? won't he come? Oh, how cruel he is!" Suddenly an opening is made in the spectators, to admit a fresh couple, *such* a handsome couple.

"Hallo! how's this?" cries Hugh, coming up behind, "has your partner forgotten you?"

"I—I believe so," with my lips trembling.

"Never mind, there's as good fish in the sea, as ever came out of it; you'll have to put up with me, after all."

"Oh, no! no!" I cry, turning my shoulder to him; "I don't want, please not."

Sir Hugh is rather obtuse.

---

1 Wearing a low cut gown, so that the throat and shoulders are exposed (French).

"*You* a wallflower[1] of all people! I couldn't think of such a thing."

I have not spirit to resist further, nor can I trust my voice, so we join the whirl, and whirl too. Hugh dances well; does it with all his heart, and mind, and soul, and strength, as he does everything he puts his hand to—the great secret of his happy cheery life is that he never does anything by halves. I get giddy at last, so we stop and watch our neighbours spinning away like so many peg tops, to the sound of "Il Bacio."[2]

Some dance in time; some dance out; some dance hoppily, like parched peas; some dance smoothly; some go jog trotting along, like old cart horses to market; some go racing pace. Amaryllis Coxe and a long gawky,[3] all arms and legs, come floundering into us.

"Oh, I beg your pardon; I hope I did no harm." Then lumber off again; hobble-de-gee, hobble-de-gee. Another couple passes us; racers these; and I bite my lip till it bleeds, as I look after them. Dolly in maize tulle, and pomegranates in her hair; smooth cheeks like living rose leaves; her scarlet lips half apart, is floating down the long room, lying restfully in Dick's arms, with her head on his shoulder. Dolly has a most reprehensible style of dancing; *I* think though Dick does not seem to think so, as they swim fleetly round, with the most complete agreement in their supple movements. Dolly is the sort of woman upon whom Mr. Algernon Swinburne[4] would write pages of magnificent uncleanness.

"Where were we this time last night, eh?" roars Hugh sentimentally, for we are close to the recess where the band is placed.

"I'm rested!" I say, abruptly; I *cannot* stand any tender reminiscences. So that dance ends, and another and another follow quickly.

The patient chaperones sit biding their time, like a row of old hens, roosting in a hen house, with here and there a superannuated chanticleer crowing feebly to enliven them. A knot of men hang about the door, talking *horsily* and *doggily*, and fling out a

---

1 At a dance, a woman who is sitting by the side of the room (i.e., by the wall), not dancing.

2 "The Kiss" (Italian), an 1862 waltz by Luigi Arditi.

3 That is, a long, gawky fellow.

4 The poetry of Algernon Charles Swinburne (1837-1909) was particularly known for its sexual impropriety.

careless word of commendation in the equine tongue, as some filly, more promising than ordinary, flies by, wafting twenty yards of tulle against their faces.

"Why aren't you taking a more active part in these gay doings?" asks the naughty old gentleman, who is known amongst men by the name of Sir Phillip Leroy, to the widowed Mrs. Marryat, who has effected an ingenious compromise between the memory of the enskied one,[1] and the desire not to let grief be too disfiguring in the eyes of his successor in *posse*,[2] by a judicious combination of the funeral black and the bridal white in her attire.

"*I!* Oh, no! no!" with a glance at her black dress, and a sigh.

"Perhaps," (letting himself gently down on the bench beside her), "perhaps you object to the pleasant knocking down of old-fashioned barriers in the present style of dancing; it certainly is what would have been called in *our* younger days, —— (How to write a whisper), don't you think so?"

"Take care! take care! somebody will hear you."

I have been guiding heavy youths who *would* give their left hand, when they ought to give their right, and their right hand when they ought to give their left, through the labyrinth of the Lancers, and the mazes of the gay quadrille. Men seem to like fern wreaths, and red heads, and ignorance. It is quite a new light to myself that I am a beauty, but I am so fortunate as to overhear that the bay filly[3] is considered quite one of the best things out. I have been scampering round the room with almost every man in it, with one melancholy exception.

Dick has been scampering largely too; with the three Miss Coxes of course; a quadrille with Mrs. Coxe—who makes her steps and chassés[4] as the world chasséd in the days when she was Miss Martha Harris—with Miss Gifford, Miss Seymour and half a dozen other Misses; then again with Dolly.

"I so seldom meet anyone whose step suits mine; it *is* such a treat!" I hear Dolly saying very softly, while she looks at him as I fancy Delilah looked at Samson, when she tried to wile the secret of his strength from him. Dolly reminds me of

---

1 A made-up word for one who has gone to heaven (the sky); i.e., the widow's late husband.
2 Potential (Latin).
3 A young female horse of a reddish brown color.
4 Gliding dance steps (French).

"—The maid of Cassivelaun,
Whom Gwydion made by glamour out of flowers."[1]

"Sandy! The canny Scot! Daddy Longlegs!" say I to myself
indignantly, recalling all the ignominious epithets that she had
heaped on the man, at whom she is now looking with the eyes of
a hundred "Laises"[2] rolled into one. Oh, if I could but tell him!
How I wish that she had had the small-pox in her youth; she
might have been a good, worthy, useful woman then; making
flannel waistcoats for poor people; wheeling the old dad's chair
to the fire for him, and being my confidant.

The room is getting so hot; too much of a good thing is as
undesirable as a little of a bad one; the smell of the gilly-flowers
and roses is getting past a joke; it makes one's head ache and
one almost wishes to exchange it for a little bone-dust or guano.
Some one—a young person—opens a window, and some one—
an old person, Lady Lancaster, I think it is—shuts it again. Lady
Lancaster has that rooted aversion to fresh air, which characterized the last generation.

The girls fan themselves vigorously, and the men mop their
foreheads, and a whisper goes through the room that the door
of the supper-room is open. Unhappy Patres Conscripti[3] who
have been dragged hither at their wives "chariot wheels," begin
to console themselves with the reflection that their sufferings are
at all events half over.

"Come, Capel, you lazy beggar!" says Sir Hugh coming up,
and tapping that ornament to the Peerage on the back; "why
don't you make yourself of some use? take one of those old girls
down to supper with you; oh, yes, there is Mrs. Coxe; take her;
won't she 'my lord' you!"

"What, that female Daniel Lambert![4] No, no, my good fellow; it makes one hot to look at her; and I'm 92 in the shade,
as it is!"

However, he obeys, and others go and do likewise. Dowager

---

1 See "The Marriage of Geraint" in *Idylls of the King* (1859), by Tennyson.
2 Lais was a famous Greek courtesan who lived around the fourth
   century BC.
3 Fathers "drafted" against their will (to go to the ball) (Latin).
4 In the late eighteenth century, Daniel Lambert was famous as the
   heaviest man in England.

after dowager sweeps by to receive the reward of her faith. The musicians retire to refresh themselves, and I need hardly say that the man who plays the bones gets drunk.

"Been to supper?" asks Hugh, who is conveying one of the first detachment back again.

I have freed myself from all my admirers, and am sitting in a humped-up, disconsolate attitude like a fowl on a wet day.

"No, I don't want any!" looking down uneasily, and plucking at the wooden bracelet that adorns my left wrist.

"Oh, nonsense! we must have half a dozen more spins by-and-bye. I have got through all my duty dances,[1] and you'll never be up to them without lots of champagne; we mustn't let her starve herself, must we, mother?"

Mother waggles her old head, while the family diamonds (even *they* don't render me unfaithful to Dick) make a restless light on her withered neck, and says "No, indeed!" she is always an advocate for a good deal of nourishment for young people.

For the second time, I am vanquished, and am walked off to the supper-room, where I find my fellow creatures like cattle before rain—

"Forty feeding like one";[2]

and where I am compelled to swallow chicken and tongue that sticks in my throat, and champagne that is of all drinks the one most abhorrent to me. The evening wears on, with no improvement in my circumstances.

I get so weary at last of the everlasting "tum te tum! tum te tum!" The room is getting strewn with long strips and fragments of gauze and tulle; and the garlands flag and droop. The girls' hair is getting loosened, and their complexions red and flushed; all the freshness is gone from their faces and their toilettes; there is something of the Bacchante,[3] I always think, in the look of a woman at the end of a hard-fought ball; the men wear better, but

---

1 As host, he is obligated to dance with all the eligible women at least once before repeating.
2 See "Written in March" (1801), a poem by William Wordsworth.
3 A priestess of Bacchus, god of wine. Bacchantes were pictured as drunken, disheveled and lustful women.

they look rather limp too, and inclined like La Motte Fouqué's "Ondine"[1] to melt away into running brooks.

"That's in honour of me!" says little De Laney, as the "Guards' Waltz" peals out, and we prepare to embark on it, "a very pretty compliment of Lancaster's isn't it?"

"You are like the man that got up and bowed, when the people cheered the king as he came into the theatre," I say laughing, for there is something contagious about light-heartedness.

· "Who's the girl in the blue top knot; one would have to have a piece added on to one's arm, before one could hope to get round *her* waist."

"Miss Coxe."

"Any relation to the Army Agent, because if so, I would ask her to put in a good word for me with her papa."

"I don't know, I'm sure."

"One struggle more and she'll be free, whoever she is."

Amaryllis is candour and generosity's self in the display of her anatomy. One faint gleam of hope comes to me that evening; but it is like the little yellow glimmer of light that comes out on a hill-side in wintry weather, no sooner seen than swallowed up again in the dull murkiness. I am dancing a quadrille, with that ever-lasting, excellent, intolerable Hugh, and Dick, very much against his will, is my *vis-à-vis*.[2] We meet in the dance; "What on earth *have* I done?" I say, with tears in my voice, and throwing all my eager soul into my misty blue eyes, as I look up in his dear sulky patrician face. He glances down at me doubtfully, half inclined to be mollified.

"Now, Miss Nelly! now, Miss Nelly!" (how enraging to be called "Miss Nelly") "what are you thinking about? we ought to have been half through this figure by now!" cries Sir Hugh catching hold of my hand, and the opportunity that looked so promising is lost. It is a mistake to suppose that it is the wicked that make this world such a sad and weary place, it is the good, blundering dunderheads! "How our wishes do mock us!" I think to myself, as I follow Lady Lancaster and her sleepy covey up the broad shallow staircase to bed. "I should have thought that to meet Dick at a ball was the acme of human happiness, and now——"

---

1 Friedrich de la Motte Fouqué (1777-1843) wrote *Undine* (1811), a tale of a mermaid who (unhappily) marries a human knight.

2 Face to face with, or in relation to (French). Here, dance partner.

I wake next morning, stiff as a doll that refuses to bend anywhere but in the middle, and with great difficulty there; with my head feeling like a ton of lead, and my eyes swelled to the size of well grown walnuts.

"What an object!" cries Dolly, lifting up her slim hands, as she comes into my room, in an innocent-looking white *peignoir*,[1] looking as fresh as a daisy. "Rachel weeping for her children! Charlotte at the tomb of Werther! Agrippina over the urn of somebody![2] I thought how it would be, so I came to see."

"You'll—you'll be the death of me, Dolly," I say whimpering, "and—and then you'll be sorry!"

"The jury will bring it in *felo de se*,[3] I think!" says Dolly, tripping daintily across to the window, and pulling up the blinds, the better to examine into the condition of my countenance. "Good heavens, child! you are worse than I thought; not all the Eau de Cologne, and rouge and pearl powder[4] in England could make you presentable; you would defy Madame Rachel;[5] you must not attempt to go downstairs."

"I don't mean to!" I say sobbing, "you shall have it all your own way; go and tell him some more *lies* about me, and I'll st-st-stay up here, and—and *die!*"

CHAPTER XXIII

I went dinnerless that day at Wentworth—a thing that even in deepest grief one is seldom willing to do—dinnerless, unless the

---

1 A light dressing gown.
2 All of these weeping women were popular subjects for sentimental paintings. Rachel weeping for her dead children, massacred by Herod, appears in Jeremiah 31:15-17. Charlotte weeps for the dead Werther, the hero of Johann Wolfgang von Göethe's novel, *The Sorrows of Werther* (1774). Agrippina was the wife of Germanicus, a Roman General who died around 19 CE, possibly on orders of the emperor Tiberius. She returned to Brindisi, accompanied by her sons and carrying the urn containing her husband's ashes.
3 Suicide (Latin).
4 Cosmetics. Ladies of the upper and middle classes were not supposed to wear cosmetics in this period, but many apparently did.
5 In the mid-nineteenth century, Madame Rachel was a famous cosmeticist. In 1868 she was imprisoned for fraud.

cud of sour and bitter thoughts which I chewed might pass for the festive meal that forms the nucleus of day's dearest interests in most people's lives. Nor did I appear at all till the evening was well on towards ten o'clock. If I had listened to the voice of nature, I should not have appeared at all, but should have retired straightway to bed, and paid the consideration that was due to it, to my most painful occiput.[1] But then we were to leave Wentworth next day, and I could not afford to lose my last chance of reconciliation with Dick.

At all risks, at the risk of my head splitting in two, I must go down to keep a watch upon the wily Dorothea's movements. So I rose, and bathed my cheeks with fresh water, whereby they became and remained as red as the new pulpit cushions in Lestrange Church; I twisted up my hair, and crowned it with a bush of ivy, put on a white frock, girded myself with a rosy sash, and went down.

I stole into the bilious drawing-room, in a mouse-like manner, in the wake of a brace of giant footmen, bearing tea, nor did any one perceive my modest entry. Three-fourths of the party were, I found, tightly packed round a table, employed in one of the senselessest modes of wasting time, that man (ingenious in frittering away his little day) has ever invented—a round game.

Every one was speaking at the utmost pitch of their voices, and laughing with all the force of their lungs. Some were squabbling over counters, some were making oeillades[2] behind clubs and spades and diamonds, some were facetiously trying to cheat, and others were getting cross with them for so trying.

Every man spoke, and no man listened. Surely, surely, ombre and quadrille and brag[3] must have been delectabler games than their posterity, commerce and chow-chow,[4] or they never could have seduced the Lady Betty Modishes, Lady Bridgets, and Lady Annes,[5] into keeping such rakish[6] hours, and indulging

---

1 Part of the skull.
2 Winks (French).
3 Ombre, quadrille and brag were games popular in the eighteenth century. Ombre was an ancestor of bridge; quadrille was a variation. Brag was more similar to poker.
4 These are all card games.
5 Lady Betty Modish is a character in Colley Cibber's play, *The Careless Husband* (1705). Lady Bridget and Lady Anne are likewise characters from this period.
6 A "rake" is a person (usually, but not always, a man) of loose morals.

such naughty passions for their sakes, as we are led by the Spectator[1] to suppose they did.

"Sympathy, or antipathy?"[2] says Sir Hugh, in his stentor's[3] voice, interrogatively, to the sharp young lady beside him.

"Oh, antipathy!" she answers venomously, "I always say antipathy; it pays much the best, I find."

"I like sympathy best; don't you?" sighs Miss Seymour, to a very Anglican young divine, who is beaming over his barnacles, pastorally at her, and her lean collar bones.

"Six upon sympathy!"

"Six upon antipathy!"

"Six upon sympathy!"

"You owe me thirty-six."

"How do you make that out?"

"Have 'rouge et noir,'[4] Sir Hugh!"

"Do! It's such fun."

"No, no, *have* blind hookey!"[5]

"No, pips!"

"Take my advice, Lancaster, don't have pips! dealer always loses."

Such, and many similar ejaculations, uttered simultaneously, in keys varying from *forte* to *fortissimo*,[6] assail my mazed ears. Dick is not among them, Dolly is; Miss Lestrange is off guard; she is a little out of her reckoning, and is enjoying a false security, under the impression that I am tossing in anguish on a bed of pain up-stairs, out of the way of handsome paupers.

She is no longer the shrewd, worldly-wise woman of two hours ago, whose sentiments might have been those of a French Marquise of fifty, *temp.* Louis Quinze,[7] and could hardly have belonged to any one younger or less world-polluted. She is trans-

---

1 *The Spectator* was an enormously influential eighteenth-century literary magazine. Although it continued for many years, it was most famous in its early years under the direction of Joseph Addison and Richard Steele (1711-14).

2 Gambling moves.

3 A powerful voice. After Stentor, the Greek herald in *The Iliad*.

4 Red and black (French). Gambling card game.

5 A gambling card game in which one bets before looking at the cards.

6 Strong to very strong (Italian). Used in music to indicated loudness.

7 Louis XV (1710-74) was famed for his vices.

formed into the innocentest, childishest Marguerite;[1] one could well fancy her picking the daisy petals to pieces, to find out whether her lover loved her *un peu, passionément,* or *point de tout.*[2]

The guiltless author of this metamorphosis was a very young cotton lord, with a fleshy nose, and a retreating chin, who was willing enough to be Faust; willing, though not eager, because no young gentleman that is a real young gentleman, ever is eager about anything now-a-days.

Dolly's whole infantine soul was immersed in her miniature speculations; her soft cheeks were flushing shyly, and the full pink lips, and the velvet eyes, were saying, with a triumph of simplicity, "I should like always to be your partner, you bring me such good luck." The old game! The old game! It wearies me! But where is Richard? Is he dead, or gone to bed? My eyes roam over the yellow sea, but fail to descry him; then I bethink me of the folding-doors, and the adjoining saloon.

Is that—can it be the top of a human head appearing above the back of an arm-chair, in the dim distance? It is worth investigating. I investigate. The head is Dick's. Dick lying back, holding a book topsy-turvy in his hand, and looking as bored and as sulky as any one of Her Majesty's servants need look.

"I came to look for *you—Dick!*" I say in a small meek voice, diffidently.

"Indeed! Very good of you, I'm sure!" rising ceremoniously, and trying very hard, but vainly, to be ironical. One must either be, or appear to be, in a good temper, to be successfully ironical.

"I thought I'd come and try to make friends," say I conciliatorily.

"Have you asked Sir Hugh's leave?" says he, acrimoniously.

"What do you mean?"

"What I say."

We stand and glare irefully at one another. I cool first. "Oh dear, oh dear! how soon Dolly has turned you against me, poor me!" I cry plaintively.

"You never were more mistaken in your life; on the contrary, Dol—, your sister, I mean—tried her best to make excuses for you; said you were young and changeable, and foolish!"

---

1 In Goethe's play *Faust* (first part published in 1808), Marguerite is the innocent working-class girl seduced and ruined by Faust. She also plays the "daisy game," and marguérite means daisy in French.
2 A little, passionately, or not at all (French).

Who likes being called foolish? none of us minds being called wicked; we take it rather civilly than otherwise; but who does not resent the imputation of folly? "Young and foolish, am I?" I cry, at white heat; "and what is she, pray? Would you like to know? Shall I tell you: she's a *mean liar*, that's what she is, there?"

Dick gnaws his moustache savagely; my nervous English displeases him. "Calling names is very easy," he says, angrily, "blackening another person to whitewash yourself; it's not quite so easy proving your assertions."

I come quite close to him, in my eagerness, and lay a hot white hand on his coat sleeve.

"Is not a liar a person that tells lies?" I ask.

"Of course."

"Well, did not she tell a lie, a villainous black lie, when she told you the day before yesterday that I wanted Hugh to drive me? Don't I hate Hugh? Don't I think him the dullest, tiresomest, botheringest, gray-headedest old fogey that ever existed? She knows I do, and you know I do, only you're b-b-bent on br-breaking my heart."

So I finish with symptoms of imminent whimpering. Exeunt[1] sulks and scowls from my lover's face.

"Is that true, Nell?"

"True! to be sure it is! Am I a liar, like Dolly?"

"On your honour?"

"On my honour."

"On your soul?"

"On my soul."

"You did not want to drive with him? You are *sure*."

"Not I, indeed! I was in such a rage that I would hardly speak to him all the way to Wilton, only he is such a dunderhead that I don't think he perceived it; how *you* ever could have believed such a transparent falsehood, passes my comprehension."

The gray eyes look rather ashamed of themselves, but very much pleased all the same.

"Was not it natural I should think you'd prefer a rich beggar like him to a poor devil, who has not got two halfpennies to rub together, like me?"

"Does one value one's friends in proportion to the depth of their money bags? If one did, I should have but a poor opinion of myself and my dear old father," I say gravely.

---

1   They leave (Latin). Used in stage directions.

There comes a fresh burst of maniac mirth from the votaries of chow-chow.

"He's cheating; he's cheating!" "Will you sell your deal?" "I'll give you half-a-crown for it." "Three shillings." "Twelve and ten is twenty-two, I'm up!" "No thanks; I'll stand!" etc., etc.

"Come into the verandah, Nell," says Dick, taking my most willing fingers in his; "we cannot hear each other's voices for this Babel,[1] can we?"

We pass into the verandah upon which the *salon* "gives,"[2] to use an Anglicised Gallicism. Roses, red and white; roses, full-blown and over-blown and budding; rugosa, with her old-fashioned scented clusters, and her redder sisters, climb and clamber up the wooden trellis work; clematis weaves her tendrils in amongst them, and jessamine stars stud the deep green of ivy leaves. And through creepers and trellis work the moon looks down, benignant and gracious, and large and full, turning the night into a mellow softened feminine day.

She fell full on a beautiful passionate face (not mine, I don't mean), and on a form such as one may fancy those were that wrestled in blue and green on the bloody sand of the arena, before the pitiless Roman world,[3] when (the cruel thumbs being turned down) many a gladiatorial Hercules bit the dust. Good God! how happy I was, lying in his arms, and with the top of my tall wreath scratching his handsome nose.

"I'm a jealous idiot, aren't I, pretty one?" he asks, raining kisses on my lips, thick as leaves in autumn, or the whirling Simois.[4]

"Yes, Dick, I think so."

---

1 See Genesis 11. According to Genesis, when the people of the earth tried to build a tower tall as heaven, God punished their presumption by imposing multiple languages on the builders, so they could no longer communicate with each other. (Before this time, the entire earth spoke a single language.) The word has come to mean a place of noisy confusion.

2 In French, as in other Romance languages, a door "gives" upon or into the street or another room.

3 In ancient Rome, gladiators who vanquished a valiant enemy could allow the crowd to decide if the loser should be killed. Traditionally, the crowd is believed to have decided the loser's fate by displaying the thumb's up sign (to spare him), or down (to kill).

4 The Simois river features prominently in Greek mythology. This reference is from Tennyson's poem "Oenone" (1833).

"You'll never think the same of me again, of course?"

"Oh, no, never!" (shaking my head with solemnity).

"But still, bad as I am, you like me a little bit better than Lancaster?"

"I should like you very little indeed, else."

"You little foolish girl! think of preferring me with twopence a year to him with a fine house, and a handle to his name."

"That's just what Dolly says; as you both say the same thing, there must be some truth in it; but it's never too late to mend, is it? The big house and the handle are still within reach, you know; will you come and see me when I'm Lady Lancaster?"

"No, I'm d—d if I will!"

I see the gray eyes flash in the moonlight at the bare idea of that visit.

"Nelly Lancaster! Eleanor Lancaster! how pretty it sounds!" I cry, pensively, plucking a moon washed rose, and sniffing at it.

"Nelly Lestrange is prettier, and Nelly M'Gregor is prettiest of all, isn't it, darling?" asks Dick, gathering me closer than ever to himself.

"What love is in the moon's eternal eyes
Leaning unto the earth from out the blissful skies."[1]

Did she look with love at us two poor fools, who, spendthrift-like, were devouring our whole portion of bliss in one half hour; that portion, which, spread in a thin layer, over long years, ought to have afforded us a decent competence during our lives? Silent we stood there, passion-drunk; did we remember then, in our perfect wonderful satisfaction, who it was that has said "this is not your rest?" The night wind sighs past; it is bearing, perhaps, some weary soul to the land that is very far off, it rocks the heavy-folded roses, and whispers to us some vague sweet tale that we heed not.

"Oh, Dick!" I murmur, "I wish to God I could die now. I shall never, *never* be so happy again!"

Dick shudders through his strong young frame.

"Don't talk of dying, my darling! Your life is only just begun, you poor little child!"

---

1   Compare "A Life-Drama" in *Poems* (1853), by Alexander Smith (1830-67).

"M'Gregor! M'Gregor! where are you?" sounds the stentor's voice[1] of our worthy host, breaking prosaically on our touching dialogue at this point. "Where the devil is the fellow gone?"

"The fellow" makes no sign; he lies as quiet as a partridge between two turnip ridges. Then a dark head and a body issue from the saloon,[2] and step through the French windows, on to the verandah.

"Oh, you're here, are you?" in a voice of anything but gratification at the discovery.

"Yes, my good fellow, you made such a row over your game, all of you, that we had to come out here for a little peace and quietness—hadn't we?" turning to me, with softened voice, and eyes fondly possessive. I say "yes," and mumble something, in an indistinct manner, about its being late, and going to bed, and— headache, and shuffle off, very red in the face, leaving my two lovers to decide their rival claims to the possession of my person, by single combat, by lots, or by heads and tails, whichever they chose.

CHAPTER XXIV

Why do I tell my poor little story so circumstantially, I wonder? Will any one care to read it? Is a dissected heart worth looking at, even though it be rather a foolish one? They say that love is the recognizing something of oneself in another person. Will any one, I wonder, recognise in me some of their own foolish fancies and thoughts and notions, and love me for being as silly as themselves, and for owning to them that I am? The old yellow-bodied barouche,[3] and the two victims to spavin and spring-halt,[4] are slowly creeping up "the long back" of a hill; the old coachman is flicking spavin's fat flanks gently with his whip, which that worthy beast does not mind a bit. The sunlight lies patchily on the dusty road; here and there a big tree intercepts it, and holds it in his great branches; a little white-haired child stands at a cottage door

---

1 A powerful voice. After Stentor, the Greek herald in *The Iliad*.
2 Alternate spelling for salon, or parlor.
3 A four-wheeled carriage with a collapsible top.
4 Both diseases of horses. Spavin causes lameness, and spring-halt causes leg spasms.

eating bread and treacle, and clapping his little brown hands at the horses; bees are buzzing drowsily about straw hives; "wine-dark" auriculas are blowing in the little borders; a woman is feeding a pig. We are going home; Wentworth lies three miles behind us, and I am thinking of the past, and smiling.

How plainly I see that group gathered on the stone steps to bid us God-speed. Lady Lancaster, in a brown silk so stiff and thick that it could well stand by itself, without the support of her ladyship's body inside it, leaning forward to give me a motherly salute (her beard meanwhile pricking me rather), while she says, in her prim old woman's voice—

"I hope we shall see you very often my dear, *now!*"

Dolly, with one foot on the carriage step, giving a small, smooth lavender hand to Sir Hugh, and saying good-bye to him so softly, as if she was so sorry to part from him; Dick, leaning one great shoulder against the door-post, and smiling a tender, flickering smile under his heavy moustache, and all around a great glory of sunshine, and young green leaves, and blue summer sky. Dick is going to Cork to-day, to join his regiment (happy, happy Cork!) but he is going to write to me, and I am to write to him; is not this brick and mortar enough to build quite a big Spanish castle[1] with? I am so building now as we jog along in the sleepy sunshine.

"My darling! my darling!" I am saying to myself over and over again, like the refrain to a song; "how I love you!" My hands are clasped together in my green cotton cap, and my eyes are looking up to the grand blue dome above, in a great rapture and gratitude and joy. Was it his beauty I loved him for? Should I have loved him so much if he had been little and black and ugly? If his comely looks were to go away from him now, would my love go away too? No, no, *no!* If he were to lose arms and legs, and eyes and nose and ears, he would still be my Dick, my beautiful, strong King Olaf.

In my mind I was drawing a little picture—a little picture with two figures and a dingy background. A bare barrack-room (barrack-rooms were always bare, I imagined, and of course we should not be able to afford lodgings) with no curtain, perhaps, and a bit of drugget in the middle of the floor, and a green baize[2]

---

1 A "castle in the air," a fantasy.
2 Cheap coarse cotton or wool fabric, with a fuzzy surface.

table-cloth. A good fire though there was in the picture, and an elbow chair beside it; Dick in the elbow chair in full regimentals (I had an adoration equal to any boarding-school miss's for

"The pomp and circumstance of glorious war"),[1]

and I, on a low stool at his feet, with my arms resting on his knees, looking up alternately at his face and his medals—my hero had three of those insignia—and making little tender speeches to him—speeches that I never hitherto had summoned resolution to utter.

When by myself I was eloquent enough, eloquent as Ulysses or Burke,[2] but when with him the passion of his eyes struck me dumb. It would be different when we were married. I should then be able to speak to him without that shy thrill; should be able to tell him what he was to me; to find words to syllable my great pure love.

Then the scene shifted. Dick was ousted from among the *dramatis personæ*;[3] I reigned in the elbow chair instead; I, dressed simply yet elegantly, holding a levée of officers of every grade and standing in Her Majesty's army; colonels, majors, and captains clustering in reverent admiration around me.

With what modest dignity should I comport myself in my difficult position; with what simple yet spirited answers should I parry their complimentary remarks.

Married at nineteen! How interesting, and like a story-book! Mrs. M'Gregor! Nelly M'Gregor! Major and Mrs. M'Gregor! I would write it down in my blotting book as soon as I got home, to see how it looked.

I suppose my lips moved visibly as I articulated my own and husband's names softly under my breath, for Dolly, who had not uttered a word before since we left Wentworth, now turned to me—Dolly in a neutral-tinted gauzy bonnet, with one blood-red carnation resting on and contrasting her shiny sombre hair; thus she spoke in her harmoniously round, full tones—

"Are you engaged in prayer?"

---

1 See Shakespeare's play *Othello* (first printed 1622).
2 Ulysses of Greek myth and British politician Edmund Burke (1729-97) were both noted for their persuasive eloquence.
3 Cast of characters (Latin), as in a play.

"No"; said I, rather cross at being roused from my reverie; "why on earth should I be?"

"Your lips were moving, so I thought you might be breathing a short prayer, as people do in the 'Sunday at Home,'[1] you know—for me, perhaps."

"No, I wasn't," said I; "I was talking to myself, which is much pleasanter than praying; at least I find it so." (Merciful God! I don't think so now!)

I turned my head away, and watched the cloud-shadows travelling swiftly over the green wheat fields, turning their laughing golden green into dull blue green as they passed; at the blackbirds gobbling cherries in the farm orchards we were driving by.

"Is it thinking of its lover?" pursued the angel in the gauzy bonnet.

"Yes," said I, briefly, "I am."

I would not stand any impudence from Dolly any longer, I was resolved. I should soon be a married woman, and able to patronize spinsters all and sundry.

"So it has got its big wax doll after all, has it?" asks she, with a sneer, "curly wig and long legs, and all!"

I am roused to retort. I turn and rend her.

"Sour grapes!" cry I, with red cheeks, and in an elevated key; "don't you wish we could say—

"Miss Jenny and Polly
Had *each* a new Dolly?"[2]

Dolly smiled sweetly, but her long sleepy eyes gave one little flash.

"Yes, dear, I do," she said with candour, "only I don't think I should care about playing dolls in a workhouse, which I fear will be your portion."

"I believe you would sell your soul for gold," said I, with my nose in the air, in lofty disdain.

"I certainly would," answered my sister, sedately; "one's soul

---

1 Probably the periodical known as *The Sunday at Home*, which began publication in 1854 and continued until 1940.

2 See "The New Dolls" in *The Daisy, or, Cautionary Stories in Verse, Adapted to the Ideas of Children from Four to Eight Years Old* (1810), a children's rhyme by Elizabeth Turner.

does not do one much good that I could ever find out; if I could have my body left me, my nice, pretty, pleasant body, with plenty of money to keep it well fed and well dressed, I'd give my soul its *congé*[1] with the greatest *sang froid*[2] imaginable."

I felt feebly shocked at Dolly's sentiments, but too lazily and sovereignly indifferent to what she or her soul said or did to contest the point with her, so we relapsed into silence, and preserved a sort of armed truce, till we reached the rook-haunted old house blinking sleepily from its ivy mantle amid its sunny crofts, with the gray-blue smoke curling straight up into the air from the queer old chimney-stacks.

The library windows at Lestrange look out on the gravelled sweep before the door; small-paned, casemented windows they are; and as we passed them I leaned forwards eagerly, to blow kisses at my father, whose face I saw leaning out among the roses and the bowery clematis to greet us. What a sad old face it was! What a yellowing tinge—like a sere November leaf's tinge, that spake of waning life and waxing sickness—was stealing over it. Poor noble old face! how often I see you now in my dreams, looking out from among the fresh pink rose-bunches! I ran to my sire with "effusion," and hurled my substantial young person into his arms; he bore the charge with equanimity.

"Well, little lass!" he said, with his sorrowful smile, sorrow-fuller than any tears, "have you seen a great many fine people, and got a fine new lover, and are you very sorry to come back to the dull old house and the dull old man?"

"Of course I am," said I, with a fresh series of ursine[3] hugs; "I should not have come back at all if it had not been that I knew the Cochin cock was to be killed to-morrow, and I thought I must come back and bid him good-bye, poor dear fowl, before he died. Come, dad," I continued, coaxingly, thrusting my arm through his in its threadbare gray coat-sleeve, and dragging him to the door, "let us come and see the pigs and the chickens, and I'll tell you all about it."

So we went, my daddy and I—went, and found the doomed chanticleer scratching and scraping peaceably on the dunghill, advertising the treasures he found there, now and again, to his

---

1 Notice of leave, holiday or termination (as from a job).
2 Cold blood, composure (French).
3 Bearlike.

harem, by one lordly cluck. The pigs and we exchanged civilities, and then I began, and narrated all things in order to my parent; how we had gone a pic-nicing, and how I had been upset out of a dogcart, and how I had fainted, and how funny it felt, and how disagreeable it was spending all the night in that little pothouse, reading the "Great Tribulation," and "waiting for the waggon" (my father looked unaccountably grave, I thought, at this stage of my narrative); what a lot there was for dinner every day; what smart gowns old Lady Lancaster had on, with many more interesting particulars concerning the Wentworth *ménage*;[1] nor had I the modesty to hide or in any way qualify the fact that Sir Hugh, the middle-aged, the desirable, the much-hunted, was the captive of my bow and spear. Then breath failed me, and I stopped, and threw damaged rice among the chickens.

"So you're going to be a great lady, are you, Miss Nelly?" said my father, playfully. "You won't speak to your poor old father, I suppose, when you are Lady Lancaster!"

That little bit of news had cheered him wonderfully; he looked less old, less bowed, all of a sudden, somehow. I leaned my elbows on the pigsty wall, reflectively.

"But, dad," objected I, "I've only said that Sir Hugh liked me; I have not said I liked him; that is a very different pair of shoes!"

My father did not heed my interruption.

"Lancasters and Lestranges!" said he to himself, as if the union of the two names was pleasant to him; "more like the old times! more like the good old times!"

A cold chill crept over me, as I thought of the baggage-waggon, and the barrack-room, and twopence a year.

"You seem very anxious to get rid of me, dad," said I, picking bits of lichen from between the slatey gray stones. "Why do you want me to marry Sir Hugh?"

"My poor little lass," said my father very pitifully, "because I'm wearing my life out, thinking every day, and all day long, what is to become of you when I'm dead and gone—gone to be with the little mother, Nell; I pray God," he said, very reverently, taking off his hat; "and also," he added, a minute afterwards, straightening himself, and looking every inch the proud old gentleman he was, "because I believe that to see you raised to your

---

1 Household (French).

right level again, and doing something towards bringing the old family back into its right position in the county, would add ten years to my life; upon my soul, I think it would!"

I could not dash his hopes—could not tell him that I was engaged to a man money-less, position-less, expectation-less; perhaps I ought to have done so, but I could not find it in my heart. So we turned homewards, I a saddened woman, sore perplexed. The chickens still scratched and pecked happily on the dunghill; the pigs grunted in the ineffable content of warmth and repletion; but to me the sunlight had gone out of grass and trees and shining pebbles.

CHAPTER XXV

Am I wrong in thinking that memory is the cruelest gift ever vouchsafed to man? Perhaps I am wrong to say any gift can be cruel, seeing who it is gives all the gifts, both the sweet and the bitter ones. But I cannot help thinking so. How happy we might be, any of us in our very lowest, forlornest state, if we had no recollection of ever having held a higher joyfuller one. If we had no remembrance of the treasures of love and youth and friendship we once owned, how happy we might make ourselves in the dearth or total absence of those good things. We might bask and roll, oh so lightheartedly in the young spring sun, and sniff at the pretty spring flowers, and drink in the lark's long rhapsody, if the brightness and the sweetness and the melody were not all dashed by the memory of how much grandlier the sun shone, how much fragranter the primroses smelt, how much sweetlier the birds sang long ago, when we had some one to feel and smell and listen with us. For my part, if any fairy were to offer me the choice of a gift, as she did to the hero of the sausage tale, I would not hesitate one minute; I would beg her to give me a great full brimming cup of the wine of forgetfulness, and *how* greedily I would drink it up! Maundering again! How prosy I am getting! I am afraid I am painting the little cabinet pictures of my life too minutely, too elaborately; like a Dutch painter,[1] I am reproducing the cabbages and onions, the pots and pans of every-day life, *exactly*, and without elevating them.

---

1 Dutch painters were famed for realistic still-life paintings, in which food was often portrayed.

If I could, I would fain make a brilliant dashing Turneresque[1] sketch; great breadths of colour, infinite nobility and harmony, in few strokes; but that is above me; if I were to attempt it, I should make but a patchy, blotchy daub. No; I must put in numberless fine lines, carefullest shading and copying, before I can produce anything like Nature; not very like even then.

Here is another Dutch picture. Dolly's bed-room; a little sanctuary of innocence and purity, and maidenly bread-and-buttery thoughts you would say, were you privileged to enter and survey it; a small white bed, spotless enough to shelter the slumbers of St. Agnes;[2] with dimity[3] curtains; field flowers in white vases, good little devout prints on the walls; Timothy and Samuel, and the eternal three choristers;[4] Ary Schefferian[5] photographs, and illuminated texts. Texts do impress one so much more, don't they, when they are picked out in blue and yellow, and are playing hide and seek amid numberless twirls and scrolls and flourishes? Dolly is sitting at the dressing-table brushing her hair, which, black as night, thick as a mermaid's, waveless, rippleless, lies heavy on her shoulders.

I am sitting on the open window sill, and my small pale face looks out from amongst a bush of curly warm tinted fuzz. We are enjoying a little sisterly chat at our *coucher*;[6] it is about a week after our return home.

"I wish," says Dolly, brushing away with vigour, "that people would sometimes manage to get the right end of a story."

"How do you mean?" I ask, a little absently.

---

1 Joseph Mallord William Turner (1775-1851) was perhaps the most famous of Romantic English landscape painters.

2 A virgin martyr. On the Eve of St. Agnes's day, maidens would often participate in certain rituals in order that St. Agnes would grant them a dream vision of their future husbands.

3 A cotton fabric with a raised pattern.

4 Biblical subjects considered appropriate for a pious young maiden's décor. The "three choristers" are probably the three righteous Jews who were cast into the fiery furnace because they refused to engage in idolatry. They were preserved by God because they sang a song of praise. Depending on the version of the Book of Daniel, their names were Hananiah or Shadrach, Mishael or Meshach, and Azariah or Abednego.

5 Ary Scheffer (1795-1858) was a German painter, sculptor and printmaker.

6 Bedtime (French).

"Oh, nothing particular," she answers lightly, "only Mrs. Smith has been giving me rather a garbled version of yours and Hugh's adventure, which she says is all over the country."

I frown. "What do I care?"

"Of course not," says my sister, smoothly combing out her long dusk locks, "only I don't think it is very pleasant to think of all the grooms in the neighbourhood making merry over Sir Hugh's huggings and kissings and weepings over you, that time you were insensible; are you sure you were quite insensible, dear?"

I toss my ruddy mane in a fury.

"If I wasn't may I be struck dead this instant, and be insensible for ever with a vengeance."

Dolly lays down her implements, and smiles good humouredly.

"Poor little wooden-headed Damon!"[1] she says, "you'll have to marry him after all, Nell, to stop people's mouths, and prevent their spreading all manner of naughty tales about you and him; what fun!"

"Have to marry a man because I happened to be pitched out of a dogcart with him?" I say, with a snort, and a withering laugh. "Ha! ha!"

"No, dear," replies my elder, gravely twisting up her great black hair coils, with warm dimpled hands; "not because you were upset out of a dogcart with him—people *will* forget that—but because you spent twenty-four hours alone in a little road-side public-house with him, and because everybody knows it, and will not forget it."

A moth floats in from the cool night, and frizzles himself to death in the candle. I feel quite glad. I am in the sort of humour when one is pleased at anything bad happening to anything. Dolly, good Dolly, drew her Bible to her, and looked out the evening lessons.

"By-the-bye," she said, after a pause, "have not you heard from Major M'Gregor yet?"

"No, not yet," I have to own, rather reluctantly.

"Rather odd, isn't it?" asks Dolly, carelessly.

"Not the least odd," I say sharply; but all the same, I do think, and for every hour of the last four days have been thinking, that

---

1 Damon and Pythias were famously close friends in Greek mythology. Damon was also a common name for a male lover in pastoral poetry.

it is odd, dreadfully odd; "of course he would be busy when first he got back to his regiment; of course he'd have a thousand things to do."

"Well, my dear, if you're pleased, I'm sure I am."

Dolly read her chapters piously all through, the dark long fringes shade the eyes that travel so devoutly along the sacred lines; how peaceful and holy the fair clear peach face looks. Why upon earth don't I go to bed, instead of sitting swinging my small slippered feet, ill-temperedly, to and fro? How still the great night outside is; the owls are snoring a little in the high elm tops, but that is all. Dolly's Bible clasps close with a little click.

"How very ill papa's getting to look," she says, looking up serene after her devotions, with a face

"Bright as for sins forgiven."[1]

"so much worse than before we went to Wentworth, even. Poor old gentleman! it makes me quite low to look at him."

I bounce off the window sill, and walk hurriedly up and down, my long blue dressing-gown floating behind me like a toga.

"Did you say that only to frighten me, or because you really think it?" I ask agitatedly.

"Because I really think it, of course," replies she, gently; "is my sole *métier*[2] in life to lacerate your feelings?"

"Seriously ill, do you mean, Dolly?" I ask very falteringly.

Dolly rises and stands by the window; how like a tall garden lily she looks, in her long soft white draperies.

"So ill," she says, emphatically, "that unless some one leaves him a legacy, or some piece of good luck happens to him, he'll be a dead man this time next year; those bills, and his anxiety as to what is to become of us—of *you*, I mean—after his death, are knocking a great many nails into his coffin."

Life without the old man! That was the very first time that that awful, awful thought presented itself to my mind.

"Dolly," said I, with tremulous eagerness, grasping her arm, "would it do him any good, do you think, would it comfort him at all, if I were to tell him about Dick?"

"Comfort him to know that you had found a man magnani-

---

1 Unknown source.
2 Occupation (French).

mous enough, or selfish enough, to be willing to starve with you, and effectually prevent your doing anything towards raising the poor old family again, as it has been and is his dearest wish that it should be raised," said my sister, with trenchant satire. "Yes, of course, it would comfort him immensely, no doubt. I know nothing more calculated to inspire consolation; good night, Nell."

Dolly sinks on her knees, and prepares to engage in evening prayer, and I slink off to bed, and cry myself to sleep.

CHAPTER XXVI

I had gone to sleep weeping, as the night does; I awoke smiling as the morning. The troubles that had seemed so gigantic at 11 p.m., had contracted themselves to very moderate dimensions at 7 a.m. From mountains they had become, not indeed quite molehills, but very gentle elevations. Dolly had a way of touching people on the raw; of course it was to her interest to make me believe Dick unfaithful; and as to my father, why he *did* look rather ill and droopy of late. I had been thinking so, myself, darling old thing! but then the hot weather never suited him; it always made him flag, as it did the flowers; when fresh winds came and cool cloudy skies, both he and they would hold up their heads again, and brighten.

My code of morals, my system of rewards and punishments was very simple, the story book code; later on in life we find that the human race's kicks and halfpence are not administered in strict accordance with the rules of that code. The good boy gets cakes and ale; the naughty boy gets a whipping. There seemed to me an antecedent improbability in the idea of such an enormous grief being laid on the poor slight shoulders of a harmless girl, whose life, as far as overt acts of wickedness were concerned, was a sheet of white paper. It seemed like putting a camel's load on a fly's back. An enormous grief always does seem improbable when it is the first of its family. Its brothers and sisters excite less astonishment, though perhaps no less anguish.

"I saw two magpies yesterday." I say to myself, "that is a good omen; my letter will come to-day." I am standing before my looking-glass, sticking up my dead-leaf cables,[1] with long hair pins. I

---

1 That is, her dead-leaf colored braids.

don't look in the least the sort of woman that anything remarkable is likely to happen to; a fair, soft, foolish woman made to say loving inanities to a husband, to make socks for his children, and be utterly hum-drum and common-place and happy. The loud whir-ir-ring of the gong comes sounding upstairs, deadened by the thick oak doors; I run down in a hurry. My father is always up and out very early, long before any of us; while the house is yet in the housemaid's possession. He is out now, and I have to read prayers. I sit down with dignity in the old oak arm-chair, nearly black with age and varnish, and of the most uncompromising straightness of back—what strong spines our ancestors must have been blessed with, for apparently they never indulged in the luxury of leaning—open the ancient calf-backed Bible, in which twenty-one and nineteen years ago respectively, my father recorded the doubtful blessing of his daughters' births.

Opposite me, on a long bench, sit the servants, in clean caps and aprons, and behind them open windows, and the sun, and the green trees, and the June airs at play. It is a very long chapter; all about the Israelitish wars, how Joshua and his host took Ai and the king thereof, and the people thereof, and killed them all; and then went off to Libuah, and did the same there, and then on again ditto. *How* tired they must have got of cutting and hacking those poor Aborigines![1] About the middle of the bloody annals I look up, and take a glance off through the window over the servants' heads, and see the old postman with the swinging gait and the withered-apple cheeks, shambling down the drive. He is earlier than his wont. I lose my place and grope hopelessly for it with eyes and fingers, for about five minutes. Having found it, I set off at a hard gallop and race through Thursday morning, third week in Thornton's "Family Prayers,"[2] skipping the "Queen, the Clergy, and the Children of this family" altogether. I come to Amen at last; and before the servants are off their knees, I am at the Hall door.

The old postman has gone again; he is halfway up to the gate by now; he knows our manners and customs and has left the bag

---

1 See Joshua 8. As he did to Jericho, Joshua demolishes the city of Ai. He massacres the inhabitants, burns the city and hangs the king, exposing the body afterward on the stones. He does this to several other cities as well. Aborigines here simply means the original inhabitants, though the use of the term in this context suggests a comparison to Britain's colonies.

2 A book by Henry Thornton, first published in 1834.

hanging on the bell. I tear it open; the Times and a Pamphlet; half-a-dozen blue envelopes in the usual sprawly tradesmen's hands for Sir Adrian Lestrange—poor darling Sir Adrian, I wish I might pitch them all at the back of the fire—a pink note, and two letters for Miss Lestrange, and one letter for Miss Eleanor Lestrange.

One letter, but alas! alas! not the right one! It is, as I find out later, when I have patience to read it, from a sister of my mother's, an excellent "*mère de famille*,"[1] and its purport is chiefly to tell me that dear Cecilia has had the nettle-rash, and that dear Archie has passed for the Line,[2] and has come out 41st, and, indeed, no wonder, considering the way in which he has been reading for the last three months. Now I throw it down and stamp upon it.

"What's the matter," asks Dolly, coming tripping downstairs; and the young June morning is not fresher or fairer than she. Dolly does not often favour us with her company at our morning orisons.

"Everything's the matter," I say exhaustively, picking up my aunt's effusion, and flinging it to the other end of the room.

"Not got your letter yet?"

"No."

"Dear me! how odd! are you sure it has not slipped inside that Magazine?"

"How *could* it?" I say gruffly.

"Perhaps you forgot to give him your direction?" (How likely!)

"No, I didn't."

"Perhaps you did not write it clear enough?"

"I wrote it as plain as a pikestaff!"

"Hm! perhaps he is ill?"

"Don't say that!" I cry eagerly, turning pale, "I'd rather he'd have forgotten me than that; no, I don't think that I would either; oh Dolly, Dolly, what can be the matter?" I sink down on the bench and cover my eyes with my hand.

"Perhaps it'll come to-morrow," says Dolly; turning away, and in a kinder voice than usual.

"It'll never come!" I say tempestuously, flinging down my head on my arms, on the cold wooden table.

---

1 Mother of a family, matron (French).
2 Men had to pass exams to graduate from college or to secure officer positions in the military.

"Sh! Sh! don't make a scene! here's papa!" By a great effort I throw off my own trouble, for the time; defer it to a more convenient season; I can always do that for *him*, and then I go to the old man and put my arms about him, and thank him for the flowers he has brought—he always brings me a little pretty bunch, summer and winter—and kiss the old pale weary face so lovingly. The dew and the moist night airs have lifted up the heads of the plants and shrubs that drooped so yesterday, but I misdoubt me this old scathed tree will never hold his head up again bravely, till the dear Lord transplants him to a kindlier, warmer clime.

"This is the day of the Coxes' croquet party, isn't it?" says Dolly, as we sat at breakfast, his "*Fate Shompater,*"[1] as Mr. Coxe resolutely calls it; "we need not go till about four I should think, need we?"

"I shall not go at all!" I say doggedly.

"Nonsense," says Dolly, severely, "you must go; you cannot treat people in that way, accepting their invitations, and then never going near them, it's *too* bearish!"

"I don't want to go!" I say plaintively, turning towards my father, and stretching out my hand to stroke his.

"You want to stay with the old man, do you, Nell? So you shall! So you shall! there's plenty of people to go to the Coxes' fine party without you."

"Just as you please, of course," says Dolly, very coldly; "children of nature are not accountable beings, I suppose; poor Sir Hugh! I'd sooner meet a bear robbed of her whelps, than him in the state he'll be in to-day!"

I frown at her to stop, but the mischief is done.

"Is Sir Hugh Lancaster to be there?" asks my father, lifting up his head.

"Yes, to be sure he is, he is coming all the way down from town, on purpose to see—Amaryllis Coxe."

We all held our tongues for a minute.

"I think, Nell," says my father, rising slowly to leave the room; "I think perhaps, you had better go, they are civil people, and there's no use giving offence."

★ ★ ★ ★ ★

---

1 Fête champêtre, or country feast (French). Dolly mimics his poor pronunciation.

"I suppose," says Dolly, as we entered the Coxian Park gates that afternoon; "I suppose, we shall finish up with a dance, for I heard Coxe *père*,[1] telling Lady Capel that his daughters were 'so uncommonly fond of cutting capers, that if they could not have a 'op anywhere else, they got up a kick-up at home.'"

As we drive up to the door, I see a faint pitying smile flitting over the countenances of the butler and footmen as they glance at our equipage, but they are too well drilled not to stifle it instantly. Mrs. Coxe receives us in the white and gold drawing-room; the gorgeous glare of which makes one's eyes water this bright day. Mr. Coxe tells us that "he is 'appy to see us in '*is* 'ouse," and that "he believes his young ladies are out in the front, and would not we like to join them?" Ploughboys, parsons, doctors, and lawyers may have sons and daughters, but the

"Lord and Ladies and the Miss O'Gradys,"[2]

alias, the Upper Ten Thousand,[3] and the Coxes have "young gentlemen and young ladies." In Mr. Coxe's vocabulary, a room is an apartment, a house is a mansion or a residence, and a wife is a lady or a partner. He does not mean to be pompous in the least; he can no more help talking Manchester than a dog can help barking. So we step out through the great plate glass windows, which are thrown high up, out on a broad urned and statued terrace, and thence on to the croquet ground, which is mown as short as a convict's hair, and where we find Mr. Coxe's "young ladies and gentlemen," as well as many other people, disporting themselves.

It is hardly saying too much to put croquet[4] as an invention on a level with gunpowder and printing; it certainly is more unmixedly beneficial to the human race than either of the others. Who can be sufficiently loud in praise of a common standing ground, where man and woman can meet without man being effeminate, or woman masculine. It requires a strong effort of memory to realize

---

1 Father (French).
2 See "Mr. Barney Maguire's Account of the Coronation," a comic poem by "Thomas Ingoldsby," pseud. for Richard Harris Barham (1788-1845).
3 The phrase refers to the families of the elite.
4 A game played on grass, using long mallets to hit balls, which roll on the ground through hoops.

the barren time when women struggled through their long weary days, unassisted by those gracious twins, croquet and afternoon tea. At the Coxes' croquet party, I need hardly say that there were a great many more women than men. I never yet was at a croquet party where such was not the case, for admirable pastime as it is, no man that is a man, and not a curate, will ever be induced to put his hand to a mallet, unless he has absolutely nothing else to do.

"There was Lady Grease Wrister,
And Madam Van Twister,
Her Ladyship's sister,
Lord Cram and Lord Vultur,
Sir Brandish O'Cultur
With Marshal Carowzer,
And old Lady Mowzer,
And the great Hanoverian Baron Pansmouzer."[1]

All the fashionable men are up in town[2] of course; so are Lord and Lady Capel. They have gone to the Palace Hotel for a month; a poor equivalent for the house in Park Lane, but better than nothing. So is Lady Lancaster; entertaining kindred frumps and foozles in Eaton Square.

The Scots Greys are still to the fore, for "England expects every man to do his duty," and their duty is at present to guard the Cathedral Close and Minor Canons of Nantford from invasion. Little De Laney is here too, much to his own disgust. Instead of leaning his jolly little smooth face out of the modest bow-window of his corps' club, he is dancing attendance on a moribund uncle for whose gouty[3] shoes he is lying in wait, the mercenary infant!

---

1 See *The New Bath Guide* (1776), a humorous collection of poetry by Christopher Anstey. Bath was a fashionable spa town, to which the rich and famous traveled to consult physicians, take the local waters (thought to have healing properties), and to see and be seen.

2 The London "season" coincided with the sitting of parliament in spring and summer, with which many men of good family were involved. Families with marriageable daughters usually moved to London for the season, so they could be seen at the many social festivities which took place during that time.

3 Gout is an acute inflammation of the joints, often of the toes or ankle. It is often associated with the intake of rich food and alcohol and is more frequent in the elderly.

"Ammy! Ammy! Amaryllis, my dear!" cries Mrs. Coxe, as we appear on the scene—Amaryllis is mistress of the ceremonies, and is flitting about in an elaborate Parisian toilette, eminently suited for a Chiswick breakfast or a Horticultural Fête, and looks as she mostly does, all nose and bust—"here are the Miss Lestranges, my dear; I hope you can make up a set for them!"

Amaryllis looks doubtful; there are five or six sets in full force already, and how to provide the gentle stimulus of a man or two for each game, is the problem which has been making her curse the day on which she was born for the last half hour. What to do with our pauper population[1] is a joke to it. All the parish priests, and all the redcoats, with whatever carefullest economy expended, have been used up.

"There are Mortimer Spencer, and the two Miss Lestranges and myself, that's four," she says slowly; "but that would be so dull for them; there's Sir Hugh Lancaster and Mr. De Laney, but they won't play; my sisters asked them to join their game some time ago, but they would not; they said they did not know how."

"Perhaps," Dolly suggests, with a suave little smile, "perhaps if you ask them again, and make a great favour of it, they would not be so obdurate; people must not be allowed to be lazy on an occasion like this." Amaryllis shakes her head and goes reluctant; two minutes more, and she returns in triumph, leading the two culprits. Hugh, as I am well aware, would be most happy to play dolls, marbles, jack-straws, anything were I to be his assistant.

"Little birds that can sing and won't sing, must be made to sing," says my sister playfully, putting out a ready sisterly hand to Hugh, so "your lordships have condescended to yield to our importunities; we were meditating going on our knees, if that were necessary."

"The little birds are quite game for singing till they crack their little throats if anybody'll show 'em how," says De Laney, putting in his little oar. Hugh is never strong at badinage, he has as heavy a hand at it, as a bad cook has with onions. On the present occasion, I appear to have taken away his elderly breath, for he is staring at me as a school boy at a mince pie, as a pig at acorns. Really it is too bad of him, when he has been having the handsomest women in England, in the becomingest dresses, passing

---

1   One of the great social questions of the period was what to do with the very impoverished, or pauper, population.

in review before him every day for the last week, that he should be gaping like a bird in the pip[1] at a simple country girl in a little straw hat.

"What sides? what sides?" asks Amaryllis, "Morty, dear, put that hoop straight."

I go up to Mr. De Laney, who is arranging a little delicate bouquet of heliotrope and geranium in his button hole. "Will you be sure and play with me?" I say eagerly.

The young fellow looks slightly surprised.

"*I*, of course I will; proudest moment of my existence; only I think it fair to warn you that I never got through a hoop in my life."

"Miss Coxe," I say, lifting up a trembling voice and blushing, "Shall you and I and Mr. De Laney play the other three?"

"That would not be fair," puts in Dolly, with slight asperity in her tone; "you are such a good player; you have given us much the weakest side; you had better let me take your place, that would make it nearly equal!"

"I think," says Amaryllis, coming to my rescue, "that Miss Eleanor Lestrange's arrangement is the best on the whole; Mortimer is much better than I am, and I suppose that Sir Hugh and Mr. De Laney are about equal."

Dolly is too well mannered to oppose the fiat of the mistress of the ground, and she bites her lip, and says smiling, "Well, 'never say die' must be our motto, and Mr. Coxe won't scold us *very* much if we do get him into disgrace, will he?"

Mr. Coxe junior wears barnacles, and his complexion is spotted as the pard's;[2] but his heart is tender. Dolly never puts all her money on one horse; she has many irons in the fire, and Mortimer Spencer De Laney is her last and smallest one.

"Blue begins; Morty, give Miss Lestrange the blue."

I make an inward resolution that where my boy goeth, I will go; that the hoop or the tunnel, or the bell that bids defiance to his inexperienced chocolate ball shall do the same to my practised green; so that I may have an excuse for sticking close into his pocket; it is the first time that the dear little fellow has ever been used as a chaperon, I fancy.

---

1 Pip was a poultry disease characterized by thick mucus on the tongue (thus, sick birds often rested open-mouthed).

2 A pard is a leopard.

"I did not think I should see you again," I say, very friendlily, anxious to engage in conversation, and edging up to where he stands, dishonestly trying to kick his ball into position without being detected. "I thought you were going back to Windsor."

"So did I, but *l'homme*[1] proposes, and *l'homme's* great uncle by marriage disposes."

"How tiresome for you; have you got to stay long?"

"Oh, I suppose till the old party up there," jerking his head in the direction of his uncle's place, "takes himself off to Abraham's bosom, which he does not seem in any hurry to do at present."

"You don't seem very sorry for the poor old gentleman," I say, laughing rather nervously and squinting out of the corner of my left eye, to discover the whereabouts of my Sir John Suckling.[2]

"How can he expect one to be sorry for him, when he takes to dying at such an ungodly time? if he had put it off a month now, it would have suited me down to the ground; there's never much doing in July."

"That's the way somebody will be talking of you by-and-bye," I say with a smile.

"Not a doubt of it, unless I give them the slip by being cut off in my youth and beauty beforehand," he says, with a grin at the thought of his own demise.

The Coxian croquet ground is to other croquet grounds what the garden of Eden is to other gardens; it is the realization of a croquet player's dream. Flat as a billiard table, big as a race course, with a fountain plashing coolly into a stone basin in the middle, and with lime trees round it. They are all in flower now, and their yellowish, greenish, whitish blossoms make the air almost too heavy. The women in their blue and green and white dresses look like big pretty flowers starring the sunny grass.

Further off, a very smart marquee spreads its flag to the wind—of which, by-the-bye, there is uncommonly little—there, later on, we are to flourish the festive heels. Mr. Coxe comes strutting out presently with his little fat hands in his breeches pockets, and that face which would be of such eminent service to him in a Jacquerie,[3] or French Revolution, stamping him so unmistakably as of the people.

---

1 Man (French). The saying is, "Man proposes, and God disposes."
2 Suckling (1609-42) was a court poet with a reputation as a playboy.
3 A peasant revolution in France which took place in 1358.

"Well, Miss Lestrange, and how are we getting on? progressing eh? ha! ha! progressing?"

"Not progressing at all, I'm afraid, Mr. Coxe!" says Dolly smiling; "on the contrary, retrograding, I think!"

"I'm afraid you don't find my son a very efficient coadjutor," continues Mr. Coxe pompously, putting his hands under his coat tails, and standing with his legs rather wide apart. Mr. Coxe will probably be among Lord ——'s next batch of lords.[1]

"*Quite* wrong!" says Dolly, glancing up under her little wild rose-wreathed shepherdess hat at the blushing Mortimer. Bagging Mortimer is like rook shooting, Dolly thinks; the poorest of all sport, but still it is sport. Then half-a-dozen extra-sized footmen come stalking along, bringing ices and Badminton[2] on superb trays, and we stop pounding one another for a few minutes, and by the aid of these refreshments endeavour to bring ourselves down from boiling point. I see Sir Hugh pouring out a tumbler of Badminton for himself; a nice cooling drink; I hope he'll take a great deal of it. Soon we return to our game with renewed vigour.

"Send her away over there! tight croquet; *I* should; she plays next." This is a most unnecessary piece of brutality, for I, with my Grenadier, am struggling for the second hoop, far in the background, as I resolved at the outset I would be.

"We stick together like leeches!" the boy said to me, just now, very innocently; "Damon and what was the other f'la's name—something beginning with a P.[3] you know." My poor green goes spinning off under the limes, disturbing the bees, and I, of course, have to go after it.

"My mother sent her love to you," says a too, *too* well known voice at my elbow. Hugh is not like himself to-day, somehow; he has not made a single joke, and he looks sheepish, and tail-between-the-legs-ish. Being in love is sadly unbecoming to a man; particularly to one who is not in the bloom of youth. Little Dresden shepherds[4] in pink coats and blue breeches look pretty

---

1 Commoners could be ennobled for being of special value to the country. To be ennobled was considered highly desirable, and the practice was somewhat cynically manipulated by those in power for political benefit.
2 A kind of light alcoholic punch.
3 Damon and Pythias.
4 Dresden was famous for its china. Pastoral subjects, such as shepherds and shepherdesses, were popular subjects for china figures, as well as painting and poetry.

when they are casting sheep's eyes at little fat shepherdesses in powder, and red cheeks; but a real live man, sunburnt, hirsute, broadclothed, looks ridiculous. Flight, without the most flagrant incivility, is out of the question.

"I'm sure I'm very much obliged to her."

"I only came down from town last night."

"Oh!"

"I came down on purpose for this—what d'ye call it—this croquet thing."

"Oh!"

"Do you suppose I came down to see the Coxes?" Hugh never pays much attention to the requirements of Mrs. Grundy;[1] he is talking now with much more earnestness than the subjects that mostly come up at a croquet party, are calculated to engender.

I look down very demurely, and make a little excavation in the smooth turf with my mallet. "I don't know, I'm sure."

"Cannot you guess who I came to see? you are sharp enough generally." (He *must* be in love to call me sharp; he might as well compliment Dolly on her piety.)

"I don't know, I'm sure!" I say very pettishly; for I perceive that we are the objects of a good deal of amused notice, and I even detect my little naughty soldier chuckling all to himself behind his pocket-handkerchief.

"I cannot bear being asked questions; will you move, please?"

I give my ball a great vicious hit, which sends it flying back to the haunts of men; and I fly after it, at the top of my speed. Hugh follows me, more surprised than sorrowful; he *cannot* and *will* not understand. His notions of courtship are like Samson's, who went down to Timnath,[2] and saw a woman that pleased him, and told his parents so, and after that it was all plain sailing. Our game comes to an end at last. Despite heroic efforts on the part of Amaryllis, our side is beaten. It would have been very odd if it had not been; seeing that I had been riding a donkey race, holding in my own jackass, and goading on my adversary's.

"Now for the muffin worry,"[3] says De Laney, as we stroll towards the house, having thrown down our implements of warfare.

---

1 Fictional arbiter of respectability.

2 See the story of Samson in Judges 14:1-15:6. Actually, it doesn't go as well for Samson and the woman of Timnath as Nell seems to believe.

3 Humorous name for a tea party (also, "tea fight").

"Yes," I say laughing; "we are all being walked off to have clean bibs and tuckers on!"

The Muffin Worry is an Aldermanic feast; a dinner in all but the name. Everything that a hundred-guinea cook, silver epergnes, gold plate, hot-house flowers, grapes as big as plums, and pines as big as pumpkins could do was done, and yet it all seemed to fall rather flat and dead somehow. Perhaps this was owing to the large preponderance of the fair sex; half a score of women being obliged to come huddling in together. I am led into the room, where first Dick locked away my foolish heart, by Major Somebody—I did not catch the name—he wears galoshes and his brother officers always talk of him as "she." On my other side is Violet Coxe. Ill-natured *he*-friends have christened the three Miss Coxes "Free and Easy," "Freer and Easier," "Freest and Easiest," Violet is "Freest and Easiest." Violet smokes Regalias,[1] and calls men by their surnames to their faces. Lily smokes cigarettes, and Amaryllis does not smoke at all, because it makes her sick. Image to yourself the ne-plus-ultra[2] of vulgarity, fastness, and good nature, and you have the gentle Violet.

"I never asked you about your spill the other night," she says, in her loud voice; "I had other fish to fry; ha! ha! you pitched on your head, didn't you, and kept flourishing your legs in the air, till Hugh Lancaster came and turned you right way up again."

"Oh, hush! hush!" I say in an agony of fear lest she should be overheard.

"Why it was not your fault, though I did hear some cock and bull story the other day, about the horses not having run away at all, and its being all my grandmother!"

I flush crimson, and my eyes fill with tears.

"How cruel people are!" I say; "what a dreadful world it is!"

"Lor' my dear! he didn't mean to be cruel; he only thought you did it for a lark; *I'd* have done it as soon as look."

"Who was it said so?" I asked indignantly.

"'Pon my honour I forget—oh yes, to be sure, it was that old rip Leroy—I remember now, because M'Gregor pitched into him so, when he said it, gave it him right and left."

My heart begins to beat wildly; I see the muslin of my dress

---

1 A type of cigar. Victorian women were beginning to smoke, but it was considered a sign of loose morals.
2 The ultimate (Latin).

agitated by its quick hard pulsations; here is an opportunity for getting some news of him.

"Mr. M'Gregor has gone to Ireland, I believe," I say faintly.

"Yes, poor old boy! he was as sick as a cat, I daresay, crossing; he's an awful bad sailor; we all cried when he went, and Ammy took to her bed, goodness knows why, for he never looked the same side of the room as her; good-looking fellow isn't he? I always say that those destroying angels[1] ought not to be let walk about loose, without tickets on their backs marked 'dangerous.'"

"He *is* handsome!" I say, turning away my head.

"Morty heard from him this morning, I saw his handwriting; and what did I do but open the letter and read every blessed word in it—wasn't Morty in a stew, oh no! not at all—and he sent his love to us all; wasn't it nice of him?" (He is not ill then; he can write to other people.)

The room swims round me for a minute, then I seize a glass of water, and drink it.

"Was he—was he—pretty well?" I gasp.

"Oh, yes; he seemed very bobbish! he said Cork was very jolly quarters, and there were heaps of pretty girls—goodness me what's the matter with you? why you are as white as the tablecloth—are you going to *die?*"

I do not die, though I almost wish to. Oh cruel, beautiful King Olaf! are you tired of me already? I knew that a poor stupid ignorant girl like me, was not a fit mate for you!

The long dull feast comes to an end, and the dancing begins in the marquee. There is the same band that they had at Wentworth; clack clack go the bones, and the fiddles squeak, and the everlasting weary tum te tum, tum te tum goes on again.

God knows I had not much inclination for dancing; but even tearing round and round, with dragging feet, and a heart as heavy as lead, is better than the inevitable alternative sitting out with Hugh. I have to dance with him of course.

"Come and take a turn outside," he says, drawing me towards the scene of our late contest, where the limes' long shadows have

---

1 See Psalm 78:49, "He let loose on them his fierce anger, wrath, indignation, and distress, a company of destroying angels." These were the plagues God sent to Egypt in order to free the Israelites from bondage. Violet suggests that men so handsome as Dick are like a plague.

thrown themselves all along upon the dewy grass, like black-stoled nuns in prayer; and where the fountain is splashing and falling drip, drip, in silver showers in the moonlight.

"No, no!" I say hastily, drawing back, "I don't want to; the grass is wet."

"You did not seem to find it so just now, when you were sitting on those stone steps with De Laney ever so long," he says, rather affronted.

"Please don't tease!" I say with irritation.

"But there's something I want to say to you," he urges pertinaciously, catching my hand.

"For goodness sake, don't!" I say rudely; "I'm sure I should not like to hear it."

As we drove home that night Dolly said,

"Did Sir Hugh propose to you to-day, Nell?"

"No," said I shortly, "and if he has a grain of sense he never will."

CHAPTER XXVII

I kept a journal in those days; if I wished I could tell you, oh my friends, all I did, and a little of what I thought every day for the next six months. But I think even the patientest among you would go to sleep, or at least would yawn very widely, were I to test your powers of endurance with such an infliction. On the contrary, oh kind unknowns! I will take a great leap in my narration, a leap as big as Pedro Alvarado's;[1] a leap from June to December; the next picture in my little homely Hollandish[2] series is a winter one.

Oh, cruel six months! They have stolen so much from me, and they have given me nothing in return. They found me very rich in hope and love, and pleasant thoughts; they left me nearly bankrupt in them all.

---

1 On 1 July 1620, the Aztecs temporarily conquered the forces of Cortez. Captain Pedro Alvarado, unhorsed, was driven back against a canal and all seemed lost for him, until he pole-vaulted over the water using his lance and escaped. He went on to do a great deal of damage in Guatemala.

2 As in the Dutch paintings Nell mentions earlier. (See p. 184, note 2; see also p. 237.)

I am standing by my bedroom window, looking out listlessly. The white dimity curtains look chilly and cheerless, and there comes in a draught that would turn a mill under the ill-fitting door; the mignonette in the green box is dead, and the birds are silent. Outside also it looks very dreary. Winter has not come in prettily this year, with his ermine cloak and his ice-diamonds; he is an ugly fellow enough; he has come in meekly, wetly, muggily; the meadows are all sponge, and the roads all pomatum. A green Christmas, they say, makes a fat church-yard, and this Christmas is very green.

Now and again great strong west winds sweep and riot over the land, not cold, but noisy, blowy, blustery, crashing down great tree-limbs, and making chimney-pots and tiles clatter down from house tops and church roofs. I turn away disconsolately from the spectacle of nature's life in death, and look vacantly in the glass.

Can that be the same round, dimpled, laughing face that met me in that same mirror six short months ago; the curse of the daughters of Zion[1] seems to have fallen upon me; "burning instead of beauty." Hollow cheeks; the corners of the mouth drawn down, and the lines about it puckered up, as if with continual weeping; dark deep shadows under the eyes, the great wistful blue eyes that seem to see everything now mistily, dimly through unshed tears; the hair twisted up with such negligent untidiness, as if nobody cared or thought about it any longer; and the figure, the pretty, tall figure drooping and nerveless.

What is it has dimmed and marred my fair looks so? What evil thing have the rolling hours brought me? What is the cause—what are the causes of the breaking heart that looks out so wanly from that small young face? Shall I tell you? First, then, and oh, far, far foremost, my father is very ill—dying. God is going to take away my dear old dad from me; the old man with whom I walked long ago in the pleasant fields gathering buttercups, in a white frock and a blue sash—the old man with whom I have had so many little jokes, and such loving little tiffs, he who seems to be woven into the fabric of my very life. Warp and woof must be

---

1 See Isaiah 3:16-24. The prophet states that because the daughters of Zion are more concerned with appearance than righteousness, they will lose their wealth and their beauty and will be afflicted with terrible and disfiguring illness.

parted now; the threads of his life be dissevered from mine, for He who made has uttered His fiat of recall; He who gave is about to take away.

When first this terrible thought came home icily to my heart (it was one night, weeks ago, as I knelt at my evening prayers—those prayers out of which one name must so soon drop) I rebelled fiercely against it, pushed it violently from me, it could not, would not be—it was too bad to happen—and my soul went up agonizedly to the great God above me, in intercession for that dear old life, as so many souls have gone up before me, but that prayer found no acceptance.

In nightly vigils on my dark bed, I wrestled and strove with that grisly phantom; I would stand in the breach between him and my old man; he should not come at him, should not smite him with that mighty blade that lays the generations low; but to what purpose? He has put me aside, he is drawing ever nigher, not stealthily, insidiously, but openly in the eye of day, so that all may count his strides, and mark his coming.

So my dear old father is going away from me on a long, long journey, and I don't rightly know what I am to do without him. Is not this enough to make me sad? But besides this greatest cause for woe, I have yet another sore grief, which, but for the advent of the yet more unbearable one, would have seemed to me unendurable; my lover has forsaken me. He on whose love I should have rested, he on whose strong young heart I should have leaned in this bitter hour, has forgotten me; not once in all these weary months has he written to me.

How many days there are in six months, how many post times! Just so many times have I had to undergo the pangs of a most grievous disappointment, a sharp smart stab at first, then a long, dull, weary ache. And I had written to him, oh, so often! very joyfully and very lovingly first; very anxiously and very lovingly next; then grievedly, bitterly, but lovingly always, and at last I had ceased writing and had sunk into the dumbness of despair.

Dolly did not exult over me much; she reminded me, indeed, that she had warned me against him, and opined that perhaps next time I should be more inclined to take her advice, but on the whole she was good-natured, and tried to comfort me on the same grounds as would have afforded herself consolation in a like case, viz., his poverty and consequent undesirability; the vanity and nothingness of the passion of love, and lastly, her invariable *corps de réserve*[1]—Sir Hugh.

And now, oh my friends, do not be very hard upon me; do not call me ugly names, as fickle and heartless; do not sit in judgment upon me when I tell you that I myself have of late been thinking much of this same Sir Hugh; not with more love or less loathing than of yore, but as my possible, probable fate. I wanted to do right, God knows! I thought it must be right to do this, because it was so hard, so difficult, so revolting. I see *now* that I was wrong, but *then* my head was full of Iphigenia and Jephtha's daughter-like ideas.[2]

The doctor said that perfect exemption from all care and anxiety *might*, probably would prolong my father's life for weeks, nay months; and to win so dear, so inestimably precious a boon as his presence among us, for even a few days longer than I otherwise should have it, I was willing to sacrifice all my future years, willing to give my shrinking body to Sir Hugh's arms, and my abhorring soul into his custody, though both body and soul clave still with desperate ineradicable passion to that other.

Since I drew my last life-picture our affairs had become quite desperate; the children of Israel had come down upon us like locusts; a dreadful man with a hook nose, thick lips, and a greasy Hebrew face had come to take an inventory of the furniture and movables. To spare our feelings and obviate the unpleasant necessity of having a strange man quartered upon us, our own man-servant had been turned into a bailiff[3] for the nonce.

My father could not move outside his own pleasure-grounds. "I suppose they will let him pass by to his grave," I thought bitterly. Bills and duns showered like hail about our ears, and there we stood, helpless, defenceless, without hope or refuge. An old dying man, and two poor young daughters in such a case. What could be pitifuller? Mrs. Smith has just been telling me that

---

1   Reserve troops (French).
2   In Greek myth, Agamemnon was supposed to sacrifice his daughter Iphigenia to appease Artemis, but she was miraculously saved. In Judges 11:34-40, Jephtha had to make a burnt offering of his daughter to fulfill a promise to God. She was not miraculously saved.
3   Anti-Semitic description of the moneylenders, who are preparing to seize the estate for its debts. The lenders have considerately allowed one of the Lestrange servants to be sworn in as a legal agent to watch the property.

"she's mor'lly certain there'll be a hexecootion[1] in the 'ouse afore the week's hout; that there will, drabbit 'em all!"

An execution! Won't that put the finishing stroke to the work of decay and sickness? Will that enfeebled frame ever be able to bear the rough world's jeers at the yawning rifts and rents in the poor old family's sides; those rifts that through so many tired years he has been painfully trying to draw a tattered covering over. Will not the poor gray head be driven to take refuge before its time in the restful grave? I clench my hands. I *must* do it; I must. My face looks back hard and rigid from the glass at me; "I must, I must"; it seems to say too. As I stand thus in an attitude worthy of Lady Macbeth,[2] the door opens, and Dolly enters hurriedly, without knocking.

"Sir Hugh's here," she says rather hesitatingly; she does not quite know how I shall take her bit of news; once or twice, lately, I have turned savage under her exhortations and beseechments. I do not turn savage now; I say nothing, only the rigid face in the glass grows rigider. My resolution is to be put to the test soon indeed!

Dolly's beauty is nowise dimmed by grief; sorrow has dug no ugly hollows in her cheeks, nor dulled the sleepy splendour of her eyes. She looks a little pale and anxious, but she manages somehow to do even that becomingly. Nor is her appearance less soignée[3] than it was; her dress is simpler indeed than it used to be; as simple as it can be; but that only serves to make her look younger, more innocently girlish. She wore now a thick black serge gown almost as plain as a riding-habit.

"It will do so nicely for mourning with a little crape[4] on it," had been the thought in Dolly's mind when she bought that dress—the unexpressed thought, but by some instinct, I had divined that she had so thought, and I hated her for it.

"For God's sake, be civil to him!" she says now, coming up and laying an eager hand on my shoulder, "he is our only hope!"

"I know it," I say coldly.

---

1 Execution. The writ allowing the formal seizure of property for payment of debt, or the process of seizing the property itself.
2 See *Macbeth* (first printed 1623), a play by Shakespeare.
3 Trim, tidy (French).
4 Also called crepe, this is a thin, transparent fabric. Often, black crepe was used to trim mourning dress.

"For pity's sake don't snub him! be good to him! do think of somebody beside yourself for once." (Dolly, of all people, to give that advice.)

"I don't mean to snub him; I mean to be civil to him; I have made up my mind," I say resolutely, with that dull pain tightening round my heart.

"Made up your mind to *marry* him! You don't mean it?" cries my sister joyfully, while the prettiest carmine wave ripples into her soft cheeks. "*Bon Dieu!*[1] how thankful I am!"

"Don't!" I say harshly, pushing her away; her mirth grated horribly somehow on my tense nerves.

"Do make yourself a little bit tidy before you go to him," she says, untying the blue ribbon that binds her own inky hair waves, and preparing to insinuate it among my curly wig. But I resist.

"No," I say doggedly, "leave me alone; I won't be made up for sale; if he chooses to bid for this piece of goods, he shall see all the flaws in it. I don't want to cheat him in his bargain." So I went, limp and crumpled, to meet my fate. Before I had given my resolution time to cool, I found myself in the library facing my *futur*.[2]

He was standing with his back to the fire, whistling softly to himself. Evidently he had called in on his way back from hunting; he had on a very shabby stained old red coat, and very splashed spattered breeches and tops, but somehow he did not look at all a bad fellow, nor an ill-looking one either. When he saw me, he stopped whistling, and dropped his coat tails.

"Well, how is he to-day? Not worse, I hope?" he says it very heartily; there is a true ring in his deep voice, as if he really meant it.

"No, not worse. I think much the same, thanks!"

I sit down in my limpness on the sofa, and feel as if I were going to have a leg or an arm cut off, and as if Hugh was the operator, and I wish he would make haste and begin. Oh, if I could but take a whiff of chloroform, and awake to find the limb amputated, the process over, the wooing accomplished. The fire glows ruddy in the wide old chimney; the flames go curling, spiring, quivering upwards. I gaze at the steel dogs in the hearth,[3] and await the operation.

---

1 Good God! (French).
2 Future (French).
3 The metal holders upon which material for burning is placed.

"You've grown very thin since last I was here." That is how it begins. The surgeon is taking off his coat, and rolling up his shirt sleeves.

"Very likely," I say, bitterly. "Lying awake at night, and having worries, and being miserable, does not conduce to putting flesh on one's bones!"

"I wish to Heaven I could take half your worries for you; God knows I would if I could; will you let me try?" The kind honest tones, and the kind simple words upset me quite; I am easily upset now-a-days. I pull out my pocket-handkerchief; my face undergoes the odd, droll, ugly contortions and workings of a person about to cry, and I burst into bitter tears. My nose reddens, and my eyelids get pink, and I sit rocking to and fro, and feeling a very desolate little girl indeed.

"Won't you let me go halves in all your troubles, dear?" he asks, very gently.

He has come and stood close before me in his eagerness, and intercepts my view of the steel dogs. I look up through my tears straight at him. I am relieved that we are getting to business so soon.

"Do you mean that you want me to marry you?" I ask, bluntly.

"Yes, I do," he says, simply; "you know I do; you know how long I have been wishing and longing for it."

There is a little pause—a little minute, when my thoughts go back miserably to that curled Greek head, to those dark, passionate, gray eyes that looked so true and were so false; then I say very slowly and with infinite difficulty—

"I will—do as you wish, if—if—you will—lend me—give me—some money—*a great deal*; oh dear—oh dear!"

My sobs burst out fresh, I feel so degraded in my own eyes. He did not ask me what I wanted money for—no doubt he divined; only the jollity died out of his honest face, and a pained look took its place.

"Of course you know," he said, very heartily, "I hope I need not tell you that—that you are welcome, most welcome to every farthing I possess, to make ducks and drakes of,[1] if you like; but—but I don't want you to marry me for that."

"If I take money from you I must marry you," I said, calmly. "I could not do it else."[2]

---

1   To waste or to spend frivolously (slang).

2   A lady could not accept money from a man who was not a relative.

It seemed to me the most matter-of-fact piece of barter in the world; so much young flesh and blood for so much current coin of the realm.

"Why, won't you try and like me?" he says, passionately.

It seems hard to him that his house, and his lands, and his dirty money should count for more with me than his loving heart, and his tender, faithful eyes; and as he speaks he throws himself on the sofa beside me.

"I *will* try and like you," I say, conquering myself, setting my teeth, and vanquishing my intense desire to say something very rude, and rush away from him; but even as I speak I shudder at his proximity.

"We might be so happy"; he says, rather plaintively. "I am not a very hard fellow to live with, I don't think; I've never had a word with mother all these twenty years, and you'd be easier to get on with, I fancy, than she is, poor old lady!"

"We *will* try and be happy," I say, firmly, and I give him my hand.

The operation is nearly over now, and I am alive after it. Then I am gathered to the middle-aged heart, to the stained red coat, and the gray knitted waistcoat, and kissed, and thanked, and blessed, and adjectived. I tear myself away at last, and escape to my room, where I fling myself on my bed, and scrub my desecrated countenance, and wail, "Oh, Dick, Dick—oh, my love, my love!" to the unresponsive pillow.

CHAPTER XXVIII

Sir Hugh must have abandoned the pursuit of the wily fox at an early hour on that memorable afternoon, seeing that it was but half-past two, when, the deed being done, he rode off on his long-raking bay mare—rode off to go and tell his mamma of his prowess, and of what a lovely, willing bride he had achieved. Only half-past two; there was therefore ample time for my father and me to take our daily stroll; that stroll which we still took, though it had become such a woeful piteous shadow of what it used to be. No earthly persuasion could induce my father to give in to being an invalid, to stay in bed and have a doctor. Every day he *would* get up and dress; *would* come downstairs, and sit in the library; *would* sit in his usual chair, and read his usual books; but every day the dressing and the coming downstairs took longer; every day the wheels of the chariot drove more heavily; every day the silver cord loosened—loosened;[1] every day the frail vessel of that dear life drifted ever faster—faster out, into the great desolate homeless sea of Death. As well as any one could tell him, he knew that he was dying—knew that the few last sands of his hour glass were dribbling slowly out; no need to break the news to him. To "break" implies that the news is bad; but to him this was not ill news; to him it seemed an evangel—"good tidings of great joy."[2] But though he so well knew that solemnest fact—perhaps the more so because he did so know it—he seemed now to taste a deeper, tenderer joy than ever, even of yore, in Nature's sweet presence; even in her leafless trees, her riotous western breezes, and her chill December suns.

And thus it came to pass that we two who were so close to each other now; we, who, a month hence, should be severed far as time is parted from eternity, walked out together every day, gravely and lovingly.

At first our walk comprised pleasure ground, farm-yard, and home wood; but then, after a little, we had to drop the wood, had to say a long good-bye to it—to the pleasant wood with its oaks, and its tangled briars, and its crimson dogwood—for it lay on a rising ground, and taxed too hardly the poor struggling, difficult breath.

A week more, and the farm-yard is abandoned for a like cause. Every day the walk grows shorter, the steps slower, the end nearer! God! What torture can be comparable to that of standing, with one dearer to us than life, on the edge of that awfullest, blackest gulf, seeing him slipping, slipping down into it, unable to stretch out a finger to prevent him; to help him back again up the kindly hither bank.

On the afternoon of my betrothal, we were as usual creeping with tedious lagging steps along the gravel walk, round the flowerless flower-beds, stopping every ten paces to take breath.

---

1   See Ecclesiastes 12:6-7. "6: Or ever the silver cord be loosed, or the golden bowl be broken, or the pitcher be broken at the fountain, or the wheel broken at the cistern. 7: Then shall the dust return to the earth as it was: and the spirit shall return unto God who gave it."
2   Compare Luke 2:10. The tidings are news of the birth of Christ, and thus of salvation.

My father was wrapped up in his old great-coat, (ah me, how he used to eschew great-coats in bygone days!) and I, with my arm passed through his, am trying to help on his tottering steps, without his finding out that he is so helped.

"I think you seem to be walking a little better to-day, dearest old man!" I say.

"Am I, Nell? I'm not a very grand traveller, I don't think."

We stop, and look over the wire fence at the drenched-looking grass, at the rich, wet, loamy earth.

"If this mild weather lasts, we shall be seeing the crocuses out in flower here, in another month," I say.

"I shall never see the crocuses again!" says my father, simply.

A rush of tears blinds me, and through them I look up at the yellowing sunken face—the face that is so immeasurably more to me than all the world besides,—more, ten thousand times, than even my beautiful false lover—and I *know* that he speaks truth; that I shall be looking at the crocuses' golden blaze *alone*. In a few minutes I swallow back my tears; I have all the rest of my life-time to weep in, but they must not come now; not now! not now! I say, gently pressing the dear arm that leans so feebly on mine.

"You must not say melancholy things to-day, darling old daddy, for I have got such a nice piece of news for you!"

"News! Have you, Nell?" says he cheerfully. "Why, little lass, you're getting like the Athenians,[1] that spent their time in nothing else but either to hear or to tell some new thing."

Some spirits can jest and joke even on the verge of that gulf that swallows time and space, nor with any irreverence towards the Great Presence, in whose antechamber they stand waiting

> "Like infants, sporting by the roar
> Of the·Everlasting Deep."[2]

Such was my father.

---

1   See Acts 17:21. Paul speaks to the people of Athens, whom he sees as idolators. The text states that Athenians spend their time gossiping and chasing novelty, so they are interested in what Paul has to say.

2   Probably a misquote of the following lines from the poem "The Holy Innocents" (1866), by theologian John Keble: "Like infants sporting on the shore,/That tremble not at Ocean's boundless roar."

"This is a real bit of news," I say, smiling; "good news too," I add, though the words go nigh to choke me. We are walking on again slowly, beneath the great ash trees that spread black skeleton arms to the low dun sky.

"Good news has forgotten the road here, I think, Nell, for this long and many a day," says my father, with a weary sigh. I look down and fumble with the lowest button of my jacket.

"Sir Hugh Lancaster has been here again to-day," I say, in a coy, low voice. My father stops suddenly, and leans both hands on the top of his stick.

"Has he?" he says, eagerly; "is your news about him, Nell!" I blush.

"Yes, he asked me to marry him; or I'm not sure that it was not I that asked him to marry me," I say, with rather dreary merriment; "anyhow, we settled it between us: it *is* to be!"

"Thank God!" says my father, very reverently, under his breath; "then there'll be somebody to take care of my little lass when I'm gone!"

"Is it good news, dad? did I say true!" I ask, throwing a pair of loving young arms about his neck, and laughing hysterically.

"That it is!" he says, heartily, and the strength seems to have come back into his voice. "I can say, 'Nunc dimittis,'[1] with all my heart *now*, Nell; I could not have departed quite in peace before, when I thought of leaving my little Nell to be a poor little ill-used governess; but now," he said, with a dash of his old pride, "she'll be able to hold up her head among the best in the county, as she ought, God bless her!"

"What good will it do me to hold up my head as high as Haman's,[2] if you're not by to see it and be glad of it?" I ask, desolately. Long dreary years, forty, fifty, sixty perhaps, flash before my mind's eye, years of a bondage whose full horrors my innocent young soul but vaguely takes in; years *with* Hugh, and *without* papa.

Oh, why could not I die of consumption, like that girl I took

---

1   Permission to depart (Latin; literally, "now dismiss [your servant].") Also the name of a hymn.
2   In the book of Esther (from the Apocryphal books of the Bible), Haman was Mordecai's chief minister and an enemy of the Jews. He was hanged—the usual context for the reference is to hang someone "as high as Haman."

the jelly to yesterday?[1] Why could not I cough myself out of the world, as she was doing so fast? "On the —th instant, at Lestrange Hall, Eleanor, younger daughter of Sir Adrian Lestrange, of rapid decline, aged nineteen." And Dick would see it in the *Times*, and be compunctious, and his grand deep eyes would fill with remorseful tears, and he would rush away to the wars— those vague wars of which I always had so convenient a stock in my mental *repertoire*[2]—and die, covered with wounds, and kissing my photograph.

This was the gloomy form my castle-building took now; a picturesque death was the only thing I seemed to have strength to long for.

"Nell," says my father, breaking in upon a paragraph descriptive of Dick's glorious demise, in

"Wild Mahratta battle,"[3]

that I was composing, "Do you remember my reading 'King Lear'[4] to you once?"

"Yes," I reply, wondering a little, "long ago; and you used to call me your little Cordelia; I remember,"

"Well, darling," he says, with a pensive little smile, "do you remember what Kent says when the poor old King is dead—

"'He hates him that would on the rack of this tough world Stretch him out longer.'"

"Oh, dad! dad!" I cry in the bitterness of my soul, clinging about

---

1   Although many diseases were identified as consumption, the term most frequently referred to tuberculosis, which often killed young adults and was characterized by weight loss, coughing, and heightened color of the facial features. As a clergyman's daughter and as a member of the upper class, one of Nell's duties is to visit the sick and bring them charity, and for invalids, that would include nourishing, easily digested foods such as calves'-foot jelly.

2   List, repertory (French).

3   There were three Mahratta wars between 1776 and 1819 that resulted in Britain's acquisition of India.

4   King Lear has three daughters, only one of whom is loyal: the youngest, Cordelia. See Shakespeare's play *King Lear* (first printed in 1608).

him. "Why cannot you take me with you? Oh, we have been such friends, haven't we? Oh, you're not going to leave me behind!"

"Hush, hush!" says he, soothingly, patting my hot wet cheek. "What will the fine new lover say if we let you wash all the colour out of your eyes with crying; God knows best, Nell! God knows best! we must try and think that!"

"I cannot think it," I say, desperately, "and I won't; I don't believe it."

After that we walk along in silence to the hall-door; I saying over and over to myself, in utter heart sickness, "He doesn't know best! He doesn't! He doesn't!" and dashing myself like a little foolish useless wave against the great adamant rock of the Omnipotent Will.

CHAPTER XXIX

"A still small voice spake unto me.
Thou art so full of misery,
Were it not better not to be?"[1]

Is there any one among us, who, at some moments of their lives, has not heard that voice asking them this despairing question? Is there any one who, at some moment or other, has not been tempted to answer "Yes, far, far better!" Is there any one, whoever thinks at all, that has not had black minutes and hours—minutes and hours when he says blankly, hopelessly to himself, "There is no God: there can be no beneficent Deity to love us and take care of us, or he never would let us be so very, very desolately wretched." Sometimes we feel that we must curse God and die; it would be such a relief to us; curse God, as Job's wife is supposed to have urged her much enduring lord to do, as a cure for his boils;[2] that is, if she did not urge him to *bless* God and die, as the word has either signification: in which case the poor woman's character for piety has been shamefully taken away for the last three or four thousand years.

---

1 See "The Two Voices" (1833), a poem by Tennyson.
2 See Job 2:9: Job is afflicted by God, who chooses to test his faith. His wife advises him to curse God and die. Nell points out that the interpretation of the original text is ambiguous.

Sometimes we say to ourselves that surely some malevolent tricksy demon must have the world's government reins in his fiend hands—some demon that delights in thwarting our poor little plans, in inventing new and ingenious diseases to rack our poor patient bodies. Our very wishing anything seems to drive the object wished for farther away; our very dreading anything seems to draw the dreaded object magnetically nearer. In every newspaper we take up, we see "melancholy suicides," "horrible murders," "fatal accidents," "economic funeral companies"; and often we lay it down with a dull numb feeling that the world is all out of joint; all discord and jangling dissonance.

But there is a Book,[1] a simple, old-fashioned eloquent Book, that tells us that "the fashion of this world passeth away,"[2] the fashion—the old, old fashion that we are all so weary of—the fashion of being wicked, and being sick and disappointed and heart sore; and whoso believeth that it is so passing, straight way there is to him harmony and peace and order. Never through all the monotonous self-repeating centuries, during which this old globe has gone lumbering round the sun, has there been an instance of instinct misleading any of the creatures in which it has been planted; and as surely as some inner voice whispers to the swallows, telling them then it is time for them to come flying over the foamy green seas to the English spring trees and fresh fields, so surely does some higher instinct, proportioned to our higher, nobler nature, bid us plume our wings for a flight, when life's winter is over, to some distant spring land, where great melody and sweet health and content are waiting for us; some land where "all crooked things shall be made straight, and all rough places be made smooth."[3] But great sorrows are in their nature like mountains, closing in the horizon, preventing our catching a glimpse of any of the fields, where

---

1 The Bible.
2 Compare I Corinthians 7:31. Paul exhorts the members of the Corinthian church to keep their mind on eternal things, rather than worldly matters.
3 See Isaiah 40:4: "Every valley shall be exalted, and every mountain and hill shall be made low: and the crooked shall be made straight, and the rough places plain." See also Luke 3:5: "Every valley shall be filled, and every mountain and hill shall be brought low; and the crooked shall be made straight, and the rough ways shall be made smooth."

"You scarce can see the grass for flowers,"[1]

of the summer waves tumbling and joyfully tossing up red sea-tang on sun-lit yellow sands, of feathery larch woods, and blue rushing brooks, that there may be, that we know are, beyond them.

I seemed now in my complete life-hatred and bitterness to be prisoned in some narrow black valley—some deep gully between great frowning granite peaks. I could not climb up their smooth slant sides, to see the sunrise washing the low morning clouds, and the gray morning billows with his flamy streams. I was groping with hands stretched out before me blindly, among the boulders and the pit-falls, and the sullen black pools in the valley bottom; and I must stay groping there as I felt, till the oil of my life's lamp were burned out, till I sat down and died there amid the darkness and the doleful beasts and the murky stagnant waters.

"If," thought I, "I had been an old roué[2] of seventy, who had dedicated all my three score and ten years to the debasing of soul and body, I could hardly have incurred more woeful penalties than my nineteen summers of insipid innocence had drawn upon my devoted head." Not even the consciousness of having made a sacrifice that raised me (at least in my own estimation) to a level with the Jewish maiden I have before alluded to;[3] not even the consciousness of having been "high heroical" supported me much. I did not grudge the sacrifice I had made; if it had to be done over again, I should do it over again; but I thought myself entitled to make as many wry faces over it as I felt inclined, and their name was legion.

One day, Dolly entering, cat-like, in her long, straight serge[4] gown, found me grovelling—lying all along on the floor, prone, while tears rushed in rivers from my foolish blue eyes, and laid the dust on the carpet.

"Are you dead, Nell?" she asks quietly, holding the door in her hand; "because if so, I'll send for the coroner."

"No," say I, blubbering noisily, and burrowing still farther

---

1 See "The Two Voices" (1833), a poem by Tennyson.
2 Debauched man, man of loose morals (French).
3 Jephtha's daughter.
4 A strong wool with a diagonal weave.

into the dim blue squares of the old Kidderminster.[1] "Worse luck—I wish to God I was."

"Are your bowels yearning[2] still over the big wax doll?" she asks, jeeringly. "Have you retired into your chamber to weep there?"

"Yes," I say, angrily, lifting up my head, and pushing back my wet, fuzzy locks; "and since it is *my* chamber, and not yours——"

"You'd thank me to 'absquatulate,' as the Yankees say," interrupts she, laughing and showing the sweetest, shortest, whitest little set of teeth that ever set dentist at defiance. "Well, I will in a minute; but 'I have an errand unto thee, oh, captain.'"[3]

"I wish your errand was to tell me that I was going to be hanged, or that you were; I'm sure I don't know which would give me the most gratification," growl I, squatting still Job-like in the ashes.

"You're a little fool, my sweet Nell," says my sister, playfully. "I don't believe you'd relish a bit of whipcord round your little neck any more than I should; but really," she went on, gravely, "I wonder you have not more spirit than to be boo-hooing about that scoundrelly longlegs; if any man had served me such a turn," she said, clenching her right hand into a small white ball, while her sleepy eyes woke up into beautiful fierce life, "I might have killed him, put a pinch of strychnine[4] into his tea, or stabbed him in the back on the sly—indeed, I'm sure I should; but cry over him, put my finger in my mouth and pipe my eye, never, never, never!" (a *crescendo* scale, ending in *fortissimo*).[5]

"If you talk of meanness," I cry, springing to my feet and stamping, "I wonder what can be meaner than selling yourself like a bale of goods or a barrel of beer, as I'm doing. Oh, what

---

1 A carpet. Kidderminster was a town in the county of Worcestershire in England famous for its rugs and carpets.
2 In ancient texts, including the Bible, the bowels or stomach were often described as the seat of emotion, rather than the heart.
3 Compare II Kings 9:5. The prophet Elisha's errand is to announce to Jehu that Jehu will be king of Israel.
4 Used as a rat poison. Victorians were fascinated with women poisoners, and occasional court cases throughout the period fed that fascination.
5 Musical terms: crescendo (literally "growing") means getting louder; fortissimo means strongest or loudest (Italian).

do I care how mean I am! What sin is there so big that I would not commit it this minute, and commit it most gladly too, if I could but have him back here this minute in this room. Oh, he has not forgotten me! I know it! I know it! There's some mistake, I'm sure, and I shall find it out when it's too late—when I'm in hell!"

I fling myself down again, and cry aloud; my punishment seems greater than I can bear. Dolly walks to the window and looks out.

"Oh, Dick, Dick!" I groan, "where are you? where are you? Oh, my darling, are you dead? Oh, come back to me, for God's sake!"

I forget even Dolly's sneering presence, I forget my father, forget everything but that one man that made earth first heaven—then hell for me!

Dolly goes to the wash-hand stand and pours some cold water into a basin.

"Stop crying," she says, harshly; "you have made your bed, and you must lie on it. Sir Hugh is here again—of course he has a right to come now; and you'd better try and bathe the swelling and redness out of your eyes, if we are to get any money out of him. You don't look a choice morsel to bribe any man with as you are now."

Her cold voice calls me back to myself. I rise and pick up my heavy cross, and prepare to stagger along a little farther under it. I sponged and mopped my face, and scrubbed it with a Turkish towel, and then I looked in the glass; and then I mopped and scrubbed again, and tried to persuade myself that I did not look as if I had been crying.

Half an hour after I am sitting on the green settee by the library fire, with the gentleman by whose library fire I am to sit through my life, with what patience I may.

His arm is round my waist, and he is brushing my eyes and cheeks and brow with his somewhat bristly moustache as often as he feels inclined—for am I not his property? Has not he every right to kiss my face off if he chooses, to clasp me and hold me, and drag me about in whatever manner he wills, for has not he bought me? For a pair of first-class blue eyes warranted fast colour, for ditto superfine red lips, for so many pounds of prime white flesh, he has paid down a handsome price on the nail, without any haggling, and now if he may not test the worth of his purchases, poor man, he *is* hardly used! As for me, I sit tolerably still, and am not yet actually sick, and that is about all that can be said of me. Presently the situation becomes too warm for me.

"May I move a little, please?" I say, edging away out of my owner's arms. "I'm rather—rather hot, please—the fire, I mean."

"All right," says he, cheerily; "it *is* a fire to roast an ox, isn't it? let's move the settee back a bit, and then we shall be all serene—shan't we, love?"

So we move the settee back into the shade, where the fire glow cannot reach us, but my blood does not grow any the cooler, for that accursed, girdling arm is still round me—my buyer's arm—that arm that seems to be burning into my flesh like a brand.

"Jolly this, isn't it?" whispers Strephon,[1] chuckling; "and it'll be jollier still when we're married; it'll be *always* like this then."

When we're married! Merciful Heavens! If the prologue is so terrible, *what will the play be?*

"If you please," I begin again meekly; "I—I think I'd rather sit on a chair by myself; you—you—hurt me rather."

I remove myself, unopposed, to a distant chair, and breathe freer.

"I thought you promised you'd try and like me, Nell," says Hugh, rather ruefully, by-and-by.

"I *will* try, I will indeed," I cry eagerly, clasping my hands, "only—oh do, *do* give me time!"

"Give you time, indeed," says Strephon, grimly, glancing at his own weather-beaten face in the glass; "all very fine, but I have not so much time to give; by the time you have made up your mind whether you like me or not, I shall be a drivelling old fool, past caring for any woman's liking."

I answered him to never a word, I agreed with him so fully as to his great age.

"One would think," pursues he, stalking up and down in a fume, "to hear you talk, that I had a humpback, or a club foot, or some great natural deformity"; and then he steps before me, and says with a certain rough pathos in his voice, "Won't you tell me, Nell, what there is about me so repugnant to you, that I may try and mend it?"

---

1 A stock name for a male lover in pastoral romance. In the eighteenth century, the name was often also used in parodies of such
romances.

A terror seizes me; beaked Israelitish faces swarm before my mind's eye; am I recklessly tossing away salvation in the shape of those signed cheques on Coutts' Bank,[1] that are lying in simple beauty on the table.

"Don't talk nonsense," I cry pettishly, giving my head a little ill-humoured jerk; "when did I say there was anything about you repugnant to me? Cannot you understand that it is not so easy to get very fond of a person all in a minute, when you have not been thinking of anything of the kind before; I told you I'd try and like you, and I will: what more can I say? Oh please, *please* have patience with me!" I cried, piteously.

"Haven't I been patient already?" he asks, sorrowfully. "I'm not an impatient fellow ever; it isn't my nature. I don't expect to sow and reap the same day, but I don't know how it is, you seem to like me less and less every time I come."

No answer: a guilty head hangs down low, lower, till it droops on a guilty breast.

"If," says Hugh, quite gently, though his honest face is working a little, as with some strong smothered emotion, "you feel that you can never have anything but a bare toleration of me, say so at once, child? I'm old enough and strong enough to bear a little disappointment; we can't expect to have everything our own way in this world, and I know I'm not quite the right cut to take a girl's fancy; it would be better you should speak out, while it's time, than that we should make each other miserable for all our lives."

I gaze long and earnestly into the fire, before I answer; watch the little firescapes crumbling, dissolving, and reforming, while my hot white hands twist and wrench and generally maltreat each other. Shall I take him at his word? Oh God! how delicious it would be; it would be like exchanging the fetid stifling air of an eastern dungeon for the free gales rioting under the blue April heavens.

Shall I get off the altar, where, *à la* Jephtha's daughter,[2] I am lying bound; slip the cords off my wrists, and walk lightly away? Shall I still be able to think of that laughing *debonair* glorious face, without stabs of despair—of those strong arms where I may yet find heaven, without deadly sin? Shall I defy the might of

---

1 Old and reliable British bank.
2 See p. 256, note 2.

Israel? Shall I let the "hexecootion" have its way? Shall I kill my old dad? *Never.* For him I have begun this great sacrifice; for him I will complete it; for him I will go to hell. So I speak quite firmly, even though I feel myself paling to the lips—Sir Hugh's lips.

"No, I have said it, and I mean to stick to it; let us try and make the best of one another; it's a very puzzling world, and it's very hard to know how to live through it; but I suppose if we try to do our best, it'll all come right in the end."

So I, in my despair.

Then he says, with some difficulty, and flushing scarlet, despite his nine lustres[1]—

"If you're only marrying me on account of that dirty money——"

I interrupt him, hastily.

"Nonsense," I cry, "say no more about it; I mean to be your wife, and I suppose we shall manage to scratch on pretty much as other people do." But to my own heart I say that "I would that I were dead."[2]

CHAPTER XXX

There is a great sacrifice to the fore; a hecatomb offered at the altar of filial affection; a pretty white lamb is being led out, be-figged,[3] be-ribboned, be-filleted to the slaughter. Pipe and tabor[4] go too-tooing before her, and the butcher, with his sharp knife gleaming, walks behind her. But the lamb knows that she is going to the sacrifice, and she bleats very piteously.

Now for the key to this graceful metaphor. I am the lamb, Hugh is the butcher, Dolly is the pipe and tabor, and the slaughter is our nuptials. I had looked upon our marriage as a distant possible evil, huge and horrible indeed, but rendered indistinct and vague by extreme distance; much as we look upon the Day

---

1 A lustre is a period of five years. He is forty-five years old.
2 From Tennyson's 1830 poem "Mariana." Mariana wishes herself dead when the lover she waits for does not come.
3 Dressed up, costumed.
4 A pipe is a wind instrument and a tabor is a small drum. Representations of sacrifices on ancient pottery often represented a garlanded animal being led by a festive procession, playing music; see John Keats's "Ode on a Grecian Urn" (1820), for example.

of Judgment, or the day of our death, and lo! here it was at the very doors.

One day, very meekly and diffidently, for he began to perceive that his turtle dove had not much coo in her, Sir Hugh suggested that there was no possible reason why our marriage should be delayed; that there was, on the contrary, every reason why it should be hastened. But mild and deferential as was the poor fellow's mode of address, I blazed out upon him; thrust the idea miles away from me, and snubbed him for his want of feeling, in talking of marrying and giving in marriage, when my father was in the state he then was. That was in the morning; in the afternoon, my father repeated Sir Hugh's very words almost.

The daily walk had been given up by this time: all day long my old man sat in his leathern arm-chair, waiting—waiting. The pitcher was breaking very fast now; it would go but few more journeys to the fountain.

All day nearly, I sat beside him on a low stool, holding his hand, kissing it every now and then, and watering it with tears, as the Magdalen did that tender God-hand,[1] that is stretched out ever to heal all wounds.

> "'I'm wearing awa', Jean,
> Like snow when it's thaw, Jean,
> I'm wearing awa', Jean,
> To the Land o' the Leal,'"[2]

says my father softly, brokenly; for speech is getting difficult, breathless to him. "It's rather hard work, Nell, 'wearing awa''; I wish I could be quicker about it." My hot tears and kisses fall on the worn hand I must so soon loose for ever, but I cannot answer him in words. "Hugh is a good fellow, isn't he?" says my father, presently. "I like to think of his being so fond of my little girl; I wish you and he were married, Nell!"

"Do you, Dad?" I say, choking.

"Yes, little lass, and then he could take you home and comfort you, when I'm gone!"

---

1 Compare Luke 7:38, where the sinful woman washes Jesus' feet with her tears. Often this woman is believed to be Mary Magdalene.
2 See the Scottish ballad, "The Land of the Leal" (circa 1798), attributed to Carolina Oliphant Nairne.

"Cold comfort, I think, Dad," I say, laying my russet head on the arm of his chair, "but if—if it'll give you any pleasure, I'll marry him to-morrow." And this was how it came about.

"The Queen laid her white throat on the block,
Quietly waiting the fatal shock."[1]

The parson has been advertised, the licence and the ring have been bought, and we are to be made one, as fast as bell, book and candle can make us. How sound I slept on the night before my bridal; people going to be hanged, or guillotined, or beheaded, always do, they say. I slept, and I had a very fair dream; a vague sweet dream of flowers—great, beautiful flowers, crimson and white and azure, and of a garden. And among the flowers, and in the garden, I saw Dick; saw him in all his beauty, saw

"The knotted column of his throat,
The massive square of his heroic breast,
And arms on which the standing muscle sloped";[2]

saw him coming quickly over the springy green turf to meet me, with a great glory of sunshine about his stately head; and I stretched out eager arms towards him, and cried, "I'm coming, love, I'm coming!" and so crying, I woke to find myself embracing the empty air; woke as Nelly Lestrange for the last time in my life.

"This is my wedding day." With what trembling rapture, with what shy shrinking from her own great passionate joy, has many a girl said this. I felt no tremor, no shyness; only a huge loathing, an infinite despair! One forgets to be coy and maidenly, when one's every pulse and nerve is thrilling with a mighty horror; when, loving one man frenziedly, one is about to be delivered over, bound to the tender mercies of another.

No friends came together to see me wed; there was no sound of mirth or music about the dim old rooms: this was no time for

---

1 Refers to the execution of Anne Boleyn, one of Henry VIII's queens. Tamar Heller identifies this passage as a misquote from Harrison Ainsworth's *The Tower of London* (1840).
2 See "The Marriage of Geraint" in *Idylls of the King* (1859), a poem by Tennyson.

merry-making, when the head of the Lestranges was nearing his last dark home. This ceremony was, we all felt, but the precursor of a solemner, sadder one. Only one uncle, a selfish bachelor colonel, had been drawn down reluctant, from his clubs and his comfortable chambers in the Albany, into the murk, wintry country, to give me away.

Eleven o'clock was the hour, at which the poor lamb's throat was to be cut; the female martyr ascend the pyre. As the time drew near, Dolly and Mrs. Smith and Mary the housemaid, all came bustling and fussing about me, in my little shabby, chill chamber; giving a tweak here, and a pull there, and a jerk somewhere else, to one or another of my wedding garments, as seemed good in their eyes. I, meanwhile, stood gazing stonily at myself in the glass. I was dressed in a white muslin gown, as simple as a nun's, a white cloak and a little white bonnet, and I looked as like a snow-drop as possible; as fair, as cold, as passionless. My face was not distorted and blurred with tear marks now; my tears seemed all shed: I had been a spend-thrift of them lately.

To-day, I could not have wept to save my life. A very miserable looking face the looking-glass gave back to me, but a very lovely one, as I could not help seeing: lovelier in its colourless, hopeless wistfulness, with its great blue eyes, and its ruddy billowing hair, than even Dolly's in its subtle Eastern sweetness.

"I'm worth my price," I say to myself, bitterly.

Then they get me downstairs somehow, and into the Noah's ark of the family coach. As we drive along to the church, I sit staring blankly before me, while my uncle, the Colonel, a little withered spick-and-span cock-sparrow, chirrups small old-world *politesses*[1] to Dolly,—whom he thinks "a monstrous fine woman, egad,"—his style of commendation savouring of the Regency[2]— and who takes them suavely, honiedly, as she would take the vilest, most opprobrious epithets ever applied to woman to-day, being, forsooth, in highest good humour.

The air is full of snow; flakes are sailing crookedly down

---

1 Courtesies (French).
2 The Regency of George IV (1811-20) was the period during which he ruled in the stead of his father, who had been declared insane. He ruled as king for 10 more years after his father's death. The term is more loosely used to designate the turn of the nineteenth century and its first three decades, marked by the Napoleonic Wars, lavish aristocratic lifestyles and, it was believed, lax morality.

to join the other flakes lying already on tree, and hedge-row, and field. There seems no horizon to-day, no definite boundary to the prospect—sky and earth are mixed and jumbled up together; it is freezing and thawing, freezing and thawing every five minutes.

At the lych gate[1] we get out. My uncle gives me his arm, and leads me up the narrow gravel walk, where half a dozen perished school-children, three blue-nosed, pinched old women, and a purple hobbledehoy[2] are assembled as witnesses of this gay show. There is a thin white shroud stretched over the sloping green mounds, thin and scant as a beggar's cloak; the snow has dropped her chill, pure pall over the quiet dead as they lie slumbering together in families and households.

Sir Hugh—*my* Sir Hugh, my own—and his best man, the large-headed young cotton lord, meet us at the church door; Sir Hugh in a blue frock-coat, a blue tie, and a red-brown countenance, which all set each other off very nicely.

There was colour in his cheek,
There was lustre in his eye,"[3]

and there was a bouquet as big as a haystack in his hand, a bouquet of delicatest hot-house ferns and whitest hot-house flowers, flowers waxiest of petal and heaviest of scent. This posy he immediately presented to me, and Lord Stockport, of the many mills, did likewise with a lesser haystack to Dolly. I said, "thank you," coldly, took it and held it in my hand, without its ever occurring to me to smell it or notice it any further.

Then we arranged ourselves before the altar. Of course, Hugh disposed himself on the wrong side of me, and had to be pushed, and nudged, and scolded into his right place. Then Mr. Bowles, whose long nose was redder than a plume reft from the flamingo's wing, and whose teeth I heard like castanets played by a skilful

---

1　Roofed gateway to a churchyard, used traditionally as a resting place for coffins before burial.
2　A hobbledehoy is a boy in the awkward stage of adolescence. He is purple from cold.
3　Compare "The Execution of Montrose" (circa 1857), a poem by William Edmonstone Aytoun (1813-65).

hand, opened the prayer-book, and began to tie the first loop of the Gordian knot.[1] I paid but small heed to his exhortation; my eyes kept wandering from Sir Adrian Lestrange, who "*obdormivit in pace, ætat 26*,"[2] in gray marble at my right, to Sir Brian, who "departed this life in the 24th year of his age," in white marble at my left. *He* was deeply regretted; Sir Adrian was *not* apparently. We were not a long-lived family, any of us.

"I require and charge you both, as ye shall answer at the dreadful Day of Judgment, when the secrets of all hearts shall be revealed," said the Rev. Bowles.

He read at a hand-gallop, and very much through his nose, but, try as he would, he could not take quite all the dignity and awe out of that solemnnest adjuration. It called back my straying thoughts; it stirred my apathy. The cold, vault-like air crept through my thin clothing, and chilled the marrow of my bones; and a colder, bitterer chill grasped at my heart, as I listened to the grave, grand words.

Then Sir Hugh was asked whether he would "take this woman to be his wedded wife," and he said, "I will," in his strong bass voice, heartily, loud, out, as if he meant it, and as if he was glad to be asked. And the same question was put to me with regard to "this man," and I said "I will" also; but said it with as much life and animation as a doll shows when she opens her eyes, the string at her side being pulled.

So he, Hugh de Vere, takes me, Eleanor, "till death us do part," and I, Eleanor, take him, Hugh de Vere, and do it with a bad grace, as if I would not have taken him if I could have helped it, and then Hugh put the ring—pledge of a worse than Egyptian bondage[3]—over my cold, reluctant fingers, and the bells clashed out, and we were man and wife, and I knew that now I could reach my darling's arms only through the billows of sin or the floods of death.

The deed being done, and Mr. Bowles having made his

---

1 In Greek mythology and history, a knot tied by Gordius which could not be untied. An oracle said that he who could untie the knot would rule all Asia. Alexander the Great cheated, cutting it in two with his sword.
2 He rested in peace, age 26 (Latin).
3 Israel was enslaved by Egypt for four hundred and forty years, according to Exodus 12:40. Because marriage is not dissolved even by death, Nell believes her marriage is worse than Egyptian bondage.

congratulations as intelligibly as his chattering teeth would allow him, we signed our names—Hugh de Vere Lancaster, very bold and firm; Eleanor Lestrange, very wobbly and illegible; and then Hugh hurried me off into his brougham, which was waiting at the gate.

"God tempers the wind to the shorn lamb," says the proverb, and I thanked God devoutly that that drive was but a short one. During it I spoke not a word; if I had attempted to utter, I felt that I should have shrieked aloud in my great agony.

I find my father in the hall, come out to welcome back his little daughter. He has put his old Sunday coat on to do me honour—the coat that I remember so many years, and which is so much too big for him now, hangs about him in such pitiful folds and wrinkles.

I throw myself passionately into his arms.

"Kiss me, dad—kiss me!" I cry, a little wildly. "I don't feel like myself to-day, somehow. I'm *your* Nell still—aren't I?—though I *am* married."

My father holds out his hand to Sir Hugh, and smiles his pleasant, tender smile.

"She has been made such a pet of all her life, you see," he says, with gentle apology.

(Death is smoothing all the little asperities out of him, dear noble old father.)

"She has been her old father's spoilt child—haven't you, Little Nell? You'll be good to her—won't you? She has been a very loving little daughter to me, and they say good daughters always make good wives—don't they?"

Then he stops, out of breath.

"I will be good to her, indeed, Sir Adrian," says Hugh, solemnly, "so help me, God."

And he has been good to me, honest fellow—he has kept his word.

CHAPTER XXXI

I may put away all the bright colours out of my paint box, for they have gone out of my life; so I need no longer lake, or carmine, or ultramarine. My few more pictures are dark as Rembrandt's; without his forges, and fires, and patches of crimson light to set them off. I made but one stipulation with my husband; and that was that immediately after the ceremony, he should return to Wentworth, *en garçon*,[1] and leave me in peace, to tend and nurse my father, until—I did not express in words, until what; hardly to myself did I dare give shape and substance to my woe—until the end. I had sacrificed myself, in order to prolong my old man's life, and on the day but one after my wedding, he died.

Thus it is with our little feeble plans and designs, in this troublesome world. The sacrifice had been offered in vain. I have told you how strenuously my father opposed all endeavours to make an invalid of him. Well, on that last day he had to succumb: the stout spirit had to give in to the failing flesh; One, mightier than he, overcame him.

So he lay in bed, very quietly, very patiently, waiting,—waiting, and panting sorely. During all those dragging, weary hours, I sat by him, holding his hand; as if *that* could keep him back from the gulf he was nearing. The snow floated down noiselessly on the window sill, and rested there, soft and flaky: the clock ticked monotonous, and the short wintry day sloped westward towards the night.

"It's all up with me, Nell," said my father, faintly; "I'm getting a very broken-winded old horse, aren't I?"

By-and-by I got mother's old Bible, with her dim faded pencilmarks; the shabby little Bible he always used; and read him bits out of it; comfortable, tender promises suited to the weakness of approaching dissolution; and he said,

"Thank you, little lass, it's very nice"; but he could not attend to me long. It is hard work dying; a bitter weary tussle; but ah! surely it is harder seeing another die. I sat and listened to the gasping breath, that grew ever quicker, harder, shorter; it made me out of breath myself to hear him labouring, panting so. O God! how I longed to be able to

"Give him half my powers,
To eke his being out."[2]

Then day died, and the snow lay thicker, and the darkness fell. Presently Mrs. Smith came in with ostentatious tiptoe tread, and

---

1 As a bachelor (French).
2 Tamar Heller identifies this as an adaptation of Thomas Hood's poem, "The Death Bed" (1831).

came creaking over, with a cup of tea for me, and turned away with big tears on her old cheeks; (there were none on mine). And then the doctor came in, with long face, and lowered voice, and told me he was sinking fast—God! as if I did not know that—and poured out some brandy into a glass for me to give him. But I said I would not, rudely, angrily; pushed it away from me; told them he should die in peace, and that they should not torment him—I hated to see that careless indifferent stranger come to gape and croak over him, in his mortal weakness.

So they left me and my old man alone together; we had always loved to be together, hadn't we? The wind rose a little at nightfall, and came sighing, sobbing, *keening*, about the old eaves and gables, and the snow turned to sleet, and beat and pattered against the panes. It seemed so hard to die on such a night; so hard for a poor bare soul to go shuddering out into the great dark void. I could have let him go from me better, I thought, on some bright warm summer nooning, when you could almost see heaven's gates a long way up in the azure depths.

Gradually he sank into a stupor; He who does all things well, took away from him all knowledge of past, present, and to come; all consciousness of his pains and aches; of his debts and his sorrows, and even of his little pet daughter, kneeling by his bedside, with her head in the counterpane, choking and shaking in her sobs.

The night deepened, waned; the candles flared tall and yellow, and the wind sank: still I knelt on, holding the hand that was ever growing colder, colder, with my eyes riveted on that sunken face, that looked so old, so gray, and so very peaceful: I was learning off every pathetic line and hollow in it; printing it on my icy desolate heart, against the time when I should have but memory left of him.

The breathing had grown fainter, fainter; sometimes it paused quite, for a second or two, then laboured on for a space, intermittent, feeble; the pauses grew longer—longer; the gasps lower—weaker—weaker—then stopped! And about the fourth watch of the night came One into that upper chamber—One that had not been there before. A great quiet awe stole over me: I rose from my knees very gently, reverently, and bent over him.

"He is gone!" I said to myself—when suddenly the old kind eyes opened once again *wide*, with an infinite glad surprise in them, as if they saw some pleasant jocund sight—My old man!

God grant that it was so!—and then the eyelids closed again very softly, and he was not.

So the family vault of the Lestranges was opened, and the good gray head went down into the dust, whither all heads go at last. I hope they'll bury me with him when I die. I should like that last grand trumpet blare to find us together. And they carried him away—*him*, that dead coffined weight—ah! not *him*, not *him*, really—away from his pretty old house, and his books, and his wretchedest, wretchedest "little lass." As they bore him slowly under the great elms, beneath whose shade he and I had so often walked, holding sweet converse, the snow fell heavy and thick, whitened the black pall, and sent its feathery, icy flakes against my face, as I walked behind.

I ought to have cried, I suppose, that day; Dolly did; even Mrs. Smith and the other servants did; and I looked at them with a certain stolid surprise. I did not cry; I was not the least inclined; I felt no particular pain or grief, only an infinite, numb apathy. So they bore him through the lych gate, and into the church, and we said the solemn good-bye words to him—he lying there deaf, unheeding of our farewells; and then they laid him in the yawning grave (we standing round), and the snowflakes fell on the coffin-plate, that told how Sir Adrian Lestrange departed this life on the 30th day of December, 186-. And then we turned away and left him, and I was sorry as one that had no hope.

CHAPTER XXXII

"I remember, I remember
The house where I was born;
The little window where the sun
Came peeping in at morn.
It never came a wink too soon,
Nor brought too long a day,
But now I often wish the night
Had borne my breath away."[1]

When next the sun comes peeping through my little dim-paned window, he will find no Nelly Lestrange to greet him. He will

---

1 See "I remember, I remember" (1826), a poem by Thomas Hood.

miss the girl whom he has watched grow up from a little toddling pinafored child, to a fair, tall, comely woman—will miss the happy, foolish innocent face that has smiled back to him across the hay-field, on so many dewy June mornings. Nelly Lestrange, with her light heart, her tumbledown Spanish castles, and her silly little tender jokes, has gone away, not from that room only, but from the world.

They buried her yesterday in that dull chamber, where Death is holding his carnival among the Lestranges, and have left only a very heavy-hearted Nell Lancaster in her stead.

I am sitting in my father's bedroom, on the floor; by the bed whereon he died, and am kissing it. God has vouchsafed to me to-day the gift of tears. After he was dead, when the warmth was gone out of the heart that would have bled less, had it been colder, when his sickness was so sore, that there was no breath left in him. I had cut off a bit of his hair, and now the sight of the thin gray lock, so sparse, so almost white, recalled to me with such bitter force the head from which it was severed, that he being dead, yet spake. Oh God! is there any verse that ever was penned by mortal fingers that grasps so at the universal sympathies of this whole tearful world, as this one.

"Oh Christ! that it were possible
For one short hour to see
The souls we loved, that they might tell us
What and where they be."[1]

Before, when my old man had gone away from me, though he was beyond the reach of my fond arms, beyond the province of the eye and the ear, I could yet picture him to myself amongst familiar human surroundings; could imagine him sitting and walking, making his kindly jests, and talking his clever pointed talk; *now* the vagueness and the doubt rebuffed me.

So far as I had gone with him, he had had a good journey, thank God! for he had parted from me smiling; but alas! that was but a very little way on. I could but take him to the great gates, and send him out into the night, and stand peering with eager aching eyes after him, as he went forth into the blackness *alone*.

It is afternoon, and, but for the servants, I am alone in the

---

1 See "Maud" (1855), a poem by Tennyson.

house. Hugh is gone over to Wentworth, whence he is to return later to fetch me, and Dolly is gone. Dolly has been very busy all the morning, going about the house, and picking up a little bit of china here, and a little bit of plate there. She has no particular right to them, although she says very feelingly, that "poor dear papa" gave them to her, and so of course she cannot bear the idea of their being put up to sale for any dreadful common creatures; but when a house is in the confusion attendant upon an owner lately dead, a little petty larceny is excusable, almost laudable.

Half an hour ago, she set off on a long visit to some of her numerous friends; she made a very pretty exit, crying a little, but not enough to disfigure herself at the railway station, and shaking hands with all the servants. I have cried myself into a state of semi-insensibility; my head is resting on the counterpane, and my lock of hair is lying in silver paper on my lap, when the door opens, and Mrs. Smith says, very gently, "If you please, my lady, Sir Hugh's come back."

If I had thought about it, I should have recollected that there was nobody but myself in the room; but somehow it never occurred to me to take the unfamiliar appellation to myself. Mrs. Smith comes a little further into the room, and repeats a tone or two louder.

"If you please, my lady, Sir Hugh's come and would like to speak to you," I stare up at her, *dully* scared for a minute; then jump up, throw my arms about the old woman's neck, and lay my head on her kindly bosom.

"Don't call me *that*!" I say whispering; "don't! I hate it; call me Miss Nell *always*; do you mind?" Mrs. Smith kisses my swollen face, and strokes my disordered hair; it was homely, but very lovingly done, as Sir Thomas More said of the maid Dorothy Collis, who embraced him as he went to execution.[1]

"I'll call you what you like, my dear, in course; but indeed— indeed you should not take on so; it's not right, it *is* not indeed; it was the Almighty's will as he was took," she says very shakily,

---

1 The name may also be Dorothy Colley. Sir Thomas More was executed in 1535 because he refused to countenance Henry VIII's adulterous marriage of Anne Boleyn. (Henry split off from the Catholic Church when the Pope would not grant him a divorce so he could marry Boleyn. He then declared himself head of a new state church and granted himself a divorce. Later, he had Boleyn executed.)

"and, oh dear! he has been worritted a deal, poor gentleman; I don't think you had oughter wish him back!"

"I don't! I don't!" I cry, sobbing hysterically; "I'm not so cruel! do you think I'm a *fiend*; but I only wish they'd—let me—let me—go to him; it's not wicked to say that is it?"

"Not a bit wicked!" says Mrs. Smith, soothingly, "and so you will in the Lord's good time; so we all shall, I 'ope; and for my part so as we was prepared, I don't much care how soon." Hugh, manlike, is getting impatient. I hear him calling

"Nell! Nell!"

It is not the same voice that was wont to come ringing up these stairs; it is a younger, stronger, commoner one; the contrast comes coldly home to my heart.

"I don't want to see him," I say; pitifully to Mrs. Smith, and speaking as if I had a very bad cold in my head; "go and ask him to give me half an hour more."

Mrs. Smith looks mild disapprobation.

"Nay, my dear, I don't think you had oughter keep him waiting; he's your 'usband, you know, and he raly is as good a gentleman as ever trod shoe-leather; we cannot expect everybody to be like them as is gone."

I have been rather meek and biddable from my youth up, so I go. Hugh is standing at the foot of the stairs, whistling very softly to himself; it is almost as inveterate a habit with him, as with Mr. Chick.[1]

"What a figure you have made of yourself, you poor little girl!" he says, surveying rather ruefully, the purple-eyed, red-nosed, hollow-cheeked prize that he has acquired.

"I cannot help it!" I say, doggedly. "Do you want me? Mrs. Smith said you did."

"I'd walk on my head from here to Wentworth, if it would do you any good," he says, disregarding my question, and looking sympathetic, as a really good-natured man would in the presence of a grief which it was equally beyond his power to measure or assuage; "but you really ought not to fret like this, you'll be laid up, and you know it's—it's *Godalmighty'swill*."

Hugh is very shy of pronouncing his Creator's name, and now does it with a jerk, running the three words into one very rapidly. I don't feel much consoled by the information, and go and sit

---

1 See *Dombey and Son* (1848), a novel by Charles Dickens.

down listlessly, on the end of the servant's prayer-bench. I have eaten nothing all day, and am as weak as a cat.

"What time will you be ready to start?" asks Hugh, seeing that his theological gun has missed fire.

"Oh, must we go yet?" I cry, clasping my hands in despair, "I wanted to bid good-bye to all the old place!"

Hugh looks down and pulls his grizzling moustache.

"The days are so short, you see," he says "and it takes two hours to get there; I don't want to bring the horses in hot; and mother will be getting anxious if we are not back by dinner time!"

"How soon then?" I ask, giving up the point as I would give up any point to-day.

"Well, as soon as you can pop on your bonnet then. I'll go to the stables and tell him to put the horses to; they're uncommon likely to take cold if they stay there long, for it's as damp as a——" *Vault*, he was going to say, but it occurred to him, that, under the circumstances, it might sound unfeeling.

I rise and move towards the stairs again, dragging my legs after me.

"Oh, by-the-bye, Nell, which would you like to go in? the brougham or the double dogcart—they are both here?"

"Oh not the dogcart!" I say with an involuntary gesture of disgust.

"Why? it is not cold!"

"It reminds me of that dreadful day," I say without thinking. (I somehow attribute all my ills to that day.) I was enough to try the patience of the ten best husbands in Britain, wasn't I? but then I was so miserable.

Sir Hugh's kind, good-natured face clouds a little.

"Those were not the same pair," he says, "and the cart cannot run away of itself."

He does not relish the idea of a fourteen mile drive in a stuffy close carriage, with a crying woman; even though she is his bride.

"As you wish," I say indifferently, "it's all one to me."

So the dogcart it is, and into it I get; a limp, nerveless figure, on which a great deal of crape is hung, and over whose face a crape veil falls black and thick as a December night. There has been one of those rapid changes in the weather, which are common in our climate, so rich in unpleasant surprises. The snow is all melted out of the sky, and the bitter wind has whistled and moaned itself away to some other quarter of the earth. The air is as warm as April, and the atmosphere that of a vapour bath.

A dank blue mist hangs over the church-yard. It is not raining, and yet the tombstones are all streaming with wet, and great drops hang from the old ash's naked boughs. I strain my neck back as long as the dim gray tower, and the great dripping yews are in sight.

"Good-bye old dad!" I say to myself over and over again, "good-bye," and then I cry under my veil, bitterlier than ever.

For the first five miles Hugh leaves me pretty much to my own devices; does not bring "*God-Almighty's-will*" to bear on me again; he makes several remarks of a friendly nature to his horses, urging them to steadiness of conduct, and throws out an inquiry or two as to the mode of their entertainment at Lestrange to the groom.

But he holds his tongue as far as the veiled statue beside him is concerned.

The veiled statue unveils herself presently, and stows away her pocket-handkerchief in her pocket, having exhausted all the tears in her lachrymatory. The lamps are lit, and we go spinning through the darkness—it is quite dark by now. Splash! splash! go the horses' hoofs through the mud; a light twinkles here and there cheerily, from a cottage window.

"So shines a good deed in a naughty world."[1]

Immediately on perceiving this change in the weather, Hugh passes the reins into his right hand, and puts his left arm round me. I am Sir Hugh's lawful wife now; so this proceeding does not amuse the groom so much as it would have done on that former drive; it tickles him a little however.

"That's right, old woman!" says my husband kindly; "cheer up! what's done cannot be undone; but things are never so bad in this world that they might not be worse."

The near horse shies; the arm is withdrawn, "Steady old boy! Steady!"

It is very unwifely of me, but I feel inclined to say *Ta*[2] to that timid quadruped.

---

1 See *Merchant of Venice* (first printed 1600), a play by Shakespeare.
2 Meaning "go."

"I suppose, Nell," says Hugh—he thinks that now that the ice is broken, a little cheerful conversation will be highly salutary for me—"I suppose, Nell, that poor Dolly has got to her journey's end by now."

"I suppose so."

"How long is she going to stay there? do you know?"

"No."

"What is she going to do with herself afterwards?"

"I don't know." (My tone said "I don't care either.")

"Poor girl! it's very sad for her not having a hole or corner to put her head in!"

"She has lots of friends."

"Oh, ay! *friends* very likely; and people are very glad to have a girl with them for a month, or *two* even; but one cannot *live* on one's friends; that was what she was saying to me this morning. We had a long talk before she went; I don't think I ever was so sorry for any one in my life."

(The objects of compassion which Hugh meets whene'er he takes his walks abroad are few apparently.)

"Did she tell you what her plans were?"

"Well, no! I don't think she had made up her mind; she came to ask my advice, poor thing! and she seemed so cut up too, about this—this—affair," says Hugh, rather at a loss for an expression, and jerking his head vaguely in the direction of my father's death.

"Awfully!" I say, ironically; "I don't suppose she'll ever get over it." Hugh does not heed my sneer. When once he is off on a train of thought, he runs along it like a mad dog; turning neither to the right nor to the left.

"Do you know what my advice was, Nell? I suppose I ought to have asked you first, but I felt sure of not meeting with much opposition from you—the old lady is the only difficulty; she is so *ratchetty* now and then, and always hates new faces, too!"

"What was your advice?" I ask, startled.

"Why to come and keep house with us, till she marries—that'll be sure not to be long first!"

"Oh!" say I, blankly, and my tone is not exultant. Hugh was right just now; there is no state of things so bad but that it may not be worse.

"Seems such a natural arrangement! own sister!—parents dead!—no home!" says Hugh, becoming ejaculatory, and not quite so certain of my approbation as he was five minutes ago.

"It was very kind of you," I say, gently.

I feel that I am receiving what he intended as a pleasant surprise for me, rather ungraciously.

"Oh, no! not at all! she is a great ally of mine; she has always been a good friend to me, even in the days when you used to snub me, Nell!"

"Yes."

"Of course, I don't mean to say that my principle motive in asking her, was not that I thought you would be pleased to have such a nice companion, and one that you have been used to all your life too; mother is all very well in her way, of course—I don't mean to say a word against her—but I should not think that you and she would be likely to have many ideas in common, and of course I cannot be with you all day; there's the farm, you know, and hunting five days a week, and—and——" says poor Hugh, rather discomfited at the ill-success of his little benevolent scheme, and trying to make out the best case he can for himself.

"It was very good of you!" I say again very gratefully; "and what answer did she make?"

Hugh looks rather foolish.

"Oh, poor girl! why I really think she hardly knew what she was doing; she cried and wanted to go down on her knees to thank me, only of course I could not stand that"; (wretched as I am, I laugh grimly to myself, as I picture the little tableau— Dolly going gracefully down on her knees, and poor Hugh in dire confusion hauling her up again; I think if she had reflected that it would in all probability go back to me, she would have refrained from that little bit of melodrama) "and that of course it was a great boon to a poor homeless girl like her, and that she dare say'd she should not trouble us long. I don't know what she meant by that, I'm sure, unless she has got somebody in her eye—and—and that she'd come, I suppose!"

I say "Oh!" again, and the subject drops.

I feel that it would seem unnatural in me to object, and I could as soon fly in the air as express any elation at the intelligence. My legs feel very stiff, and I am weary, as Hugh lifts me down at Wentworth Hall door.

Last time I saw that door, Dick was leaning against it—I don't even think of Dick to-day somehow. I follow Hugh into the library, where lights are blazing and the curtains are drawn, and a tall old lady in black—she has put on complimentary mourning—receives me in her arms, and kissing me, says with prim stateliness, but very kindly withal, "Welcome home, my dear daughter!"

Alas! she is the only person whose daughter I am now.

CHAPTER XXXIII

They tell us, don't they, that one of the mercifullest dispensations of Providence is our facility for forgetting—the ease and quickness with which we get over things? To me it seems that what points the sting of every grief, is the thought that a time will come when we shall grieve no more. It is terrible enough, God wot,[1] for a person to drop out of our lives; but to drop out of our hearts too. Ah, poor dead ones! is not that hard?

As long as their memory is with us fresh and green—as long as it lives with us, as they themselves lived with us, coming in and going out, in the house and in the street, in talk and in silence, on Sundays and on week-days—so long do we seem to keep a little portion of them with us; they do not seem quite gone away from us.

But the same thing happened to us all. Strive and resolve as we may to keep our sorrow fresh and new and glossy, it is all to no purpose; it grows insensibly old and stale and shabby, like the crape round our hats. Have not you, oh friends, before now, seeing some acquaintance who had just issued out of great tribulation, laughing and talking, apparently unchanged—have not you said within yourself—how unfeeling he is! how different I should be!

And lo! the apple of *your* eye is taken away from you, and in a week or two you also are laughing and talking—the river of your life flows on smooth, unruffled, as if that new-made grave were razed out of creation.

"Out of sight, out of mind," is true to a certain extent of all of us. We cannot be always thinking of what we never see: that is the very thing that makes it so difficult for us to rest our minds on heaven, and heaven's high King; we cannot see them, and so we but feebly, transiently realize them.

---

1 "Knows" (archaic English).

The people we see, who talk to us, and we to them, whom we can hear and touch and feel, gradually fill more and more of that vacant space: the overpowering force of time saps our woes, as a little wave, plashing through long aeons, wears and hollows at last the great granite rock.

But oh! we don't forget, really! I don't mean you to think that. The wound heals over slightly; we could not all walk about with great gaping gashes, could we? The world's work could not get done if we did; but beneath the surface that looks all fair and even, there is a great dull ache going on always—an ache that takes the taste out of our life's savoury meats, and makes us call our short day all too long.

A month has gone by—a wintry, sleety, dreary month. People have got tired of talking of Sir Hugh Lancaster's wedding, and Sir Adrian Lestrange's death. Other men and women have been wed and died since; and new subjects have supplanted those two, which were of intensest interest to but one or at most two people. And there has been a sale at Lestrange; the old oak chairs and tables have been knocked down to the highest bidder; scattered among the neighbouring sons of Manchester and Liverpool: and the old rooms look strange and piteous and unfurnished without them.

And greasy Jews[1]—the offscouring of the earth—(my one point of sympathy with the *moyen âge*[2] barbarians is their loathing and maltreatment of the accursed Israelitish dog)—have been prowling about, trading, as is their wont, on the miseries and weaknesses of poor humanity. And Hugh, good old fellow, has bought the old leathern arm-chair for me: I am sitting in it now; I hope I shall die in it.

I have been transplanted from Lestrange to Wentworth, and the transplantation has not killed me. I am a hardier plant than I thought I was. I don't cry all day, by any means, and I laugh now and then when anything in my husband or his belongings strikes me in a ridiculous light, which is not seldom. I am hungry and eat, I sleep sound, I still have likes and dislikes, I make jokes occasionally; I squabble about every two days with my mamma-in-law, when she tries to give me lectures on deportment, and *le bon Dieu* still gives me energy to snub Hugh as seemeth good unto

---

1 See p. 92, note 4.
2 Middle Ages, the medieval period (French).

me. Do you suppose from this that I accepted my fate meekly, that I was beginning to get reconciled to it? Not I!

My father's death I should have got over in time perhaps: it is natural that parents should go before their children, and I might have got to think of him without torture, with a gentle eternal regret and "sehnung,"[1] as the Germans say. I doubt even that; doubt my ever forgetting my old dad even if I had had Dick to kiss away my tears, and supply the place of all other loves by his great passionate one. Now that the first *éclat*[2] and excitement of my sacrifice were over—*now* that I knew for certain that I had slain myself in vain, knew that he for whom I had been offered up was sleeping with his fathers beneath the chancel of Lestrange, never to be wakened by my loudest, piercingest cries, then my misery rose up before me, huge, unnatural, gigantic; terribler "than ever woman wore." I was like Jonah when his gourd died down. I said, "I do well to be angry, even unto death."[3] "Why," I cried, "was I to be picked out from among all women, to be pre-eminently wretched?"

The little worthless earthenware pitcher, picked a quarrel with the potter who framed it. I did not love Hugh one bit; it is not easy to love two men at once; to tell you the truth, I did not try much, sometimes I loathed him. And yet he was very good to me, as good as could be. I verily believe that he loved me as much as he could love any created thing; it was not his fault, poor fellow, that he was not made of the finest porcelain, but was only good, useful, ugly Delf.[4] He was not to blame that Providence had made him a little, dark, middle-aged baronet, instead of a great beautiful fair dragoon.

I am sure that he appreciated my varied excellences, and even ruggednesses, as much as man could; and was fully alive to the advantage he had gained in having a pretty young white face opposite to him every day at dinner, instead of an old yellow ugly one. He was a most loving husband; horribly, needlessly, irksomely loving, I said to myself. One has not much power of

---

1 Longing (German).
2 Glamor (French).
3 Compare Jonah 4:9. God gave Jonah a gourd, to shade him, but then afflicted the gourd with a worm, and it died.
4 Delf or Delft china was made in Holland, and was cheaper than some other kinds of china.

simulation or dissimulation at nineteen; but I did my best to hide my disrelish for my lord, and to receive his blandishments with as good a grace as I could.

I was his chattel as much as his pet lean-headed bay mare, and I felt that he had justice on his side. If he might not insinuate his arm round my *waist*, round whose waist might he? Sometimes I will confess to you that I wished he would transfer his amities to some other person, even if it were the cook. I'm sure I should not have been jealous. All Sir Hugh's other servants, if they disliked their situations, or got tired of them, might give warning and leave; but I, however wearied I might get of mine, could never give warning, could never leave. I was a fixture for life. So I said to myself sometimes, and ground my teeth, and snarled like a caged tiger.

I had indulged a mild vague hope that the very words of the marriage ceremony read over me, would have a cabalistic[1] charm to prevent my ever thinking of any man but Sir Hugh, after we were man and wife. I had heard that only very bad wicked women ever cared for anybody but their husbands after they were married, and I hoped I was not a very bad wicked woman.

However, I discovered pretty soon with some chagrin that I must reckon myself among that naughty band; that I was not one of those "who love their lords"; not "a matron of Cornelia's mien."[2] I found that I thought of Dick infinitely more; more regretfully, passionately, longingly, now that I was Lady Lancaster, and it was criminal of me so to think, than I had done as Nelly Lestrange, when it was only unwise and unworldly. Nor was this mere womanly perversity, hankering after the unattainable; nor did it spring from any idea that it was rather fine to be immoral. I thought of him because I had nothing else pleasant to think of. The one person who had ever halved my heart with him was gone from me.

I *hated* to think of my father, not having that living faith accorded to some, which enables them to say from their hearts,

---

1 The Cabala, or Kabbalah, or Qabalah (there are many spellings) are Jewish mystical texts. In this period, there was great curiosity among British people about many forms of Eastern religion and mysticism.

2 See "Childe Harold's Pilgrimage" (1812-18), a poem by Lord Byron. Cornelia was a Roman matron who was widely respected as an embodiment of matronly virtue and dignity. She lived circa 1 BCE.

that their dead ones are "not dead but gone before."[1] My father *was* dead to me, dead as the old dog who died the other day licking my hand. I *knew* I never should see him again.

How did I know whither he was gone; how did I know whether he had gone to any good place; and if he had, what right had I to think that I should ever rejoin him there? I did not believe in any heaven with sufficient strength to make me strive very strenuously to attain it.

Life seemed to me a great vast chaos, through which men stumbled and tottered to a big black pit at the end. So I thought on the forbidden theme all the day, and sometimes all the night; and truly there was not much at Wentworth to distract my thoughts. A lap-dog would have thought my existence paradise; for I had plenty of the best to eat, and big fires to bask in; but for myself, I thought it a very dull gehenna.[2]

All through the wintry morning I sat on a gilt chair, clad from head to foot in thickest silk and blackest crape, in the yellow drawing-room, every stick of whose ugly furniture spoke to me of *him*; while my mother-in-law knitted socks for her beloved son—she was a thrifty old soul, and would fain have had me do likewise—and narrated to me apocryphal tales of Hugh's extreme beauty in infancy; thrilling anecdotes of his childhood, and of how he caught the measles; of his habits and customs at various periods of his history; of how often he had broken his collar-bone, etc., etc.

In the afternoon I either went behind the fat coach-horses, to pay solemn calls to neighbouring matrons, accompanied as before, by our mamma, or else, when it was not a hunting day, I pottered about the premises with Hugh, heard his horses' pedigrees, and thought, with a frosty chill at my heart, of those other saunters at Lestrange, about shabbier stables, with the dear old man who was not.

Sometimes, but very rarely, I managed to shirk out by myself, to put on the dowdiest cloak and hat I could find, to take off my ring, and dawdle and wander and scramble about the park, and be Nelly Lestrange—in my own eyes at least—once again.

In the evenings, we two women stitched and interchanged

---

1 See "Human Life" (1819), a long poem by Samuel Rogers.
2 A word deriving from Hebrew that came to mean hell or the underworld.

amicable nothings or mild sparrings, while Hugh, having bestowed on me such post-cenal[1] caresses as he felt inclined, went to sleep, and mostly snored.

We were so sitting one evening after dinner—Lady Lancaster, senior, click-clacking away at that eternal knitting; Sir Hugh not quite asleep yet, but reading the *Times* as a narcotic; and Lady Lancaster, junior, toiling unlovingly at a smoking-cap for her master, and glancing now and then from him to his mother, from the lean grizzling head and bristles to the yellow front and wrinkles, and crying out to herself—

"Oh, how sick I am of you both. Oh, if I could but get away—oh, if I only could!"

Then Hugh spoke.

"Mother, do you recollect M'Gregor?"

"M'Gregor, my dear boy; what M'Gregor?—there are so many M'Gregors. There is your poor father's friend, Sir Malcolm, and there's General M'Gregor?"

"No, no," interrupts her son, "none of those old fogies. I mean a big, good-looking fellow that was here last year. Don't you remember?"

"To be sure," says mamma, calmly; "he spilt a cup of coffee over my lavender satin—I had to have the breadth taken out; and I remember remarking that he seemed very attentive to Dorothea Lestrange. Yes, I remember the young man perfectly."

"Do you happen to recollect the number of his regiment?" says Hugh, who is widely, brilliantly awake by now.

"—th Dragoons," interpose I, breathlessly; "what about him?"

"Nothing, darling," says Benedick,[2] looking at me with lazy rapture, "only I see it's ordered to India."

"Ordered to India!"

I rose and rushed hastily out of the room, very nearly falling foul of the butler, who was bringing in tea, and disconcerting that grave functionary considerably.

Next day, Sir Hugh and his mother went to dine and sleep at a house in the neighbourhood. My deep mourning of course

---

1 After dining.

2 See *Much Ado About Nothing* (first printed 1600), a play by Shakespeare. Benedick is the lover of Kate, who resists his advances for much of the play.

excused me from accompanying them, and a proud woman was I when their backs were fairly turned. I had begged and entreated of my mother-in-law not to stay, or let Hugh stay at home on my account; and she had commended my unselfishness, and had driven off in high good humour with "her boy."

"Thank God!" said I, standing at the hall-door, and watching the carriage lamps go twinkling down the dusky avenue. Then I returned slowly to the saloon, and let my countenance fall into any woe-begone dejected curves it chose, there being nobody by to remark upon them.

"Ordered to India—ordered to India!" Those three words had been dwelling in my ears for the last twenty-four hours, ceaselessly; the gilt clock on the mantelpiece seemed to be ticking them now. "Going to India to have his young life scorched away, and I should *never* see him again." It was not that I should not see him again for a year, or for two, or for twenty years, but—*never*. I should never know how, why, or for what other fairer, lovabler woman he had deserted me.

An overpowering, mad longing seized me to go to him to ask him why he had been so cruel to me, to ask him to take me with him to that far sultry land. What did I care how wicked I was? My old man would never know it,

"For he was chill to praise or blame."[1]

It seemed to me, then, that the best thing we can do in this grievous world is to snatch whatever present bliss we may, seeing that the past is all torture and the future all nothingness. "Let us eat and drink, for to-morrow we die,"[2] seemed to me the profoundest philosophy then. "If there is eternal justice somewhere," said I to myself, "why is my punishment so much heavier than my sins? I ask for so little; I don't expect, don't ask to be happy—I only beg for exemption from bitterest, sharpest pain; I only ask for an easy death and quick annihilation. Oh, to lay down my head in the kindly dust—not in a coffin, a heavy, stifling, dreadful coffin—but in the fresh-scented, dark-brown earth, and with 'life's fitful

---

1 See "The Two Voices" (1833), a poem by Tennyson.
2 See I Corinthians 15:32. Paul suggests that without the belief in eternal life, all people have is the present. But the members of the Corinthian church must remember that they do have eternal life.

fever'[1] for ever cooled, sleep on and on, till my body 'returns to the earth as it was,'[2] and my spirit—ah, can *it* sleep?"

The fire burnt cheerily; the wax candles shed a soft lustre round them; the old china on mantelshelf and table and cabinet looked comfortable and snug and homelike; but I felt stifled, choking. I went to the window, opened it, and stepped out into the verandah. A great gust of rain-laden wind comes driving roughly against me, the French window behind me bangs to, and I stand out on the wet flags, and watch the black clouds go scudding, hurrying across the sky, for the moon is up and gives me light. It was not cold, and I felt to breathe freer, leaning my face among the wet ivy, that climbed and twisted round the further pillar of the verandah.

"It was here he kissed me; it was here he took me in his arms," said I to myself, nestling my head among the dripping green. "I thought I was going to spend my life with him, and now I am alone, alone for evermore! Great God—how unbearable!"

Suddenly there comes a lull between two rain-bursts; the moon comes sweeping out from behind a great cloud shoulder; the Portugal laurel beside me shakes and rustles; and from behind it a man steps out suddenly—steps out into the moonlit gravel walk, where the pebbles are glittering like so many diamonds.

CHAPTER XXXIV

Need I tell you who the man was? For a second, I did not know myself; for a second, I stood paralyzed by terror; then he came close up to me, and I knew him; and a great flood of wicked, wonderful joy streamed into my soul and nearly drowned it; as I looked up at the young giant with the haggard, beautiful, angry face that was stooping over me.

"I have been prowling about like a thief or a poacher," he says, harshly; "I have watched that fellow, your husband, out; I was determined I *would* see you before I went." The cloud rack blots out the moon again; it is very dark.

---

1   See the play *Macbeth* (first printed 1623), by Shakespeare.
2   Compare Ecclesiastes 12:7. "Then shall the dust return to the earth as it was: and the spirit shall return unto God who gave it."

"Is it you, Dick, *really*?" I say, faltering, and then I push back the window, and the light from fire and candle flashes on him, as he stands there, wet to the skin, big, shaggy, miserable. My heart goes out with a great yearning pity to him; "come in," I say, hastily; "you're so wet; don't stand out there!" I step back into the warm, scented room, and he, after hanging back a minute, as if irresolute, follows me. We give each other no polite greeting; we stand by the crackling, cheery fire blaze, and say nothing for a while; only we look into each other's eyes, with passionate, desperate longing across the mighty chasm that yawns between us. At length Dick says groaningly, as if the words were wrenched from him—

"Oh, Nell! Nell! why did you do this? why did you jilt me when I loved you so?"

The blood rushed boiling, surging into my cheeks and forehead and throat. I was a mean-spirited woman; till he said that, I had absolutely forgotten his ill-treatment of me.

"How dare you ask that?" I cried vehemently, "you, who have blighted all my life for me; you, who have been crueler to me than ever man was to woman before; you, who never sent me word or sign, all through those weary six months; you, who had not even the bare civility to answer the letters I wrote to you in my misery!"

I stopped, suffocated.

"What—*do*—you mean?" said Dick, very slowly; he was spreading his broad hands to the blaze, and his drenched pilot-coat was steaming in the warmth; at my upbraidings, no remorse, only intensest surprise came into his face. "I never had but one letter from you, and *that* one you most solemnly adjured me not to answer. Here it is! I have carried it about with me, night and day, ever since I got it."

He put his hand into his breast pocket, and pulled out a letter. I snatched it eagerly; it was like my handwriting, but it was not it; it was neater, carefuller, more ornate. I turned to the signature; there was none; then I read it through:—

"My dearest,—It seems so odd and so pleasant, sitting down to write to you; but oh! I'm grieved to have to tell you that this first letter must also be the last; at least for ever so long. Don't be angry with me, but I told papa all about you; you know how I love him, and I could not bear to keep anything from him. Well! he was *very* angry at first; would not hear of it at all; said it was all nonsense, and that we had both behaved shamefully; but at last, after a great deal of trouble and begging, I got him to come round so far as to say, that if we both remained in the same mind for a year, he would then listen to us; only he stipulated that we must neither see nor write to each other during the year. I did my very best, as you may imagine, to make him change his decision, but all to no purpose! It seems a little hard, doesn't it? and I cannot help crying a little sometimes, when I think of neither hearing from, nor seeing you for so long; but, after all, a year will soon be gone, and just think how happy we shall be then. Good-bye, my darling; God bless you! "Ever your own.

"P.S.—I adjure and implore you not to answer this: *I beg it of you as a proof of your love.* Papa would be sure to see the letter, and then we should be in worse case than we are now even. Good-bye again, my own darling."

"I never wrote a word of it," said I, compelling myself to speak very calmly, though I clutched hold of a chair-back for support. "Never; it's all a forgery; this is Dolly's doing!"

"What?" said he, gasping, and his strong frame staggered as under a mighty blow; "you never wrote this!"

"Never," said I, very solemnly. "I wrote you plenty of other letters to tell you how much I loved you, and to ask you why you never wrote to me, as you promised to do?"

"And I never got one of them," he said; and as he spoke, the blood retreated from his lips, and left them livid.

We stared at one another blankly; we were as if stunned.

Presently he asked, hoarsely, "What made her do it?"

"Oh, I see it, I see it all!" I groaned, wringing my hands. "She was determined I should marry *him*," (I could not mention his hated name), "and I've done it; I have fallen into the trap she laid for me! Oh! I cannot bear it! I cannot bear it!"

I burst into loud sobbing, and throwing myself on the ottoman, buried my head in the cushions.

"She-devil," said Dick, grinding his white teeth, like a wild beast in his rage and agony, "I wish to God I had her here now, I'd tear her limb from limb, though she is a woman; by G— I would!"

"If my heartiest, bitterest curse," said I, vindictively, "can do her any harm, she has the comfort of knowing that she has got it"; and then I flung myself on the floor, and wept afresh—wept till I was exhausted, and till my eyes had nearly disappeared from their situations.

He, meanwhile, stood with his elbow on the mantel-piece, watching me, with his angry, hopeless, passionate eyes; he did not attempt to give me any comfort; he could not give what he had not got, poor fellow! and besides was not I another man's wife? It was Sir Hugh's business to dry my tears, not his.

"And so it's all a mistake! all a mistake!" he said at last, very brokenly, as if to himself; and the gilt clock changed its tune, and went ticking on, "all a mistake, all a mistake!"

Then I rose from off the floor, and went and sat down on the ottoman again, and forgot Sir Hugh's existence altogether. The rainy wind still blustered and wailed and stormed outside; but yet the storm within our breasts was mightier.

"I cannot stand it any longer," Dick said, vehemently, clenching his hand, and bringing it down like a sledge hammer on the marble slab. "I must go, or I shall make a beast of myself. Nell! I'm sailing for India to-morrow; say one kind word to me before I go. Oh, Nell! Nell! you belonged to me before you belonged to him, damn him!"

Looking into his haggard, beautiful, terrible face, I forgot all I should have remembered; forgot virtue, and honour, and self-respect; my heart spoke out to his. "Oh, don't go!" I cried, running to him, "don't you know how I love you? For *my* sake stay; I cannot live without you!"

I clasped both hands on his rough coat sleeve, and my bowed head sank down upon them.

"Do you suppose I can live in England and see you belonging to another man?" he asked, harshly; "the world is all hell now, as it is; but that would be the blackest, nethermost hell! No, let me go," he said, fiercely, pushing me away from him roughly, while his face was writhen and distorted.

"If you go," I said in my insanity, throwing myself into his arms, "I'll go too. Oh! for God's sake take me with you."

He strained me to his desolate heart, and we kissed each other wildly, vehemently: none came between us then. Then he tried to put me away from him.

"My darling," he said, "you don't know what you're saying; do you think I'm such a brute as to be the ruin of the only woman I ever loved?" and his deep voice was sorely shaken as he spoke.

But I would not be put away: I clung about his neck, in my bitter pain.

"I'd rather go to hell with you, than to heaven with him!" I cried, blasphemously. "Oh, don't leave me behind you! You're all I have in the world now. Oh, take me, take me with you!"

My hair fell in its splendid ruddy billows over his great shoulder, and my arms were flung about the stately pillar of his throat.

He set his teeth hard, and drew in his breath; it was a tough ordeal.

"I won't," he said, hoarsely; "for God's sake stop tempting me. I'd sooner cut your throat than take you. Do you think it would be loving you to bring you down to a level with the scum of the earth? Oh, Nell! Nell! you ought to be my good angel. Don't tempt me to kill my own soul and yours!"

The reproachful anguish of his tones smote me like a two-edged sword. I said no more; I lay passive as a log in the arms that must so soon loose me for ever, while the madness died slowly, frostily out of me.

"I'm very wicked, I know," I whispered piteously; "you don't hate me, Dick, do you, for wanting to go with you?"

"Hate you! my poor pretty darling; if you could but look into my heart, and see what it is without you!"

Great tears are standing in his honest, tender, agonized eyes—tears that don't disgrace his manhood much, I think.

"Go now," I whisper, huskily, "I can bear it. God bless you, darling!"

"My little Nell! My own little snow-drop!" he cries, and then he kisses me heart-brokenly; and as he so kisses and clasps me, a great blackness comes over my eyes, and I swoon away in his arms.

When I come back to life—come back with trouble, and sighings, and pain, I find myself lying in my long heavy black draperies on the sofa; find the candles burning low, and the fire nearly out; find that he is gone, and that I am alone—alone for evermore!

CHAPTER XXXV

Hugh and his mamma returned next day; the red and brown leaves were whirling and dancing about, and the tree-arms were creaking and grinding. Standing listlessly by my boudoir window, about four o'clock, I see the family coach and the bays coming with slow majesty though the park.

Hugh in his brown great-coat driving; our parent uprighter than one of her own knitting-needles, and her *femme de chambre*[1] inside; the valet and the footman in the dickey.[2] Here they all are! welcome, welcome home! I had spent the last night lying all along upon the earth, as David did when he was interceding for the life of his little son.[3] I was interceding for the sparing of no life; I was but interceding for the taking away of my own. The rough west wind kept dashing the ivy sprays against the window pane, and I lay with my face buried in the deep piled carpet, while my darling went away from me through the night; went away forlornly, in his soaked pilot coat, with his dripping golden hair, and his true desolate heart.

As for Dolly, I had made up my mind about her. She had sown, and she was about to reap; she had laboured, and she was about to enter upon the reward of her labours.[4]

"No! *that* she shall not! so help me God!" I cry out in my rage and pain, and the dying fire gives one sleepy flicker of surprise at my vehemence. I would go to Hugh, and would tell him all. I had been dishonest to him all along; I would be honest now; I had been sailing under false colours; *now* I would run up my own black pirate flag. I would go to him, and tell him all my little bitter story; I would hide no detail; gloss over none of my own vast wickedness. I would tell him how I had thrown myself into that other man's arms, and begged him with tears and prayers earnester than ever mother sent up in behalf of her dying child, to take me away with him, to make me utterly vile and enormously happy. And I would also tell him— for to *this*, that other anecdote would be but the necessary preface, of my sister's ingenious and newly discovered accomplishment of imitating her neighbour's handwriting; an accomplishment which would have twisted her graceful neck a hundred years ago.[5]

---

1 Chambermaid (French).
2 Seat outside the back of a carriage.
3 See II Samuel 12:16. God punishes David for taking another man's wife by sending sickness upon his son. The child dies, despite David's abasing himself by fasting and sleeping on the ground.
4 Compare I Corinthians 3:8. "Now he that planteth and he that watereth are one: and every man shall receive his own reward according to his own labour."
5 A century earlier, forgery was a capital offense and Dolly could have been hanged.

Hugh would turn me out of doors of course. I was fully prepared for that; I should not think it the least severe of him. I could see the old woman sweeping away her stiff lavender satin from contact with me, and looking at me with her stern Puritan eyes, as the Pharisees long ago, under the blue Palestine sky, looked at the woman, to whom our dear Lord Christ said, "Neither do I condemn thee!"[1] I should be turned out of doors, and should have to go about begging my bread, in greenish rags and a whine.[2]

There was almost a relief in the idea; it would be a fit expiation for my crime. Moreover, what hardships, what ignominy, what painfullest, lingeringest death, would not I have embraced *laughing*, to have baulked Dolly of the pay for which she had so diligently served her master, the Devil. Cowardly, chicken-hearted woman as I was—and there were few more so between the three seas,—terrifiedly as I had always shrunk from physical pain; in that first frenzy of agonized hate, I would have hung all day beneath an Eastern sky, nailed hand and foot to a cross, while soul and body parted slowly—slowly—in unimagined anguish, would have been sawn asunder, stoned, burnt, readily, yea, most joyfully, if thereby I could have purchased for myself the power to be fitly revenged on her who had turned the jocund garden of my young life into a desolate wilderness.

"I will tell him to-day—to-morrow" I say to myself, as I stand drumming with my fingers on the sill, and watching my own fine carriage, the carriage for which I have paid the longest price ever carriage fetched, sweeping dignifiedly up to my own Hall door. Hugh helps his mother out dutifully—"my boy" is a good son—and then I hear him coming running upstairs three steps at a time.

"Well, old girl, how are you? Why did not you come down to meet us? I was looking out for you at the Hall door."

"I—I—don't know, I'm sure," I say, feeling horribly guilty, "I never thought of it."

"Very glad to get home again," says Hugh, pulling off his dog-skin gloves, and precipitating himself into a minute cane

---

1   See John 8:11. The woman, an adulterer, was brought to Jesus for judgment. He pardoned her and told her to sin no more.
2   Nell seems to be referring to common representations of the fallen woman, who becomes a homeless beggar.

arm-chair; for, if you remark, men always select the smallest chair they can find to deposit their persons upon. "I wish my neighbours all the good in the world, but I don't seem to care how little I see of them now-a-days."

"Don't you?" with a feeble smile.

"Next time anyone invites me to his house, I think I shall say 'I have married a wife, and therefore I cannot come,'[1] eh, Nell?" (I have turned a wife out of doors, and therefore I cannot come, will be a more valid excuse, I think bitterly.) "I say, Nell, what do you say to running downstairs, and saying something civil to the old lady; I suppose it would be a proper attention, wouldn't it? and old people are such sticklers for their dignity."

"Oh, yes—oh, to be sure—I was forgetting!" I cry, and I turn to go and greet my "mother," while Hugh follows me.

We find the old dowager sitting in the library; she has not yet laid aside her toga, and is reading her letters.

"I hope you have had a pleasant visit," I say, rather timidly.

"Charming, my dear, charming!" (rustling her letter, and giving me a fond but prickly kiss. It is a dreadful thing living in the house with two moustaches nearly related to you, I find). My version of the little touching hymn to our mammas, that we all commit to memory in early life would be

"Who ran to help me when I fell,
And kissed the place and *stabbed* it well,
My mother."[2]

"They always arrange their parties so nicely, no mixtures; one never runs any risk there of having any of these *nouveaux riches*[3] forced willy nilly upon one; the dear Bishop, and Lord and Lady Brandreth—oh, by-the-bye, Lady Brandreth asked a great deal about you, was so sorry to miss the opportunity of making your acquaintance; we must positively return her call next week, my dear."

---

1 Compare Luke 14:20. These are excuses offered by guests invited to a feast, in Jesus' parable. The host then invites the beggars and the unfortunate to the feast instead. The lesson is that, when invited to salvation, one should choose faith over worldly commitments.

2 From a verse by Ann Taylor (1782-1866). The original line reads, "and kissed the place to make it well."

3 Newly rich people (French). It carries a connotation of vulgarity and is derogatory.

"Yes, certainly, if you wish." (By next week, I shall have assumed the greenish rags and the whine.)

I did not tell Hugh on that day, nor on the day after, nor on the day after that. Do not we all know, how without having faltered in our resolution to do a disagreeable thing, we keep putting it off, from one day to another. And meanwhile, the said excellent Hugh pursued the even tenor of his way, doing his duty to God and to man, according to his own ideas of what those duties were. Went to church and read "Bell's Life"[1] on Sundays; hunted, and drained, and liquid-manured, and steam-ploughed on week days.

As for the little tiffs in his seraglio[2]—for little tiffs there were even in those early days, little tiffs there must always be, when an old woman and a young one hold divided sway—as long as they were not obtruded on his notice, he treated them with the sublime indifference with which Zeus, the cloud compeller, resting on the topmost peak of Olympus, or going to have a snug dinner with the Ethiopians, might have treated a squabble between those two arrant shrews, cow-eyed Here, and gray-eyed Athene.[3]

If my eyes were red, why it was the east wind, or a touch of influenza. If I did not talk, why he concluded philosophically that I had nothing to say, or at least nothing to say on the subject that he was wont to delight in. For be it known that Sir Hugh was in the habit of keeping a hobby horse,[4] saddled and bridled in his mind's stable; and on this docile animal he frequently cantered up and down, and took healthful exercise. As often as not, this hobby horse was some pet grievance, which went to sleep and underwent decent burial, as long as the hunting and training and liquid-manuring were in full force, but was resurrectionized whenever they were found insufficient to employ all the powers of his intellect.

---

1 A popular weekly magazine.

2 A harem.

3 Zeus was the leader of the Gods. Here, or Hera, was his wife, and Athene, or Athena, his daughter. "Cow-eyed" and "gray-eyed" is how these Greek goddesses were repeatedly described in Homer's *Odyssey.*

4 This is a child's toy horse, but the term is also used to describe a topic in which one is disproportionately interested (and therefore bores others with).

At present the grievance was a projected railway, that was to intersect a part of his property. It was to run only for about a mile and a half through one or two outlying farms, and it was of no earthly disadvantage to him or his, and he knew it; and yet to hear him talk, you would have imagined that it involved the ruin of the whole Lancastria Gens.[1]

"It is too bad!" he is saying now, in a quasi-injured voice, as he sits cracking walnuts at his comfortable dinner table; "one cannot call a foot of one's property one's own now-a-days; one can never be safe from having one's land cut up by these rascally projectors, for their beastly lines that nobody wants."

"Disgraceful!" echoes the acquiescent Dowager, who like lovely Thaïs,[2] sits beside him, with her head unlike lovely Thaïs, I imagine, crowned with one of those weird erections of black velvet and steel that old women delight in. "I suppose it is all these dreadful Radicals; I'm sure I don't know what the country is coming to; I suppose they will bring their horrid railways through one's drawing-room next."

"It's such a confounded swindle!" pursues Hugh, applying the nutcrackers viciously to a walnut as if it had been a director's head; "the merest bubble! Only people are such fools; they will be taken in, try as one may to open their eyes; and if they do get it—and they won't get it so easy as they think, *I* can tell them—it will never pay them sixpence in the pound."

"Won't it, dear?" say I, starting into sudden interest, for I imagined that my husband addressed his last remark more particularly to me; but I am mistaken, it is only that having finished his walnuts, his eyes are gazing straight before him, and consequently, unavoidably take me in their range of vision.

"Don't you remember, mother," he goes on, after a few minutes devoted to sipping claret, bringing his eyes to bear on his mamma, and thereby putting his wife off guard; "don't you remember, they were talking about this line once before, five years or so ago. There was some sense in it then, because the Tadcaster and Milton branch was not open then; but when that was opened it did away with all need for this—for that—I mean, don't you see?"

---

1 Lancaster Family (Latin).
2 See John Dryden, "Alexander's Feast" (1767). Thaïs was a courtesan who accompanied Alexander the Great.

He ends, for he perceives that the relative pronouns are getting too many for him.

"These horrid companies get everything their own way now-a-days! I declare it is quite shocking! it seems to me that no one can do anything for themselves in these days, but must have a company to help them. We shall be having praying companies, and going to bed companies soon."

Our prophetic parent ceases and adjusts her diadem, the point of which is veering gently round towards her left ear.

"Lord ——made such a capital speech in the House yesterday, upon these infernal railways; shows 'em up so completely, brings 'em down to chapter and verse, don't you know. *I don't care what any one says*," pursues Sir Hugh, looking round on his harem with a determined air, "but I stick to it, that he is the best speaker they've got now; out and out, *out and out*, I say."

"Ah!" says the senior occupant of the seraglio, deferentially, "won't you read it to us, dear Hugh? at least any part of it that you think we could understand; we should like it so much, should not we, Nelly?"

I again start and blush; I always am starting and blushing of late, and say very nervously, "Oh, yes, to be sure dear—so much—oh do!"

So we migrate to the drawing-room, and Ariel,[1] *alias* Tomkins, having fetched to-day's "Times," dear Hugh begins to read through two and a half columns of statements and statistics, and representations, all gilded by the lambent glow of Lord ——'s wit. Meanwhile "mamma" having assisted her spectacles to mount her long nose, draws her parish bag towards her, and begins to clothe the naked "hear, hear's" and "cheers," and asks the reader is he sure he is not tired, begs him not to make himself hoarse, and offers to get black-currant lozenges for him.

I work too, and do my best to keep my attention somewhere within a mile of those big sheets; to laugh and express surprise and horror at the right places; not to laugh where I ought to express horror, not to express horror where I ought to laugh; and by dint of care and always taking my cue from the dowager, I succeed admirably. I could not sleep that night for the wind; it kept roaring so, and groaning in the great Scotch fir close to my bed-room

---

1 Ariel is the spirit-servant of the magician Prospero, in Shakespeare's play, *The Tempest* (first printed 1623).

windows. It shook the window frames, and came banging with impotent fury against the stout stone walls.

That was a blowy time; many and many a coast was strewn with wrecks and stranded vessels.

"What an awful night!" my mother-in-law had said, as we came up the deep carpeted stairs to bed, "how thankful we ought to be, my dear, that we have no one dear to us at sea."

(Oh yes, so thankful, of course.) What did it matter to us that the "Euryalus" sailed from Cork for India four days ago, with the —th Dragoons on board. God help that poor ship to-night, labouring through a wintry sea, with the great greenish-gray waves, with their angry white crests towering high above her mast-heads! God help the one passenger that for me that ship contains! The man in the drenched pilot coat, with the set white face, that day and night I see so plain, that I shall see when the damps and dews of death are coming dankly down upon my own.

The wind lulls every now and then for a minute or two, to gather fresh strength for the onset; then comes tearing, howling, shrieking like a hundred lost spirits over the wintry wolds. Oh God! He'll be drowned! he'll be drowned! Perhaps he is drowned already! Perhaps the crabs and scrawls, and noisome, shapeless sea beasts are already gnawing at the heart that beat with such passionate agony against mine a week ago.

Towards morning the hurricane moderates, and I fall asleep heavily, and dream confusedly of churchyards, and of my father as alive again, while yet I know somehow all the while that he is dead—of tombs and drowned men. I sleep on late, and my eye-lids are purple, and my eyes look as if they had been put in with a dirty finger, when I go down late—a great crime at Wentworth—to breakfast.

"I hope you have not waited; I'm so sorry!" I say apologetically, as I make my tardy entrance.

"I think, my dear, that it would be as well if you could try and be down for family prayers," says Lady Lancaster, stiffly; "it is a bad example for the servants when the mistress is absent, and it is no great hardship to be dressed by nine o'clock; at least it used not to be considered so in my young days."

"Come, come, mother, we must not be too hard upon her," says Hugh, taking my hand fondly, "she is not so tough as we old stagers are; and the wind kept her awake, poor little woman! She is half asleep still, isn't she?"

To prevent any wrangling over my unprayerful spirit, I betake myself to my letters, which are lying in a little heap beside my plate. My correspondence is not of much interest generally. The first that I take up has a very broad black edge,[1] ostentatiously broad, like the Pharisees' phylacteries.[2] I look at the handwriting, frown, tear it open, and read. It does not take long reading.

"My dear Nelly,—As you and *dear* Hugh, to whom I can never be sufficiently grateful, have been so kind as to offer me a home, I write to ask if you will allow me to take shelter there, early next week. I trust that my coming will be no annoyance to dear Lady Lancaster, but indeed I shall try hard to be in nobody's way.
"Your affectionate sister,
"DOROTHEA LESTRANGE."

The evil day has come then; the match must be put to the train of gunpowder, which is to blow the reputation of the Lestranges, and the domestic peace and honour of the Lancasters into the air. Shortly after breakfast I go and knock, with trembling knuckles, at the door of Hugh's snuggery, where he and his bailiff hold their Witenagemotes,[3] and transact the affairs of the Wentworth nation.

"May I come in, Hugh?"

"Come in! Of course you may!"

I enter.

"What do you mean by knocking, Nell? have you forgotten that uncommon cold day, not so long ago, when I endowed you with all my worldly goods? I did not make any exception in favour of this sanctum, did I?"

"I wanted to speak to you," I say, coming over to the table, with my eyes glued to the carpet.

"All right! Fire away! Only come a bit closer to the fire, and don't stand there looking like a little undertaker's assistant."

"I have heard from Dolly!"

---

1 People in mourning used stationery with black edging.

2 See Matthew 23:5. Phylacteries are leather cases worn on the forehead and arm, which usually contain prayers or scriptures written on parchment. Jesus accuses the Pharisees of making their phylacteries broad and their fringes long; that is, of turning religious articles into ostentatious ornaments.

3 A council of wise men, a legislature (Anglo-Saxon, Old English).

"Oh! we shall have to have your tongue slit like a magpie's,[1] Nell, to make you talk a bit faster; she's coming, I suppose."

"She wants to come next week."

"Poor Dolly! I'm sure I shall be very glad to see her; and I suppose you have come to talk about what rooms she is to have, and that sort of thing; but you had better settle all that with the old lady; she'll be fit to be tied, if she is not taken into council."

I make a great plunge; it is like taking a header into a cold tub on a frosty morning.

"Hugh!" (Twisting a rosary of jet beads that I have about my neck, round my fingers.) "Would you mind my telling her not to come?"

Hugh opens his brown eyes very wide, wider than ever Providence intended those windows to his worthy soul to be thrown open.

"Tell her not to come! After having offered her a home, to slink out of it; leave her, poor girl, without a roof to shelter her pretty head in! why, Nell, you must be joking!"

"Joking!" I cry, passionately; "if you knew all, you would not think it a joking matter. I cannot *breathe* in the same house with her!"

Hugh comes over, and pulls me down on the sofa beside him. "You must have a slate off this morning, Nell! Wind blew it off last night! Ha! Ha! cannot breathe in the same house with your only sister! Such a big house too; you *must* require a deal of fresh air! You have been squabbling by post, I suppose!"

"It's no case of squabbling!" I say, very earnestly, while I feel my white cheeks getting crimson; "oh, Hugh, I have something to tell you—something I *must* tell you—oh, I wish it was not so hard!"

"If it is anything about Dolly; anything she has done wrong, or any scrape she has got into, I don't seem to care about hearing about it!" says Hugh. "I daresay she'd sooner I didn't, you know, and there is no use crying over spilt milk."

"It's about myself, too!" I say, in great agitation.

Hugh puts his kind arm round me, and looks with incredulous amused eyes at my half averted face. "Some dreadful crime you have been committing, eh? Not said 'Amen' loud enough in church, or pitched into Bentham, for giving your back hair a tug?"

---

1 It was believed that in order for a magpie to learn to talk like a parrot, its tongue should be cut.

His utter unsuspiciousness stabs me.

"Oh, don't, don't laugh!" I cry, piteously; "you wouldn't if you knew."

There is nothing on earth that Hugh hates so much as a scene, and he fears that one is imminent. "I've got something to tell you too," he says, cheerily, rising and walking towards his *escritoire*;[1] "and as mine seems to be the pleasantest piece of news, I'll have it out first; *yours* will keep, I'm sure!"

I remain sitting on the sofa where he left me, twisting my hands about, and wishing, oh how heartily! that this confession, of the gravity of which my husband is so utterly unsuspecting, were well over, and I turned out of doors once for all. Presently he comes back with a small red leather case in his hand, and sits down again beside me.

"Do you remember, Nell," he says, composing his jolly face to a decent gravity, befitting, as he thinks the subject; "do you remember telling me once that you had nothing but a photograph of—of—your poor father?"

"Yes," I say, wincing; "don't talk about him!" (nobody ever mentions his name to me now, I cannot bear it).

"I won't, I won't!" says Hugh apologetically; "not more than I can help at least, but I have had this done for you, and I want you to take one look at it, if you don't mind."

He unfastens the case, takes out a large gold locket, with the monogram A.L. in diamonds upon it, and after fumbling a little about the spring, opens it with his big, kind, clumsy fingers.

I look half reluctant, and in an instant the tears come rushing to my eyes. I see again the kind blue eyes; the humorous tender smile that the coffin lid hid away from me six dreary weeks ago; it is my old man come to life again, only that the artist has painted out half the weary care lines; my old man, as he was before his troubles came upon him; as he will be—oh, no! he will look yet nobler and beautifuller, and peacefuller then—when he comes to meet me at the golden gates.

I throw my arms round Hugh's neck; it is the first time that I ever kissed him voluntarily in my life. Poor Hugh! my emotion is hardly of the pleasurable kind that he had hoped and intended. He looks uneasily concerned, and I see his mouth forming itself into his favourite whistling shape.

---

1   Writing desk (French).

"I did not mean to upset you like this, Nell!" he says, by-and-by.

"Oh, you are so good to me!" I cry, incoherently; "and I'm not at all good to you! Oh, I do so wish that I liked you better! I do so wish that I had always liked you!"

Hugh pats my hair very fondly.

"My dear old woman!" he says, "let bygones be bygones! don't let us rake up any old grievances; it don't make much odds if you hated me like poison once, so as you don't hate me now!"

We sit silent for a few minutes. Hugh whistles "Polly Perkins"[1] very softly to himself, while doubt and vacillation enter my mind.

My husband's words keep ringing in my ears. "Let bygones be bygones!" Is he right? Would not it be better to "let the dead past bury its dead?" Have I not done him enough injury already, coming to him so meanly, taking all his love and his kind words and caresses, and giving him nothing in return but sour looks and peevish tears, and dimmed beauty; without lacerating that honest heart unnecessarily, by telling him that his wife is unfaithful to him; if not in deed, at least in heart and thought?

The temptation is gone, never to return; why not let that secret remain between God and my own heart? But if I abandon my confession, I must also abandon my revenge; the one involves the other.

"I often think," says Hugh, with more gravity than is his wont, "that one great cause of there being so much unhappiness in married life is people's expecting too much of one another, I don't want us to split on that rock, Nell. I should like you to look a bit happier certainly by-and-by; and to seem a bit gladder to see me, when I come to speak to you, if you can; but if not, why we must rub on as we are, and I'm very thankful to Providence for having given you to me at all!"

"Providence made you but a shabby present!" I say, with contrition.

"Not much to brag of, I daresay"; says Hugh playfully, pulling my ear, "but you see I am easily pleased. Well, I must be going out; I cannot stop molly-coddling away half a morning at a foolish little woman's apron strings; and I say, Nell, you go and talk to the old lady about Dolly, and drop the poor girl a line to tell

---

1 "Pretty Polly Perkins of Paddington Green" (1864), a song composed by Harry Clifton (1832-72).

her we shall be very glad to see her any day she likes to come; and don't let me hear any more nonsense about envy, hatred and malice and all uncharitableness!"

"But I *do* hate her! I have every reason to hate her! Hugh! Hugh!" I call after him eagerly, but he has beaten a hasty retreat, to avoid further discussion of the subject.

CHAPTER XXXVI

"Vengeance is mine; I will repay, saith the Lord!"[1] Of all the texts of scripture, that is the one that kept saying itself over and over again to my heart, as I sat that morning listening in respectful silence, while Lady Lancaster went on purring about Lady Brandreth's crochet needles, and the fleecy wool she had to send to Glasgow for—could not get it in England, my dear, tried every shop in Regent Street.[2]

Do you know that after all my blustering and threats and big resolutions, I am beginning to think that I must leave that said vengeance in the hands of Him to whom it appertains; that I must not meddle with the attributes of the Omnipotent. I have cooled down from my first fever of indignant hate. I am not the stuff of which Jaels[3] are made. My fingers would have trembled so that I could never have hammered the nail into my prostrate enemy's tired brows. I should have fallen to pitying him; lying there so weary, so helpless, so trustful. I am beginning to doubt whether I will bring the last of the old name—name for ever hallowed by my father's having worn it, to disgrace and shame, whether despite all her misdoings, I will turn her out adrift and homeless on the world.

I am beginning to see my own sins very clearly, and not only other people's. Will not Dolly's tormenting presence in my house, the sound of her silky voice, the sight of her subtle beauty triumphing over the ruins of my life, be a fit penance for my own wickedness? Can any expiation be too hard, too bitter, for the

---

1   See Romans 12:19. Paul exhorts the faithful of the church not to give way to anger, but leave vengeance to God.
2   Street in London famous for its shops.
3   In Judges 4 and 5, Jael kills Sisera, the leader of an enemy army, by driving a spike through his head as he sleeps.

woman who fell so low, as to ask another man to run away with her from her husband? who was only saved from utter shipwreck by the untainted nobility of soul, the selfless devotion and honour of her lover himself.

"Your sister Dorothea had a charming crochet *tricoter*[1] pattern, when last she was here, my dear, she seemed a beautiful worker, quite different from you, Nell; by-the-bye, I am afraid that the hunting season will be over before poor dear Hugh's waistcoat is finished; she will be a great assistance to me, I fancy, when she comes to us next week. Did she say what day we were to expect her, my dear?"

"No."

"Have you written to her, my love? because if not, had not you better go and do so immediately?"

"There's plenty of time," I say indolently, "it is not near post hour."

"There is never any use in procrastination, my dear, as my dear mother used often to say to me, when I was your age, and besides, I shall want you to come and pay a few calls with me this afternoon. You really must try and exert yourself a little more than you do, Nell; there is something almost lethargic about you at times."

So I retire and write a little icy note to my sister; telling her that my husband bids me say she is welcome to come any day she chooses, and that I am hers sincerely, Eleanor Lancaster.

The day of Dolly's advent comes, and the carriage is sent to the station for her. Hugh had suggested to me, to go to meet her in it; an honour which I steadfastly persist in declining. Lady Lancaster is writing letters in her own room, almost effacing with her long old nose the characters that she forms with her fingers. I am buried in an arm-chair in my boudoir, reading a novel. It interests me rather, for it is all about a married woman, who ran away from her husband and suffered the extremity of human ills in consequence.[2] I have made several steps in morality of late

---

1 To knit (French). Here, a crochet pattern.
2 Scholars have often speculated that Broughton has in mind Ellen Wood's popular novel *East Lynne* (1861). I am indebted to Catherine Pope for pointing out that novelist Florence Marryat in *The Nobler Sex* (1892) refers to *East Lynne* as a "rechauffe of a forgotten romance by Mrs Marsh [Anne Marsh-Caldwell] called *The Admiral's Daughter*" (1834), and indeed Marsh's novel is a likely source for Broughton.

I flatter myself, but even now, I can hardly imagine that I should have been very miserable if Dick had taken me away with him.

The naughty matron is just dying of a broken heart and starvation in a Penitentiary, when I hear carriage wheels. Postponing the last dying speech and confession of the faded flower, I jump up, run to the window, and peep behind the blinds. I am in time to see Dolly descend gracefully—my sister can get in and out of a carriage with any woman in England, not so easy an accomplishment as one might think—and hold out two little black hands effusively to Hugh.

Dolly gives one an impression of extreme blackness altogether. "Poor dear Papa" is written all over her, in best paramatta[1] and deepest crape. Even the slender shapely legs that I caught a glimpse of a minute ago on the carriage step, look as if they belonged unmistakably to a mourner.

"Nell! Nell!" shouts my domestic Stentor,[2] but I respond not. Then I hear my husband's and sister's voices approaching me.

"She's not here, I'm sure," Hugh is saying, "or she would have answered when I called; she always does; she's out, I'm afraid." He opens the boudoir door. "She is here after all; why, old woman, what has become of your manners? Come and say how do you do to Dolly?"

Dolly is advancing rapidly to precipitate herself on my neck, but something in my face keeps her back, and alters her intention.

"How do you do?" I say very coldly, not even holding out my hand to her.

Hugh looks from one to the other puzzled and uncomfortable.

"Well, I suppose you two have got a hundred and one things to say to one another, and would only be wishing me at the other end of nowhere if I were to stop, so I'll make myself scarce," he says cheerfully, and then he goes out, and shuts the door behind him.

We stand opposite each other like two fighting cocks for a minute or so; then Dolly sinks into a chair.

"As you don't appear to intend to invite me to take a seat, I suppose I must invite myself," she says, smiling; "you certainly

---

1 Finely woven cotton and wool blend.
2 After Stentor, the Greek herald in *The Iliad*.

have the *manière prévenante*,[1] Nell, which is becoming so rapidly extinct."

"I have, have I?"

"You know how to welcome the coming, and I should imagine also how to speed the parting guest."

"I do, do I?"

The delicate carnation is deepening in my sister's cheeks; those cheeks that look smoother and clearer than ever in their crape setting.

"I hardly know how to break the news to you, but I'm afraid I shall not be able to trespass on your hospitality long."

"Hm! are you going to betake yourself to a better world?" I ask ironically; "you certainly are too good for this."

"I'm going to make a home for myself!" says my sister, with calm triumph; "I am going to marry Lord Stockport."

I stand for a moment dumbfoundered, aghast. Where, where is my story-book code of morality? Where is the whipping for the naughty boy? Here is a young woman who has told lies, has forged, has wrecked the happiness of her sister's whole life, and she is punished; how?—why by marrying a lord with £80,000 a year. Truly poetic justice is confined to poetry indeed; and comes down never to the prose dealings of everyday life.

"Lord Stockport!" I ejaculate, "happy man!"

An angry scintillation flashes from Dolly's superb black eyes.

"He is to be pitied, isn't he, poor man? His wife cannot bring him the ample stock of affection and fidelity that Sir Hugh Lancaster's did him! Of course not! that goes without saying."

"She can bring him a large stock of accomplishments though!" I say quickly, breathing short and hard.

Miss Lestrange looks as if she did not exactly see the drift of this observation; she says *"Après?"*[2] interrogatively.

"Lady Stockport's list of talents will be longer than Desdemona's[3] even"; I say very bitterly. "So delicate with her needle! an admirable musician!—oh, she would sing the savageness out of a bear—of so high and plenteous a wit and invention—*and can imitate her neighbour's handwriting so excellently.*"

---

1 Obliging or attentive manner (French). Here used ironically.

2 After (French). Here meaning, and? what more?

3 Desdemona is the wife of Othello, in Shakespeare's play of the same name.

Dolly gives a start, a perceptible start, but recovers herself immediately.

"What do you mean?" she asks quietly; "you ought to be published with a key or a commentary!" But I see her fingers tightening their hold upon the back of her chair.

I go over to my writing table, and take out a letter. "This is what I mean!" I say, very slowly, holding it up before her; "I am sure Lord Stockport will prize the gift of your hand all the more, when he sees how clever it is! I intend to keep this to show him!"

The carmine retires rather rapidly from my sister's cheeks, and from her full lips also as she scans the document.

"Are you quite so sure that you will be Lady Stockport now?" I ask very softly.

We are silent a minute; then Dolly says very sharply—none of the old sweetness in her tone, "How did you get this? you must have been seeing that man again?"

It is not a bad idea carrying the war into the enemies' quarters, is it?

"It is not much matter to you how I got it; it is enough for you to know that I have got it."

"Of course! of course! only it is a pity that any detail should be wanting to complete such a pretty story."

"It will be quite complete enough for Lord Stockport, I daresay!" I say very drily.

"And for Hugh?" asks Dolly, with a little vicious smile.

"We will be impartial!" I say coldly, "they shall both hear it."

Dolly laughs softly, and the colour comes back with a deeper, fuller rush to her face. "Resurrection of Daddy Longlegs! A tragedy in two acts," she says derisively. If I have expected to overwhelm my sister with the damning proofs of her guilt, I am disappointed. As the petrel[1] is popularly supposed to rejoice in the storm, so Dolly appears almost to riot in the war of the moral elements; "to be put on the boards of the Wentworth theatre, what day, Nell? Let us be exact!"

"To-day!" I cry, raising my voice, my hard kept composure giving way, and merging into honest passionate anger, "there is never any use in delaying the exposure of crime."

---

1 The petrel is a sea bird believed to like stormy weather; it flies close to the surface during rough weather in order to feed.

"Impossible, my dear!" says my sister, with a shrug, "one of the principal actors will be absent. Stockport does not come till Saturday!"

"Poor man!" I say compassionately, "it will be a pleasant surprise for him discovering that his wife is a *forger*." Dolly subsides into gravity.

"I never objected to people calling a spade a spade; I suppose I am a forger; but to my thinking, the end justifies the means, and has done so in this case; there is one commandment I am sorry for having broken, and only one!"

"Which?"

"The eleventh, peculiarly appropriated to woman's use. 'Thou shall not be found out!'" replies Dolly with composure.

"Unfortunately you *have* broken it!" I say, struggling to emulate her calmness, "and now you must pay the penalty!"

"Don't let us have any threatening, it is not ladylike; let us be ladylike whatever we are!" says Dolly, standing up, and sweeping gracefully over towards the door. "Have me up for forgery if you like—'Scandal in high life'; it would make the fortune of the *Nantford Advertiser*; drag the old name through the dirt; it will annoy you far more than it will me, to tell you the truth. I have never been very much in love with either Stockport or respectability, so that the loss of neither will *quite* break my heart."

A knock at the door.

"May I come in?" in an old croaky voice, and without waiting for permission, a long reddish nose, a pair of gold-rimmed spectacles and a beard make their appearance.

We both look rather foolish, like little naughty boys whose pockets have been found bulging with the illicit marble, or the succulent bull's-eye[1] in church. Simultaneously, we vault off our high horses.

"I am afraid, I'm interrupting a pleasant *tête-à-tête*!"[2] says the old lady, pokerishly, "but I heard your voice, my dear Dorothea, and I thought I must come in and just say how d'ye do to you. Are not you very tired after your journey, my dear child? those cross-lines are so fatiguing; so many changes, and having to look after your own luggage too. I suppose it is an old-fashioned notion on my part, but I never can reconcile myself to the idea of young people travelling alone. So many unpleasant *contretemps*

---

1 A kind of hard candy.
2 Intimate conversation (French; literally "head to head").

have occurred of late, too; no communication between the carriages, and since that dreadful affair of Mr. Briggs[1] too!"

"You did not interrupt us at all, dear Lady Lancaster," says Dolly, whom the old woman's babble has given time to recover her *aplomb*;[2] "we had nearly finished our chat, hadn't we, Nell?"

CHAPTER XXXVI

It is the twentieth day of February, in the year of our Lord 186-. The violets, like Noah's dove, are poking their noses out of doors, to see what sort of weather it is. They are beginning to quit their wintry lodgment.

> "Where they together
> All the hard weather
> Dead to the world, keep house unknown."[3]

White ones—plenty of them—are peeping out modestly, from among freshest green leaves, on the sunny south side of Lestrange churchyard, above the prone heads of the human flowers, to whom the spring time of Resurrection is long in coming. Sir Adrian Lestrange loved them so dearly; every spring he used to come with his little daughter Nell to look for them, and smile his friendly welcome to them and the celandines that carpet goldenly the space beneath the old black-budded ashes.

Sir Adrian does not come this spring; he is "away" good man! He has travelled to a land where there are better flowers than his pretty violets, and where he and his little Nell can walk about together in peace, without any "cloaked shadow" coming between to part them, as they have been parted for just a little space—a little bitter minute—here below.

The celandines are spreading their gaudy carpet also beneath the elms and sycamores in Sir Hugh Lancaster's garden at Wentworth. They are flaring and flaunting away with such confident pertness; just for all the world as if they were real garden

---

1 Thomas Briggs was murdered in July of 1864 on the North London Railway, in the five-minute period between two stops.
2 Balance, self-possession (French).
3 From "The Flower" (1633), a poem by George Herbert.

flowers, and did not deserve to be extirpated every bit as much as the poor daisies that were always being ruthlessly spudded up.

The first breath of spring is blowing about the land; she is raising herself a little out of winter's snowy lap, waking up and rubbing her fair eyes. I have been late for prayers again, and have received a mild jobation[1] in consequence.

Breakfast is over now, and Lady Lancaster and I are standing at the Hall door, watching our Hugh mount his hack to ride to a rather distant meet. Hugh looks his best a-cock-horse; one does not see how short he is, and he has the best seat in ——shire.

"How well Hugh looks on horseback!" exclaims the Dowager, never weary of admiring her son, though the spectacle is anything but a novel one to her.

"He does not look amiss in pink," I respond, less rapturously, but still with commendation in my tone; for to give myself my due, I am growing to love Hugh with all love

"—except the love
Of man and woman, when they love their best
Closest and sweetest—"[2]

The last vestige of my lord's red coat having disappeared round a bend in the drive, I turn away and stroll up and down the terrace by myself. The sun is getting a little power; he beats quite warmly on my uncovered head, and I saunter and potter about slowly, and watch the crocuses, yellow, and purple, and striped forcing their way up through the rich red earth. A small fat cock robin is sitting on the stone balustrades, singing his little heart out. I stand pensively listening to him.

"I wish I was as happy as you!" I say to myself; "I do indeed! it would be so pleasant!"

There is a little sound of pebbles being swept along, and looking up, I see Dolly coming along to meet me; Dolly in a tight fitting black dress, which shows every curve and turn of her exquisite figure, and relieved about neck and wrists by the nattiest of white linen collar and cuffs. It is not every one that can blend the afflictive and the becoming as our Dolly can. Dolly looks lovelier

---

1 Scolding.
2 See "Lancelot and Elaine" in *Idylls of the King* (1859), a poem by Tennyson.

in the early morning, in her everyday gown, than when dressed, or undressed—as the *mode* now has it—for ball or opera.

"Delicious morning, isn't it?" says my sister, stopping beside me, and sniffing the sweet fresh air, with her little Greek nose.

"Yes."

"What a pretty place it is!" surveying admiringly the wide formal gardens, where terraces, gravel walks, Deodaras,[1] urns recur with almost as tedious a monotony as the knops and flowers in the Tabernacle decorations.

"Not particularly, I don't think!"

"If people only knew what was for their own good!" with a gentle sigh, "you ought to be a very happy woman, Nell!"

"You have done your best to make me so, at all events!"

"I did evil that good might come, as I told you yesterday, when that exemplary old tabby interrupted us—by-the-bye I hope she had not been eaves-dropping—and good *has* come," says Dolly steadily; "*à propos*[2] of that, I have something to tell you; Stockport comes to-day."

"Well?"

"Oh nothing particular, of course; only I thought I had better tell you, so that you might have your weapon ready to stab the poor soul with, as soon as he arrives."

Dolly is not agitated, she never is; "wise men never wonder,"[3] and "with the wisdom of the children of this world"[4] none can deny that Dorothea is dowered. Perhaps it is my fancy that there is rather an anxious light in the great dreamy sensuous eyes, that the flush on the oval cheeks is deeper than what the soft south wind has brought there.

"Thanks," I say, very coldly; and then I go and lean my arms on the balustrade—our talking has scared away the robin—and look wistfully off over the landscape, winking in the morning sun, to the East, whither my heart has gone. One would have thought, wouldn't one, that Dolly having told her errand, would straightway have returned again whence she came, but such does

---

1 A kind of cedar.
2 Pertaining to (French).
3 Old saying.
4 See Luke 16:8. Jesus says that the children of this world are more cunning, or "wiser," than the "children of light," but that the faithful will be rewarded in the end.

not seem to be her intention. She comes, on the contrary, and leans on the rough cold stone beside me.

"Let us understand one another, Nell," she says, with some slight hesitation, "are you *really* bent on exhibiting that unlucky document, or is it only a *bogy* that you are keeping to frighten me into good behaviour with?"

"I thought we had understood each other perfectly the other night, and that there was no need for fresh explanations," I say icily, "I imagined that I had made my meaning tolerably clear then."

"And about yourself?" she says quickly; "have you considered what awkward inquiries it will entail, inquiries too from a person who has the best right in the world to make them, and who cannot be put off, as you have put off me with, 'it is enough for you that I *have* got it.' Hugh must be more or less than human if he is not a little curious to know how you came by it. Lords with £80,000 a year don't grow on every hedge; it is worth while eating a little dirt for one of them, isn't it?"

I turn round and face her.

"Do you think," I say eagerly, "that if it entailed the loss of my life, I should very much care? Thanks to you, I may say, with Agag,[1] 'surely the bitterness of death is past.'"

Dolly looks down and draws geometrical patterns with her slender pointed foot.

"I know you won't believe me, so it's rather wasting breath asseverating," she says slowly, "but I give you my word of honour I did it for the best; I thought that it was a childish besotment you had for that man; a sort of calf love, that it would be a real kindness to help you out of."

"Without an *arrière-pensée*[2] for your own advantage of course; it would have been truer kindness to have cut my throat for my own good!" I end passionately. My voice shakes and wavers in my intense self-pity; I am afraid of breaking down into weeping before her, into "howling," "blubbering," "snivelling," as she in her dry-eyed contemptuousness would graphically phrase it; so I rush away, away to the house, and up to my chamber, like Joseph,[3] to weep there. For an hour or more I sit with my

---

1 See I Samuel 15:32. Actually, Agag seems to be pleading for his life in this passage. Samuel hacks Agag to pieces.
2 Ulterior motive (French).
3 See Genesis 42:21-22 and 43:29-31. Joseph weeps (happily) when he is reunited with his brothers, who sold him into slavery in Egypt.

two hands holding my head, buried in thought. Woe is me if my mamma-in-law catches me; small opinion has she of thought as an employment for the female sex, and then I rise, unlock the drawer of my writing table, take out the "unlucky document," as its parent leniently calls it, and go downstairs with it.

I find Dolly sitting by the library fire, her small white left hand on which Lord Stockport's great diamond betrothal ring is flashing and sparkling in the fire-light—bitter, bitter will be the parting between Dolly and that jewel of price—is pushed in amongst the black wealth of her scented hair; she is staring with her great dark velvet eyes at the shining bars; her cheeks and small round ears are getting burnt a dull red, but she does not seem to heed that. I go up close to her, and stoop over her.

"Dolly!" I say with solemnity, "I have thought a great deal about my revenge upon you; I have lain awake at night planning it; it has seemed meat and drink to me for the last week. I have finished planning it out now, look!"

As I speak I toss the letter into the fire's innermost heart, and watch the flames catch hold of it, and then shoot up high; watch it turn brown; then writhe like a thing in pain; then shrivel away utterly. Dolly jumps up and throws her arms about my neck.

"Don't," I say, gently disengaging myself; "keep your blandishments for the lover you have *saved*; I think he would appreciate them more."

So you see I gave up my revenge; I did not carry the stone in my pocket for seven years; then turn it, and carry it for seven years more.[1] I yielded up my injuries unto Him, who claims the redressing of all the injustices that have been wrought since the world was. I had been clamouring for justice, bare justice. Alas, if bare justice is all I myself get, in that day when the world's long tangled accounts are made up, where shall I be?

"What shall I, frail man be pleading?
Who for me be interceding
When the Just is Mercy needing?"[2]

---

1 A proverb: "Keep a stone in thy pocket for seven years: turn it, and keep it seven years more; but have it in hand to cast at thine enemy when the time comes."

2 From a thirteenth-century hymn, "Dies Irae," by Thomas of Celano, translated from Latin as "Day of Wrath" by William J. Irons in 1848.

"A very worthy young man, my dear, I don't doubt," says Lady Lancaster to me, a morning or two afterwards, à propos of my brother-in-law elect, as we sit pecketting at our work in the morning room—Hugh's waistcoat is making rapid strides towards completion—looking at me over the top of her spectacles, "very worthy, indeed! does not seem to have very much to say for himself perhaps, but that is a fault on the right side in these days, when all young people seem to think that they cannot have too much of the sound of their own voices!"

"He is rather silent!" I say, which is certainly putting it in a very mild form, seeing that I could count with ease on the fingers of one hand the remarks he has made since he entered our hospitable portals.

"Dear me!" pursues the old lady, wandering off into reminiscences, "how well I remember his grandfather's shop to be sure! He was a hosier, you know, my dear, in Bond Street, a very civil old man with a bald head, I recollect—this young man has a look of him now and then—he used to come out to one's carriage-door to take orders, and that sort of thing, my dear!"

"It is a very up-py and down-y world!" I say sententiously.

"If he had told me then," continues my companion, making her speech more emphatic by uplifted and outspread right hand, "that forty years from that time, my son and his grandson would be marrying two sisters, I should have withdrawn my custom from his shop for his impertinence."

I laugh.

"It is a rise, whose suddenness is only paralleled by Dick Whittington's and his cat;[1] in fact, it beats them, for Dick was only Lord Mayor after all, and Stockport is Lord, without the Mayor!"

Meanwhile, the "worthy young man" and Dolly are strolling up and down the terrace. Dolly seems to like to keep within view of the windows. I fancy that the young Viscount's amenities become ponderous, when freed from the restraint of the public eye.

So Dolly is to be wed; she is to be made a Viscountess of; to be elevated to a throne among the Gods. King Cophetua has given

---

1 Dick Whittington is a character in a children's story based on the real Richard Whittington who served three terms as Lord Mayor of London. His cat helps make his fortune by catching rats.

his hand to the Beggar Maid,[1] and she is tripping daintily up to seat herself beside that august and condescending monarch.

But when is it to be? When are the festive poles to be run up, and the "healths to the houses of Stockport and Lestrange" to float in the breeze?

At first, Dolly stoutly maintained that no earthly power should induce her to allow her marriage to be celebrated till a full year had elapsed, since "poor dear Papa's" death.

"O, impossible! Quite out of the question! So disrespectful to his memory! Did he suppose she had no natural affection?" etc., etc. When first the subject was hinted, she retreated from the room with her handkerchief to her eyes; not angry, but so *hurt*.

This I hear from Hugh.

"Completely upset, poor girl!" he says, pulling his thick moustache, and staring at his boots, which are stuck out straight before him; "so Stockport tells me. He thought he had put his foot into it with a vengeance, and that she was not going to speak to him again for a month of Sundays."

The text about polishing the sepulchres of the Righteous[2] occurs to me, but I keep it to myself.

"If ever I have any daughters," says Hugh—I look down—"I hope they'll be as fond of me as you two were of *him*."

(You *two*! classing us together! My God! that is hard to bear!)

"I'm sure I wish she would marry him, and have done with it," continues Hugh, yawning. "Great Sawney![3] I'm getting dog-tired of seeing his ugly mug about the house; seems to be in every room at once too, like a bird; he's a thundering lout, that's what he is!"

"If you *will* be so Quixotically[4] generous as to bring all your wife's relations, like a hornet's nest, about your ears, you must take the consequences," I say, a little maliciously.

---

1 The legend goes that King Cophetua could find no woman to please him, but then fell in love with a beggar maid, and married her. The first source is unknown, but Shakespeare references the story.

2 Probably Nell is thinking of Matthew 23:27, where Jesus accuses the Pharisees of being like "whitewashed sepulchres"—beautiful outside, but filled with corruption.

3 A fool, simpleton.

4 From Miguel de Cervantes' novel *Don Quixote* (1605). To be quixotic is to be idealistic and impractical.

Time does wonders, and time and Lord Stockport succeeded in softening our Dolly's tender scruples.

"One cannot always consult one's own feelings in this world," I overheard her saying one day to Hugh, "else, (with a gentle sigh) things would be very different, but for poor Stockport's sake—he really is getting so miserably unsettled and fretful—ah, I know some one who can feel for him; some one who was not *too* patient himself once, a hundred years ago—that I am afraid it will tell upon his health; *that* would not be fair, would it? And so"—(with down-dropped eyes and a blush). And so a judicious compromise has been effected between the bridegroom's eagerness, and the bride's filial devotion. He had clamoured for April, and she had stickled for December. June is a happy mean between the two, and June it is to be.

I had begged that the wedding might be a very quiet one; the idea of a great gathering, of all the onerous duties of mistress of a great house coming upon me for the first time, of feasting and merry making in the midst of my deep mourning was utterly repellent to me. But I am overruled by my mamma, as I have been on many other occasions.

"Life is too short to be spent in vain repinings, my dear," she says to me one morning, after we have been indulging in a mild wrangle on the subject; "there are duties owing to the living as well as to the dead, and we should not selfishly neglect the former for the latter." I make no answer, but bend my head in silence over my work. "It seems to me," pursues the old lady, rather exasperated by my silence, "that there is something *unchristian* in such exaggerated grief; it is a sure argument of an ill-regulated mind; you seem to forget that there is such a virtue as Resignation, one of the most beautiful of Christian graces, or that our Heavenly Father knows what is best for us!" Lady Lancaster has none of her son's shyness in mentioning the Deity. On the contrary, her Heavenly Father plays a large part in her conversation, particularly when she is angry.

"It's very easy to be resigned to one's Heavenly Father, when he does nothing to vex one," I cry passionately, ignoring the fifth commandment, or perhaps imagining that it does not apply to parents-in-law. The Dowager rises very stiffly, and makes her flat back flatter than ever.

"If you are going to be blasphemous, my dear," she says, "I have nothing more to say; we must drop the subject, if you please!" and she sweeps out of the room with dignity. Dropping the subject means that I apologize, and that the old lady gets her own way. And so March, and April, and May—blowiest, tearfullest and sweetest of the daughters of the year—steal past us; march quickly by to join the other dead months and years; go over to the majority as the Romans have it.[1] And there comes a sultry day in early June—day when my sister's life began to open, and mine, I think, to close.

"'Happy the bride that the sun shines on,' the proverb says, doesn't it?" asks Hugh that morning, lying staring lazily out of window at the pale blue sky, and the Scotch firs, and the rooks cawing and flapping about their windy homes; "if that's the case, I'm afraid you have not a chance of coming in for much luck, have you, Nell? You had not a ha'porth of sun from 'Dearly Beloved,' to 'Amazement.'"

I am up and dressed already.

"Proverbs often tell lies," I say carelessly. "Honesty is the best policy; It is better to be good than pretty; Early birds pick the worm; what can be greater fiction than those three?"

"We shall have the house to ourselves to-night, Nell!" says Hugh cheerfully, "that'll be a comfort, won't it?"

"Ye-es," I say rather doubtfully, "at least do you know, Hugh, I sometimes wish that somebody would take it into their head to marry your mother; some meek-minded old gentleman that she could rule with a rod of iron, and make muffetees[2] for, and read 'A Voice from the Pit,' or 'A few plain words about sinners,' to."

Hugh bursts out into a loud haw! haw!

"Oh! I say, Nell! too bad! what's the Mater[3] been doing now? Slanging[4] you, or giving you good little books to read?"

"A little of both, perhaps!" I say, laughing.

Wentworth Church is a mile from Wentworth House; just outside the park it stands; ugly, square-windowed, ivy-less. Sir Hugh's work-people and tenants have been as zealous in doing honour to his sister-in-law, as if she were a real Lancaster. There is a big arch at the first gate; a bigger at the second, and a biggest at the church gate.

---

1 To die.
2 Knitted wristlets, worn for warmth.
3 Mother (Latin).
4 Scolding.

June has such a wealth of roses that she can spare a good many to scatter under Dolly's feet, without missing them. The deer raise their slender smoky heads to look surprisedly at these monstrosities that have sprung up like mushrooms after rain, and then go leaping lightly away through the deep bracken.

The churchyard is full of people; there is quite a struggle for the vantage ground of the high flat tombstones, that give one always an idea of grim ghastly boxes. The children have had their faces washed as if it were Sunday; the women are bobbing curtseys, and the men pulling shaggy forelocks, as we float and rustle up the scarlet cloth put to the chancel door. There are twelve bridesmaids, six innocents in blue, and six in pink; it has been a work of some labour and thought to get that spinster dozen together.

Female friends Dolly has none, holding—was it Cowper's[1] opinion—that women's friendships were leagues of folly and interest; and it has been difficult to collect, at least in a country neighbourhood, twelve young ladies of fit standing, to walk behind Lady Stockport to the altar. It is rather a scratch team after all; we have been obliged to eke it out with an old maid and a child.

Little De Laney is best man; not that he has any peculiar affection or admiration for the bridegroom, as indeed he told me afterwards that he was "the biggest fool out," but because Lord Stockport once shed the radiance of his presence over the corps of which De Laney is a member.

A bishop in very clear lawn-sleeves[2] and on painfully thin legs, with two High Church rectors, officiate. They all read very fast, and leave out as much as they possibly can, so that whatever else it is, at least the service cannot be said to be tedious. And so the "august ceremony," as the county newspapers said next day, is consummated, and Dolly draws a sigh of relief. I think she is glad that the costly brittle cup has reached her red lips in safety at last. And then we all get into our carriages and bowl home,

---

1 William Cowper (1731-1800) was a poet and classicist. Tamar Heller identifies the sentiment here as actually being from Samuel Boswell's *Life of Johnson* (1791), rather than Cowper, though the Boswell passage refers to friendship in general.

2 Lawn is a very fine, very sheer cotton fabric. The sleeves were cut amply, so they draped gracefully.

with the "ugly duckling" transformed within the last quarter of an hour into a swan leading the way.[1]

"This is the room we danced in last year, isn't it?" Lord Capel says to me, at breakfast.

"Yes," I say, "it looks so different without its furniture, doesn't it?"

Lady Lancaster, like the fisherman's wife, Ilsabil,[2] has had her own will, and the gathering is as large as even she could wish.

Looking down the long table, on either side of the forest of ferns and flowers and pyramidal fruit, I see happy people—*these* in Elise-ian[3] bonnets—*those* in Poole-ian coats—laughing and talking nonsense.

The bridegroom is doing neither; he is eating "poulet au truffes"[4] and looking solemnly amorous, and amorously solemn. I fancy that his impending speech is weighing on his mind, and he is wishing that a fellow might be allowed to get married without having to jaw about it. Happiest, noisiest, gorgeousest of apparel, frequentest of laugh among the guests are the Coxes; all except Mortimer Spencer De Laney, behind whose barnacles the bitter tear of disappointment keeps swelling.

The Coxes are not presentable certainly, but I insisted on their being asked. I have a kindness for them; they were good to my poor Dick.

"There have been a good many changes since then," says Lord Capel, pleasantly thinking of my marriage.

"Indeed, there have!" I say, with a slight shudder.

"Everyone that was here last year is here now!" he continues, looking round on the assembled faces; "with one exception."

"Who is the exception, Capel?" asks De Laney, who is on the other side of me, "proves the rule, doesn't it, eh?"

---

1 A fable, memorialized by Hans Christian Andersen in 1844, in which a duckling thought very ugly turns out to be a changeling swan. Here, Nell uses it ironically to describe the transformation of her sister from spinster to married woman.

2 From a fable usually called "The Fisherman and his Wife." A magic flounder grants the fisherman wishes, and the wife, who is very greedy, continually demands that he ask the flounder for grander requests.

3 Elise is named in Chapter 4, probably Madame Elise and Co., Limited, Court Dressmakers. Nell puns on "Elysian," from the Elysian Fields, in Greek mythology—an afterlife of ideal happiness.

4 Chicken with truffles (French).

"No, nonsense! M'Gregor, don't you recollect poor M'Gregor?"

"Why *poor*?" I ask, trying to smile; "for not being here?"

"Haven't you heard? oh, I thought you were sure to; I'm sorry I mentioned the subject."

"Why?" I ask, hoarsely.

"Oh, because it's a shame to introduce melancholy subjects on an occasion like this; bad omen, you know. Stockport would not thank me."

"You had better go on, now you have begun," says De Laney, "or we shall think it something worse than it is."

"Well then, poor fellow! he is dead! I heard of it a day or two ago, from a man who was quartered on the same station with him; died of fever and ague at Lahore![1] Very sad thing! Nobody he cared a straw about near him."

"Dead!" cries Violet Coxe, overhearing, in her hard loud voice; "poor M'Gregor! Lord! how sorry I am!"

The bride suddenly rises from her seat, and comes rushing over to me.

"For God's sake, don't expose yourself!"

I hear her whispering very eagerly, and then there sounds a loud buzzing in my ears; a deadly sickness comes over me, and I faint away, as I fainted away five months ago, in those strong arms that will never more embrace any bride but corruption.

> The knight's bones are dust,
> And his good sword rust,
> His soul is with the saints, I trust."[2]

CHAPTER XXXVIII

June 7th, 186-. I am coming to the last in my series of pictures from a life that has been, alas!

> "Failure, crowning failure, failure from end to end."[3]

---

1 A large city in India (now in Pakistan), site of a battle in the Indian Mutiny, or Sepoy Rebellion.

2 See "The Knight's Tomb" (1834), a poem by Samuel Taylor Coleridge.

3 See "Last Words of a Sensitive Second-Rate Poet," a poem by Owen Meredith, pseud. for Lord Edward Robert Bulwer-Lytton (1831-91).

My foolish little tale has been dull enough in the telling, I'm afraid; it was not dull in the acting, Heaven knows! It is two years and a half ago now, since that wintry night, when, in my wicked madness, I wanted to sacrifice soul and body to my one, my only love; since he said to me, but in tenderer, more impassioned words,

"I could not love thee, dear, so much,
Loved I not honour more."[1]

Since then, I have been sorry for my sin; at least I have tried to be. I have been a good wife to Hugh too; I think he would tell you so, if you asked him. It has been up-hill, tiring work, and I have often got out of breath, but it is nearly over now. Yes, my friends, I ask you to bid me God speed, for I am going very far journey, *"je vais chercher un grand peut-être."*[2]

I am dying, and the great smith who strikes off all fetters, is knocking off mine. In the Litany,[3] you know, we pray for deliverance from sudden death, and my prayer has certainly been answered. Never did anyone leave the world with more lagging, lingering feet, than I am going. I am able to watch the steps of my own dissolution. My beauty and my strength are gone from me: they were sorry to go, I think; they went so slowly and I shall not be long after them now.

Until last winter, I always thought I should live to be an old woman,—like my mother-in-law, perhaps; bony, grenadier-like, hirsute of lip, and baggy of cheek,.

"With a little hoard of maxims,
Preaching down a daughter's heart."[4]

But about last Christmas, the idea struck me, came home to me, that never should gray hairs and I make acquaintance; that my head would be laid down in its ruddy glory, before very long,

---

1 See "To Lucasta, Going Off To the Wars" (1649), a poem by Richard Lovelace.
2 "I go to seek a great perhaps" (French). "Perhaps" refers to the uncertainly of the afterlife. The quote is from François Rabelais (1490-1553).
3 See the Anglican *Book of Common Prayer.*
4 See "Locksley Hall" (1842), a poem by Tennyson.

in the chilly sombre vault of the Lancasters. (Oh, if they would but lay me among mine own people!) I looked very well, certainly—Hugh's men friends complimented him (so he told me) on his wife's beauty; such rosy cheeks I had too;[1] I, who used to be pale to a proverb; and my rosy cheeks did not come out of the rouge pot, as the Dowager's wigged compeers curiously hinted to that irate old matron.

But surely, surely I was getting oddly, unaccountably thin: my rings took to slipping off my fingers, and rolling into remote corners, and all "me frocks," like Glorvina's,[2] of lovelorn memory, "had to be took in." Also I somehow stopped very often, and leant against the carved banisters; as I went up the shallow, broad oak steps of the grand staircase. One day I spoke out my thought.

"Mother," I said, (Hugh liked me to call her mother), "don't you think I'm getting to look very like Jane Stevens, that died of consumption at the West Lodge, last year?"

"Nonsense, my dear," answered the old lady, very hastily, "you should not get fanciful; young people of your age often look delicate in such cold weather; don't imagine anything so silly!"

But she was very much flurried as she spoke, her old nose got red, and two big tears dropped on to her eternal knitting. I asked no more questions; I said no more on the subject, but from that day, I knew that my fate was sealed. So I was going to die; going to be erased from the number of the warm kindly living; going to be numbered with the cold, cold dead, whose battle is over, whose race is run. In their successive generations,

"God's finger touched them and they slept."[3]

Soon, that dread finger would be laid upon me, and there could be no shrinking from under it. I could see quite plain a new tablet over our pew, in Wentworth's dark old church: I could read the black letters traced distinctly on the white marble, "*Hic jacet Eleanora.*"[4]

---

1 One of the symptoms of tuberculosis was the "hectic flush" on the cheeks, and brightness of the eyes.

2 Glorvina O'Dowd is a character in William Makepeace Thackeray's novel *Vanity Fair* (1848).

3 A rephrasing of a line from Tennyson's long poem, "In Memoriam" (LXXXV, l.20).

4 Here lies Eleanora (Latin).

The next Lady Lancaster would be spelling out the Latin words, instead of minding her prayers, would be picturing to herself this dead Eleanora to whom but two and twenty summers had been vouchsafed.

But where should I myself be at this time? Oh, thought full of unspeakable awe! How that prayer comes home to the souls of all us miserable sinners; a thousandfold more, then, to those of us, who are on the verge of that dark, dark flood!

"Rex tremendæ majestatis
Qui salvandos salvas gratis
Salva me, fons pietatis."

"King of majesty tremendous,
Who dost free salvation, send us
Fount of Pity! then befriend us."[1]

Oh, noble verse! simple utterance of a soul trembling and abased to the dust before that King of kings, that Lord of lords. Those must have been holy men, those monks, who put together those grand words. No doubt they agonized to enter at that straight gate;[2] no doubt they sinned, and suffered, and wept as we do now; and oh! in mercy let us hope that they are—

"Where God for aye
Shall wipe away
All tears from every eye."[3]

I wondered much within myself whether I were going to a good place; I rather fancied not; I certainly had no ground for hoping that I was. Heaven had shared but few of my thoughts hitherto.

All the love and aspirations I had to bestow had been squandered on that intense earthly passion which seemed to be eating up body and soul. It was too late to mend now, but I was sorry it had been so.

---

1 From the Mass for the Dead, also in "Dies Irae," by Thomas of Celano, translated from Latin as "Day of Wrath" by William J. Irons in 1848.
2 Compare Matthew 7:14. "Because strait is the gate, and narrow is the way, which leadeth unto life, and few there be that find it." That is, the road to salvation is difficult.
3 See "The Three Sons" a poem by John Moultrie (1799-1874).

Yet still, on that one subject which had dominated my whole life, I felt easier and more comfortable than I had been for a long time. I no longer wept in secret, nor felt a gnawing, wearing, mighty longing to see that one face again. He was gone from me but a very little way; just—

"From this room into the next."[1]

I had known I could not live without him, and I was not going to do so. God was very good and pitying; he was going to release me from the long pain of existence, and through the grave and gate of death I should pass to my beloved; should see his hero face immortal *then* in its beauty, so that "decay's effacing fingers"[2] could never sweep its hues.

"You'll be all right again, when the spring comes round, darling little girl!" Hugh would say to me, cheerily, now and then, and would smooth my hair with his kind brown hand, and I always said,

"Yes, dear old fellow, I dare say I shall!" though my all right was different from his.

Would not it be all right, would not it be passing well with me, when I had gone away with great gladness to be with my beloved for evermore?

"*June 20th.*—I am going so fast! oh, so fast! These are the last words I shall ever write; it is hard, laboursome to me to hold the pencil, but I do not want to leave the story of my poor life incomplete; incompleter at least than the story of all lives must be. Some other hand must put 'Finis' I know.

"It is night, and I am sitting in my old dad's chair, watching the stars silently taking their allotted places in the firmament. I have been gazing up into those depths of air unfathomable by mortal eyes, wondering how far up in those measureless tracts of ether, or whether in that direction at all, lie the spreading fields of light, rise the walls and towers, shine the golden streets of the holy city. 'A land where the inhabitant shall no more say I am sick.'[3]

---

1 See "The Grandmother" (1859), a poem by Tennyson.
2 See "The Giaour" (1813), a poem by Lord Byron.
3 Compare Isaiah 33:24. The prophet promises that God will give the righteous a land of beauty and plenty, in which no one suffers or is ill.

"What a pleasant thought. That text never struck me particularly when I was well. I suppose now that I am so full of aches and pains it comes home to me more. Oh God! *am* I going there? If I could but know for certain!

"'In my father's house are many mansions.'[1] Perhaps that text has something to say to me; into one of the lowest of those mansions, perhaps into the very lowest of all, the Great Householder,[2] who is ever holding his Marriage Feast, and calling thither who-so hungers, and is weary, may let me creep in, even me, for am I not weary, most weary? I have been trying (oh, vain endeavour) to picture to myself that land of unpictured, *unpictureable* passionless bliss—trying, with narrow human brain, to compass and take in the idea of the ineffable joys of the blessed souls of the just, in those unfading abodes which they have climbed up the steep ladder of faith to, at last; trying to conjure up before my mental vision—

"'The shores where tideless sleep the seas of time,
Soft by the City of the Saints of God!'[3]

"O Lord Jesus Christ! let me be in that city by this time to-morrow night! Grant me entrance there! Open to me when in fear and trembling I knock."[4]

FINIS.

End of Volume 2

1 Compare John 14:2. Jesus reassures his followers that they will go to heaven: "In my Father's house are many mansions: if it were not so, I would have told you. I go to prepare a place for you."
2 Compare Matthew 22. In this version of the parable, the king invites guests to a marriage feast, but his guests do not treat the invitation with the seriousness it deserves and so, again, he invites people from the street. But some of the people again are not worthy; one who comes without a wedding garment is cast out. Salvation is an open invitation, but not everyone will recognize its worth, or be personally worthy of it.
3 See the long poem *Tannhäuser; or, the Battle of the Bards* (1861), by poets Edward Robert Bulwer-Lytton and Julian Charles Henry Fane.
4 Compare Phillippians 2:12, wherein Paul exhorts the members of the church to continue their spiritual work in his absence: "Wherefore, my beloved, as ye have always obeyed, not as in my presence only, but now much more in my absence, work out your own salvation with fear and trembling." See also the gospels passim (see, for example, Luke 11:9: "And I say unto you, Ask, and it shall be given you; seek, and ye shall find; knock, and it shall be opened unto you").

Appendix A: The Publication of the Novel

1. Serialization in *Dublin University Magazine* (1866-67)

[The original version serially published in *Dublin University Magazine* was considerably shorter, at 28 chapters, than the 38-chapter version published by Bentley and Son in two volumes in 1867. The additional material was added in whole chapters; only a few words were corrected in the original 28 chapters, with the exception of some added matter at the end of the original last chapter (see appendix A2, below). Here I give the breakdown of the original chapters' serial publication.]

Dublin University Magazine	Bentley and Son
July 1866 volume LXVIII number CCCCIII Chapters 1-5	1-5
Aug. CCCCIV Chapters 6-8	6-8
Sept. CCCCV Chapters 9-11	9-11
Oct. CCCCVI Chapters 12	12 (Chapters 13, 14, and 15 are new)
13	16
14	17
15	18
Nov. CCCCVII Chapters 16-17	19-20 (Volume 2 begins here. In the two-volume set, Chapter 20 is Chapter 1 of Volume 2)

Dec. CCCCVIII

	(Chapters 21 [2] and 22 [3] are new)
Chapters 18	23 [4]
19	24 [5]
20	25 [6]
	(Chapter 26 is new) [7]
21	27 [8]
22	28 [9]
23	29 [10]

Jan. 1867 volume LXIX
   number CCCCIX

Chapters 24–28	30, 31, 33, 34, 38 [11-15]
24	30 [11]
25	31 [12]
	(Chapter 32 is new) [13]
26	33 [14]
27	34 [15]
	(Chapters 35, 36, and 37 are new) [16-18]
28	38 [19]

2. Epilogue to the Serial Version of the Novel (1867)

[In the serial version, the chapters in which Dolly marries and Nell learns of Richard's death (pp. 300–29 in this edition) are omitted. The following epilogue is instead added to the end of the last chapter, directly after "Open to me when in fear and trembling I knock."]

The M.S. ends here; a stronger hand must put "Finis" to it, for the Almighty hand has written Finis to the poor life it tells about. On that same last night Lady Lancaster was roused from her solemn thoughts by the entrance of her husband. He came over to her in silence, nor did he ask, as his invariable custom was, tenderly after her health; and when she looked up at him, she saw a "light of horror" in his kind eyes; a shocked, grieved, awed look, as of one who had heard freshly evil tidings.

"What is it, dear?" she asked gently; she knew that nothing he could tell her would have power to grieve or wound her now.

"Oh, Nell!" he said, not seeing any necessity for hiding this bad news of his from her, and his hearty voice sounded low and solemn, "I have just heard such an awfully sad thing; I cannot tell you how cut up I am about it; poor M'Gregor is dead—died of cholera at Lahore; not a soul he cared about with him. I don't know when I ever heard anything that shocked me so much!"

"Dead, is he?" said Nell, softly, and her voice sounded very sweet and clear, and she half rose from her chair, and stretched out her slight arms, while a very tender smile came rippling over her face. And then she sank back quietly, with eyes closed, as one that slept—but it was that sleep from which there is no waking here—and, her weary course at last ended; Hugh Lancaster's fair wife was not.

Round her neck, lying on her cold breast, they found a small, simple, paltry locket—for it had not been bought with her husband's money, but with a few hardly-scraped shillings of her own—and in it two locks of hair—one rich and thick, and golden brown; one thin and grey.

They had not the heart to rob it out of the thin dead hand that guarded it so jealously, and so poor pretty Nell was allowed to carry it with her when she went coffined and pallid to her dark home among the Lancasters.

I wish they had laid the "little lass" beside her "old dad," but they could not spare such a fair flower from their Death Garden.

3. Correspondence from the Bentley Archives (1866)

[These quotations are taken from the Bentley papers, containing correspondence between the publisher and his reader, Geraldine Jewsbury, regarding Broughton's work. (c) British Library Board. All Rights Reserved. Bentley Papers vol. XCVIII, Brit. Library, Additional Mss 46,657.]

On *Not Wisely but Too Well*. 2 July 1866, Bentley archives. "There is undoubtedly a certain force of strong epithets ... in a picture of unregulated sensual passion it is lifelike enough—but the story is absolute and unredeemed nonsense and the interest is of a kind that I shd carefully keep it out of the hands of all the young people of my acquaintance. I am sorry you have accepted it and I am sorry it is going to be published at all—the interest is of highly coloured and hot blooded passion—pretended to be quenched in a few drops of luke warm rose water sentimentality ... it is nothing but a series of love scenes (if love it can be called) & the point of interest turns upon the man being a "big [unclear] Litare" with "brawny athletic arms" ... "... broad shoulders" ... —a thorough blackguard.... It is the most thoroughly sensual tale I have read in English in a long time." G.E. (Geraldine) Jewsbury

In a follow-up letter on 3 July, she repeats that it is "a *bad* story please have nothing to do with it—It will not do you any credit—indeed people will wonder at a house like yours, bringing out a work so *ill* calculated for the reading of decent people."

Appendix B: Contemporary Reviews of the Novel

1. *The London Review* (16 March 1867) 324-25

There are dull stories which have the merit of being natural, and there are improbable stories, the unreality of which is redeemed by the charm of their execution; but the flippant nonsense entitled "Cometh Up as a Flower" belongs to neither one class nor the other. There is nothing lifelike about it; the men and women who figure in it are mere distorted, dislocated puppets; the pictures of society with which it favours us are clumsy caricatures; its pathos is artificial, its facetiousness is depressing, its philosophy consists in the utterance of worn-out platitudes, and its tone is unhealthy throughout.... There is something far from agreeable in this vague transition from flippant jesting to prayer, but it may have been sincere on the part of the author, by whom it has possibly been made with tears gathering in the eyes. In that case we may trust that her taste will be improved as the years go by. At present it stands in decided need of careful training. The unmaidenly manner in which the heroine constantly dwells upon her lover's physical charms is not pleasant; and her conduct after she has married another man, with whom she can find no fault except that he is too fond of her, in entreating that lover to elope with her, is simply abominable. There is no excuse for allowing the imagination thus to run riot. Such a scene represents nothing that is real or true to nature, unless it be the ravings of a lunatic, and its introduction serves no good purpose whatever.... The description of Dolly, the wicked sister, has some artistic merit, but it would have fitted some Italian lady in the middle ages, of noble birth, and with a propensity for poisoning, better than the daughter of a kind old English rector.

2. *Athenaeum* 2060 (20 April 1867) 514-15

That the author is not a young woman, but a man, who, in the present story, shows himself destitute of refinement of thought or feeling, and ignorant of all women either are, or ought to be, is evident on every page. The style of the book is bad, and full of slang; the story itself is not one to be put into the hands of girls with a view to what some one calls "their beneficial amusement." There is an all-pervading coarseness of thought and expression which is startling in its free and unrestrained utterance.

The descriptions which the young lady gives of her love-scenes would be coarse and flippant even as the confidential narrative of a fast young man of the order of "jolly dogs" to a kindred companion. There is a mixture of slang and sensuality, which, setting aside all other considerations, is in the worst possible taste. Of good feeling, or ordinary good principle, there is not a trace. There is a sensual sentimentality, self-indulgent emotion, a morbid skepticism, with dashes of equally morbid religious emotion. Of all true love or noble sentiment, the story is destitute. We are sorry to see a book of this kind making its appearance among our works of fiction; it is a thoroughly bad style of book, and it is not redeemed by talent: there is no knowledge of life or character or human nature displayed. The only two phases of existence which the author, in his assumed feminine character, seems to think women recognize, are, the delight of being kissed by a man they like, and the misery of being kissed by a man they don't like. These two points seem to fill up his idea of the whole duty of women.

3. *The Times* (6 June 1867) 9

"We are led to make these remarks after reading the strikingly clever and original novel whose curious title stands at the head of this article. We should judge it to be the authoress's first essay in the arena of fiction, and feel assured that if she should go on as she has begun, barring certain imperfections which we propose to point out as we process, she will attain to inconsiderable popularity....

... [A]n error into which many female novelists fall [is that they] ... are so proud of the mastery which they have acquired over masculine slang and masculine forms of expression that they treat the reader with these delicacies on every possible occasion....

The story is by no means the strongest part of *Cometh Up as a Flower*, being of the ordinary conventional type. We must confess that we have no patience with these tiresome young ladies who marry the man they don't love and make the poor fellow miserable all through the honeymoon with their sighs and tears and dismal faces. The real merits of this commonplace tale consist in the powerful, vigorous manner of its telling; in the exceeding beauty and poetry of its sketches of scenery, and in the soliloquies, sometimes quaintly humorous, sometimes cynically bitter, sometimes plaintive and melancholy, which are uttered by the heroine. Nor must we omit to add that the love-passages abound in warmth and passion. They are anything but milk-and-watery conventionalities. A real man appears before us clasping a real woman in his arms. Reverting to the soliloquies, it may be observed that, though the ideas expressed in them have been uttered a hundred times before, still there is a freshness and raciness about them exceedingly refreshing after the lumbering commonplaces which so often encumber the novel-reader's path....

There is no want of vivacity in this book; in fact, there is rather too much of it—too great a straining after clever sayings and effective hits. The exuberance of the language might have been pruned, and the colouring toned down. But we are not at all sure that a more quiet and sober manner of writing would increase the authoress's popularity; because a simple, straightforward, unadorned narrative is deemed insipid at the present time; our stories, however commonplace they may be, must be told in a smart and surprising manner.

Habit accustoms us to so many strange phenomena that we can hardly realize how greatly the ladies' novels of the present day differ from the ladies' novels of 20 or 25 years ago. Let us suppose that a copy of such a book as the one now before us could be placed in the shadowy hand of some departed instructress of youth, some worthy soul who believed, in the simplicity of her heart, that the *beau-ideal*[1] of female excellence differs as much from the *beau ideal* of male excellence as the glory of the sun differs from the glory of the moon. Such a teacher would desire that her pupils should be as ladylike as possible, she would prefer that they should remain in ladylike ignorance concerning many topics of masculine discourse. Our worthy friend would vainly search for any traces of this "ladylike ignorance" in the pages of modern female novelists, for they penetrate everywhere, and describe everything; they have the argot of the sporting world at their fingers ends, they know the prices and qualities

1 Beautiful ideal, the ideal type (French).

of cigars, they can repeat the conversation which takes place in the smoking-room after the ladies have retired upstairs.... Our ideal governess would be shocked at the "plain Saxon" of Miss Nelly Lestrange.... On some parts of the book the prim instructress of youth would look with still graver displeasure. She would certainly desire to expunge a passage in the second volume descriptive of Dolly's dancing, and we hope she would consider the following tirade ungenerous and unworthy:—

> "And greasy Jews—the offscourings of the earth (my one point of sympathy with the *moyen age* barbarians is their loathing and maltreatment of the accursed Israelitish dog)— have been prowling about, trading, as is their wont, on the miseries and weaknesses of poor humanity."

Such defects as these, however, will not lessen the popularity of this book. Habitual novel readers are not the wisest of mankind, and they will like the book all the better for its tone of knowingness, and its highly-coloured love-scenes. For ourselves, we prefer the authoress in her calmer and more serious moods— when she is sitting by her poor old father, weighed down with debt and disappointment; or when she is striving to solve some of the many puzzles of our existence. One great merit of the book is that every topic, whether trivial or serious, is treated heartily and enthusiastically....

The popularity of *Cometh up as a Flower* is more likely to be injured by its sorrowful ending. We cannot admit this to be a serious artistic defect, for there must be tragedies as well as comedies. Still, the modern public is very soft-hearted.... It is very true that poetical justice is seldom dealt out in real life, but for that very reason we like to have it dealt out in a story-book. We feel vexed that Nelly, after being cruelly deceived, should be left to die of decline, while her "she-devil" of a sister—as King Olaf forcibly styles her—lives to marry a peer with 80,000£. a year. No childish audience, listening to a "make-up" story, would allow us to conclude thus; and children are excellent judges in these matters.

4. *The Spectator* 2051 (19 October 1867) 1172-74

... [T]he writer, of whom we know absolutely nothing, cannot be a man, though she may have learnt much from some man's mind.... She is the novelist of revolt, and it is in this revolt, scarcely indicated in words, but penetrating and flavouring every sentence, that the curious charm, the nuttiness, the vanilla flavour of her tales consists. She expresses through fiction an emotion, a doubt, a sentiment—call it what you will—which has rarely been expressed except in poetry, but which surges up now and again in the mind of every human being with a mind at all ... —a feeling not only that all is Vanity, but that all ought not to be, that there is some mistake, some misarrangement, some failure in the grand scheme.... In each story the central figure is the same—a girl of a full and noble nature, round as to her lines mentally and bodily, with full bust and an exuberant mental life, despising conventionality and contemning the usual cut-and-dry formulas for living, ensnared, but not stained, by a burning passion for a man who cannot, or does not, become her husband,—by a real love, a sovereign entrancing hunger such as few feel in real life, and all civilized men believe at heart they might feel.... In each of the novels, the heroine dies of that want.... The love in each case is as an emotion marvelously described, though for some readers it will have perhaps too much realism; there is too clear an intrusion of the sensuous—we do not mean the impure—too much of clinginess and the disposition to embrace.... [T]he love-making is wonderfully vivid, so vivid that we believe the success of Cometh Up as a Flower is due far rather to that, to its appeal to a perennial instinct in men, the thirst to be loved to madness, than to the occasional audacities of thought and expression of which the reading world made so much. These audacities are due,—with an exception or two traceable to that curiously permanent consciousness of sex which infects the writing of all the ablest women,—rather to feebleness than to force, a straining to express what can hardly be expressed in prose.... When Cometh Up as a Flower first appeared, there was great dispute in quiet households as to its morality. It fluttered women as Jane Eyre did, and almost for the same reason, but we should no more pronounce it immoral than Jane Eyre. The author indulges, as we have said, in certain audacities of expression, sometimes witty to an enjoyable degree, sometimes profane, sometimes feebly flippant, and some of these audacities reveal, like some passages in Villette, in the Mill on the Floss, in many another work of female genius, a consciousness of sex which in its persistency is not either healthy or realistic. But we cannot admit that the general drift of these two books is in any degree immoral. Each has for a subject a love which might have ended in adultery, but in each the love is so treated as to create a horror of that consummation. Miss l'Estrange, married, offers herself to her lover, but the reader feels that the offer is made under maddening mental pain, and its rejection is, for women at all events, the sternest of moral lessons.

Appendix C: Contemporary Reviews of Sensation Fiction

[*Cometh Up as a Flower* was originally identified as a "sensation novel," a controversial genre of the 1860s. The following excerpts offer a range of opinions on the sensation genre from contemporary publications.]

1. "Sensation Novels," *Blackwood's Edinburgh Magazine* 91 (May 1862) 564-84. Attributed to Mrs. Oliphant

The violent stimulant of serial publication—of *weekly* publication with its necessity for frequent and rapid recurrence of piquant situation and startling incident—is the thing of all others most likely to develop the germ, and bring it to fuller and darker bearing....

We have just laid down a clever novel, called "East Lynne," which some inscrutable breath of popular liking has blown into momentary celebrity. It is occupied with the story of a woman who permitted herself, in passion and folly, to be seduced from her husband. From first to last it is she alone in whom the reader feels any interest. Her virtuous rival we should like to bundle to the door and get rid of anyhow. The Magdalen[1] herself, who is only moderately interesting while she is good, becomes, as soon as she is a Magdalen, doubly a heroine. It is evident that nohow, except by her wickedness and sufferings, could she have gained so strong a hold upon our sympathies. This is dangerous and foolish work, as well as false, both to Art and Nature. Nothing can be more wrong and fatal than to represent the flames of vice as a purifying fiery ordeal, through which the penitent is to come elevated and sublimed.

The rise of a Sensation School of art in any department is a thing to be watched with jealous eyes; but nowhere is it so dangerous as in fiction, where the artist cannot resort to a daring physical plunge, as on the stage, or to a blaze of palpable colour, as in the picture gallery, but must take the passions and emotions of life to make his effects withal....

---

1 From the Biblical Mary Magdalen, generally used to refer to a fallen woman, either an adulteress or a prostitute.

2. "Sensation Novels," *Medical Critic and Psychological Journal* (1863) 513-19

... [I]t appears to us that the love of excitement incidental to the idle members of prosperous communities is showing itself, to some degree, in a direction new to the present generation, and in an extent which, although vastly exceeding anything ever before witnessed, is only commensurate with the immense increase and wonderful diffusion of wealth and superficial knowledge. People with nothing to do, and with sufficient money to live in luxury, have always had, and from the nature of the human mind always must have, a strong desire for "sensations"—a desire that has invariably found gratification in the acts and sayings of conspicuous criminals....

We have said already that the craving for excitement has taken a direction in one respect new to the present generation. We refer to the interest excited by sexual immorality....

There is, moreover, some ground to believe that the interest felt by the educated classes in sexual immorality increases in proportion to the increasing variety of the offence. There have been times, not very remote, in English history, when immorality was uninteresting and prosaic, simply by reason of its universality. In the present day, ladies of station who offend, place themselves by a single effort in the position of distinguished criminals, and excite a share in the concern felt about the conduct and welfare of such persons as Mr. Leopold Redpath or the late Mrs. Manning.[1] We see no reason to fear that this concern will in the least degree tend to increase the crimes of swindling or homicide; and we do not fear either, that the eager perusal of the unsavoury revelations made before Sir Cresswell Cresswell[2] will, as a rule, in any appreciable degree undermine the virtue of our wives and daughters. Perhaps the ladies may learn many things about

---

1 Leopold Redpath was convicted in 1857 of fraudulently obtaining funds intended to construct London's underground railroad. He was transported for life to Australia. Mrs. Maria Manning was convicted for conspiring with her husband to murder her lover, and she was hanged in 1949.

2 Sir Cresswell Cresswell (Cresswell Easterby, 1794-1863) was a lawyer and judge. He presided over the divorce court, and so the "revelations" made before him would be of wives' sexual infidelity and husbands' domestic brutality.

which they would have done better to remain in ignorance. But among other things, they will at least learn the unerring action of the Nemesis that waits upon sin.... The world, it is trite to say, moves fast, evil of every sort is rampant, and unconcealed around us; and it is possible that "Sensation literature" may become a substitute, not altogether to be despised, for the didactic teaching that was in vogue with an earlier generation.

3. "Sensation Novels," *Quarterly Review* 113 (1863) 481-514. Attributed to H.L. Mansel

"I don't like preaching to the nerves instead of the judgment," was the remark of a shrewd observer of human nature, in relation to a certain class of popular sermons. The remark need not be limited to sermons alone. A class of literature has grown up around us, usurping in many respects, intentionally or unintentionally, a portion of the preacher's office, playing no inconsiderable part in moulding the minds and forming the habits and tastes of its generation; and doing so principally, we had almost said exclusively, by "preaching to the nerves." It would almost seem as if the paradox of Cabanis,[1] *les nerfs, voilà tout l'homme*,[2] had been banished from the realm of philosophy only to claim a wider empire in the domain of fiction—at least if we may judge by the very large class of writers who seem to acknowledge no other element in human nature to which they can appeal. Excitement, and excitement alone, seems to be the great end at which they aim—an end which must be accomplished at any cost by some means or other, "si possis, recte; si non, quocunque modo."[3] And as excitement, even when harmless in kind, cannot be continuously produced without becoming morbid in degree, works of this class manifest themselves in belonging, some more, some less, but all to some extent, to the morbid phenomena of literature—indications of a widespread corruption, of which they are in part both the effect and the cause; called into existence to supply the cravings of a

---

1 Pierre J.G. Cabanis (1757-1808) taught that the brain was an organ that digested impressions and secreted thought. One of the French ideologues, he believed that the mind and thought should be approached scientifically, and on a biological basis.
2 The nerves, there you have the entire man (French). That is, humanity is located in the nervous system.
3 If it is possible, rightly; if not, by whatever means (Latin).

diseased appetite, and contributing themselves to foster the disease, and to stimulate the want which they supply.

The sensation novel is the counterpart of the spasmodic poem.... The one leans outward, the other leans inward; the one aims at convulsing the soul of the reader, the other professes to owe its birth to convulsive throes in the soul of the writer. But with this agreement there is also a difference. There is not a poet or poetaster of the spasmodic school but is fully persuaded of his own inspiration and the immortality of his work.... Not so the sensation novelist. No divine influence can be imagined as presiding over the birth of his work, beyond the market law of demand and supply; no more immortality is dreamed of for it than for the fashions of the current season. A commercial atmosphere floats around works of this class, redolent of the manufactory and the shop. The public wants novels, and novels must be made—so many yards of printed stuff, sensation pattern, to be ready by the beginning of the season. And if the demands of the novel-reading public were to increase to the amount of a thousand per season, no difficulty would be found in producing a thousand works of the average merit....

Various causes have been at work to produce this phenomenon of our literature. Three principal ones may be named as having had a large share in it—periodicals, circulating libraries, and railway bookstalls. A periodical, from its very nature, must contain many articles of an ephemeral interest, and of the character of goods made to order. The material part of it is a fixed quantity determined by rigid boundaries of space and time; and on this Procrustean bed the spiritual part must needs be stretched to fit. A given number of sheets to print, containing so many lines per sheet, must be produced weekly or monthly, and the diviner element must accommodate itself to these conditions. A periodical, moreover, belongs to the class of works which most men borrow and do not buy, and in which, therefore, they take only a transitory interest. Few men will burden their shelves with a series of volumes which have no coherence in their parts, and no limit in their number, whose articles of personal interest may be as one halfpennyworth of bread to an intolerable quantity of sack, and which have no other termination to their issue than the point at which they cease to be profitable. Under these circumstances, no small stimulus is given to the production of tales of the marketable stamp, which, after appearing piecemeal in weekly or monthly installments, generally enter upon a second stage of their insect-life in the form of a handsome reprint under the auspices of the circulating library.

This last named institution is the oldest offender of the three; but age has neither diminished the energy nor subdued the faults of its youth.... The manner of its action is indeed inseparable from the nature of the institution, varying only in the production of larger quantities to meet the demand of a more reading generation. From the days of the "Minerva Press" (that synonym for the dullest specimens of the light reading of our grandmothers) to those of the thousand and one tales of the current season, the circulating-library has been the chief hot-bed for forcing a crop of writers without talent and readers without discrimination.... Subscription, as compared with purchase, produces no doubt a great increase in the quantity of books procurable, but with a corresponding deterioration in the quality. The buyer of books is generally careful to select what for his own purposes is worth buying; the subscriber is often content to take the good the gods provide him, glancing lazily down the library catalogue, and picking out some title which promises amusement or excitement....

The railway stall, like the circulating library, consists partly of books written expressly for its use, partly of reprints in a new phase of their existence—a phase internally that of the grub, with small print and cheap paper, externally that of the butterfly, with a tawdry cover, ornamented with a highly-coloured picture, hung out like a signboard, to give promise of the entertainment to be had within. The picture, like the book, is generally of the sensation kind, announcing some exciting scene to follow. A pale young lady in a white dress, with a dagger in her hand, evidently prepared for some desperate deed; or a couple of ruffians engaged in a deadly struggle; or a Red Indian in his war-paint; or, if the plot turns on smooth instead of violent villainy, a priest persuading a dying man to sign a paper; or a disappointed heir burning a will; or a treacherous lover telling a flattering tale to some deluded maid or wife. The exigencies of railway travelling do not allow much time for examining the merits of a book before purchasing it; and keepers of bookstalls, as well as of refreshment rooms, find an advantage in offering their customers something hot and strong, something that may catch the eye of a hurried passenger, and promise temporary excitement to relieve the dulness of a journey.

These circumstances of production naturally have their effect on the quality of the articles produced. Written to meet an ephemeral demand, aspiring only to an ephemeral existence, it is natural that they should have recourse to rapid and ephemeral methods of awakening the interest of their readers, striving to act as the dram or the dose, rather than as the solid food, because the effect is more immediately perceptible. And as the perpetual cravings of the dram-drinker or the valetudinarian for spirits or physic are hardly intelligible to the man of sound health and regular appetites, so, to one called from more wholesome studies to survey the wide field of sensational literature, it is difficult to realise the idea which its multifarious contents necessarily suggest, that these books must form the staple mental food of a very large class of readers....

Regarding these works merely as an efflorescence, as an eruption indicative of the state of health in the body in which they appear, the existence of an impure or a silly crop of novels, and the fact that they are eagerly read, are by no means favourable symptoms of the conditions of the body of society. But it is easier to detect the disease than to suggest a remedy. The praiseworthy attempts of individual proprietors of circulating libraries, to weed their collections of silly or mischievous works, have been too partial and isolated to produce any perceptible result, and have even acted as an advertisement of the rejected books. A more general and combined attempt in this direction is a thing rather to be wished than expected. Could a taste for the best class of fictions be cultivated in the minds of the rising generation, it might, perhaps, have its effect in lessening the craving for this kind of unnatural excitement; and could any check be imposed on the rapidity of production, it might improve the quality of the article produced.

4. "Novels," *Blackwood's Edinburgh Magazine* 102 (September 1867) 257-80. Attributed to Mrs. Oliphant

... [T]here can be no doubt that a change has passed over our light literature.... The change perhaps began at the time when Jane Eyre made what advanced critics call her "protest" against the conventionalities in which the world clothes itself. We have had many "protests" since then, but it is to be doubted how far they have been to our advantage. The point to which we have arrived now is certainly very far from satisfactory.... What is held up to us as the story of the feminine soul as it really exists underneath its conventional coverings, is a very fleshly and unlovely record. Women driven wild with love for the man who leads them on to desperation before he accords that word which carries them into the seventh heaven; women who marry their grooms in fits of sensual passion;[1] women who pray to their lovers to carry them off from the husbands and homes they hate; women, at the very least of it, who give and receive burning embraces, and live in a voluptuous dream, either waiting for or brooding over the inevitable lover,—such are the heroines who have been imported into modern fiction.... Now it is no knight of romance riding down the forest glades, ready for the defence and succour of all the oppressed, for whom the dreaming maiden waits. She waits now for flesh and muscle, for strong arms that seize her, and warm breath that thrills her through, and a host of other physical attractions, which she indicates to the world with a charming frankness. On the other side of the picture it is, of course, the amber hair and undulating form, the warm flesh and glowing colour, for which the youth sighs in his turn; but were the sketch made from his point of view, its openness would be somewhat less repulsive. The peculiarity of it in England is, that it is oftenest made from the woman's side— that it is women who describe these sensuous raptures—that this intense appreciation for flesh and blood, this eagerness of physical sensation, is represented as the natural sentiment of English girls, and is offered to them not only as the portrait of their own state of mind, but as their amusement and mental food. [This literature] ... has reinstated the injured creature Man in something like his natural character, but unfortunately it has gone to extremes, and moulded its women on the model of men, just as the former school moulded its men on the model of women. The heroine of "Cometh Up as a Flower" is a good case in point. She is not by any means so disagreeable, so vulgar, or so mannish, as at the first beginning she makes herself out to be. Her flippancy, to start with, revolts the reader, and inclines him to pitch the volume to as great a distance as is practicable; but if he has patience a little, the girl is not so bad. She is a motherless girl, brought up in the very worst way, and formed on the most wretched model, but yet there is a touch

---

1   This probably refers to Mary Elizabeth Braddon's novel *Aurora Floyd* (1863).

of nature in the headstrong creature. And this of itself is a curious peculiarity of fiction generally. Ill-brought-up motherless girls ... have become the ideal of the novelist. There is this advantage in them, that benevolent female readers have the resource of saying, "Remember she had no mother," when the heroine falls into any unusual lapse from feminine traditions; but it is odd, to say the least of it, that this phase of youthful life should commend itself so universally to the female novelist.... And here let us pause to make a necessary discrimination. A *grande passion*[1] is a thing which has to be recognized as possible wherever it is met with in the world. If two young people fall heartily and honestly in love with each other, and are separated by machinations such as abound in novels, but unfortunately are not unknown in life, and one of them is compelled to marry somebody else, it is not unnatural, it is not revolting, that the true love unextinguished should blaze wildly up, in defiance of all law, when the opportunity occurs. This is wrong, sinful, ruinous, but it is not disgusting; whereas those speeches about shrinking bodies and sexless essences are disgusting in the fullest sense of the word.... After our free-spoken heroine has come to the climax of her fate, she becomes consumptive and reflective after that loftily pious kind which generally associates itself with this species of immorality; for sensual literature and the carnal mind have a kind of piety quite to themselves, when disappointment and incapacity come upon them. The fire which burned so bright dies out into the most inconceivably grey of ashes; and the sweetest submission, the tenderest purity, take the place in a second of all those daring headstrong fancies, all that will and self-indulgence. The intense goodness follows the intense sensuousness as by a natural law....

Hair, indeed, in general, has become one of the leading properties in fiction. The facility with which it flows over the shoulders and bosoms in its owner's vicinity is quite extraordinary. In every emergency it is ready for use. Its quantity and colour, and the reflections in it, and even the "fuzz," which is its modern peculiarity, take the place of all those pretty qualities with which heroines used to be endowed. What need has a woman for a soul when she has upon her head a mass of wavy gold? ... the hue is gold or red. When the conception demands a milder shade of colouring, auburn, and even chestnut (with gold reflections) are

1 A great passion (French).

permissible, but when a very high effect is intended, red is the hue *par excellence*.[1] Red and gold, in all its shades, are compatible with virtue; amber means rich luxurious vice, whereas the pale and scanty locks are the embodiment of meanness and poverty of character.... [I]t is the female novelist who speaks the most plainly, and whose best characters revel in a kind of innocent indecency, as does the heroine of "Cometh Up as a Flower." ... Nasty thoughts, ugly suggestions, an imagination which prefers the unclean, is almost more appalling than actual depravity, because it has no excuse of sudden passion or temptation, and no visible boundary. It is a shame for women so to write; and it is a shame to the women who read and accept as a true representation of themselves and their ways the equivocal talk and fleshly inclinations herein attributed to them.... Women's rights and women's duties have had enough discussion, perhaps even from the ridiculous point of view. We have most of us made merry over Mr. Mill's crotchet on the subject,[2] and over the Dr Marys and Dr Elizabeths;[3] but yet a woman still has one fundamental duty to her country and her race which cannot be over-estimated— and that is the duty of being pure. There is perhaps nothing of such vital consequence to a nation.... [T]here can be no possible doubt that the wickedness of man is less ruinous, less disastrous to the world in general, than the wickedness of woman.

---

1 To a (high) degree of excellence (French).
2 John Stuart Mill wrote *The Subjection of Women*, a key feminist text of the period, in 1869, but had advocated for women's rights long before then.
3 Women were still excluded from becoming doctors in Britain in this period, but some studied abroad and then returned to practice in various capacities. Dr. Elizabeth Blackwell was the first woman doctor to practice legally in Britain, having earned her qualifications in the United States in 1849 and returning to practice in Britain in 1858. Dr. Elizabeth Garrett Anderson qualified in London in 1865, the first woman to be allowed to do so.

Appendix D: Punch Magazine's Parody of the Author

1. From "Prefatory Correspondence," *Punch* (18 March 1876) 98-99

[The following is taken from the parodied "Prefatory Correspondence" which appeared in *Punch* before the serialization of *Gone Wrong. Punch* (18 March 1876) 98-99. Upon being asked for a novel, the author, "Rhody Dendron" responds, as follows:]

From Miss R.D. to the Editor.
Dear Sir,
Do you object to tremendous Love interest? If not, I have the very thing for you.
Yours Truly,
R.D.

Ed. to R.D.
My Dear Young Lady,
I never object to "tremendous interest," even up to fifty per cent. Yet permit me to observe, as a matter of business, that, when the interest is extraordinary, the risk is proportionately large....

Dear Sir,
I take you at your word. You are willing to accept a high interest with proportionate risk. Of course I do not write for milksops, and I am sure that you would not wish either yourself or your readers to come under that designation. My object is to raise a rosy cloud of Love and maddening witchery round you, to make your veins throb, and your pulse beat with ecstasy, as I guide you onward, with my enchanter's wand-pen, into the very presence of divine ambrosial loveliness.... As to "pointing a moral," my dear Sir, depend upon me for that. I am proud to say there is not one of my novels which has not been written with the highest possible aim....

Good, my dear Sir, you shall have it. Man wants but little here below, but that little, strong.
Yours Sincerely,
R.D.

P.S. "That Little—Strong" wouldn't be a bad title. But I prefer either popular songs, or a bit of a proverb. I have had my eye on several song titles, such as "Tommy make room for your uncle," which might be cut into "For Your Uncle"; also "Don't be Sorrowful, Darling" which could come out well as "Sorrowful Darling" * * * Stay! I have just put my hand on what I am told is quite a catch phrase about town now, and that will be half the battle of popularity. It is "There's another good man gone Wrong." You can therefore announce my new Novel as

"Gone Wrong"

And you can advertise the first number for your next.

2. From *Gone Wrong*, serialized in *Punch* from 25 March to 3 June 1876

Burnand, F.C. [as Miss Rhody Dendron] Authoress of *Cometh Down like a Shower, Red in the Nose is She, Buy Sweet Tart!, Not Slily, But Don't Tell. Gone Wrong. A New Novel.* "Our Shilling Novel Series." London: Bradbury, Agnew and Co., 1881. (reprint from *Punch*).[1]

Neither wholly red, nor purely golden, are her electro-plaited locks, which gleam with all the brilliancy of an autumn walnut in a dank wood. She is just settling in her mind which colour it is to be, and has done her sister the honour of consulting her. She makes a soft pillow for her little glossy head on the window-sill. Thought made her head ache.

"I do not want to dye yet!" she murmured plaintively.

"There is no necessity for it," I say. I always say whatever Bella wishes—it is my *rôle* in life, and I take a good look at her as she twines her shapely fingers in among her sunset tresses. She has big grey eyes, in which, at first sight, there appears to be a considerable amount of green. She has the small upward turned nose of a person who is passing through Cologne, or through a back street of the Seven Dials in the hottest summer time, with

---

1 This seems to parody the opening of *Not Wisely but Too Well* (1879), another bestselling Broughton novel. The other titles parodied here are *Red as a Rose Is She* (1870), and *Good-bye, Sweetheart!* (1872).

two little heart shaped dimpled nostrils, that are the very extinguishers for men's souls....

All men who looked once at Bella's mouth, thought twice. It seemed to expect life to be one long pleasant dinner of ever-varying dishes, with luscious fruits for the dessert, and then the whole movement *da capo* from the *potage à la Reine*.

There is a lurking gravity in her low forehead which most men have wondered at; and her full, unblushing cheek, men admire still more, but wonder at less. This face is nicely set on a warm round throat, not too white, nor like unliving marble, but like a large, well-turned, soft, consistent, roley-poley pudding, with the veins of raspberry jam within, indicated on its warm, soft surface.

As for Bella's figure,—well, she has told me, her Sister Jenny, that five thousand a year would be about her figure, if the *parti* were in other ways suitable.

Appendix E: Attitudes Toward Women and Marriage in Victorian Society

[*Cometh Up as a Flower* takes up the relation of marriage to ideals of romantic love and to economic and social responsibilities. This was a topic of wide interest in the period, and the excerpts below offer a range of commentary on the moral and practical concerns of choosing a spouse.]

1. From Sarah Stickney Ellis, *The Daughters of England, Their Position in Society. Character and Responsibilities.* [1842] London: Fisher, Son and Co., 1845

In speaking of friendship, I have said nothing of that which might be supposed to exist between the two sexes; because I believe, that, in early youth, but little good can accrue to either party from making the experiment ... man, in his intercourse with woman, seldom studies her improvement; and that woman, in her's [*sic*] with man, is too much addicted to flirtation. The opinion of the world, also, is opposed to this kind of intimacy; and it is seldom safe, and never wise, to do what society unanimously condemns. Besides which, it is exceedingly difficult for a young and inexperienced girl to know when a man is really her friend, and when he is only attempting to gain her favour; the most serious mistakes are, therefore, always liable to be made, which can only be effectually guarded against, by avoiding such intimacies altogether.

Again, it is no uncommon thing for men to betray young women into little deviations from the strict rule of propriety, for their own sakes, or in connection with them; which deviations they would be the first to condemn, if they were in favour of another. Be assured, however, that the man who does this—who, for his own gratification betrays you into so much as the shadow of an error—who even willingly allows you to be placed in an exposed, a questionable, or even an undignified situation—in short, who subjects you, for his own sake, to the slightest breath of censure, or even of ridicule, is not your real friend, not worthy so much as to be called your acquaintance.

Though truth should be engraven upon every thought, and

word, and act, which occurs in your intercourse with the man of your choice, there is implanted in the nature of woman, a shrinking delicacy, which ought ever to prompt her to keep back some of her affection for the time when she becomes a wife. No woman ever gained, but many, very many have been losers, by displaying all at first. Let sufficient of your love be told, to prevent suspicion, or distrust, and the self-complacency of man will be sure to provide the rest. Suffer it not, then to be unfolded to its full extent....

2. From Mary Wollstonecraft, *A Vindication of the Rights of Woman: with Strictures on Political and Moral Subjects*, vol 1. 2nd edition. London: Printed for J. Johnson, 1792

My own sex, I hope, will excuse me, if I treat them like rational creatures, instead of flattering their FASCINATING graces, and viewing them as if they were in a state of perpetual childhood, unable to stand alone. I earnestly wish to point out in what true dignity and human happiness consists—I wish to persuade women to endeavour to acquire strength, both of mind and body, and to convince them, that the soft phrases, susceptibility of heart, delicacy of sentiment, and refinement of taste, are almost synonymous with epithets of weakness, and that those beings who are only the objects of pity and that kind of love, which has been termed its sister, will soon become objects of contempt.

Dismissing then those pretty feminine phrases, which the men condescendingly use to soften our slavish dependence, and despising that weak elegancy of mind, exquisite sensibility, and sweet docility of manners, supposed to be the sexual characteristics of the weaker vessel, I wish to show that elegance is inferior to virtue, that the first object of laudable ambition is to obtain a character as a human being, regardless of the distinction of sex; and that secondary views should be brought to this simple touchstone....

The education of women has, of late, been more attended to than formerly; yet they are still reckoned a frivolous sex, and ridiculed or pitied by the writers who endeavour by satire or instruction to improve them. It is acknowledged that they spend many of the first years of their lives in acquiring a smattering of accomplishments: meanwhile, strength of body and mind are sacrificed to libertine notions of beauty, to the desire of establishing themselves, the only way women can rise in the world—by marriage. And this desire making mere animals of them, when they marry, they act as such children may be expected to act: they dress; they paint, and nickname God's creatures. Surely these weak beings are only fit for the seraglio! Can they govern a family, or take care of the poor babes whom they bring into the world? ...

How grossly do they insult us, who thus advise us only to render ourselves gentle, domestic brutes! For instance, the winning softness, so warmly, and frequently recommended, that governs by obeying. What childish expressions, and how insignificant is the being—can it be an immortal one? who will condescend to govern by such sinister methods! "Certainly," says Lord Bacon, "man is of kin to the beasts by his body: and if he be not of kin to God by his spirit, he is a base and ignoble creature!" Men, indeed, appear to me to act in a very unphilosophical manner, when they try to secure the good conduct of women by attempting to keep them always in a state of childhood. Rousseau was more consistent when he wished to stop the progress of reason in both sexes; for if men eat of the tree of knowledge, women will come in for a taste: but, from the imperfect cultivation which their understandings now receive, they only attain a knowledge of evil.

Children, I grant, should be innocent; but when the epithet is applied to men, or women, it is but a civil term for weakness. For if it be allowed that women were destined by Providence to acquire human virtues, and by the exercise of their understandings, that stability of character which is the firmest ground to rest our future hopes upon, they must be permitted to turn to the fountain of light, and not forced to shape their course by the twinkling of a mere satellite....

To speak disrespectfully of love is, I know, high treason against sentiment and fine feelings; but I wish to speak the simple language of truth, and rather to address the head than the heart. To endeavour to reason love out of the world, would be to out Quixote Cervantes,[1] and equally offend against common sense; but an endeavour to restrain this tumultuous passion, and to prove that it should not be allowed to dethrone superior powers, or to usurp the sceptre which the understanding should ever coolly wield, appears less wild.

---

1 *Don Quixote* by Miguel de Cervantes (1605 and 1615).

Youth is the season for love in both sexes; but in those days of thoughtless enjoyment, provision should be made for the more important years of life, when reflection takes place of sensation. But Rousseau, and most of the male writers who have followed his steps, have warmly inculcated that the whole tendency of female education ought to be directed to one point—to render them pleasing.

Let me reason with the supporters of this opinion, who have any knowledge of human nature, do they imagine that marriage can eradicate the habitude of life? The woman who has only been taught to please, will soon find that her charms are oblique sun-beams, and that they cannot have much effect on her husband's heart when they are seen every day, when the summer is past and gone. Will she then have sufficient native energy to look into herself for comfort, and cultivate her dormant faculties? or, is it not more rational to expect, that she will try to please other men; and, in the emotions raised by the expectation of new conquests, endeavour to forget the mortification her love or pride has received? When the husband ceases to be a lover—and the time will inevitably come, her desire of pleasing will then grow languid, or become a spring of bitterness; and love, perhaps, the most evanescent of all passions, gives place to jealousy or vanity.

I now speak of women who are restrained by principle or prejudice; such women though they would shrink from an intrigue with real abhorrence, yet, nevertheless, wish to be convinced by the homage of gallantry, that they are cruelly neglected by their husbands; or, days and weeks are spent in dreaming of the happiness enjoyed by congenial souls, till the health is undermined and the spirits broken by discontent. How then can the great art of pleasing be such a necessary study? it is only useful to a mistress; the chaste wife, and serious mother, should only consider her power to please as the polish of her virtues, and the affection of her husband as one of the comforts that render her task less difficult, and her life happier. But, whether she be loved or neglected, her first wish should be to make herself respectable, and not rely for all her happiness on a being subject to like infirmities with herself.

The amiable Dr. Gregory fell into a similar error. I respect his heart; but entirely disapprove of his celebrated Legacy to his Daughters.

He advises them to cultivate a fondness for dress, because a fondness for dress, he asserts, is natural to them. I am unable to comprehend what either he or Rousseau mean, when they frequently use this indefinite term. If they told us, that in a pre-existent state the soul was fond of dress, and brought this inclination with it into a new body, I should listen to them with a half smile, as I often do when I hear a rant about innate elegance. But if he only meant to say that the exercise of the faculties will produce this fondness, I deny it. It is not natural; but arises, like false ambition in men, from a love of power.

Dr. Gregory goes much further; he actually recommends dissimulation, and advises an innocent girl to give the lie to her feelings, and not dance with spirit, when gaiety of heart would make her feet eloquent, without making her gestures immodest. In the name of truth and common sense, why should not one woman acknowledge that she can take more exercise than another? or, in other words, that she has a sound constitution; and why to damp innocent vivacity, is she darkly to be told, that men will draw conclusions which she little thinks of? Let the libertine draw what inference he pleases; but, I hope, that no sensible mother will restrain the natural frankness of youth, by instilling such indecent cautions. Out of the abundance of the heart the mouth speaketh; and a wiser than Solomon hath said, that the heart should be made clean, and not trivial ceremonies observed, which it is not very difficult to fulfill with scrupulous exactness when vice reigns in the heart.

Women ought to endeavour to purify their hearts; but can they do so when their uncultivated understandings make them entirely dependent on their senses for employment and amusement, when no noble pursuit sets them above the little vanities of the day, or enables them to curb the wild emotions that agitate a reed over which every passing breeze has power? To gain the affections of a virtuous man, is affectation necessary?

Nature has given woman a weaker frame than man; but, to ensure her husband's affections, must a wife, who, by the exercise of her mind and body, whilst she was discharging the duties of a daughter, wife, and mother, has allowed her constitution to retain its natural strength, and her nerves a healthy tone, is she, I say, to condescend, to use art, and feign a sickly delicacy, in order to secure her husband's affection? Weakness may excite tenderness, and gratify the arrogant pride of man; but the lordly caresses of a protector will not gratify a noble mind that pants for and deserves to be respected. Fondness is a poor substitute for friendship!

In a seraglio, I grant, that all these arts are necessary; the epicure must have his palate tickled, or he will sink into apathy; but have women so little ambition as to be satisfied with such a condition? Can they supinely dream life away in the lap of pleasure, or in the languor of weariness, rather than assert their claim to pursue reasonable pleasures, and render themselves conspicuous, by practising the virtues which dignify mankind? Surely she has not an immortal soul who can loiter life away, merely employed to adorn her person, that she may amuse the languid hours, and soften the cares of a fellow-creature who is willing to be enlivened by her smiles and tricks, when the serious business of life is over.

Besides, the woman who strengthens her body and exercises her mind will, by managing her family and practising various virtues, become the friend, and not the humble dependent of her husband; and if she deserves his regard by possessing such substantial qualities, she will not find it necessary to conceal her affection, nor to pretend to an unnatural coldness of constitution to excite her husband's passions. In fact, if we revert to history, we shall find that the women who have distinguished themselves have neither been the most beautiful nor the most gentle of their sex.

Nature, or to speak with strict propriety God, has made all things right; but man has sought him out many inventions to mar the work. I now allude to that part of Dr. Gregory's treatise, where he advises a wife never to let her husband know the extent of her sensibility or affection. Voluptuous precaution; and as ineffectual as absurd. Love, from its very nature, must be transitory. To seek for a secret that would render it constant, would be as wild a search as for the philosopher's stone, or the grand panacea; and the discovery would be equally useless, or rather pernicious to mankind. The most holy band of society is friendship. It has been well said, by a shrewd satirist, "that rare as true love is, true friendship is still rarer."

This is an obvious truth, and the cause not lying deep, will not elude a slight glance of inquiry.

Love, the common passion, in which chance and sensation take place of choice and reason, is in some degree, felt by the mass of mankind; for it is not necessary to speak, at present, of the emotions that rise above or sink below love. This passion, naturally increased by suspense and difficulties, draws the mind out of its accustomed state, and exalts the affections; but the security of marriage, allowing the fever of love to subside, a healthy temperature is thought insipid, only by those who have not sufficient intellect to substitute the calm tenderness of friendship, the confidence of respect, instead of blind admiration, and the sensual emotions of fondness.

This is, must be, the course of nature—friendship or indifference inevitably succeeds love. And this constitution seems perfectly to harmonize with the system of government which prevails in the moral world. Passions are spurs to action, and open the mind; but they sink into mere appetites, become a personal momentary gratification, when the object is gained, and the satisfied mind rests in enjoyment. The man who had some virtue whilst he was struggling for a crown, often becomes a voluptuous tyrant when it graces his brow; and, when the lover is not lost in the husband, the dotard a prey to childish caprices, and fond jealousies, neglects the serious duties of life, and the caresses which should excite confidence in his children are lavished on the overgrown child, his wife....

Business of various kinds, they might likewise pursue, if they were educated in a more orderly manner, which might save many from common and legal prostitution. Women would not then marry for a support, as men accept of places under government, and neglect the implied duties; nor would an attempt to earn their own subsistence, a most laudable one! sink them almost to the level of those poor abandoned creatures who live by prostitution. For are not milliners and mantuamakers[1] reckoned the next class? The few employments open to women, so far from being liberal, are menial; and when a superior education enables them to take charge of the education of children as governesses, they are not treated like the tutors of sons, though even clerical tutors are not always treated in a manner calculated to render them respectable in the eyes of their pupils, to say nothing of the private comfort of the individual. But as women educated like

---

1 Milliners (hatmakers) and mantuamakers (dressmakers) were very poorly paid women workers and thus often seen as vulnerable to seduction.

gentlewomen, are never designed for the humiliating situation which necessity sometimes forces them to fill; these situations are considered in the light of a degradation; and they know little of the human heart, who need to be told, that nothing so painfully sharpens the sensibility as such a fall in life.

Some of these women might be restrained from marrying by a proper spirit or delicacy, and others may not have had it in their power to escape in this pitiful way from servitude; is not that government then very defective, and very unmindful of the happiness of one half of its members, that does not provide for honest, independent women, by encouraging them to fill respectable stations? But in order to render their private virtue a public benefit, they must have a civil existence in the state, married or single; else we shall continually see some worthy woman, whose sensibility has been rendered painfully acute by undeserved contempt, droop like "the lily broken down by a plough share."

It is a melancholy truth; yet such is the blessed effect of civilization! the most respectable women are the most oppressed; and, unless they have understandings far superior to the common run of understandings, taking in both sexes, they must, from being treated like contemptible beings, become contemptible. How many women thus waste life away, the prey of discontent, who might have practised as physicians, regulated a farm, managed a shop, and stood erect, supported by their own industry, instead of hanging their heads surcharged with the dew of sensibility, that consumes the beauty to which it at first gave lustre; nay, I doubt whether pity and love are so near a-kin as poets feign, for I have seldom seen much compassion excited by the helplessness of females, unless they were fair; then, perhaps, pity was the soft handmaid of love, or the harbinger of lust.

3. From Marie Corelli, *The Modern Marriage Market*. London: Hutchinson & Co., 1898. Originally published in *The Lady's Realm*, 1897

Most women of Society find it more than difficult to carry out the good intentions with which they have perhaps begun their careers; and the more exalted their position, the less, as a rule, are they able to withstand the temptations, follies, and hypocrisies which surround them. Follies, temptations, and hypocrisies surround in a greater or less degree all women, whether in Society or out of it,—and we are none of us angels, though to their credit be it said, that some men still think us so. Some men still make "angels" out of us in spite of our cycling mania,—our foolish "clubs," where we do nothing at all,—our rough games at football and cricket, our general throwing to the winds of all dainty feminine reserve, delicacy, and modesty,—and we alone are to blame if we shatter their ideals and sit down by choice in the mud when they would have placed us on thrones. It is our fault, not theirs. We have willed it so. Many of us are more "mannish" than womanly; we are more inclined to laugh at and make mock of a man's courtesy and reverence than we are to be flattered by it. The result is that nowadays we are married, both men and women alike, for what we *have*, and not for what we *are*.

It is one of our many hypocrisies to pretend we do not see things that are plainly put before us every day, and also to assume a fastidious disgust and horror when told of certain "barbarisms" still practised in Europe, barbarisms which we consider we have, in our state of ultra-civilisation, fortunately escaped. One of these "barbaric" institutions which moves us to shudder gracefully and turn up the whites of our eyes, is slavery. "Britons never, never shall," we say. British women shall never, for example, stand stripped in the market-place to be appraised and labelled at a price, and purchased by a sensualist and ruffian for so much money down. No British man shall ever stand with bound hands and manacled feet, shamed and contemptible in his own eyes, waiting till some luxurious wanton of the world, with more cash than modesty, buys him with her millions to be her fetch-and-carry slave till death releases him from the unnatural bondage. These things are done in Stamboul. True. Stamboul is barbaric. What of London? What of the "season," when women are as coolly "brought out" to be sold as any unhappy Armenian girl that ever shuddered at the lewd gaze of a Turkish tyrant? What of the mothers and fathers who force their children thus into the open market? Come—face the thing out—don't put it away or behind you as a matter too awkward and difficult of discussion. It is an absolute grim fact that in England, women—those of the upper classes, at any rate—are not to-day married, but bought for a price. The high and noble intention of marriage is entirely lost sight of in the scheming, the bargaining, and the pricing.

What *is* marriage? Many of you have, I think, forgotten. It is not the church, the ritual, the blessing of the clergyman, or the ratifying and approving presence of one's friends and relations at the ceremony,—still less is it a matter of "settlements" and expensive millinery. It is the taking of a solemn vow before the Throne of the Eternal,—a vow which declares that the man and woman concerned have discovered in each other his and her true mate,—that they feel life is alone valuable and worth living in each other's company,—that they are prepared to endure trouble, poverty, pain, sickness, death itself, provided they may only be together,—and that all the world is a mere grain of dust in worth as compared to the exalted passion which fills their souls and moves them to become one in flesh as well as one in spirit. Nothing can make marriage an absolutely sacred thing except the great love, combined with the pure and faithful intention, of the human pair involved. They have to realise first of all that a God exists; and that before that God, Whom they solemnly acknowledge and believe in, they are One.

What has the cash-box to do with this? The reply will be that in order to live, one must have the wherewithal for living. Quite so. But then, if it be once fully realised that there is a Supreme Creator of things, to Whom we are answerable for the breaking of any of His laws, we shall understand that no two human beings have a right to share each other's lives at all, if the result of such sharing should be to *drag each other down*. Marriage is intended to uplift—to consecrate—to inspire,—and while these noble duties cannot altogether be properly fulfilled if extreme poverty bars the way, and starvation looks in at the door, it is not at all necessary that the married pair should be so grossly and vulgarly wealthy as to be free of every shadow of difficulty. Shadows of difficulty show best where love's sunshine falls. We are never as strong, as sweet, or as true as we might be if we lack the divine difficulties which nerve us to fresh endeavour. It is as easy—perhaps easier—to be happy on five hundred a year, as on five thousand, and a study of the faces of those who possess a hundred thousand a year will move us more to compassion than envy....

... Mothers teach their daughters to marry for a "suitable establishment": fathers, rendered desperate as to what they are to do with their sons in the increasing struggle for life and the incessant demand for luxuries which are not by any means actually necessary to that life, say, "Look out for a woman with money." Heirs to a great name and title sell their birthrights for a mess of American dollar-pottage,—and it is a very common every-day sight to see some Christian virgin sacrificed on the altar of matrimony to a money-lending, money-grubbing son of Israel.

Bargain and sale,—sale and bargain,—it is the whole *raison d'être* of the "season,"—the balls, the dinners, the suppers, the parties to Hurlingham and Ascot. Even on the dear old Thames with its delicious nooks, fitted for pure romance and heart betrothal, the clatter of Gunter's luncheon-dishes and the popping of Benoist's champagne-corks remind the hungry gypsies who linger near such scenes of river revelry that there is not much sentiment about—only plenty of money being wasted....

... There can be nothing more hideous, more like a foretaste of hell itself, than the life-to-life position of a man and woman who have been hustled into matrimony, or rather, as I prefer to put it, sold to each other for so many thousands per annum, and who, when the wedding-fuss is over, and the feminine "pictorials" have done gushing about the millinery of the occasion, find themselves alone together, without a single sympathy in common,—with nothing but the chink of gold and the rustle of bank-notes for their heart-music,—and with a barrier of steadily-increasing repulsion and disgust rising between them every day.

And this is what happens in nine cases out of ten in fashionable modern matrimony. "A marriage has been arranged" is a common phrase of newspaper parlance,—and it has one advantage over most newspaper forms of speech—namely, that of being strictly and literally true. A marriage is "arranged" as a matter of convenience or social interest; lawyers draft settlements and conclude the sale,—and a priest of the Most High God is called in to bless the bargain. But it is nevertheless a bargain,—a trafficking in human bodies and souls, as open and as shameless as any similar scene in Stamboul.

And yet there *is* liberty in our land if we will only avail ourselves of the glorious privilege. Women are free to assert their modesty, their sense of right, their desire for truth and purity, if they only will. Is it too much to ask of them that they should refuse to be stripped to the bosom and exposed for sale in the modern drawing-rooms of the "season"? Is it too much to ask that, in their natural and fitting desire to be suitably wedded, they should look for men rather than money,—love rather than an "establishment,"—mutual sympathy and understanding rather than so much heritable property in houses and lands? And may not it even be suggested that men should be manly enough to refuse to set themselves forth in the market as "Heir to the estate of So-and-So, worth so much in hard cash"—or "Only lineal descendant of the Earl of So-and-So,—anxious to sell title, with body and soul attached to it, to any woman who can give the adequate millions necessary for immediate purchase"? A man who marries a woman for her money only is really one of the most despicable objects in existence. He who by natural law was intended to be the supporter, becomes the supported,—he who by every proud prerogative of manhood is formed to be the conqueror and protector, is tamed and tied like a feeble nursling to a woman's apron-string,—he loses the right to exert his independence, and must submit to be hen-pecked, "nagged at," or else treated with a callous indifference, and sometimes an infinite contempt.

The woman who marries for money is quite as blameworthy, and is likely to find her position equally as aggravating, only in another way. The man who has the "chinks" will never throw her poverty at her as a fault in the blunt and coarse terms which many a wealthy woman uses to a dependent husband,—but he will involuntarily show her, by a thousand little unmistakable signs, that he knows he has bought her,—and even in the very lavishness of his gifts to her she will gradually come to realise the "position" she holds with regard to him—namely, one of social dummy, household figure-ornament,—while he, free as air, amuses himself with other women, and soothes any pricking of his conscience by the reflection that after all, as his wife, she has everything she wants in the way of dress and jewels, food and firing, and that, in all the necessary items of sustenance and comfort, he has done his duty by her.

The real fact of the matter is that marriage is nothing more nor less than a crime if it is entered upon without that mutual supreme attraction and deep love which makes the union sacred. It is a selling of body into slavery,—it is a dragging down of souls into impurity. The passion of love is a natural law,—a necessity of being,—and if a woman gives herself to a man in marriage without that love truly and vitally inspiring her, she will in time find that the "natural law" will have its way, and attract her to some other than her lawful husband, and drag her steadily down through the ways of sin to perdition.

I am addressing myself especially to women. In a woman's life *one* love should suffice. She cannot, constituted as she is, honestly give herself to more than one man. And she should be certain—absolutely, sacredly, solemnly certain—that out of all the world that one man is indeed her pre-elected lover, her chosen mate,—that never could she care for any other hand than his to caress her beauty,—never for any other kiss than his to rest upon her lips,—and that without him life is but a half-circle, waiting completion.

How much of this kind of "certainty" enters into the "arrangements" of a fashionable marriage? How many women, as they pass up to the altar in all the glory of their bridal finery, are actually proud and happy to take the vows of love and fidelity? Very few. Yet it *should* be a proud moment for any woman; it should be the height of her life's triumph to submit to the mastery of love. Only, unfortunately, it is seldom this divine mastery of love which dominates her; it is a weak compound of toleration and resignation, mixed up with pounds, shillings, and pence,—a farce of society fuss and feigning, in which poor Love gets crowded out altogether, and hastily spreads his wings for flight. He is the last of all the mythical gods to be tempted or cajoled by lawyers and settlements, wedding-cake and perishable millinery. His domain is Nature, and the heart of humanity,—and the gifts he can bestow on those who meet him in the true spirit are marvellous and priceless indeed. The exquisite joys he can teach,—the fine sympathies,—the delicate emotions,—the singular method in which he will play upon two lives like separate harps, and bring them into resounding tune and harmony, so that all the world shall seem full of luscious song,—this is one way of love's system of education. But this is not all: he can so mould the character, temper the will, and strengthen the heart, as to make his elected disciples endure the bitterest sorrows bravely,—perform acts of heroic self-sacrifice, and attain the most glorious heights of ambition; for, as the venerable Thomas à Kempis tells us, "Love is a great thing, yea, a great and thorough good; by itself it makes everything that is heavy light, and it bears evenly all that is uneven. For it carries a burden which is no burden, and makes everything that is bitter sweet and tasteful. Though weary it is not tired, though pressed it is not straitened, though alarmed it is not confounded, but as a lively flame and burning torch it forces its way upward and securely passes through all."

Is not such divine happiness well worth attaining? Is the cash-box better? And will the possession of jewels, gold, and estates, be of any avail as consolation in the hours of pain and loss? Think well about it, fair women, before deciding your destinies; and if you are inclined to shudder at the way in which your human sisters are sold in Stamboul, put a stop to the preparations you are making for selling yourselves. The London market will be open to you in May, and the bidders will assemble as usual. They will consider your value in face, figure, skin, eyes, hair, and general complexion. They will note in slang parlance as to whether you are "well-groomed" (i.e., well-dressed), just as they note the condition of their thoroughbred mares. They will look at you with the egotistical tolerance of men who have money and know that they are worth marrying. Your pretty ways, your little smiles, your blushes, your graceful attitudes, will be discussed at the clubs and restaurants in various forms, as, "She knows how to do it," or, "She is laying a neat trap for me," or, "I expect I shall have to give in to her in the long run," and certain other chuckling assertions of a like kind; and if you come up to the expectations of the Jews or the Gentiles, who are thus estimating your qualities, you will be sold.

That is, if you choose to be marketable commodities. It rests with you. You are not bound to listen to one of your own sex who asks you, as I do, in plain words *not* to sell yourselves. But if you do listen, albeit only for a moment, I shall not have written quite in vain. I want you to refuse to make your bodies and souls the traffickable material of vulgar huckstering. I want you to *give* yourselves ungrudgingly, fearlessly, without a price or any condition whatsoever, to the men you truly love, and abide by the results. If love is love indeed, no regret can be possible. But be sure it *is* love,—the real passion, that elevates you above all sordid and mean considerations of self—that exalts you to noble thoughts and nobler deeds,—that keeps you faithful to the one vow, and moves you to take a glorious pride in preserving that vow's immaculate purity;—be sure it is all this, for if it is not all this, you are making a mistake, and you are ignorant of the very beginnings of love. Try to fathom your own hearts on this vital question; try to feel, to comprehend, to learn the responsibilities invested in womanhood,—and never stand before God's altar to accept a blessing on your marriage if you know in your own inmost soul that it is no marriage at all in the true sense of the word, but merely a question of convenience and sale. To do such a deed is the vilest blasphemy—a blasphemy in which you involve the very priest who pronounces the futile benediction. The saying "God will not be mocked" is a true one; and least of all will He consent to listen to, or ratify such a mockery as a marriage-vow sworn before Him in utter falsification and misprisal of His chiefest commandment—Love. It is a wicked and wilful breaking of the law and is never by any chance allowed to remain unpunished.

4. From Flora Annie Steel, *The Modern Marriage Market*. London: Hutchinson & Co., 1898. Originally published in *The Lady's Realm*, 1897

This title, "The Modern Marriage Market," conveys to my ear a distinct flavour of blame when taken as a whole; but when I come to dissect its alliterations, I find myself in doubt where to lay the accent of accusation. Should it be on the "modern," the "marriage," or the "market"?

So far as the adjective is concerned: I think the plaint may be dismissed summarily. Personally I confess myself unable to see the slightest difference in the principles on which marriages are made nowadays and those on which they were made a hundred—two hundred—five hundred years ago; briefly, since chivalry beguiled the world from the straight path of duty. The theory of marriage, as set forth by Western civilisation, has practically remained the same for centuries; such theory being simply that the feeling, passion, emotion—call it what you will—which we designate as Love—with a big L—is the only reason which an honourable man or modest woman can possibly admit, even to themselves, as a reason for marriage. In other words, herein lies the only justification, sanctification, and purification of what would otherwise be unjustifiable.

I think that even the most cynical and *blasé* frequenter of house-boats at Cookham[1] would, if confronted with his own soul, admit that it had a sneaking belief in this theory; while even the most cursory glance at our literature proves that it has as many signatories as the Thirty-nine Articles. Briefly, it is and has been the foundation-stone of our marriage system.

It is scarcely fair, therefore, to blame it as modern. Nor, when we come to analyse the next word, have we any right to condemn

---

1 A popular location for pleasure parties on the river.

marriage as it is. Viewed in the purely personal aspect which is all that a marriage conducted on such purely personal lines as the mutual gratification of feeling can claim, marriage seems to touch a very high average of content. It can boast quite as much success as is consistent with the natural evanescence of all feeling.

Are we, then, to let our tongues slide over "modern" and "marriage" to dwell reproachfully upon "market"? Are we to lay the burden of blame upon the very idea of commerce in the Temple of Hymen?

One of my predecessors has used the whip of words both to buyers and sellers in this connection, and the other, while deprecating the justice of the reproof in regard to actual facts, has not denied the iniquity of barter.

Nor do I; but I would like to remind my readers that it was not only the tables of the money-changers which the scourge of the Master drove forth from the Temple, but also the seats of them which sold doves![1] I would ask them what ethical difference there is in selling yourself for love or for money, if mere personal pleasure lies at the bottom of the bargain?

I make bold to say that there is none. The girl who gives herself for exchange in pure passion is quite as mercenary as the one who sells herself for gold. Both claim their own desire, irrespective of everything but themselves. It is merely a question as to the relative dignity of their ideals in regard to such personal pleasure. A market is therefore inevitable under our present system, since, whether Mammon or Eros ratifies the bond, English girls are taught to take their equivalent in something which is valuable to themselves, and themselves only.

So it seems to me that the phrase "modern marriage market" should have no accent at all. It must be taken as a whole, or rejected as a whole. We must either say that marriage is honourable in all if we get an equivalent which satisfies our personal ideals, or we must say that neither for love nor for money have men and women the right to enter into a contract which only concerns themselves for a few short years, but which may influence the world for generations.

Which shall we do?

---

1 See Matthew 21:12. Jesus drove the moneylenders and the pigeon sellers out of the temple with a whip, as using a holy site as a site of commerce seemed to him a desecration of the temple's purpose.

To most, no doubt, the very idea of condemning the fundamental principle of our marriage system wholesale may seem more absurd even than sacrilegious. The world, they will say, has got on very well with the help of the little blind god. Lads and lasses have sold their birthright for love since the beginning of Time, and will continue so to do until Time is no more. It is natural, it is proper, it is above all easy for them to do so. The majority of such marriages are happy, decorous, respectable; and though our social morality is not quite what it should be, that has nothing to do with the question. Our qualms as to what may be going on round the corner in Piccadilly have no right to make our own voices quaver in singing about the one "which breathed o'er Eden" during a marriage service in St. George's, Hanover Square.[1]

Perhaps not; and yet the uncomfortable remembrance that the first wedding in this world was rather the reverse of a panacea for all evil makes some of us doubt if this theory of ours, of which we have spoken, is not responsible for a large portion of the confusion which undoubtedly exists in the minds of many men and women regarding what is called the relation of the sexes.

To say so may seem almost an insult to the hundreds, the thousands of honest men and women who, as their children grow up to take their place in the world, hold each other bravely by the hand till death do them part, and smile at each other even then, knowing that they have done their duty—that they have given their mortality to the immortality of the world; but the heroism, the virtue of these thousands must not blind us to the fact that the very things we admire in them—the faithful comradeship, the dutiful devotion, the self-denial—are the very things which would have been scouted as a justification of marriage long years before: must not blind us also to the fact that the passionate, absorbing Love—again with a big L—which, according to Marie Corelli, is the only safeguard against making souls and bodies "the traffickable material of vile huckstering," has in nine cases out of ten disappeared.

I shall be told that I am wrong in saying this—that it has not disappeared. It has strengthened, changed, sobered, risen into a far more excellent thing than it was at first. Then why, in Heaven's

---

1 In other words, immorality in Piccadilly (a known haunt of prostitutes) should not make us doubt the respectable marriages taking place at this popular church in a well-to-do neighborhood.

name, condemn those who prefer the gingerbread without the gilt upon it to begin with? Why should we extol the man or woman who says openly, "I expect 'Love to teach me exquisite joys,' to 'bring our lives into resounding tune and harmony, so that all the world shall seem full of luscious song.'—I wish to appropriate to my sole use and benefit that which personally makes 'my life worth living.'—I feel that I must have that 'kiss and no other on my lips,' that hand 'and no other to caress me'"?

Does not that—put, not as I put it, but as the advocates of Love as a purifying element between man and woman put it— sound quite as much like an apotheosis of personal delights as "I expect money to give me exquisite joy, to bring resounding tune and luscious song, etc., etc."?

Compare it, for instance, with the position which our present system condemns, which nine out of every ten women would be ashamed to confess. "I do not expect intense personal gratification, but I wish to marry, to have a home and children, to take my share in the glory and toil, and here is my chance." If you come to analyse this, you will find, not only that it brings with it a far higher ideal of life, but that it emphasizes something that sorely needs emphasizing: the distance—if I may be allowed so to put it—between Piccadilly and St. George's, Hanover Square. It leaves us with something more as a foundation for marriage than a mutual physical and mental attraction which overpowers other considerations: an attraction which the individual experience of nearly every man and woman in the world teaches them is evanescent. That it lasts sometimes need not be denied. But its persistency certainly seems to vary in inverse ratio to its intensity: those who feel it most keenly being, as a rule, those who are liable to feel it most frequently. This, indeed, is almost inevitable, since both the strength and the frequency argue the same cause, an emotional nature.

I shall be told, of course, that I have utterly failed to grasp the very idea of Love; that I am confusing it with passion.

I do not think I am, if the latter word is meant to carry even a suspicion of blame with it. Briefly, it is one thing to fall in love— to be, let us say, very much in love; another to think that it is not only a pleasant but a virtuous act. As a matter of fact, it is a very commonplace, a very natural one. In many cases such Love may prove quite a safe guide; but it is not a virtue to yield obedience to the instinct, as if it were the voice of God.

Yet that it is so, is the teaching which nine-tenths of us almost give to our girls. Nay, more! It is the universal teaching to both sexes on this point. Take up the most sentimental fiction of the English school, or the most realistic of the French,[1] and you will find them alike in this underlying assumption that the attraction of sex for sex is something praiseworthy. In the former the mutual self-sufficiency of hero and heroine, when it dawns upon them that they are really in love with each other, would be unbearable if it were not comic. And if Providence is kind enough to endow their superiors in age with a few sensible doubts, the young people almost burst with importance over the discovery that the course of true love never did run smooth.

The same thing is observable in the realistic novel. The blind little god's arrow is sufficient excuse for murdering one's grandmother, to say nothing of one's lawful wife. No doubt the treatment of this theory differs, but a careful reader can scarcely avoid coming to the conclusion that the emotion which leads, in the sentimental novel—after an intolerable amount of strong love-making—to wedding bells, is virtually the same as that which culminates in the necessity for propriety to use the "candle, the bell, and the book."[2]

The drama in both, begins on the old classical lines; youth, propinquity, an all-absorbing selfishness, a mental and bodily exaltation which is intoxicating as wine. Now, if this be so, the wrong—if wrong there be—must be in the end which differentiates the two similar beginnings.

But if the end in both be a purely personal gratification, it is hard to see why one should be blessed and the other cursed utterly. Still harder it is for any one to lay down the law and say, as the advocates of "all for love and the world well lost" theory do say, that you may seek the happiness of personal self-gratification through the mind but not through the body; through the sensual pleasures which can be bought by love, and not through those which are to be bought by money. The distinction is a purely arbitrary one. Self

1   French novels were famed for being more forthcoming about sexual matters than were English novels. French "realist" novels tended to emphasize the darker side of social life, including crime and illness.
2   These items were used during the ceremony of excommunication from the church. Steel suggests that it is the same emotion celebrated in the sentimental novel that leads also to women's "fall" from virtue, and which results in social "excommunication."

lies at the bottom of both decisions. The money-changers and the sellers of doves alike turn the Temple into a market-place.

Of course, the retort will once more be that I fail to understand what Love with a big L means, and that, even admitting the earthly element, which must count for something, there still remains the mental sympathy—the friendship, the honest, unselfish desire to stand by each other to do the best for each other, in every way, which is the essence of real love.

Undoubtedly it is. So much so, that I retort, in my turn, by asking why this should need the sanction of an ephemeral passion? Why, briefly, should it be right for a woman to crave a "luscious song," and wrong for her to be content with the still small voice of an approving conscience? Why should she be allowed to forget duty in pleasure, and forbidden to forget pleasure in duty?

Women have not so learnt their rights, their privileges, their duties in those Eastern lands with which I am best acquainted. There, hidden under a thousand blemishes, a million abuses, still lingers the great truth—so unpalatable to our Western individualism—that man and woman stand related, not to each other, but to the immortality of their race—that immortality which comes to the world through the generations on generations of men and women who are born into it. There, even nowadays, when error has obscured so much, marriage is not a purely personal matter, as it is with us; it is a duty to the race.

I am not, however, going to advocate the Indian system here (with child-marriage, female infanticide, and *sati* thrown in as make-weights)[1]—though my personal experience is that, even with polygamy superadded, the percentage of rational happiness derived from wifehood and motherhood is as high in India as it is in England. I only wish with all diffidence to ask each thinking woman if our present ideal of what justifies marriage does not put St. George's, Hanover Square, into dangerous proximity with Piccadilly. To use one and the same bell for weddings and exorcisms is confusing to the multitude, which has but the one sense of hearing; yet, if we admit the sanctifying power of mere emotion, it seems to me impossible to avoid so using it. For experience—

---

1 Sati was the practice of immolating the widow of a dead man on his funeral pyre. All three of these practices were frequently discussed by the British as examples of Indian abuse of women.

every-day experience of the world—teaches us that it is impossible even for the principals themselves to tell beforehand whether the Love which prompts their marriage will stand the strain. They may hope it so, wish it so, pray that it may be so; but very few men—or women either, for that matter—could truthfully say, as they stand at the altar, that they never felt a similar emotion before, or predict that they would never feel it again. Perhaps it may be said that I exaggerate this teaching. Let us go back to what has been written in these pages about it.

"What is marriage?" asks Marie Corelli; then answers the question by saying that it is the taking of a vow before the Throne which declares that the "man and woman concerned have each discovered in each other his or her true mate—that all the world is a mere grain of dust in worth as compared with the exalted passion which fills their souls, and moves them to become one in flesh as well as one in spirit."

Lady Jeune,[1] again, gives it as her opinion that with a pure and single-minded English girl, nothing has any chance in competition with "the glamour and ecstasy of a pure, genuine passion."

These are no uncertain utterances. They point unerringly to the thesis that this personal emotion—call it what you will—is in itself sufficient to warrant entering into a lifelong contract into which, to say the least of it, many other considerations should enter: a thesis which is largely responsible for making the standard of social morality in the West so low.

For it is low. Whatever the theory of twin souls may have done towards personal happiness, it has certainly not enabled us to rise one whit higher in regard to social and conjugal morality than those who hold marriage to be a thing apart from Love.

In truth, the quarrel goes deeper than a mere dispute as to the relative greed for pleasure of the Englishwomen of to-day and their sisters of yesterday. What has to be settled is the question whether, as Marie Corelli puts it, "marriage is nothing more nor less than a crime if it is entered upon without the mutual supreme attraction and deep love which makes the union sacred"; whether a marriage without ecstasy is a *selling of the body into slavery*" (the italics are mine). Is this so? Or do we touch here on the mother

---

1 Lady Jeune was another author who contributed to the forum on marriage.

error which has done more to lengthen the record of our divorce courts than any other cause, and which, even when it stops short of that, sells the soul of many a good woman into something worse than slavery,—into the loss of her own self-esteem, into a sense of perpetual degradation: the assertion, briefly, that the duties of wifehood and motherhood are in themselves debasing?

"Try," goes on Marie Corelli in her eloquent appeal, "to feel, to comprehend, to learn the responsibilities invested in Womanhood."

Never was more admirable advice given; but why stultify it by setting as the highest responsibility the duty of "being kissed" as she likes to be kissed, caressed as she likes to be caressed, of giving herself "without any consideration whatever to her pre-elected lover"?

Would it not be better advice to bid our daughters claim that right of reasonable judgment which Lady Jeune excuses in the much-abused mother—the right of remembering "that there are wider considerations in marriage than the present happiness of two people, since the destinies of unborn children have to be considered"?

It seems almost incredible that at this time of day it should be necessary to insist on such a palpable truism. That it should be so speaks volumes of blame, not so much for the Modern Marriage Market as for the theory of marriage which has inevitably led to it.

It is time this was altered. The changing conditions of woman's life in this nineteenth century of ours make it imperative that some more certain guide should be chosen than that which leads alike to Piccadilly and St. George's. In the old days, when women had little else to do, and still less to choose, this dream of personal happiness was not so dangerous as it is now, when we have begun to ask questions and insist upon answers. Take a middle-class family of girls, for instance; nice girls, good girls, pretty girls. Half of them cannot hope to marry. But which half? There is the crucial point. If, when they were born, Providence wrote on their foreheads, "This one is to be married, this one not," it would be well and good. But it can never be safe to din the claims of personal pleasure and pure passion—as they are dinned by most purveyors of fiction *"pour les jeunes filles"*—into ears which may never have the chance of listening to the passion itself, or, what is worse, may have to listen to it without the mysterious sanction of marriage.

It is always unsafe to live in the mental condition of that large section of unreasoning humanity which loves to sit in a basket and then lift itself up by the handles. Pure passion is the sanction of marriage—marriage is the sanction of pure passion. Here is the position with a vengeance!

In truth we need a surer guide, a more bracing and wholesome gospel.

We must go back to what our Eastern sisters have never left; to the sanction of home and motherhood—a sanction which there is grave danger, in this age of individualism, will soon be lost sight of altogether.

Men have already almost lost their fatherhood, from the very extent of their personal freedom in regard to it; and though this is not the place in which to discuss that aspect of the question, the fact that this is so must fill the minds of the thoughtful among us with dread, lest the emancipation of women should lead to a like loss of the highest function of humanity.

For it is the highest. The Angel of the Annunciation carries to woman the most honourable of all messages, gives her the most noble mission she can have. For the world still waits for the child that shall be born—for its greatest poet, its greatest statesman, its greatest philanthropist: briefly, for the man who shall right the wrong in all times, all places.

And it is to the thought of that child which is to come—that child with its message of peace through self-sacrifice, lying in its mother's arms, perhaps in our own—that we women must look for the solution of many a problem which now angers the world and us. As of old, the purification of the Temple will come through that message of Annunciation; but the hand of the Messiah must overthrow the seats of them that sell doves, as well as the tables of the money-changers.

5. From Susan, Countess of Malmesbury, *The Modern Marriage Market*. London: Hutchinson & Co., 1898. Originally published in *The Lady's Realm*, 1897

"Lord Thomas was a bold forester,
And a chacer of the Kings deere.
Faire Ellinor was a fine woman,
And Lord Thomas he loved her deere."

The condition of mind so artlessly described in the old ballad quoted above, belongs to the aboriginal class of emotions which is neither ancient nor modern, but co-existent with human nature, and against which education, civilisation, and luxury fight in vain. As every creature born into the world presents a fresh and sensitive surface to the impressions of experience, and only learns too late, as a rule, to profit by that of others, so the successors of Lord Thomas and Faire Ellinor, as they walk together in the vernal pageant of their youth, contemplate themselves and their heart-adventure with astonishment, awe, and an honest, hearty, wholesome belief that no one ever loved before as they do, nor ever can again so much as guess at the unearthly beauty of a light which seems to shine for them alone. Upon this simple but solid foundation the edifice of marriage mainly rests, and I fully believe that in the majority of the unions of to-day feeling plays an important part.

If any one should doubt this statement, let him spend a week in a country-house alone with any young engaged couple, chosen at random among his acquaintance. It will probably be a painful experiment, since his unhappy personality, unillumined by the Shekinah[1] of their mutual interest in one another, will remain plunged in a gloom which will seem all the darker for the brilliant radiance near at hand.

But the foundations of a building, though first in importance, are only the beginning of a complicated structure, and it is my desire to follow as closely as I can the details of an institution which has existed so many thousands of years, and has, from age to age, learnt, partly to adapt itself to the needs of a nervous and impulsive race of beings, and partly to act as a restraint on qualities, not in themselves actually bad, but hurtful when exercised without control. I wish to guess at what should and perchance might be, and at what seems practically attainable in the present state of society. But first I must glance at the three views of marriage now laid before me: the Romantic, as presented by Marie Corelli; the Social, as understood by Lady Jeune, and the Practical, of which Mrs. Steel is the prophet.

The first of these writes with a skilful pen, a warm heart, but an undisciplined mind. It is, no doubt, a happy state to be in,

---

1 In the Jewish tradition, a glowing manifestation of the spirit of God.

that in which we are unable to see more than one side of every question, and one which, in addition, seems calculated to endow the world with saints and martyrs whom it piously reveres, but whom it shows no signs, at this stage of its existence, of emulating. The fly, with the thousand facets of its eye, must be fairly puzzled at times, one would suppose, to choose its path in life, unless its brain corrects the myriad images the retina receives. It is for us, in the same manner, to order and arrange the many different facts and sides of life which pass before our gaze. A good delusion and a strong prejudice serve as a goal in the steeple-chase of our career, and as blinkers to keep us in a narrow and perhaps a useful path; but in studying a question in order to arrive at the truth, whether palatable or not, and above all in claiming to advise our own sex for its highest good, so far as is possible, every point of view should be considered, every element in the case weighed in the balance. To look at marriage from its purely romantic side, or, on the other hand, to bring its utilitarian aspects into too great relief, is unskilfully to mix the ingredients which go to form that compound of experience and intuition which we call a ripened judgment. Marie Corelli draws a pretty picture of simple, loving hearts in Sicily, but is she very sure that those whom she so touchingly describes as passing rich on over twice as much again as forty pounds a year exhibit more than the negative virtue of content? Would they refuse comfort and affluence if offered them? Comfort, which might mean life or death to either in ill-health; affluence, which would certainly afford advantages to their children such as they could not hope to obtain under present circumstances, and such as they would scarcely have the right to decline?

The sum, in truth, we have to spend is nothing: the all-important question is, What must that sum be made to buy? What are necessaries? What are luxuries? For I need hardly point out to any one who has felt the grip of an English winter, that what constitutes riches in Capri would mean poverty and privation in a climate like ours. So much depends on the class we happen to associate with, and the sky under which we live. The deprivation of accustomed luxuries, or such easements as we have enjoyed in life, is so serious a matter that it is a well-known factor in punishment as administered to criminals.

Are we, then, purely mercenary if we urge these considerations on those who have yet to grapple with reality, and have never known the crushing hug of want? To turn to another point: is there a mother in this world who, if she could prevent it, would allow her daughter to give herself "without conditions of any sort" to the first man for whom the woman-nature in her breast had faintly stirred in that slumber where it lies bound by the opiate of custom, education, and hereditary proclivities? To such dreams of Heaven, natural though they be, there is a cold awakening in the chilly dawn of human experience. Few men, worthy of the name, would accept such a sacrifice or undertake such a charge. Those who have done so, for selfish reasons, have forged fetters on their limbs of which they sometimes hear the clanking all their days. Not the most advanced woman among the vanguard which leads that section of our sisters can live happy and content under the disapproval and avoidance of those she has been accustomed to associate with. The enthusiasm which armed martyrs for the rack or death is sadly cooled by the daily pin-pricks which accompany any irrevocable step taken in defiance of custom and society, just as a heavy shower of rain will do more to disperse a mob than more heroic measures. No woman, whose heart is single, would recommend another to follow in such a thorny path.

Lady Jeune, who follows Marie Corelli in the discussion, writes from the practical standpoint of a woman who has a wide and intimate knowledge of the special class which she describes; but she confines herself to that alone. And Mrs. Steel, who succeeds her, is, by her own confession, more conversant with the matrimonial affairs of our Eastern than of our Western sisters. Moreover, she evidently considers the former to be the highest and happiest development of home-life, and that the duties of wives and husbands towards each other should be entirely or chiefly merged in their mutual care for their offspring, which, I may suggest, but for that gilt on the gingerbread which Mrs. Steel condemns, would probably never come to be a factor in the case. She is evidently of opinion, with Mrs. Malaprop,[1] that it is better to begin with a little aversion; but even that stern lady does not condemn us to indifference all our lives. Why, because a feeling is both beautiful and evanescent, are we not to enjoy and prize it while it lasts? Beauty and evanescence are two of the

---

1 In Richard Brinsley Sheridan's play *The Rivals* (1775), Mrs. Malaprop is always misusing words (from French mal à propos, meaning badly suited or inappropriate).

chief characteristics of existence—beauty which the human eye may never see, and evanescence which oft-times enhances that very beauty we desire or regret. And will the memory of love not serve to prevent our judging coldly and harshly the faults of those to whom our faith is pledged? And if that only, and no more, does it not fulfil a high purpose between a man and woman whom only death or shame can part, whose interests and whose duties are the same? Love is the fulfilment of the law, the willing, cheerful sacrifice of self for the happiness and good of others, either of a single individual or of the race. It is this that Mrs. Steel constantly confuses with passion.

Another point. Her special reference to the greater regard of Indian women for their children than is displayed by our sex in this country seems to me to be an unfortunate one. Take, for instance, the motive for bringing children into the world which is well known to exist in many cases: the belief that, if they die without descendants to perform their obsequies, their souls go into the body of an unclean beast. This is certainly purely selfish, and has its root in what Mrs. Steel ought to feel compelled to call a personal gratification, though one which we should consider imaginary. All true love, whether between parents and children or husband and wife, is, in its essence, free from self; but in both cases it is founded on the strongest and most abiding instincts of the human race. Neither can be said to be higher than the other, as they are not intrinsically good, if I may say so, nor are they bad. They are simply natural; their absence is unnatural, and tends to the deterioration, as their presence does to the preservation, of our kind, having still, as Mrs. Steel would say, a selfish origin, though on the widest basis.

All things, as St. Paul himself admits, are lawful, but all are not expedient.[1] Self-preservation is a notable example of an impulse admirable in itself and necessary to human life, which must be controlled, or sacrificed even, where wider interests are at stake. Instincts, to be useful, must be recognised as such, not placed on a pedestal and elevated into transcendent virtues, but put into harness, so to speak, and made to draw the cart of life.

---

1 See I Corinthians 6:12. St. Paul argues that for those who are saved, much is permitted. But all that one may do is not the same as all that one should do, and no practice should be retained that interferes with the focus on salvation.

Another factor in marriage has eluded Mrs. Steel's quick eye—one that is of the highest consequence to the race. It was touched upon by *Punch*[1] many years ago in his picture of the Noble Owner and his Prize Short-horn:—

NOBLE OWNER (*very attenuated*): You certainly are a magnificent fellow.

PRIZE SHORT-HORN: Well, my lord, if as much trouble had been taken to select your father and mother as you took with mine, you would be a magnificent fellow too!

History does not relate what the Noble Owner replied, but he might have pointed out that difficulties of selection increase as higher tests of fitness are required. With us not only physical, but moral and intellectual gifts are looked for, and it is a recognised, if melancholy, fact that the first and last, at any rate, rarely exist together in any high degree. Different qualities also are needed in the various ranks of life—a fact which our modern system of education does not always condescend to notice; while it is evident that certain natures require certain others as the complement to their own. "The heart of a little man," said a friend of mine the other day, "goes out like a rocket to a big woman," and we see the converse happen every day; while what he said of physical is equally true of mental gifts. The exhilarating and stimulating effect of certain minds upon our own is within the experience of most of us, while another perhaps superior intellect may leave us cold and dull.

Not even the Purdah or the Yashmak[2] can entirely disguise or obliterate a determined character or powerful will, and this we know was as true in the days of Lady Mary Wortley Montagu[3] as it is in certain notable instances at the present time.

The little tenement in which, for a few brief years, our soul crouches in unrest, and of which it is in some degree both the cause and the effect, so effectually separates us from other beings of our kind that each must live apart and die in solitude. This loneliness grips every heart that beats and every mind that

---

1 *Punch* was (and is) a comic magazine.
2 Purdah (Hindi) is the practice of concealing women from men to whom they are not related. The Yashmak was a veil worn over the face, to this end.
3 Lady Montagu (1679-1762) traveled in purdah in Turkey and wrote about it.

stretches forth a feeler in the dark. To find a sister-being one with our own, complete community of thought and aspiration, is the deep longing which consumes both men and women; and to the thoughtful mind, denied fulfilment of its holiest and dearest wish, the most convincing proof of life beyond the grave. This desolation of the soul, "divine despair," which feeds upon our inmost heart, and which spurs a noble nature to exertion, is the same force, but transformed, which drives the weaker creature to perdition. We cannot live alone, and, meeting with another isolated entity, we think to find in it the silver key to loosen our disquietude, and to unlock, each for another, the guarded secrets slumbering, scarcely dreamt of, below the surface we present to the open, if inscrutable, book of persons and events, whose pages slowly turn before our eyes. We search, as did Faust of old, for the Helen of our lives, and when, at last, like him, we say to the flying moment, "Stay! thou art so fair!" it melts beneath our touch. No reality—if, indeed, there be such a thing—can reach the beauty of our pictured thoughts, and we are doomed from childhood to smart beneath privation and regret.

This bitter discipline, rightly endured, moulds the character and develops the muscles for the Olympic Game of life. Nerve feeds on danger, and courage on necessity; while sorrow, nobly borne, weaves a steel strand into the cable of experience, which strengthens it for those who follow in our traces.

This hope of fellowship and effort to attain perfect union, the practical outcome of our solitude of heart, is the motive power which drives some of us to marriage and some of us to sin.

After an early stage of existence, men are much less likely to "fall in love," as it is called, than women, and especially girls who are less in contact with the real world, and unacquainted with its sterner side. It is therefore far more important that they should be protected against themselves, and it is certainly the plain duty of every mother to lay before her child the inevitable consequences of an imprudent marriage. Most girls in the upper classes know nothing of the value of money; they are brought up in comfortable, or even luxurious, homes, by parents generally indulgent, and are as incapable of judging of the merits of a possible husband as they would be of the points of a horse. Such a girl might, as likely as not, choose a high-stepping, flashy screw,[1]

---

1 A screw is a horse in poor condition, often broken down from hard use.

and pay for it the ruinous price of a spoilt life. It is the act of a friend, though a painful task, to tear aside the veil which ignorance or native innocence and a pure heart hang before her eyes, if by so doing she can be saved from an irretrievable blunder, the punishment for which is as heavy, alas! as for a crime.

Girls are now highly educated—so far as book-learning can make them so; they are allowed freedom undreamt of twenty years ago, and the superficial knowledge of life they thus acquire is one of the most dangerous elements in their present condition. An attitude of independence, an indisposition to listen to advice, combined with total ignorance of the real situation they are bent on creating for themselves, is a spectacle which would be ludicrous if it were not melancholy to those who know by experience the difficulties which beset a woman's life, even under the most favoured conditions. Authority being admittedly obsolete, all a mother can do is to create and maintain, with infinite patience and affection, such an influence over her child's mind as will allow of the latter being guided aright when she comes to the place where two roads branch. To know how to look for the qualities which stand the wear and tear of life in common, and to learn that all that glitters is not gold, is one of the first steps in our education. Neither brilliant personal qualities alone, nor wealth and position by themselves, can satisfy the heart which is formed to look, often against its conscious will, for something higher, for that invisible but possible perfection to which the caged bird sings its sweetest songs. It is this search for the ideal, and the fond belief that it has at last been found, which wrecks so many lives and makes the searchers do wrong in secret, or bear open shame for the sake of the treasure which they think at length is in their grasp, but which often turns to ashes in their hand.

It is therefore inevitable that marriage should produce a large amount of disappointment, which may best be overcome by reflecting on our own shortcomings rather than on those of our companion. Partners in a happy marriage must bring a certain capital of youth and health, and in addition qualities, moral and mental, such as are necessary to advance them in their condition of life.

"Choose not alone a proper mate,
But a proper time to marry."

You do not require your carriage-horses to wait at table, neither does your pet dog pay the household bills; but in human beings we are apt to look for qualities quite as incompatible as these, and to marry in the fond hope that the particular thistle we have selected, unlike all others, will bear a fine crop of figs.

Marriages between different classes in Society rarely turn out well. Early influences are seldom, if ever, eradicated, and where two people look at life from opposite points of view there must be constant straining of the tie which binds them to each other.

Those who marry into a class above their own are almost invariably huffy, and constantly on the outlook for slights. Where this is not the case they may easily become overbearing or purse-proud. When, on the other hand, they marry beneath them, they find their new surroundings impossible to conciliate, and themselves accused of pride or "airs." Most frequently is this the case where a lady marries a working man. The tie shortly becomes as irksome to him as to her, and he finds her delicate and useless, unable to do the hard work expected of the women to whom he is accustomed; while the very sense of inferiority, which constantly haunts him, renders him uneasy in her presence, and sometimes even drives him to ill-treat or desert her altogether.

I came across an instance of this kind, not long ago, in a pretty creature, still young, but roughened by toil, who had formed a union with a working man. Shunned by her own people, and finally abandoned by her husband, she had been found and rescued from the lowest depths of degradation by a kind and charitable lady.

Difference of race is generally a great handicap to contentment in conjugal life. Even between European nations difficulties are apt to arise: how much more, then, where colour prejudices step in. This sad lesson many of our girls have learnt in India, where they find their position almost untenable, while the men they marry, returning to their own people and former habits, undergo a strange and terrible transformation in the eyes, at least, of their English brides, who are awakened too late to the truth and to the inherent differences of race and inherited characteristics which even a European education is powerless to remove.

Imprudent marriages, where means of support are inadequate, are more frequent with us than on the Continent, where, particularly in France, the whole affair is treated more as a family arrangement. The position of the woman in her own house seems to gain, rather than not, by this way of looking at the matter, and on the whole the average results appear to be satisfactory.

Restrictions on marriage are common in Continental armies, where, in certain cases, officers are obliged to ask the consent of their colonel, who is instructed to institute a full inquiry into the lady's character and financial position.

With us these regulations are confined to the men, four or five per cent of whom only can marry "with leave." This does not, of course, compel the remainder to remain single, like Zulu warriors, but excludes their wives from certain privileges which those who are "on the strength" enjoy; free quarters, for instance, and such employment as can be reserved for them.

Mercenary motives are far from being confined to the upper ranks of life, and from inquiries I have made I learn that a woman of the working classes, with "a little bit of money," is just as much run after as great heiresses in Society by fortune-hunters, and just as likely to be cast aside when that little bit of money is spent.

I have said that equality in social position is an important factor, and that serious racial divergences should act as a bar to marriage. Furthermore, for the sake of any children which may be born, persons suffering with hereditary diseases ought to remain single, and the very immature unions which take place so frequently—for instance, in the East End of London—should be discouraged and prevented as much as possible.

Beyond these initial points, I hold that we ought to look for physical beauty, which in itself includes so many other qualities; for evenness of temper, and the greater moral and intellectual gifts which go to widen and heighten the horizon of our life, and which bring unfailing consolation in time of privation or sorrow. The power to occupy the mind, to divert it from cares when by no taking thought can trouble be averted or suffering relieved, is one of the most precious gifts that a man or a woman can receive or acquire, and one which must tend to sweeten the life they have solemnly undertaken to spend together.

These, I shall be told, are all counsels of perfection; but in reply I may remind my readers that he who "aimeth at the sky, shoots higher far than he who means a tree." We can at least look up, and some day hope to scale the snow-clad heights which look so inaccessible from below.

And in the meantime let us say with the Preacher:

"Two are better than one; because they have a good reward for their labour. For if they fall, the one will lift up his fellow: but woe to him that is alone when he falleth; for he hath not another to help him up."[1]

---

1 Ecclesiastes 4:9. The reader is advised not to forego family ties simply to accrue wealth, as companionship is also valuable.

Appendix F: Discourses on Health in Victorian Medicine

[*Cometh Up as a Flower* intersects with discourses on health in two ways. As a novel originally identified as "sensational," it was viewed as potentially unhealthy reading. But it also tells a typical Victorian story of a woman whose health suffers because of a thwarted emotional life. The following excerpts deal with the "nervous temperament" and tuberculosis, the disease to which Nell succumbs.]

1. From Henry Ancell, *A Treatise on Tuberculosis, the Constitutional Origin of Consumption and Scrofula.* London: Longman, Brown, Green and Longmans, 1852

The Depressing Passions [as predisposing Physiological Causes of Tuberculosis]

Louis, and many of our best observers, have enumerated mental depression amongst the predisposing causes, and regard it as one of the most efficient…. As a predisposing cause, it acts upon the blood by depressing the nervous energies, diminishing the respiratory powers, disturbing the regular process of hematosis, altering the proportions of the constituents of the blood, and diminishing its vital properties; thereby rendering it more susceptible of the tuberculous transformation…. I consider there is strong ground for the belief, that mental agencies alone, may actually induce the specific change in the blood which constitutes the disease….

… When the operation of the depressing passions is slow and long continued, among the most prominent effects we find the bloom of health disappearing, the face grows pale and emaciated, the adipose support of the eyeball gradually diminishes, and the eye becomes sunken, the fat generally is absorbed, and the muscles become weak and relaxed. They appear to diminish the vitality of the blood, and to undermine the source of all the vital energies.

2. From Sir James Clark, *A Treatise on Pulmonary Consumption: Comprising an Inquiry into the Causes, Nature, Prevention and Treatment of Tuberculous and Scrofulous Diseases*. London: Sherwood, Gilbert, and Piper, 1837

When of hereditary origin, it is manifested by a peculiar modification of the whole organization,—in structure and in form, in action and in function.

The countenance generally affords strong indications of the presence of this affection; in early childhood it has a pale pasty appearance, the cheeks are generally full.... At a more advanced period of youth, the character of the constitution is still more clearly indicated by the countenance. The eyes, particularly the pupils, are generally large, the eye-lashes long; and there is usually a placid expression, often great beauty of countenance, especially in persons of a fair, florid complexion.

... [Such persons have] great sensibility to impressions, with a corresponding acuteness of mind....

Mental depression also holds a very conspicuous place among those circumstances which diminish the powers of the system generally, and it often proves one of the most effective determining causes of consumption. Disappointment of long-cherished hopes, slighted affections, loss of dear relations, and reverse of fortune, often exert a powerful influence on persons predisposed to consumption, more particularly in the female sex.

3. From T.H. Yeoman, M.D., *Consumption of the Lungs, or Decline: The Causes Symptoms, and Rational Treatment*. London: Sampson Low, 1848

Hereditary transmission is the chief remote cause....

... The tuberculous diathesis is usually associated with a smooth, fair, and delicate skin; a rosy countenance; light-coloured, or reddish, fine hair; bright blue eyes; long eye-lashes; delicate pupils ... and in general, there is great mental sensibility and constitutional irritability....

... Mental emotion and the passions, especially those which are depressing, exert a decided influence in arousing tubercles from their lair. The effect of mental affliction instantly overthrows the whole economy of the system; an agonizing sense of oppression and tightness is experienced in the neigh-borhood of the heart and lungs, accompanied by a dreadful feeling of impending suffocation. If the sorrow be unremoved, if the heart be uncheered by hope, this disturbance continues, the health sinks under the oppression, and the mind falls into despondency.

4. From Anon., *The Causes and Prevention of Consumption*. [London]: Marchant, 1835

Mental depression also holds a very conspicuous place among those circumstances which diminish the powers of the system generally, and it often proves one of the most effectual determin-ing causes of consumption. Disappointment of long-cherished hopes, slighted affections, loss of dear relations and reverse of fortune, often exert a powerful influence on persons predisposed to consumption, more particularly in the female sex.

5. From Rowland East, *The Two Dangerous Diseases of England, Consumption and Apoplexy. Their Causes, Nature and Cure*. London: John Lee, 1842

The passions may produce this disease: deep, permanent, intense grief, the loss of a child or a fortune, the loss of the idol of the hu-man heart, whatever it may be, around which the "pleasures of memory," and the "pleasures of hope" clustered and blossomed. Some minds have such a capacity for this idolatry, that the idol becomes part of themselves. The mental emotions consequent upon this may rank among the causes.

There is another passion termed Love, not the father's love, not the mother's love; no, that is a far different feeling, but love in its common acceptation. Some say that such a disappointment may bring on a consumptive state; I do not deny it, it may. All the world would censure the novelist, or the dramatist, if his or her heroine, disappointed in love, did not expire from its conse-quences....

... But from what we know of the young ladies of this country, we think, the disease is far more likely to result from insufficient clothing, injudicious exposure to the vicissitudes of an uncertain climate, and tight lacing.

6. From Thomas Trotter, M.D., *A View of the Nervous Temperament*. 3rd ed. London: Longman, Hurst, Rees, Orme and Brown, n.d. [1812]. Originally published in 1807

The passion of novel reading is intitled [*sic*] to a place here [as a predisposing cause of nervous disease, including scrofula or tuberculosis]. In the present age it is one of the great causes of nervous disorders. The mind that can amuse itself with the love-sick trash of most modern compositions of this kind, seeks enjoyment that is beneath the level of a rational being. It creates for itself an ideal world, on the loose descriptions of romantic love. That leaves passion without any moral guide in the real occurrences of life. To the female mind in particular, as being endowed with a finer feeling, this species of literary poison has often been fatal; some of the most unfortunate of the sex have imputed their ruin chiefly to the reading of novels.... It is lamentable that three-fourths of these productions come from the pens of women; some of whom are known to have drunk deep of the fountains of pleasure and depravity.

Appendix G: Attitudes Toward Women and Sexuality

[*Cometh Up as a Flower* was heavily criticized for its representation of a woman of good family who displays desire for a man. The excerpts below offer a range of representative views on women's sexuality and behavior.]

1. From William Acton, M.R.C.S., *The Functions and Disorders of the Reproductive Organs*, 6th ed. (London: Churchill, 1875), pp. 212-16

We have already mentioned lack of sexual feeling in the female as not an uncommon cause of apparent or temporary impotence in the male. There is so much ignorance on the subject, and so many false ideas are current as to women's sexual condition, and are so productive of mischief, that I need offer no apology for giving here a plain statement that most medical men will corroborate.

I have taken pains to obtain and compare abundant evidence on this subject, and the result of my inquiries I may briefly epitomise as follows:—I should say that the majority of women (happily for society) are not very much troubled with sexual feeling of any kind. What men are habitually, women are only exceptionally. It is too true, I admit, as the Divorce Court shows, that there are some few women who have sexual desires so strong that they surpass those of men, and shock public feeling by their consequences. I admit, of course, the existence of sexual excitement terminating even in nymphomania,[1] a form of insanity that those accustomed

---

1 I shall probably have no other opportunity of noticing that, as excision of the clitoris has been recommended for the cure of this complaint, Köbelt thinks that it could not be necessary to remove the whole of the clitoris in nymphomania, the same results (that is destruction of venereal desire) would follow if the glans clitoridis had been alone removed, as it is now considered that it is the glans alone in which the sensitive nerves expand. This view I do not agree with, as I have already stated with regard to the analogous structure of the penis.... I am fully convinced that in many women there is no special sexual sensation in the clitoris, and I am as positive that the special sensibility dependent on the erectile tissue exists in several portions of the vaginal canal. [Acton's note]

to visit lunatic asylums must be fully conversant with; but, with these sad exceptions, there can be no doubt that sexual feeling in the female is in the majority of cases in abeyance, and that it requires positive and considerable excitement to be roused at all; and even if roused (which in many instances it never can be) it is very moderate compared with that of the male.

Many persons, and particularly young men, form their ideas of women's sensuous feeling from what they notice early in life among loose or, at least, low and immoral women. There is always a certain number of females who, though not ostensibly in the ranks of prostitutes, make a kind of a trade of a pretty face. They are fond of admiration, they like to attract the attention of those immediately above them. Any susceptible boy is easily led to believe, whether he is altogether overcome by the syren or not, that she, and therefore all women, must have at least as strong passions as himself. Such women, however, give a very false idea of the condition of female sexual feeling in general. Association with the loose women of the London streets in casinos and other immoral haunts (who, if they have not sexual feeling, counterfeit it so well that the novice does not suspect but that it is genuine), seems to corroborate such an impression, and as I have stated above, it is from these erroneous notions that so many unmarried men imagine that the marital duties they will have to undertake are beyond their exhausted strength, and for this reason dread and avoid marriage.

Married men—medical men—or married women themselves, would, if appealed to, tell a very different tale, and vindicate female nature from the vile aspersions cast on it by the abandoned conduct and ungoverned lusts of a few of its worst examples.

I am ready to maintain that there are many females who never feel any sexual excitement whatever. Others, again, immediately after each period, do become, to a limited degree, capable of experiencing it; but this capacity is often temporary, and may entirely cease till the next menstrual period. Many of the best mothers, wives, and managers of households, know little of or are careless about sexual indulgences. Love of home, of children, and of domestic duties are the only passions they feel.[1]

As a general rule, a modest woman seldom desires any sexual gratification for herself. She submits to her husband's embraces, but principally to gratify him; and, were it not for the desire of maternity, would far rather be relieved from his attentions. No nervous or feeble young man need, therefore, be deterred from marriage by any exaggerated notion of the arduous duties required from him. Let him be well assured, on my authority backed by the opinion of many, that the married woman has no wish to be placed on the footing of a mistress....

In strong contrast to the unselfish sacrifices such married women make of their feelings in allowing cohabitation, stand out others, who, either from ignorance or utter want of sympathy, although they are model wives in every other respect, not only evince no sexual feeling, but, on the contrary, scruple not to declare their aversion to the least manifestation of it. Doubtless this may, and often does, depend upon disease, and if so, the sooner the suffering female is treated the better. Much more frequently, however, it depends upon apathy, selfish indifference to please, or unwillingness to overcome a natural repugnance for cohabitation....

... I have given an instance of a wife refusing to cohabit with her husband because she would not again become a mother. I was lately in conversation with a lady who maintains women's rights to such an extent that she denied the husband any voice in the matter, whether or not cohabitation should take place. She maintained, most strenuously, that as the woman bears the consequences—has all the discomfort of being nine months in the family-way, and thus is obliged to give up her amusements and

---

1 The physiologist will not be surprised that the human female should in these respects differ but little from the female among animals. We well know it as a fact that the female animal will not allow the dog or stallion to approach her except at particular seasons. In many a human female, indeed, I believe, it is rather from the wish of pleasing or gratifying the husband than from any strong sexual feeling, that cohabitation is so habitually allowed. Certainly, during the months of gestation this holds good. I have known instances where the female has during gestation evinced positive loathing for any marital familiarity whatever. In some exceptional cases, indeed, feeling has been sacrificed to duty, and the wife has endured, with all the self-martyrdom of womanhood, what was almost worse than death. [Acton's note]

many of her social relations—considering too that she suffers all the pains and risks of childbirth—a married woman has a perfect right to refuse to cohabit with her husband. I ventured to point out to this strong-minded female that such conduct on her part might be, in a medical point of view, highly detrimental to the health of the husband, particularly if he happened to be strongly sexually disposed. She, however, refused to admit the validity of my argument, and replied that such a man, unable to control his feelings, ought to have married a street-walker, not an intellectually disposed person, who could not and ought not to be obliged to devote her time to duties only compatible with the position of a female drudge or wet-nurse....

Of one thing I am quite certain, that many times in the course of the year I am consulted by conscientious married men, who complain, and I think with reason, that they are debarred from the privileges of marriage, and that their sexual sufferings are almost greater than they can bear in consequence of their being mated to women who think and act as in the above-cited instances. I regret to add that medical skill can be of little avail here. The more conscientious the husband and the stronger his sexual feelings, the more distressing are the sufferings he is doomed to undergo, ultimately too often ending in impotence....

We offer, I think, no apology for light conduct when we admit there are some *few* women who, like men, in consequence of hereditary predisposition or ill-directed moral education, find it difficult to restrain their passions, while their more fortunate sisters have never been tempted, and have, therefore, never fallen. This, however, does not alter the fact which I would venture again to impress on the reader, that, in general, women do *not* feel any great sexual tendencies. The unfortunately large numbers whose lives would seem to prove the contrary are to be accounted for on much more mercenary motives. Vanity, giddiness, greediness, love of dress, distress, or hunger, make women prostitutes, but do not induce female profligacy so largely as has been supposed.

2. From Elizabeth Blackwell, "On the Abuses of Sex— II. Fornication," *Essays in Medical Sociology* (London, 1902), 1: 46-67, 51-58

One of the first subjects to be investigated by the Christian physiologist is the truth or error of the assertion so widely made, that sexual passion is a much stronger force in men than in women. Very remarkable results have flowed from the attempts to mould society upon this assertion. A simple Christian might reply, "Our religion makes no such distinction; male and female are as one under guidance and judgment of the Divine law." But the physiologist must go farther, and use the light of principles underlying physical truth in order to understand the meaning of facts which arraign and would destroy Christianity.

This mental element of human sex exists in major proportion in the vital force of women, and justifies the statement that the compound faculty of sex is as strong in woman as in man. Those who deny sexual feeling to women, or consider it so light a thing as hardly to be taken into account in social arrangements, confound appetite and passion; they quite lose sight of this immense spiritual force of attraction, which is distinctly human sexual power, and which exists in so very large a proportion in the womanly nature. The impulse towards maternity is an inexorable but beneficent law of woman's nature, and it is a law of sex.

The different form which physical sensation necessarily takes in the two sexes, and its intimate connection with and development through the mind (love) in women's nature, serve often to blind even thoughtful and painstaking persons as to the immense power of sexual attraction felt by women. Such one-sided views show a misconception of the meaning of human sex in its entirety.

The affectionate husbands of refined women often remark that their wives do not regard the distinctively sexual act with the same intoxicating physical enjoyment that they themselves feel, and they draw the conclusion that the wife possesses no sexual passion. A delicate wife will often confide to her medical adviser (who may be treating her for some special suffering) that at the very time when marriage love seems to unite them most closely, when her husband's welcome kisses and caresses seem to bring them into profound union, comes an act which mentally separates them, and which may be either indifferent or repugnant to her. But it must be understood that it is not the special act necessary for parentage which is the measure of the compound moral and physical power of sexual passion; it is the profound attraction of one nature to the other which marks passion, and delight in kiss and caress—the love-touch—is physical sexual expression as much as the special act of the male.

It is well known that terror or pain in either sex will temporarily destroy all physical pleasure. In married life, injury from childbirth, or brutal or awkward conjugal approaches, may cause unavoidable shrinking from sexual congress, often wrongly attributed to absence of sexual passion. But the severe and compound suffering experienced by many widows who were strongly attached to their lost partners is also well known to the physician, and this is not simply a mental loss that they feel, but an immense physical deprivation. It is a loss which all the senses suffer by the physical as well as moral void which death has created.

Although physical sexual pleasure is not attached exclusively, or in woman chiefly, to the act of coition, it is also a well-established fact that in healthy loving women, uninjured by the too frequent lesions which result from childbirth, increasing physical satisfaction attaches to the ultimate physical expression of love. A repose and general well-being results from this natural occasional intercourse, whilst the total deprivation of it produces irritability.

On the other hand, the growth in men of the mental element in sexual passion, from mighty wifely love, often comes like a revelation to the husband. The dying words of a man to the wife who, sending away children, friends, every distraction, had bent the whole force of her passionate nature to holding the beloved object in life—"I never knew before what love meant"—indicates the revelation which the higher element of sexual passion should bring to the lower phase. It is an illustration of the parallelism and natural harmony between the sexes. The prevalent fallacy that sexual passion is the almost exclusive attribute of men, and attached exclusively to the act of coition—a fallacy which exercises so disastrous an effect upon our social arrangements—arises from ignorance of the distinctive character of human sex—viz., its powerful mental element. A tortured girl, done to death by brutal soldiers, may possess a stronger power of human sexual passion than her destroyers.

The comparison so often drawn between the physical development of the comparatively small class of refined and guarded women, and the men of worldly experience whom they marry, is a false comparison. These women have been taught to regard sexual passion as lust and as sin—a sin which it would be a shame for a pure woman to feel, and which she would die rather than confess. She has not been taught that sexual passion is love, even more than lust, and that its ennobling work in humanity is to educate and transfigure the lower by the higher element. The growth and indications of her own nature she is taught to condemn, instead of to respect them as foreshadowing that mighty impulse towards maternity which will place her nearest to the Creator if reverently accepted....

Some medical writers have considered that women are more tyrannically governed than men by the impulses of physical sex. They have dwelt upon the greater proportion of work laid upon women in the reproduction of the race, the prolonged changes and burden of maternity, and the fixed and marked periodical action needed to maintain the aptitude of the physical frame for maternity. They have drawn the conclusion that sex dominates the life of women, and limits them in the power of perfect human growth. This would undoubtedly be the case were sex simply a physical function.

The fact in human nature which explains, guides, and should elevate the sexual nature of woman, and mark the beneficence of Creative Force, is this very mental element which distinguishes human from brute sex. This element, gradually expanding under religious teaching and the development of true religious sentiment, becomes the ennobling power of love. Love between the sexes is the highest and mightiest form of human sexual passion....

This power of sex in women is strikingly shown in the enormous influence which they exert upon men for evil. It is not the cold beauty of a statue which enthrals and holds so many men in terrible fascination; it is the living, active power of sexual life embodied in its separate overpowering female phase. The immeasurable depth of degradation into which those women fall, whose sex is thoroughly debased, who have intensified the physical instincts of the brute by the mental power for evil possessed by the human being, indicates the mighty character of sexual power over the nature of woman for corruption. It is also a measure of what the ennobling power of passion may be.

Happily in all civilized countries there is a natural reserve in relation to sexual matters which indicates the reverence with which this high social power of our human nature should be regarded. It is a sign of something wrong in education, or in the social state, when matters which concern the subject of sex are discussed with the same freedom and boldness as other matters. This subject should neither be a topic of idle gossip, of unreserved publicity, nor of cynical display. This natural and beneficial instinct of reserve, springing from unconscious reverence, renders it difficult for one sex to measure and judge the vital power of the other. The independent thought and large observation of each sex is needed in order to arrive at truth. Unhappily, however, women are often falsely instructed by men, for a licentious husband inevitably depraves the sentiment of his wife, because vicious habits have falsified his nature and blinded his perception of the moral law which dominates sexual growth.

Each sex has its own stern battle to fight in resisting temptation, in walking resolutely towards the higher aim of life. It is equally foolish and misleading to attempt to weigh the vital qualities of the sexes, and measure justice and mercy, law and custom, by the supposed results. It is difficult for the child to comprehend that a pound of feathers can weigh as much as a pound of lead. Much of our thought concerning men and women is as rudimentary as the child's. Vast errors of law and custom have arisen in the slow unfolding of human nature from failure to realize the extent of the injury produced by that abuse of sex—fornication. We have not hitherto perceived that, on account of the moral degradation and physical disease which it inevitably produces, lustful trade in the human body is a grave social crime.

In forming a wiser judgment for future guidance, it must be distinctly recognised that the assertion that sexual passion commands more of the vital force of men than of women is a false assertion, based upon a perverted or superficial view of the facts of human nature. Any custom, law, or religious teaching based upon this superficial and essentially false assertion, must necessarily be swept away with the prevalence of sounder physiological views.

3. From Eliza Lynn Linton, "The Girl of the Period," *Saturday Review* 25 (14 March 1868) 339-40

No one can say of the modern English girl that she is tender, loving, retiring, or domestic. The old fault so often found by keen-sighted Frenchwomen, that she was so fatally *romanesque*, so prone to sacrifice appearances and social advantages for love, will never be set against the Girl of the Period. Love indeed is the last thing she thinks of, and the least of the dangers besetting her. Love in a cottage—that seductive dream which used to vex the heart and disturb the calculations of the prudent mother—is now a myth of past ages. The legal barter of herself for so much money, representing so much dash, so much luxury and pleasure—that is her idea of marriage; the only idea worth entertaining. For all seriousness of thought respecting the duties or the consequences of marriage, she has not a trace. If children come, they find but a stepmother's cold welcome from her; and if her husband thinks that he has married anything that is to belong to him—a *tacens et placens uxor*[1] pledged to make him happy—the sooner he wakes from his hallucination and understands that he has simply married some one who will condescend to spend his money on herself, and who will shelter her indiscretions behind the shield of his name, the less severe will be his disappointment. She has married his house, his carriage, his balance at the banker's, his title; and he himself is just the inevitable condition clogging the wheel of her fortune; at best an adjunct to be tolerated with more or less patience as may chance. For it is only the old-fashioned sort, not Girls of the Period *pur sang*,[2] who marry for love, or put the husband before the banker. But the Girl of the Period does not marry easily. Men are afraid of her; and with reason. They may amuse themselves with her for an evening, but they do not readily take her for life. Besides, after all her efforts, she is only a poor copy of the real thing; and the real thing is far more amusing than the copy, because it is real. Men can get that whenever they like; and when they go into their mothers' drawing-rooms, with their sisters and their sisters' friends, they want something of quite a different flavour. *Toujours perdrix*[3] is bad providing all the world over; but a continual weak imitation of *toujours perdrix* is worse.

If we must have only one kind of thing, let us have it genuine, and the queens of St. John's Wood in their unblushing honesty rather than their imitators and make-believes in Bayswater and Belgravia.[4] For, at whatever cost of shocked self-love or pained

---

1 A sweet, quiet wife (Latin).
2 Pure blooded—here used as an intensifier, "as such" (French).
3 Too much of the same thing (French).
4 St. John's Wood was a neighborhood of London known for being the location of kept mistresses. Bayswater and Belgravia were middle-class and upper-class respectable neighborhoods.

modesty it may be, it cannot be too plainly told to the modern English girl that the net result of her present manner of life is to assimilate her as nearly as possible to a class of women whom we must not call by their proper—or improper—name. And we are willing to believe that she has still some modesty of soul left hidden under all this effrontery of fashion, and that, if she could be made to see herself as she appears to the eyes of men, she would mend her ways before too late.

It is terribly significant of the present state of things when men are free to write as they do of the women of their own nation. Every word of censure flung against them is two-edged, and wounds those who condemn as much as those who are condemned; for surely it need hardly be said that men hold nothing so dear as the honour of their women, and that no one living would willingly lower the repute of his mother or his sisters. It is only when these have placed themselves beyond the pale of masculine respect that such things could be written as are written now. When women become again what they were once they will gather round them the love and homage and chivalrous devotion which were then an Englishwoman's natural inheritance.

The marvel in the present fashion of life among women is, how it holds its ground in spite of the disapprobation of men. It used to be an old-time notion that the sexes were made for each other, and that it was only natural for them to please each other and to set themselves out for that end. But the Girl of the Period does not please men. She pleases them as little as she elevates them; and how little she does that, the class of women she has taken as her models of itself testifies. All men whose opinion is worth having prefer the simple and genuine girl of the past, with her tender little ways and pretty bashful modesties, to this loud and rampant modernization, with her false red hair and painted skin, talking slang as glibly as a man, and by preference leading the conversation to doubtful subjects. She thinks she is piquante[1] and exciting when she thus makes herself the bad copy of a worse original; and she will not see that though men laugh with her they do not respect her, though they flirt with her they do not marry her; she will not believe that she is not the kind of thing they want, and that she is acting against nature and her own interests when she disregards their advice and offends their taste.

---

1 Spicy (French). Here, charming or interesting.

We do not understand how she makes out her account, viewing her life from any side; but all we can do is to wait patiently until the national madness has passed, and our women have come back again to the old English ideal, once the most beautiful, the most modest, the most essentially womanly in the world.

Select Bibliography

Biographies and Letters

Black, Helen C. *Notable Women Authors of the Day*. London: Maclaren and Company, 1906. (Revised from the 1893 edition, Glasgow: David Bryce and Son.)

Peterson, Linda. "Mary Cholmondeley (1859-1925) and Rhoda Broughton (1840-1920)." *Kindred Hands: Letters on Writing by British and American Women Authors, 1865-1935*. Ed. Jennifer Cognard-Black and Elizabeth MacLeod Walls. Iowa City, IA: U of Iowa P, 2006. 107-19.

White, Gleeson. *Letters to Eminent Hands*. Derby, England: F. Murray, 1892.

Wood, Marilyn. *Rhoda Broughton (1840-1920): Profile of a Novelist*. Lincolnshire, UK: Paul Watkins, 1993.

Criticism on Broughton

Debenham, Helen. "Rhoda Broughton's *Not Wisely but Too Well* and the Art of Sensation." *Victorian Identities: Social & Cultural Formations in Nineteenth-Century Literature*. Ed. Ruth Robbins, Julian Wolfreys, and James R. Kincaid. Hampshire, England: Macmillan, 1996. 9-24.

Demoor, Marysa. "Women Authors and Their Selves: Autobiography in the Work of Charlotte Yonge, Rhoda Broughton, Mary Cholmondeley and Lucy Clifford." *Cahiers Victoriens et Edouardiens* 39 (1994): 51-63.

Faber, Lindsey. "One Sister's Surrender: Rivalry and Resistance in Rhoda Broughton's *Cometh Up as a Flower*." *Victorian Sensations: Essays on a Scandalous Genre*. Ed. Kimberly Harrison and Richard Fantina. Columbus, OH: Ohio State UP, 2006. 149-59.

Gilbert, Pamela K. *Disease, Desire and the Body in Victorian Women's Popular Novels*. Cambridge, England: Cambridge UP, 1997.

Hager, Lisa. "Slumming with the New Woman: *Fin-de-Siècle* Sexual Inversion, Reform Work and Sisterhood in Rhoda Broughton's *Dear Faustina*." *Women's Writing* 14 (2007): 460-75.

Handley, Graham. "*Middlemarch* and *Belinda*." *George Eliot Review: Journal of the George Eliot Fellowship* 32 (2001): 63-67.

Heller, Tamar. "'That Muddy, Polluted Flood of Earthly Love':
Ambivalence about the Body in Rhoda Broughton's *Not Wisely but
Too Well*." *Victorian Sensations: Essays on a Scandalous Genre*. Ed.
Kimberly Harrison and Richard Fantina. Columbus, OH: Ohio
State UP, 2006. 87-101.

———. Introduction. *Cometh Up as a Flower*. By Rhoda Broughton.
In *Varieties of Women's Sensation Fiction, 1855-1890*. Ed. Andrew
Maunder, et al. London: Pickering & Chatto, 2004.

Jones, Shirley. "'LOVE': Rhoda Broughton, Writing and Re-Writing
Romance." *Popular Victorian Women Writers*. Ed. Kay Boardman
and Shirley Jones. Manchester: Manchester UP, 2004. 208-36.

Meyer, B. "Till Death Do Us Part: The Consumptive Victorian Heroine in Popular Romantic Fiction." *Journal of Popular Culture* 37.2
(2003): 287-308.

Murphy, Patricia. "Disdained and Disempowered: The 'Inverted'
New Woman in Rhoda Broughton's *Dear Faustina*." *Tulsa Studies in
Women's Literature* 19.1 (2000): 57-79.

Pykett, Lyn. *The Sensation Novel: From* The Woman in White *to* The
Moonstone. Plymouth, England: Northcote House, 1994.

Sadleir, Michael. *Things Past*. London: Constable, 1944.

Terry, R.C. "Rhoda Broughton." *Victorian Novelists After 1885*. Ed.
Ira Nadel and William E. Fredeman. Detroit, MI: Thomson Gale,
1983. 15-17.

Criticism on Sensation Fiction

Bernstein, Susan David. "Dirty Reading: Sensation Fiction, Women
and Primitivism." *Criticism* 36 (1994): 213-41.

Boyle, Thomas. *Black Swine in the Sewers of Hampstead: Beneath the
Surface of Victorian Sensationalism*. London: Hodder & Stoughton;
New York: Viking, 1989.

Brantlinger, Patrick. "What Is 'Sensational' About the 'Sensation
Novel'?" *Nineteenth Century Fiction* 37 (1982): 1–28.

Cvetkovich, Ann. *Mixed Feelings: Feminism, Mass Culture, and Victorian
Sensationalism*. New Brunswick, NJ: Rutgers UP, 1992.

Harrison, Kimberly, and Richard Fantina, eds. *Victorian Sensations:
Essays on a Scandalous Genre*. Ohio State UP, 2006.

Hughes, Winifred. *The Maniac in the Cellar: Sensation Novels of the
1860s*. Princeton, NJ: Princeton UP, 1980.

Jones, Anna Maria. *Problem Novels: Victorian Fiction Theorizes the
Sensational Self*. Columbus, OH: Ohio State UP, 2007.

Loesberg, Jonathan. "The Ideology of Narrative Form in Sensation Fiction." *Representations* 13 (Winter 1986): 115-38.

Mangham, Andrew. *Violent Women and Sensation Fiction: Crime, Medicine and Victorian Popular Culture.* Basingstoke: Palgrave, 2007.

Maunder, Andrew, et al, eds. *Varieties of Women's Sensation Fiction, 1855-1890.* London: Pickering & Chatto, 2004.

Mitchell, Sally. "Sentiment and Suffering: Women's Recreational Reading in the 1860s." *Victorian Studies* 21 (1977): 29-45.

Pykett, Lyn. *The "Improper" Feminine: The Women's Sensation Novel and the New Woman Writing.* New York: Routledge, 1992.

Showalter, Elaine. "Desperate Remedies: Sensation Novels of the 1860s." *Victorian Newsletter* 49 (1976): 1-5.

Talairach-Vielmas, Laurence. *Moulding the Female Body in Victorian Fairy Tales and Sensation Novels.* Aldershot: Ashgate, 2007.

Taylor, Jenny Bourne. *In the Secret Theatre of Home: Wilkie Collins, Sensation Narrative, and Nineteenth-Century Psychology.* London & New York: Routledge & Kegan Paul, 1988.

Social and Historical Contexts

Armstrong, Nancy. *Desire and Domestic Fiction: A Political History of the Novel.* New York: Oxford UP, 1987.

Calder, Jenni. *Women and Marriage in Victorian Fiction.* New York: Oxford UP, 1976.

Casey, Ellen Miller. "Edging Women Out?: Reviews of Women Novelists in the 'Athenaeum,' 1860-1900." *Victorian Studies* 39.2 (1996): 151-71.

Cruse, Amy. *The Victorians and Their Books.* London: Allen & Unwin, 1935.

Davidoff, Leonore, and Catherine Hall. *Family Fortunes: Men and Women of the English Middle Class, 1780-1850.* Chicago: U of Chicago P, 1987.

Fahnestock, Jeanne. "The Heroine of Irregular Features: Physiognomy and Conventions of Heroine Description." *Victorian Studies* 24.3 (1981): 325-50.

Flint, Kate. *The Woman Reader, 1837-1914.* Oxford: Clarendon P, 1993.

Gilbert, Sandra, and Susan Gubar. *The Madwoman in the Attic: The Woman Writer and the Nineteenth-Century Literary Imagination.* New Haven, CT: Yale UP, 1979.

Gorham, Deborah. *The Victorian Girl and the Feminine Ideal.* London: Croom Helm, 1982.

Kucich, John. *The Power of Lies: Transgression in Victorian Fiction.* Ithaca, NY: Cornell UP, 1994.

Langland, Elizabeth. *Nobody's Angels: Middle-Class Women and Domestic Ideology in Victorian Culture.* Ithaca and London: Cornell UP, 1995.

Leckie, Barbara. *Culture and Adultery: The Novel, the Newspaper, and the Law, 1857-1914.* Philadelphia: U of Pennsylvania P, 1999.

Poovey, Mary. *Uneven Developments: The Ideological Work of Gender in Mid-Victorian England.* Chicago: U of Chicago P, 1988.

Russet, Cynthia Eagle. *Sexual Science: The Victorian Construction of Womanhood.* Cambridge: Harvard UP, 1989.

Schaffer, Talia. "Women and Domestic Culture." *Victorian Literature and Culture* 35 (2007): 385-95.

Shanley, Mary Lyndon. *Feminism, Marriage, and the Law in Victorian England, 1850-1895.* Princeton: Princeton UP, 1989.

Swenson, Kristine. *Medical Women and Victorian Fiction.* Columbia: U of Missouri P, 2004.

Weiss, Barbara. *The Hell of the English: Bankruptcy and the Victorian Novel.* Lewisburg, PA: Bucknell UP, 1986.